DETROIT GREEN HOUSE

ARIZONA
NEW
MEXICO Kansas City
TEXAS
OKLAHOMA
ARKANSAS
TENNESSEE
KENTUCKY
OHIO Memphis

Davenport
AR
NEW
M
Des Moines

KANSAS Columbus
ST. LOUIS NEW
MEXICO
COLORADO
NEBRASKA
INDIANA IOWA
Nashville ILLINOIS
ILLINOIS
DETROIT

DEX

Published by:
Just Dex Publishing
18530 Mack Ave. Suite, 178
Grosse Pointe, Mich 48236
E-Mail: Dex33@Comcast.net
www. JustDexPublishing.Net

Library of Congress Catalog Card No:
ISBN-10: 0-9778202-1-1

DETROIT GREEN HOUSE

Revised by DEX
Edited by DEX
Text formation by DEX
Cover concept by Midknight Graphx

Printed in the United States of America

DEX

ACKNOWLEDGEMENTS

Zaykoia Tate (Love You Always)
Sonia Miller(Thank you for your support)
Ursara Lapsley(Thanks for your support)
Sean Troy Courtney of N.Y.
Duane Merrill of V.A.
Emory Jones of N.Y.
Michel Moore (Say U Promise Publications)
Melvin London of Midknight graphx
Alonzo and DeAndre Moore

The Uncle

"Oh God no! Oh God no!" De'Anne screamed hysterically after just receiving the disturbing news her younger brother De'Andre had been shot. She tried to calm down and gather her nerves before calling her eldest brother Tywon; it was useless. De'Anne had dialed his cell phone number several times only to receive his voicemail. She continuously kept calling until Tywon finally answered the line.

"Damn! De'Anne, what do you want? I'm vacationing at bike week in Myrtle Beach."

"It's Dre, Ty! It's Dre!" sobbing uncontrollably.

"What! What happened to Dre?" he nervously asked.

"He's been shot, Dre's been shot!"

"Awe shit! By who, is he dead? De'Anne, is he..."

Heavily crying, "I don't know... I don't know..."

"I'm on my way De'Anne! Don't call momma yet, you hear me! I'll be there in two hours." "Click!"

"Damn man! Them muthafucka's shot my brother," ranted Tywon kicking his Motorcycle to the ground. "Dre knew to stay low, he knew shit was hot, damn! C'mon yawl, we got'ta catch this flight back to the D."

Tywon's childhood friend Money Bunny followed, as well as White Boy J; his suburban business partner.

Tywon spared no expense as he cashed out the first class flight tickets. Money suddenly didn't matter to him anymore, only thoughts of his brother's possible death raced in his mind. His mouth grew dry, his hands grew numb and he continuously twitched, just knowing Dre took a bullet. "Damn!"

Money stood up. "Ty, don't worry man. Dre's a fighter, he's strong. He's go'on be alright."

The two embraced for a hug. J shook his head knowing that was a hug of death and the out-come wasn't going to be good.

Tywon then sat back in his seat, looking deep through the clouds as thoughts of his childhood came to mind.

The year was 1983; Tywon Miller was 12 years old. It was a time of no worries, no pains and no problems; a time when most neighbors knew one another by first and last name; a time when violence and gunfire was only seen or heard about on the nightly news.

With caution, Tywon stood at the backdoor of Uncle Ed's Night Lounge, located on Gratiot Avenue between Seminole and Maxwell on Detroit's east side of town. His 13 year-old partner, Money Bunny as a cover, accompanied him.

Nervously looking around he mumbled. "Money man, I don't know if I should be here. My momma don't be playin' games about what she say, as her words replayed in his mind; *'Don't let my belt find out yo' ass been back in that bar, you won't like what it has to say.'* Tywon shook it off with a quiver.

Money stood with his arms folded, "Cut that crap out Ty!" he frowned. "Quit being a chicken. Yo' momma ain't nowhere around here. Plus, you promised to introduce me to Uncle Ed for a job. Are you faking on me now?"

"Naw man."

"Well c'mon then," he encouraged stepping inside the bar.

Inside the bar, the atmosphere was smooth and laid back. The lights were dim, the air was chilled, and marijuana joints were openly being puffed and passed, as Isaac Hayes 'Walk on by,' pushed out the jukebox speakers.

The bartender spoke from over the counter as the boys approached.

"Can I help y'all sweetie?" she asked.

Dang, she's pretty, thought Money. He excitedly hopped onto the bar stool like he was a grown man. With his voice deepened he answered, "Yes, I'd like a beer, Bush beer," holding back a smile.

The bartender giggled. She decided to play along with the joke. She walked towards the cooler. Money turned to Tywon smiling knowing he was about to get served. The bartender returned with a tall glass and poured the beer. Money's eyes lit up with anticipation. It would be his first drink of brew. He reached for the glass and tilted it up, ready to down it.

Suddenly, a loud, deep, threatening voice came from behind.

"I suggest you put that got damn beer down, unless you want yo' teeth knocked down yo' throat," said an older man. He snatched the glass from Money's hand, slamming it down onto the counter.

"Who the fuck told you, you could drink?" he asked with a hard stare. "This establishment is foe grown folks. What the hell yo' young ass doin' in here?" Money turned and peered into the mans yellow glazed fish like eyes. He then pointed to Tywon ready to speak, but the man cut him off.

Moving in closer, "Do you want yo' ass whooped boy?"

Money didn't say a word. He was frozen with fear. He glanced at Tywon who appeared to be in shock with his hand over his mouth. Everyone else in the small bar also sat in silence.

"Answer me boy! You here me talkin' to you! Do you want yo' ass whooped?" the man asked with intimidation.

Money struggled to shake his head, '*No.*'

"I didn't think so," pulling the stool away from the bar. "Go'on fella, hit the door, get out'ta here. C'mon back when you get some hair on them baby nuts. Until then, go and get drunk off yo' momma's tiddies."

Money slowly eased his way from the barstool. He'd never been so embarrassed in his life. Any becoming of age manhood he had was quickly dissected. Just as he was exiting the backdoor, the man weirdly called out his name, "Money! Hey Money. C'mon back here, let me talk to you."

Money turned around in confusion. *How does this man know my name?* he thought to himself. He then saw everyone in the bar beginning to laugh, including Tywon.

What's so funny? heading back.

Money approached. The man's hand was now extended for a handshake. Money was hesitant to make a move, until Tywon gave him a nod to go ahead. The two shook hands.

The gentleman then introduced himself. In a smooth tone, "Hello Money, I'm Uncle Ed. I own this joint," he said raising his hand. "Ty has told me a lot about you and how anxious you've been to work for me. Tywon's a good worker and he said you would be too."

Money eagerly nodded his head, *'Yes'* already forgetting about the incident that transpired.

"I see you got a little heart about yo'self from the way I tested you, I like that. I don't need no cry babies on my team working for me." Money, speechless, but attentive nodded, *'No.'*

Again shaking hands, "Ok good, welcome aboard young blood. Follow Tywon here and he'll show you what needs to be done."

The two youngsters headed towards the stockroom. Ed watched as the boys entered the room, closing the door behind them. It was something in Money's eyes Ed didn't like and he was usually never wrong, but he shrugged it off dismissing the fact that Money was only a kid.

Uncle Ed, *Julius Edward Brown* was a 49 year-old street player who own and ran Ed's Night Lounge for the last 20 years. In his time, he's touched every hustle known to a black man. He never married or fathered children any children with the excuse of, *'The right one ain't came along yet.'*

Uncle Ed liked Tywon from the first day he walked in the bar and asked for a job. He told Tywon he saw the ambition for success in his youthful eyes. Since Ed had no kids of his own, he decided to be a father figure or at least a mentor to Tywon.

It was only 6:00 p.m. and already Ed's Night Lounge was off the hook. The music was bumping, the crowd was building and the drinks were flowing. By this time, Tywon had trained Money for his job. He learned quickly. He was to assort the empty beer bottles by brand into their cases for pick-up.

Tywon worked on the floor clearing the empty beer bottles from the tables, the bar, and most of the time off the pool table. He worked diligently and politely. He often received large tips from the patrons for his services.

Tywon repeatedly returned to the stockroom with a bin full of bottles. Every time he came to the back, Money could hear the jingle of the change in his pocket getting louder. *Hhmmm,* he thought with a hatred feeling. *I need to be working the floor. Ty make'n all that Money while I'm stuck back here playin' with these bottles.*

Just then, Tywon again came with another bin and was returning to the floor when Money stopped him. "A Ty man, I'm tired of being back here in this darkroom. Why don't you let me collect the bottles for a while and you stay back here and sort them out," thinking of the tips he could make.

Tywon looked at Money in disbelief. "What! This is only your first day. You've worked for only an hour," he said holding the stockroom door slightly open. Disco lights from party lit up the dim room. Money tried to peek to the outside, but Tywon shut the door. "Listen Money, Uncle Ed ain't gon'na like if he sees you out there on the floor, he don't know you yet. Give it a month or two, let him get comfortable with you and then maybe, you can work the floor like me. Until then, be cool. Ok?" with his hand on Money's shoulder.

"Ok" Money agreed with a fake smile. He then continued his job.

As Tywon was walked out the door, Money turned around and shot him through the back with a handgun gesture.

Maurice Bonner a.k.a. Money Bunny was Tywon's best friend ever since they could remember. Money was a friend that might as well have been an enemy. He was self-centered, jealous hearted, envious and revengeful in this thoughts. He was a dangerous and a subtle type of kid; never giving a clue to how he really felt.

****

Ed was sitting down in the corner talking to a couple of rough looking fellows. He appeared to be upset. His voice was low, but his pointing and hand gestures were fierce. "If y'all would've killed that muthafucka Black-Knight the first time, we wouldn't have this problem, now would we?" he said to the pair with his eyes bucked out.

"But Ed, Black-Knight's kids were out there, we didn't want them to get hurt," voiced one of the men with concern.

Ed's face soured up. "What the fuck kind of killers is y'all? I don't give a fuck about Black-Knight's kids. Fuck his kids!" Ed then asked pointing, "Is they yo' kids?"

"No," the man answered.

"Are they his kids?" pointing to the guy seated next to him.

Again,"No."

"Well shut the fuck up then. Y'all suppose to have did his ass. I don't care who was around. They daddy stole from me, therefore I'm feedin' they asses. They eaten off my plate, and ain't shit on my dish for free," clenching his teeth. "So c'mon and lets get this muthafucka! Gos'ta get this pecka' wood off my back," he ended as they all got up from the table.

Ed and his men then walked out the backdoor into the parking lot of the bar just before the alley. The two men entered their vehicle ready to pull off when Ed leaned down onto the passenger window for a last word. In a raw tone, "Listen, game time is over. This shit is for real, so I expect for Black-Knight to be Dead-Knight real soon. Don't fuck it up!" now looking around like he heard something.

"Don't worry Ed, we got you," assured the man in the passenger seat. They then drove off.

Ed watched the two with an evil eye glare riding away. Something about the pair didn't sit right with him. He'd been out here too long not to know bullshit when he smelled it. But Ed couldn't dwell on it right now. He was too focused on the woman's voice he heard faintly calling his name when she suddenly appeared. "Ed!" she called tapping him on the shoulder. Ed turned around startled, caught off guard. Pissed off, he grabbed her by the throat.

"Bitch! What did I tell you about sneaking up on me like that? You know my nerves is bad."

She angrily slapped his hands. "Get the fuck off me Ed. What do you mean sneakin' up on you? I've been calling you all day, but you been ignoring me. You act like you don't want me anymore," said China.

Sympathetically, "Naw baby, you know that ain't it. I already explained the problem to you. But as usual, you never listen to me. Plus, you be havin' me all fucked up and off my game and shit, I don't like that. The women in my life have always stood ankle high to me, but you," he said snarling. "You be tryin' to run shit, you think you slick. I see how you act when you in the bar. You always in a muthafucka's face; smiling, talking, teasin,' flirtin' and shit, you know how you do." China blushed as if that was a compliment.

"But really though China, I don't have time for a bitch like you. Don't get me wrong, you still my number one hoe, but I can't fuck around with you right now."

China was unmoved and unemotional about what Ed had said. From their 18-year relationship, she was all too familiar with his shit talk but China decided she had heard enough. She simply kissed Ed on the nose and walked away.

Just then, Tywon walked outback to take the trash out. He just happened to look over his shoulder and weirdly saw Ed standing in the middle of the alley. His lips were moving but no words were coming out. He appeared to be starring at someone down alley but Tywon looking himself, didn't see a soul.

Puzzled, "Uncle Ed, what's goin' on? Why you standing out here by yourself? Who you looking at?" rapidly asked Tywon eyeing the silver compact in Ed's hand. Oddly, Ed didn't even hear him. He was zoned out. He just stood stiff and motionless.

Tywon nudged him. "Uncle Ed, are you alright? Can you hear me?" worried. Ed suddenly came back to as he sniffed and wiped his nose placing the small compact in his back pocket.

"Hey Ty baby my main man, what you need? Money! Bitches! Is somebody in there fuckin' wit you?" he asked with a serious look.

Tywon laughed knowing that was the Uncle Ed he knew.

"Naw, no-one is bothering me, but I did wan'na thank you for giving my friend Money a job." Ed was about to voice his thoughts about Money but Tywon continued. "He really ain't got nothing or nobody. His daddy ain't around and his momma acts like she doesn't care about him. Most of the time he eats at my house and wears my clothes." Tywon then began to whisper. "He even be sporting my under-wears but I just let him have them." Ed smiled. "But Money will be alright, I got his back for life," said Tywon as if he was Money's big brother.

Ed could see the love Tywon had for Money. He decided not to rock the boat with his opinions but instead, just have a little man talk on life with Tywon. The two were slowly walking down the alley when Ed asked, "Ty, How old are you? 12, 13 what?"

"I'm 12 years old," Tywon proudly responded. Ed breathed deeply knowing he was still a mere baby. That of course didn't halt his direct words.

"So, are you fuckin' yet?" he boldly asked.

Tywon was embarrassed by the question. He smiled, shaking his head '*No*' like the thought was nasty.

"Don't be shy boy. You 'bout at the baby makin' age, that's right. One of them rag headed girls gon'na think you cute and try to give you some."

"Some what?" asked Tywon playing simple minded.

"Some what? Some pussy boy! Some of that hot fire between her legs. That deep tunnel to the devils workshop. I thought you had an older sister?"

"No younger. De'Anne's only 9 years old."

"Oh" said Ed, quickly changed the subject. "What about drugs? Have you ever tried any drugs?" he asked already knowing the answer.

Tywon nodded '*No.*'

"Good…and don't you start. If nothin' else, them drugs will fuck your life up. Them pills, heroin all that shit! Ain't nothin' but acid on the brain. I seen the prettiest and the finest women get reduced down to skinny, helpless junkies," he said shamefully.

"I seen that before too," interrupted Tywon. "My momma was on that stuff, but she got help. She's alright now."

She's one in a million, thought Ed.

The two arrived at the end of the alley on Maxwell Street. They stopped, looked around and then slowly proceeded back up the alley towards the bar.

"So, Uncle Ed, since we're talking about drugs, can I ask you a personal question?" "Shoot" he replied.

"Ok. Have you ever tried drugs before?"

Ed didn't stutter, "Every damn drug on the pharmacy shelf and some." Tywon was shocked but he showed no reaction.

Without hesitation, "What about now, are you on any drugs now?"

'*Damn,*' Ed looked at Tywon. He wasn't ready for that one. He was a little offended. That information was private, but Ed knew he opened up the floodgate for questions.

With no shame, Ed responded, "Yeah, I do drugs."

"Really! I can't tell. You don't look like you do drugs," said Tywon.

"Nothing is what it seems young blood. That's the cover up of the world. That's why I'm telling you this. Every face you deal with in life is gon'na have a story, some good, some bad and some horrific. I want you to be able to decipher people when you first meet them, when you hear them talk and by how they move. I want your game to be cold. Most folks don't know how cold is cold. I want you to understand that in some cases your best friend and even the woman you share your bed with can be your worst enemy. These are the people who can bring your darkest secrets into a courthouse and get you a life sentence. These are the people who know your weaknesses and your strengths and will use them against you, to bring you down. The same people who might be jealous of you and you'll never know because they're so close. Jealousy is a dangerous emotion. It's when people feel dissatisfied with themselves because they never accomplished anything or even had a goal in life. Then they see you with your confidence, your game plan or whatever it might be as a greater power than themselves. That's when they come for blood. An old cat once told me *'The tragedy in life is not accomplishing your goal: The tragedy in life is not having a goal.'* Tywon smiled, liking that phrase as he continued to listen.

"You see Ty, a lot of these dumb-ass dudes jump in the dope game ass back-wards ending up with bullets in their heads. They all make the same repeated mistakes. They stick their dicks in the game like it's a pussy. After they make a little money, they fall in love with the game like it's a hoe. But what they don't understand is, the game can never love you back. It's a harder bitch to understand than life itself. I understood though, that's why I'm still here baby", he said fixing the collar on his shirt.

"Tywon, this shit I'm on. This shit I sell, this drug called cocaine. This some bad shit! I want you to stay the fuck away from this shit as far as you can. Don't use it, sell it, touch it, don't even get near it. Cocaine is a hella'va drug and it's gon'na make the streets worse. If you ever decide to sell some shit and I hope you never do, sell some weed. Selling a little weed ain't never killed nobody," ended Ed.

The two finally arrived back at the bar in the parking lot. Ed finished by telling Tywon to keep a goal in life and to never ever be like him, be better than him. Tywon understood. Then once again Ed pulled out his silver compact with a large E engraved on top. He again heard China White, first name; *Cocaine* calling his name. She told him she was ready to fuck. She invited him back inside the bar and into the men's bathroom. She wanted to give him the loving he and millions of others loved so much. Tywon shook his head. He now knew Uncle Ed was high off cocaine when he found him in the alley.

At that moment, an unmarked Police car came strolling up the alley cruising at 2 M.P.H. In the car, a white man in his late 20's was looking the bar up and down. His blue eyes then briefly made contact with Tywon's. The car continued to cruise up the alley until making a right turn onto Seminole Street. Tywon didn't think anything of it, he never had any contact with the law, but he was still gon'na inform Uncle Ed of what he saw, of course when Ed came down off his high.

You Raw Now?

Ed's two hit men had just arrived on Detroit's west side. They were staked out up the street from one of the Black-Knight's known drug houses. The two watched as 30 or more people purchase narcotics from the residence. Their plan; execute Black-Knight with two shots to the head, no questions asked. Their problem, they didn't know when, what time, or if Black-Knight was gon'na show up at this location. One of the men decided to call it in. He pulled the keys from the ignition and got out of the car. He opened the trunk, pulling out a hand-held C.B. radio. He hopped back into the driver's seat, turning the radio on.

"This is under-cover Officer Darryl France calling Sergeant Conrad Bantz. Do you read me?" he spoke. Sounds of distortion could only be heard from the radio. He then answered.

"This is Sergeant Conrad Bantz. Switch your radio frequency over to channel 2, it's a secure channel." Officer Darryl did as instructed. He then began explaining the Black-Knight situation. Sergeant Bantz told the Officer to hold on while he made a phone call. He soon returned on the C.B. radio informing the Officers to keep surveillance on the home. Black-Knight was scheduled to show and the hit had to be made. He also told Darryl and his partner to knock off Uncle Ed tonight as well. Bantz said Ed's abusive cocaine usage along with his poor business decision-making had cost him enough, and at this point he was now expendable.

"Plus, it ain't good for the city's image for Detroit's two biggest cocaine traffickers to be at war. Make the killings look like they're drug related retaliation hits," ordered Bantz.

"No problem" replied Officer Darryl, signing off as he and his partner sat back waiting for Black-Knight to arrive.

****

Tywon was still in back of the bar leaning against the wall. He was in thought thinking about Ed's street talk. He loved the realness and the knowledge in Ed's words without the preaching technique, words from a strong male figure. That was something Tywon didn't have in his home. Tywon didn't know his real father, but he did have a stepfather, *Ronnie Nelson.*

Ronnie was a 30 year-old drunk who always pissed his pants when intoxicated. Tywon didn't at all respect him. He viewed his stepfather as being on his level as a 12 or 13 year old kid. He only dealt with Ronnie because he was the father of his younger brother: 5 year-old De'Andre. Whenever Ronnie tried to take an authoritative position in the home, with no respect, Tywon would flick him off like a flea. De'Anne and De'Andre would soon follow.

At that moment, Tywon snapped his fingers coming out of thought. Talking to Ed, he'd forgotten about his job and Money in the stock room. He entered the bar slowly moving amongst the dancing crowd. Tywon felt a little guilty for leaving Money alone for so long, but to his surprise, Money was on the floor collecting bottles and sliding tips into his pocket. Tywon frowned. He felt a little betrayed. He then excused his feelings thinking, *'Money's my partner. He's only covering my back because I wasn't here.'*

Tywon was about to approach Money and thank him for covering his job when suddenly, he felt two painful lashes blaze across his back. Tywon's lips curled with agony. He hurried to turn around when a third struck him across the chest. "Oowww!" he cried covering himself. Money gave a smirk but kept working like he never saw or heard a thing.

Pointing with the belt in hand, "Didn't I tell you? Didn't I tell you I was gon'na beat your ass if you came back up in this bar?" ranted Tywon's mother. Both his hands were now up in a defensive position to block any further attack.

"Yeah momma you did, but... but..."

"Whap!" she lashed again. Tywon didn't have a defensive word for his case. Nor did he have any maneuvering room to dodge the strikes. He immediately took off running pushing pass the party people and out the back door. His mother was about to give chase until she spotted Uncle Ed coming out of the bathroom. Tywon's mother approached him with a look of vengeance on her face. She placed her finger 1 inch from Ed's nose.

"Listen dammit, Tywon is an under-aged minor. I've told you before I didn't want him around you or your kind. I'm raisin' mine to know right from wrong, and it ain't right, you letting children work in here like that," she said as she looked over to Money.

"And I'm telling your mother Maurice."

Money shrugged his shoulders like he didn't care.

She turned back to Ed whose eyes were glossier than freshly waxed floors. "If I see or even hear about Tywon being back in this bar, the Mayor's office is gon'na hear about this place. Mess with me if you want to and I'll have yo' ass shut down!" she ended exiting the back door.

Ed threw his hand not wanting to hear that shit. *Bitch ain't go'on do nothing, she just wan'na hear herself talk.* He then slowly steered his way to the bar. He took a seat and ordered 3 shots of crown royal. He downed all 3 drinks, lit a cigarette, crossed his legs and watched his customers all have a good time.

****

It was 9:30 p.m.; the warm August day fell into a cool breezy night. Officer Darryl and his partner were still patiently waiting for Black-Knight to arrive. The two were calm, showing no signs of agitation. They didn't break a stare from their targets place of business. The pair was suited in all black, armed with pistols and anxious to kill.

Officer Darryl looked to his partner. "Conrad Bantz can't be nothing more than a year or two older than us. How did he get in control over such a large drug operation. He's working both the east and west side of town like it's his own cartel. Who put him in charge?"

Darryl's partner was over anxious to answer.

Eagerly, "Detroit is where Conrad Bantz grew up. He knows these streets. He's been on the force almost 10 years since the age of 19. He's followed the footsteps of his daddy and his grandfather. At 22, he became 2nd in command of the Narcotics Division with over 200 busts, soon-after he was running his own drug task force entitled, 'Stress' in which you and I are now a part of," he stated proudly.

Damn, is he bitch or something? thought Darryl.

He continued, "Stress was designed to bring down major narcotics traffickers. It was created to alleviate the rising crime rate since cocaine hit the city's streets. The drug search and seizure confiscations also help with the city's budget and..."

Darryl interrupted, "And it helps to line up Conrad's pockets, that's what it does if you wan'na be real about it. Man...This white boy ain't nothing but a Gangster wit'a badge. From what I've seen, Conrad's worse than the Dope Man himself. He's controlling the distribution of drugs in the city and he's controlling the dealers. And, if a dealer shows he's useless to Conrad, Conrad then creates a beef between rival dealers and have them both hit, in-which you and I carry out."

"But that's just to protect his interest," defended his partner.

"Anyway, you know what the sad thing about all this is?" he continued.

"What's that?"

"We're all black and Conrad's white. He's just sitting back in his office, pulling our genocidal strings like were puppets and gettin' rich." Darryl and his partner just sat back in silence marinating on the hard truth.

At that point, a blue BMW passed by the two Officers. The pair knew the vehicle belonged to Black-Knight. They sunk lower in their seats peeking over the dashboard. The car stopped one house before the drug house. A broad shouldered gentleman stepped out the car with a briefcase in his hand.

"That's him," whispered Darryl. "That's Black-Knight."

Even though Darryl didn't have a clear vision on Black-Knight's face, he recognized his build. Both Officers then cocked their weapons. Darryl after-wards looked at his partner.

"Man...Do you really wan'na do this?" he asked.

His partner shook his head. "Darryl, it's too late for that now. Lets just do this thing. We'll kill Black-Knight, finish off Ed and then we can lay back and relax for a while," stated the Officer with persuasion. Darryl nodded in agreement.

Black-Knight entered the home. Officer Darryl and his partner then exited their vehicle. They began casually walking up and down the sidewalk portraying themselves to be pedestrians. Darryl walked on one side of the street, his partner on the other. The two repeated this back and fourth act many times now worried it could draw suspicion. 35 minutes had passed and Black-Knight still hadn't yet exited the home.

Damn! Where's he at? What's taking him so long? thought Darryl's partner as he tightly squeezed the handle of his pistol. He didn't care anything about Darryl's earlier speech of genocide. He was a killer. He was relentless when it came to mercenary work, regardless of race.

Darryl's partner decided on a different approach to this hit. When he reached the corner of the block, he made a right turn walking, until he arrived to the alley. There, he ran through the dark alley finally arriving at the backyard of the drug house. He tucked his pistol on his waistline, hopped over the gate and made his way down the side of the house where he waited. Darryl continued to stroll the sidewalk now realizing his partner had disappeared. He then stopped eyeing both sides of the street wondering where his back up went to.

Just so happen, Black-Knight was coming out of the dope house. As always, he checked his perimeter spotting Darryl suspiciously standing across the street.

"Who is this mutha...?" reaching around to his back for his pistol. He then proceeded to walk off the porch.

Darryl looking around didn't see Black-Knight approaching him.

"Yo! Yo! Who you lookin' foe? What you doin' 'round here?" he asked with the barrel of his gun exposed.

Darryl was caught off guard. His instinct was to reach for his own pistol, but he knew that would only be a death sentence for him-self. He quickly thought.

"I'm looking for the blow house. My partner said I could get some good nose candy from around here" he spoke.

Doubtfully, "Nose candy, huh?" Black-Knight scanned Darryl up and down.

"And I guess you need black leather gloves to do that, right? Get yo' bitch ass down on the ground!" shoving the pistol to Darryl's forehead."

Awe shit! Where's my backup.

Darryl's partner was watching everything go down from the side of the house. He was tempted to rush across the street blasting, but he knew that would jeopardize both him and his partner's life. He decided to wait. Black-Knight had laid Darryl face down on the pavement. He searched him finding his gun. Darryl was again questioned. He stuck with the same nose candy tale. Black-Knight began to pistol-whip Darryl senselessly. With-in seconds, his head was lumped with bruises. His eyes were puffed and swollen. Blood was trickling from his mouth.

Whimpering "Please, no more," he begged.

"You muthafucka! I know you was comin' to kill me for that white boy! I'm no fool! I ought'a do you right here," raged Black-Knight.

Awe hell naw! thought Darryl's partner. *Do him?* He couldn't wait any longer. It was a time to kill. He darted across the street with his gun drawn.

Infuriated, "What the fuck you doin' man!" he hollered.

Black-Knight turned with his pistol aimed. The two then squared off with their pistols aimed at one-another's face. "What it look like I'm doing?" stated Black-Knight as to say, *'As if you don't know.'* "I'm getting rid of the shit that I paid you to do."

Lowering his weapon, "I was on it."

"Well apparently not fast enough. C'mon, grab his feet. This boy is threw, lets put him in the trunk."

Darryl's partner shook his head but he gave no objections. He and Black-Knight tossed Officer Darryl into the trunk. The two then hopped in the BMW and headed towards the Detroit River.

****

Tywon was upstairs in his bedroom starring out the window into the night. He was disgusted and distraught over how his mother came in the bar and kicked his ass. The situation for him was hard to deal with, it was heart wrenching. *Damn!* he thought. *My momma embarrassed me in front of everybody; the customers, Money, and even Uncle Ed. She could've talked to me, but she just had to show out,* angrily folding his arms. Tywon now felt his mother didn't love him. In his heart, he knew that wasn't true but the anger overcame any rational thinking.

Tywon stomped towards his locked bedroom door, unlocking it. He then flung the door open slamming it against the wall. Tywon's stepfather Ronnie was sitting on the couch when he heard the loud commotion.

"What the hell!" making his way over to the bottom of the stairs.

"A Boy! You better calm yo'self down up there. Don't take it out on the house because your momma beat yo' ass in front of everybody," snickering. "She told you and I told you to stay out that bar."

You told me? Tywon thought in confusion. *Who does Ronnie think he's talking to? What he say don't mean nothin' 'round here, plus I don't even like his ass.* That was it, Tywon had enough of Ronnie's shit.

Enraged, he hollered downstairs. "Fuck you Ronnie! This my momma's house, you don't tell me what to do. You ain't my daddy, and you don't pay no bills around here. My momma already done told you, you got one foot out the door," looking over the banister.

Ronnie was about to sit down when Tywon's words struck him like a cold nerve. "I'm tired of this lil' bastard's mouth, doggin' and disrespectin' me."

De'Anne and De'Andre awoke from their brother's screaming voice. They walked out into the hallway where Tywon stood. Ronnie madly charged his way up the stairs.

Approaching, "What did you say boy! You got somethin' you wan'na say to me?" he asked with his finger in Tywon's face.

Tywon could smell the liquor reeking through Ronnie's shirt with a light hint of piss. He starred his stepfather in his eyes. The same way Uncle Ed always told him to look at the enemy.

Gritting his teeth, "You heard me. I said fuck you! Your drunk ass ain't my daddy," grimmed Tywon.

Ronnie at first was shocked. He then chuckled with his hand up to his mouth. "Damn, you raw now, huh lil' muthafucka'? Yeah…you got some hair on your nuts. Hanging down at the bar done made you a man, huh?" he said cracking his knuckles.

Tywon didn't laugh. He just stood mute with a mugged look on his face. De'Anne and De'Andre stood confused. From the exchange of swear words, they were now unsure of who was the adult and who was the child. Ronnie then walked away throwing his hand gesturing, '*I ain't got time for this shit.*'

Tywon breathed hard through his nostrils knowing he punk'd his stepfather. He then turned and headed back to this bedroom. De'Anne and De'Andre followed. Tywon was just entering his bedroom when he suddenly spinned around from a snatch by his shoulder.

"Whap!" Ronnie forcefully backhanded Tywon across the face.

"You go'on respect me boy! I'm a grown ass man! Watch your self, I'm telling you," he said pressing Tywon against the wall.

The snatch and slap happened so fast Tywon was dizzy. De'Anne and De'Andre were now screaming for their brother's safety.

Ronnie turned towards the youngsters. "Shut the fuck up!"

Just then, Tywon refocused making his move. He gripped Ronnie by the hips and kneed him in the nuts. "Oofff!"

Ronnie hunched over Tywon as he tried to run away, but was grabbed by the back of his shirt. Like a Rag-Doll, Tywon was repeatedly slammed back and fourth against the hallway walls. A couple of times he went in head first cracking the dry wall. Ronnie was loving the release of his anger and the control he held over Tywon's frail 120-pound frame.

"Stop daddy! No daddy!" cried De'Anne and De'Andre. Tywon was finally released as Ronnie flung him up the hardwood floors. He slid 15-feet, until reaching the edge of the stairs. He quickly looked back at his stepfather who was pouring in sweat and breathing hard. Tywon frantically crawled down the stairs as if his legs were broken. Ronnie was on him like a lion on prey.

"Come back here lil' muthafucka!"

The two youngsters still crying and screaming watched from the upstairs railing. Tywon reached the bottom of the stairs but he had enough. He was weak and tired and had no strength to defend himself. He turned onto this back. He at-least wanted to see his predator face to face. Ronnie took the last two steps off the stairs arriving at the bottom. He then stood over his stepson. He knelled down and pulled Tywon up by his shirt collar.

Vindictively, "I got your ass now." Ronnie balled his fists and pulled back. Tywon was wide eyed awaiting the crucial blow.

Right then, the front door flew open. It was Tywon's mother, *Faye Nelson.* She was walking up the block when she heard the cries of her children from up the street. With all of her might, Faye rushed in pushing Ronnie from over her son. He tumbled to the floor like a brick.

"What the hell is wrong with you Ronnie? That damn liquor done made you lose your mind or something?" she yelled repeatedly slapping his face. Ronnie cowardly folded up trying to block her hits. Now silent, De'Anne and De'Andre felt relieved from their mother's presence, although continuing to watch from the upstairs. Tywon was holding back a silent cry, but his tears still ran. He was breathing hard along with his quivering lips. He could no longer remain quiet as anger again took over his emotions.

"Momma! Ronnie rammed my head into the wall!" he cried. "And he slapped me. Ask De'Anne and Dre, they seen him," pointing upstairs.

Faye ceased her attack on her husband.

"He what! Ronnie what!" raving mad she asked looking up to her children. They both shook their heads confirming Ronnie's acts.

Faye stood from the floor. She took a closer look to inspect Tywon's head and face. She could see the white wall residue in her son's hair, which gave it a salt and pepper appearance. His forehead was bruised with slight blood bunts on the ends. Faye turned and starred at Ronnie as if a look could kill. Right then, she almost lost it, she almost went crazy. Ronnie tried to verbally defend his actions, but the situation was beyond explanation. His wife didn't want to hear shit he had to say.

Faye silently walked towards the front door. She opened the door and pointed, "Leave Ronnie! Just get the fuck out my house," she said coldly. Ronnie held his hands out from his side with his mouth hung open. His thoughts were twisted.

'What the fuck just happened? How did this happen?' He couldn't remember. All Ronnie knew he was being put out the house into the dark night with nowhere to go. He hung his head and slowly proceeded to walk out the door. Ronnie looked into his wife's eyes hoping for a sign of sympathy. But to no surprise he could only see lost love. The short fuse in their marriage had finally ignited and blew up.

****

Black-Knight and Darryl's partner pulled up to the edge of the Detroit River. The trunk was automatically opened from the glove box. The two men hopped out the car. They lifted the trunk laying eyes on Darryl. The pistol whipping did more damage than originally thought. He was in bad shape.

Darryl who was slipping in an out of consciousness couldn't believe it. He'd been set up by his own partner. *But why?* he so badly wanted to know, but he was too bruised and battered to talk. Darryl could only peek at his captures through his left unclosed eye.

Quamy, Darryl's partner sighed at the sight of him lying helplessly in the trunk. Quamy knew what he'd done to Darryl wasn't right, but in this line of work, there was no loyalty, there were no friends and you couldn't have a conscious. The dollar ruled this game. Darryl wasn't guilty of a thing. He was simply a victim of Quamy's greed.

Quamy continued to stare at Darryl as he went into thought that led up to this event. One month earlier while on his way to the shooting range, Quamy spotted a blue BMW traveling down 7-Mile Rd. going in the opposite direction. He stuck his head out the driver's window and turned to look.

"Is that? Yeah, that's his ass," Quamy convincingly told himself. He quickly u-turned his narc vehicle running up the curb, at the same time cutting off traffic, placing his siren light on the dashboard quickly catching up to the car, making a so-called routine stop.

Quamy exited his car. He approached the driver side window of the vehicle he pulled over.

Kindly, "Hello sir, do you know why I stopped you today?" he asked taking off his leather gloves.

"No, no I don't," calmly answered 31 year-old Black-Knight. Quamy didn't have time for games, he cut straight to the chase.

"Well Black-Knight, I stopped you because you stole 10 kilos of cocaine from Uncle Ed. You do know Uncle Ed right?"

Black-Knight almost choked. He was startled by how the Officer knew his name. Mostly at how casually he spoke of theft of the cocaine.

Black-Knight snatched off his shades and tried to exit the driver's door.

Quamy jumped back un-holstering his pistol.

"Whoa! Whoa! Hold on now cowboy, just take it easy. I'm not here to arrest you, I wan'na talk business."

Black-Knight feared a hit as he deliriously looked in every direction. Out the passenger window, in his rear-view mirror and finally back to Quamy. Black-Knight was nervous, he didn't trust shit.

"So what kind of business do you wan'na talk about?" suspiciously he asked. Quamy began telling Black-Knight of the $30,000 price Ed had placed on his life. He then lied by saying he knew who the hit man was, which supposedly was his partner Darryl.

Quamy boasted to Black-Knight how he did mercenary work. He bragged in detail about countless murders. He said his badge meant nothing to him; it was just a good cover up for his real profession. Black-Knight sat unimpressed. He only wanted to hear the real reason why the crooked cop stopped him.

After the introduction shit talk, it came. Quamy told Black-Knight he would knock-off the alleged hit man for $50,000. For and additional 40 grand, he would personally kill Uncle Ed himself.

Black-Knight didn't trust the corrupt freelance Policeman. He felt he was dumb, over anxious and greedy all at the same time. Besides Black-Knight didn't discuss murder plots out in the open, especially not with cops. But considering the unusual circumstances, he agreed to the deal without hesitation. He knew he stood to lose a lot more, possibly even his life if he didn't agree. Black-Knight was no fool. This was just another part of the game he knew he had to play in order to survive. The two shook hands, exchanged information and then took off in their separate directions.

Quamy soon came out of thought as Black-Knight nudged him.

"Yo! What's up man?" You're not getting cold feet on me now, are you?" he asked.

"Hell naw!" voiced Quamy as if his mind never drifted.

"Ok good, because remember, you approached me with this. I would hate to think you can't finish what you started," said Black-Knight with doubtful thoughts.

Quamy frowned. He felt some disrespect in that statement.

'This two-cent hustler muthafucka' dares to question my *reputation? Let me show this cat how I really get down,'* thought Quamy. He then reached for his pistol. Black-Knight didn't notice

Quamy had pulled out his gun, fumbling with the chain down on the passenger seat floor.

Rapidly, "Bbooomm! Bbooomm! Bbooomm!"

Gun smoke whisked in the rivers breeze. Silence plagued the air. Black-Knight emerged from the car with his pistol in hand.

"Man! What the fuck you shootin' at?" He then looked down into the trunk. Heavy globs of blood was running from Darryl's mouth. He was struggling to breathe. The pain was in his eyes. He clinched his fists trying to hold on but it was useless. The 3 close range 38. Magnum shots were too much for him to bare. Darryl was trembling from the shock as he took his final breath. "Hhuuuhh!" and then he was gone.

Quamy turned to Black-Knight with his pistol still smoking. "Word of advice partner, don't you ever question my credibility. Whatever I start, trust me, I will finish it," he said with a stern look.

Right then, Black-Knight knew he'd made a deal with the devil, but he had no intentions on selling his soul. He only kept in mind: *'This is still part of the game.'*

Black-Knight grabbed the chain along with a 45-pound weight. He shackled them both to Darryl's body. He and Quamy then lifted Darryl from the trunk and dragged him to the rivers edge. With no remorse, they tossed him into the cold dark river.

"Bbooosshh!" Darryl hit the water like a bomb. The chain and weight made him sink fast. Quamy then spit into the water.

"I didn't like his ass no-way," he stated walking back towards the car. Black-Knight looked at Quamy with the same mutual feeling towards him, as he followed.

Black-Knight closed the trunk and hopped into the car. The pair then took off for Ed's Night Lounge.

****

Ronnie was standing on the porch when he looked back. He was watching as his wife was shutting the front door behind him. She snarled her top lip at him like he was a piece of shit. *Ol' Bitch!* thought Ronnie.

The door was inches from closing when Ronnie stuck his foot in the entrance, preventing its closure. Faye looked down to see what was jamming the door.

"Move your foot Ronnie!" she said pushing the door with her shoulder. Ronnie refused.

"If I got'ta leave, then I'm taking De'Andre with me. That's my son!" he repeatedly yelled beating on the door.

De'Anne and De'Andre again started screaming. Tywon tried to assist his mother in closing the door, but Ronnie's strength seemed to amplify. He burst back into the front room screaming.

"Fuck that! I ain't goin' nowhere! I'm still the man of this house!"

"You ain't no man," said Tywon. "You a drunk sucker."

"Fuck you!" hastily pointed Ronnie.

"Hush your mouth Tywon, let me handle this," said his mother.

Faye could see her husband was now at a hostile point. She knew her physical strength was no match for his. She then tried to rationalize with him.

"Ronnie listen, what you did to Tywon was ignorant, childish and uncalled for. Plus, the children are upset. I think you should just leave the house tonight and come back after a week or two. Then we all could sit down and talk about this sensibly."

'A week or two? This Bitch is trying to get rid of me.' Ronnie squint his eyes. He had serious doubts about what his wife just said. Faye was a Gemini: A two headed beast. She'd flip like the wind. Ronnie dealt with his wife long enough to know she'd say one thing but would act on another. He knew once he was out that door, he was out. Ronnie wasn't buying it. He flopped down on the couch.

"Uh! Uh! Fuck that!" he said ruthlessly. "If somebody's leavin' this house tonight, it's go'on be you, Tywon punk-ass and that lil' bitch De'Anne. Y'all leave for the night and come back after a week or two. Me and Dre go'on stay right here," pounding the sofa cushion.

"Bitch! Bitch! I know you didn't just call De'Anne a Bitch?" asked Faye in disbelief. Ronnie took a swig of his drink for courage.

"I call 'em how I see 'em," he coldly stated.

"You pissy draws, stankin', broke ass, disrespectful muthafucka! This is my house, and I'm not about to sit here and let you disrespect my kids like that. Yo' ass go'on leave this house right now," said Faye as she ran into the kitchen. She could still hear Ronnie from the front room hollering he wasn't going anywhere.

In the kitchen, Faye placed a pot of hot water on the stove to boil. She then rambled through the utensil drawer, coming across the biggest cutting knife she could find. All in one step, she sprinted back into the front room wildly swinging. Any drunkenness Ronnie had or felt was altogether gone. He instantly sobered up at the sight of the sharp edge blade.

Wildly swinging the knife, "You go'on leave here got-dammit! Get out my house!" yelled Faye.

Ronnie leaped from the couch startled. He started jumping side to side in a boxing fashion dodging the knife's contact. But Faye caught him across the forearm.

"Oowww!" he screamed now wishing he'd left. Blood ran down his arm. The cut was deep. De'Anne nearly fainted from witnessing the blood spill onto the floor. De'Andre covered his eyes.

"I told yo' ass I wasn't playing Ronnie! I betcha' you'll leave now!" raved Faye.

Ronnie upset, snatched off his t-shirt and wrapped his arm. The knife wound had him timid, but he stood his ground. Surprisingly, he was ready for more, but Tywon himself had enough.

"I'm calling the Police," he said running towards the phone. Ronnie cut him off, snatching the large square phone out the wall. Tywon tried to re-direct his steps but it was too late. Ronnie was already in a swinging motion with the phone coming over top.

"Bing!" sounded the phone as it smashed Tywon on the center of his head. He fell to the floor in agonizing pain.

"Tywon!" screamed Faye, running to his aid. As she was passing by Ronnie, he stepped aside and broadsided Faye across her face with the phone.

"Wham!" She hit the floor, dropping the knife from the unexpected blow. Faye laid like a corpse as Ronnie bent down to her face.

"You ain't so tough without that knife, huh bitch? Say somethin' nah," he raved kicking her in the stomach.

Ronnie was going berserk. He knew one day, he was going to answer to the ass whooping he was passing out tonight, but for now, he felt almighty as he took his respect in the house.

De'Anne and De'Andre had long ago been tired of crying. They could no longer just sit back and let Ronnie abuse their mother. The two youngsters then ran down stairs launching a full squadron attack on their father; equipped with biting teeth and sharp nails, they both gouged into one of each of Ronnie's legs. He slapped them both off but the two kept on coming. Tywon arose from De'Anne and De'Andre's avenged attack. He knew now was the time to act. Immediately, he scanned the floor searching for the knife. He spotted it laying next to his mother who was still knocked out cold. *'Awe momma,'* Tywon felt in sorrow. He then ran to the knife picking it up, as he turned towards Ronnie whose back was turned away from him.

Tywon stood with the blade in hand. *'This is it,'* he thought. *'That muthafucka' Ronnie is dead and he don't even know it. I'm just gon'na run up and stick his ass as many times as I can, until he falls. And then I'll cut his throat. Ronnie messed up puttin' his hands on me and my family. Fuck that shit! Get em!'* Tywon viciously told himself, but he was skeptical about if or not he could murder a man. He never killed anyone before. Such a thought never even crossed his mind, he was just a kid. Uncle Ed before told Tywon, if he should ever have to kill a man, that same man will forever live in his dreams. Tywon definitely didn't want that on his conscious knowing he killed his brother's father. He lowered the weapon.

Just then, "Uuuhhh!" sounded De'Anne. Ronnie open-handedly slapped her from his leg. Tywon watched as his sister thumped to the floor. She held her face, more in shock than pain.

Tywon instantly jumped militant forgetting his thoughts.

"You muthafucka!!" he screamed charging his stepfather with the knife. Ronnie pretended not to hear Tywon's revengeful out-cry. He continued to man handle De'Andre, timing his Tywon's approach. As he neared, Ronnie suddenly turned and threw the large phone at him, bashing him on the knee. The painful blow sent him into a fall but he kept the knife in an upright position. Only half of a foot from Ronnie, Tywon simultaneously thrust the knife into his stepfather's foot as he hit the floor.

Ronnie went deep down into his gut and hollered to the heavens. The cry was loud, foreign and animal like. Tywon stabbed him so hard, the blade exited the bottom of his shoe, severing the wood flooring beneath.

In tears, "Oh, oh, oh God please! Oh God please no! Please, pull it out," mercifully Ronnie cried starring at the children. Tywon didn't speak, he was in disbelief over what he'd just done. His nerves were jittery and his blood was rushing. Stiff faced, he slowly walked backwards shaking his head 'No,' he wasn't removing the knife.

Ronnie still pleading then called on his youngest son.

With flowing tears, "De'Andre look, look at what your brother did to daddy. Please son, help me. Help your daddy. It hurts so bad," he cried squeezing his foot trying to hinder the blood flow.

De'Andre started to whimper. He was about to assist his father when Tywon halted him by the chest.

"No Dre! Stay away from Ronnie, don't go near him," he said with a mistrustful look. "Your daddy is a stranger to us all now. A matter of fact, you ain't got no daddy no more. Ronnie is nothing more than a piece of shit on the bottom of your shoe. And when you mess with shit, you're sure to get some on you." A phrase he quoted from Uncle Ed.

Tywon then smirked looking down at Ronnie's foot whose injury was painting the floor red.

Growing cocky, "Yeah...,with that knife stuck in your foot, you ain't so tough yourself, huh bitch!" he mimicked. "Look at you, cryin' like a baby. And you call yourself the man of this house. You ain't no man Ronnie, you're far from it. You know, the only reason my momma put up with you sorry, pissy drunk ass because you're De'Andre's father, that's it. Other than that, you're a useless good for nothing. You're a joke, a has-been and a wanna-be. But you don't have to worry about none of that now because your finished here," he stated reopening the front door. "Like my momma told you earlier Ronnie, you need to leave. Now get the fuck out our house," Tywon coldly stated pointing to the outside.

Ronnie still on the floor imprisoned by the knife, rather die than to let a 12 year-old kid put him out on the street. His anger began to over power his pain as he grabbed hold the handle of the blade.

Grunting, "Lil' son-a-bitch!"

He snatched the knife out freeing his foot. Blood distilled from the weapon like raindrops.

"Awe shit!" yelled Tywon. "Run!"

The kids ran up the stairs scared and screaming.

Faye had suddenly risen from her blackout. Dazed but on her feet, she too heard Tywon's warning. She first peered at Ronnie who was focused on Tywon, standing at the front door entrance. She then quietly started walking up the wooden stairs to join her children, when the stairs stared to creek. *'Damn,'* she thought hoping Ronnie didn't hear the sounds of the steps. She stopped and looked back. Ronnie was starring back at Faye like a deranged killer.

"Run momma, run!" hollered Tywon. The kids cheered the same. Faye was tempted to haul ass but she knew that would only fuel Ronnie's insane tendencies. She thought fast.

"Ronnie!" she yelled. "Quit actin' crazy, put the knife down," hoping that would disrupt his psychotic thoughts.

Waiving the knife, "Actin!' This ain't no act Bitch! I'ma kill all y'all asses starting with you first. You tryin' to put me out the house, you stabbed me in my arm and you think this is an act. Hold on Bitch, stand right there. I'm go'on show you how much of an act this is," rushing the stairs.

Faye seen and heard enough to know Ronnie was serious as she continued to sprint her way up the stairs. At the top, she screamed for Tywon to run and get help. Despite Ronnie's injured foot, he was hot on his wife's trail. Faye hurried into the bedroom where De'Anne and De'Andre were awaiting. She slammed and locked the door behind herself.

Holding her chest, gasping, "Get behind the bed" she ordered.

"Bam! Bam! Bam!" sounded the bedroom door as Ronnie kicked it. "Bam!"

"Open this muthafuckin' door!" he demanded.

Faye and the children were huddled together silent and scared. Tywon held his face in a panic. He was unsure about if, or not, he should stay and fight, or run to get help. It wasn't a second thought. Tywon knew he couldn't leave his family behind. He acted fast. He ran into the kitchen. There, he saw the boiling pot of water on the stove. He snatched the pot by the handle and headed for the upstairs.

Tywon peeped over the last step from the top. He could see Ronnie still cussing and kicking at the bedroom door, trying to gain entry into the room.

Just then, Ronnie began stabbing through the door with the knife. This fueled Tywon into action. He grabbed the pot and jumped to the top stair. He charged his stepfather this time without a word spoken. As Tywon approached, he douched Ronnie with the scalding water across the side of his face. Ronnie fell to the floor kicking and screaming, leaving the knife stuck in the door. His skin started to bubble and peel away from his face.

Tywon started beating on the bedroom door. "Momma! Momma! C'mon, I got 'em. Momma!" he called.

Faye looked up unsure if she was hearing correctly. "Tywon! Tywon! Is that you?" she asked slowing approaching the door. She heard nothing.

Suddenly, "Bam!" went the door.

Faye jumped back. The knife was snatched from the door. She then heard footsteps running away. Ronnie gave chase to Tywon down the stairs only to stop. He was in too much pain to continue. He watched as Tywon ran out the front door.

Ronnie stood in the middle of the front room sulking. He looked at his cut arm, his bloody foot and his blistering flesh. Ronnie knew he was fucked up. He knew today wasn't his day. He looked upstairs and swore he'd get even with Faye one day. Then slowly in pain, Ronnie proceeded to walk out the front door.

The Conclusion

Black-Knight and Quamy had long ago been posted up the alley from Ed's Night Lounge. They watched as all the customers exited the bar. Quamy looked to Black-Knight.

"It looks like everybody's about gone. I'm gon'na go put two slugs in Ed's head. It'll be simple. He should be high off that shit right about now. You stay here and be ready to get my $90,000 when I get back," he said chambering his pistol.

Black-Knight smiled as if that plan was official. When Quamy exited the car, Black-Knight's smile turned to a mugged look.

'Yeah, I got your money alright,' sarcastically he thought.

Quamy approached the bar. He knocked on the back door hoping his late night visit didn't draw Ed's suspicion. Ed approached the door sliding his compact back in his pocket.

Unsure, "Who is it?" he asked looking out.

"It's me, Quamy."

Quamy? he thought. *What the fuck is he doing here?*

Opening the door "Hey, hey Quamy. I didn't expect you back here tonight. It's closing time you know, what's going on?" he asked keeping Quamy posted at the door.

"Ed man...some shit jumped off with Darryl tonight that I need to tell you about," he spoke with urgency.

"Damn! Can it wait until the morning?"

"It could, but it concerns Black-Knight too."

Ed was high but far from dumb, he knew it was some shit in the game. He looked past Quamy checking the outside perimeter. Everything appeared to be cool. He then invited Quamy inside.

Black-Knight watched as the bar door closed. At that point he exited the car having plans of his own.

It was empty inside the bar making it appear bigger than it really was. There were no drinks being poured or no music playing. The spot was dead. Besides Ed and now Quamy, Money was the only one left in the bar. He was in the stock room assorting the last of the bottles.

Ed directed Quamy to sit at this table booth in the corner. There, if any trouble started, Ed had an upper hand.

"So Quamy, where's Darryl, what happened to him, what jumped off?" Ed calmly asked.

Quamy wasn't one who toyed around, he cut straight to the chase.

Pulling out his pistol, "Darryl's dead. I smoked his ass an hour ago. He's laying at the bottom of the river with the fishes. The same place you're gon'na be real soon. Now get yo' old ass up and open that safe behind the bar, before I kill your ass where you sit," he said with his gun drawn in Ed's face.

Ed expected this shit. He didn't stutter. Mugging, "Man...Fuck you! I ain't opening shit! The only thing I'm go'on open up is my zipper, so you can suck my dick! What, you go'on shoot me? Shoot the muthafucka!" he said placing his hands on the two pistols mounted underneath the table.

Quamy couldn't believe this man's arrogance. He figured the cocaine had Ed delusional to what really was going on. He then pulled out his badge, throwing it on the table.

"You see that? That's my license to kill. That's respect! This ain't no game! This ain't no joke! Wake up you fuckin' cokehead! Recognize who you're dealing with. Now get up and get that safe open!" he said ready to shoot.

Ed's face soured up. *Cokehead?* "Bbooomm! Bbooomm! Bbooomm! Bbooomm!" his pistols ripped. Quamy wide eyed didn't know what hit him. He fired a single shot as he fell to the floor. "Bbooomm!"

Ed jumped from the table bringing his guns up top, again ready to shoot. Ed unknowingly was shot in his right arm.

"What was that!" said Money in the stock room ducking down. Nervously, he crawled over to the door, cracking it open to see what happened. He could see Ed ranting standing over Quamy pointing his pistols.

"You young dumb-ass greedy punk! This my muthafuckin' house! My shit! You don't waltz your ass in a man's establishment pullin' guns, and demanding money and disrespectin' him and shit. You damn fool! You'll get shot doin' stupid shit like that!"

Quamy laid chocking, gasping in disbelief he was shot. His penis blown off. His intestines were hanging and his death's forthcoming was slowly moving in. Quamy could only suffer and listen to his murderer's un-sanctified sermon. Ed continued:

"What! You thought because you slang a badge across my table, that's respect? I, I suppose to bow down or somethin'. Well, you're a bigger fool than I thought. This street life muthafucka! This life don't respect no badge. It applies to one law only: kill or be killed, and you just got killed. You the one who should've recognized who you was dealin' with muthafucka!" he preached.

Money watched stunned and flabbergasted. He was unsure if or not Ed knew he was still in the stockroom. And if so, would Ed kill him after witnessing him kill a man. The thought made Money cold. He decided to keep it quiet and stay put.

Ed felt he'd said enough. It was time to end this. He went to the front door to retrieve a rug. As Ed bent down, his right arm went numb. His gun fell from his hand to the floor. "Damn! I'm shot" seeing all the blood from his bullet wound. He there-upon dragged the rug with his left hand placing it over Quamy's face. Ed didn't want brain fragments all over his bar.

Taking aim with the left, "I'ma do you a favor by making this quick. See you in hell muthafucka!"

Suddenly, "Bbooomm! Bbooomm!" The back door was blown open. It slammed against the wall only to slam back shut. The room stood still for two seconds. Then, "Blam!" Someone kicked the door back open, but not a soul was seen.

"Show your face you fuckin' coward!" Ed hollered.

Just then, two faces peeked back and fourth inside the door. Ed began firing his weapon. He shot out the back door until his gun emptied. Right then, "He's out! He's out of bullets! Get 'em!" ordered Black-Knight.

Six armed men one by one stormed the bar blasting their pistols. Ed took off running towards the front door where he'd dropped his other gun. Bullets were flying, bouncing and ricocheting off everything missing him only by inches. Money figured he's seen enough. He slammed the door, taking cover. Ed was nearing his gun as two bullets cut through the back of his thighs. A follow up shotgun blast ripped into his back. Ed collapsed to his knees, then forward on top of his gun. He was face down, bloodied and in pain.

Black-Knight and his six man squad rushed over to Ed with their weapons drawn. They were not taking and chances. Black-Knight stood over Ed's back. He poked at him with his shotgun several times, there was no movement. He then kicked Ed in the nuts. Still, he lay lifeless.

Black-Knight smiled. "Yeah...This old cat's done." The men all relaxed their weapons.

The quietness had Money curious. He again cracked the stockroom door. Just then, Ed turned over onto his back emerging with his pistol.

"Bbooomm! Bbooomm!" he shot, striking one of the armed men in the throat. The bullet exited out the top of his head. Black-Knight and his men began to scatter.

"Bbooomm! Bbooomm! Bbooomm!" Ed rapidly shot hitting another one in the ankle, which proved to be a mistake. The large man fell backwards onto Ed pinning his left hand to his body. But Ed continued firing only hitting the now deceased man on top of him. Black-Knight and his men returned fire from across the room. They struck Ed several times as well as their own man not caring if he was dead or alive.

Ed felt numbness all over his body. He knew this fight was to be his last. He lay defeated starring up at the ceiling fan go round and round, picturing it to be like a helicopter. Suddenly, a dark shadow cast over Ed's fascinating sight.

With the shotgun aimed looking downward, "I must admit Ed, you're hard to kill. I was for sure you were dead this time," said Black-Knight. "I knew getting close to you was gon'na be difficult but not impossible. Thanks to your fraud ass hit man laying over there, you were easy pickings. You see Ed, the number 1 rule of the game is: Don't get high off your own supply, but you ignored that rule. That China White got you all fucked up, that shit got you slipping. I had to fuck you out them 10 keys, you got too comfortable with me. Never let the right hand know what the left hand is doing."

Black-Knight again peered at the body partially covered by the rug. "I don't know how the Quamy muthafucka' lived as long as he did. I knew you was gon'na be onto his bullshit the minute you saw him at the door. That was a greedy dude. Well, it don't matter now, it appears you handled the situation. Mmph, that Bitch wasn't getting paid no way." Ed helplessly watched as Black-Knight tightened his grip on the shotgun. "Oh Ed, one more last thing. I respect you, I always have. But you're like a cat with 9 lives that's full of surprises. And Ed, I don't like surprises. "Bbooomm!"

Ed's feet flew in the air from the close range shot gun blast, and his head was nearly blown off his shoulders.

Money flipped backwards over a bin of bottles. The after math was too horrific. Everyone turned their attention towards the stockroom door. Black-Knight snapped his fingers pointing, ordering his man *Rowe* to check it out.

Money knew even a deaf man would've heard that commotion. He scrambled for a place to hide. Unfortunately, the small room didn't provide one. Money was about to panic. He thought fast. Then quickly, he again started assorting bottles like he never seen or heard a thing.

Rowe smashed his way into the storage room. Money frightened, tried to act surprise. "Who are you?" he asked. Rowe didn't answer. He snatched Money by the neck and flung him into the next room.

"It's some kid Black-Knight. He could be Ed's son. Do you want me to take him out?" he asked.

Money looked to Ed's deceased body blurting out, "That ain't my daddy! I just started working here today. My friend Ty…"

"Shut the fuck up!" yelled Black-Knight raising the shotgun to Money's head. "I don't give a shit who yo' daddy is. I wan'na know, what did you see?"

Money scared to death, started babbling. No one understood a word he spoke. Black-Knight squint his brow.

"You seen everything, didn't you kid?"

Money wanted to say 'No' but somehow his head nodded 'Yes.' Black-Knight lowered the shotgun, unsure of what to do with this kid. Money was a witness and a witness was never left alive.

"Fuck em' Knight, put one in his head," said *K.G.*, Black-Knight's best friend, who was also Rowe's brother. Black-Knights mind was made up. He held out his hand as one of his men handed him a pistol. He cocked back the hammer. Money knew his fate was sealed. He closed his eyes gritting his teeth. Then surprisingly, Money was handed the gun. Black-Knight told him to walk over and shoot Ed in what was left of his face.

Money took a deep breath glad to be alive. He was for sure he was dead, at the same time he was confused.

Why didn't Black-Knight kill me? Why does he trust me with a gun? And how can I kill a man twice? thought Money. *'Ed is already dead.'*

Money had questions, but he wasn't about to ask Black-Knight shit. He strolled over to where Ed's corpse lay. With both hands, he aimed the heavy piece of cold steal. He starred at the nearly headless body ready to throw up. It was his first time actually seeing someone dead. It also was his first time holding a gun. Money was stalling and Black-Knight could see it.

"Listen kid, you've got 5 seconds to pull that trigger or you're gon'na be laying right there next to Ed. Splinters of nerves singed over Money's face. He almost lost his legs from that statement. It was no doubt in his mind on what he now had to do.

Money wrapped his finger around the 44 magnums trigger. He turned his face and then pulled back. "Bbooomm!"

Ed's body jerked as Money's hands went upward. Black-Knight smirked, about to approach the youngster.

The jolt power of the revolver for Money was exhilarating. It felt damn good. He wanted to do it again. Since the opportunity had presented itself, Money went for what he knew.

"Bbooomm! Bbooomm! Bbooomm! Bbooommm! Bbooomm! Click! Click! Click!" He emptied the gun wanting more. Money then turned to Black-Knight and his men with a menacingly glare. They all were aiming their guns at him, unsure of retaliation against them.

Black-Knight again raised his brow. *Damn, all headshots. This lil' muthafucka' a real killer,* he thought. He then cautiously reached in snatching the weapon back from Money. Black-Knight's men all agreed one day this kid could be useful.

The bar was then ransacked and the safe emptied. At the same time, Money picked up the deceased killer's gun. He took it upon himself to repeat the same act against the deceased Quamy, loving his new tough guy image. Afterwards, Black-Knight and his men all lit cocktails. They tossed them around bar as the cocktails began to burst.

"Lets go! Lets ride!" hollered out Black-Knight.

The bar broke out into a hail of fire. Everyone scurried to the outside, except for Money. He spotted Ed's silver compact through the blaze, lying near the front door. He was unsure of what it was, all he knew is he wanted it. Money darted across the fiery room risking his life to collect his prize. He scooped up the compact and then hauled ass to the outside.

Black-Knight was impressed, but gave no appraise.

"What's your name kid" he asked.

Breathing hard, "I'm Maurice, but everybody calls me Money Bunny," he replied.

"Money Bunny?"

"Yeah...That's right."

Black-Knight laid his shotgun onto Money's shoulder.

"Well listen here Money Bunny. I don't like killing kids, but I will if I have to. I'll kill up a whole family, plus the babies. I don't give a fuck. Now, you did real good in there killing Ed for me. But, can I trust that you'll keep quiet about this, or will that be a problem?"

Money quickly nodded *No,* indicating he could keep quiet. He was still grasping the fact thinking he really did kill Ed.

Black-Knight smiled. "Ok good, because you owe me big time kid. You owe me your life, and the Black-Knight always collects what's owed to him."

Just then, Black-Knights men pulled up to a screeching halt. "C'mon Knight, time, time," yelled K.G. tapping his watch. Black-Knight hopped into the 75 Buick Electra. Hanging out the window, he slapped his chest pointing to Money. "You armor plated baby! Armor plated! Remember that!"

Money felt the energy. He too slapped his chest repeating Black-Knights chant. "Armour Plated!"

The 4-door Sedan then began to speed away making a wild right turn onto Seminole Street. So wild, it almost struck Tywon, his aunt Francine and Aunt Gladys, who also were driving up the block at a high rate of speed. They were racing the clock to save Faye and the kids from Ronnie's vicious attack, not knowing he was already gone.

Assholes, thought Tywon looking out of the rear window, catching a glimpse of Black-knight hanging out of the car. Just as they were passing the alley's intersection, "Wwhhbbooomm!" the bar exploded into flames, lighting up the night. The pressure from the blast sent Money crashing to the pavement.

Covering his mouth, "Oh no! Oh my God!" said Tywon.

Still looking out of the back window, he saw as a ball of fire dispersed into the air. He couldn't help but think of the lives of Money and Uncle Ed. Then faintly, Tywon saw a familiar image lifting from the ground, when the passing of houses blocked any further view. Tywon slumped down in the seat confused as to what possibly could have caused this to happen. He wanted to go back and check on Ed's and Money's well being, but family came first.

Right then, Francine fastly pulled up to the house sliding sideways as she came to a stop. The car doors were opened. Everyone sprinted onto the porch. The front door strangely was standing wide open. This made Tywon and his aunts feel the worst may have happened.

Standing at the entryway, "Momma! De'Anne! Dre!" sorrowfully yelled Tywon. No one answered. Gladys rubbed her nephews shoulders.

"Don't worry baby, they're alright. The Lord is in there with them," she stated. She then turned to her sister whispering. "Francine, you got the gun, right?"

Francine pulled out her nickel-plated 25 automatic. "Yeah, I got it. And soon as I see Ronnie's ass, one of these hot one's has his name on it. That Bitch already knows to keep his hands off my sister."

Francine took lead stepping into the house. She clearly could see a struggle had taken place. "Damn," she mumbled laying eyes on the heaps of blood smeared across the floor. Gladys followed behind her.

"Oh Lord, Oh Lord" she repeated horrified. She then broke down into prayer. Tywon walked away irritated by the over usage of the Lord's name. He proceeded to the upstairs tagging closely behind Francine. They both yelled out to Faye and the children, still receiving no response. Tywon first retuned to the room where his mother and siblings were last, only to be disappointed. The room was empty. Chills ran down his spine.

The two continued strolling down the hallway when suddenly, they both jumped from a starting sound. A doorknob from another bedroom was twisting and turning. Fran's pistol was aimed. She was ready to mow Ronnie down at first sight. She took a hard swallow warning Tywon as the door began to open. "Get ready nephew, this might get ugly."

Suddenly, Faye, De'Anne and De'Andre appeared from the room with smiles of relief. Tywon rushed to his family for hugs and kisses. He couldn't tell them enough times how much he loved and missed them. He excitedly began telling them how he ran a mile non-stop to his aunts house. Francine yelled to the downstairs. "Gladys! Gladys! Come quick. They're up here!"

Gladys lifted from her knees overjoyed. She then marched upstairs raving, "Don't tell me about my Lord! It's he who keeps ya' safe from harm! It's he who protects you from evil. I told y'all, don't never be ashamed to pray to your God, because the Sheppard always protects his children." She then stopped as everyone gave her a stare with tears in their eyes. Gladys now teary eyed herself, opened her arms smiling, "I'm just glad y'all alright."

The Detroit News

July 24, 1984

 After a full 1 year investigation, authorities are still no closer to having a suspect or suspects in connection with the disappearance of under cover Officer Darryl France, or about the brutal death of his partner Quamy Page, whose body was found in the remains of a suspicious east side bomb fire. Officer Pages corpse was discovered in the 8200 block of Gratiot in a now burned down, then popular local bar known as Ed's Night Lounge. The owner, 49 year-old Julius Edward Brown, a suspected narcotics distributor for Detroit's East side, was also 1 of the 4 victims burned beyond recognition in the fire. Dental records were unable to identify the two other victims. However, autopsy reports did reveal the victims were all shot. One body was even decapitated. Employees of the popular bar were all questioned, but most said they never seen or heard any suspicious activity in or around the bar. However, a week ago from today, an anonymous tip received by Police lead to the body of Officer Darryl France. Divers found him at the bottom of the Detroit River. Foul play was ruled in connection with the Officer's death. The two Officers were a part of the elite drug task force group Stress, which was headed up by 10-year veteran Sergeant Conrad Bantz. The sergeant spoke highly, proud and honorable about his two slain Officers. But when allegations arose about if Sergeant Bantz himself was a major narcotic distributor in the city, he stated, "That's bullshit! And you all know it!"

 The Sergeant finished by saying the question was an insult to his respected reputation with the department. Later, Bantz went on to apologize for his comments to the press and to the citizens of Detroit, but that apology was all too late. Soon after, Conrad Bantz was offered the opportunity for an early retirement, but when he refused, he was terminated from the D.P.D.

 Off the record, Conrad Bantz's discharge from D.P.D. played in his favor. He was called in by the Federal Government for recruitment as an F.B.I. (Federal Bureau of Investigations) Agent. From Conrad's ranked position as sergeant, from his experiences and familiarity with the streets and drug trade, to the government, he was an ideal agent for a major city-wide narcotics clean up. The job for Bantz came with a stipulation clause: He had to turn in the names of all his present suppliers, his former connections and local distributors. Conrad Bantz agreed to it all, signing a work exclusively only under the Federal Government Vision Waiver.

1988

The Break-up

The day was hot. Tywon stood at the intersection of Van Dyke and Medbury as traffic passed him by. When it cleared, he crossed the street. He strolled through Kettering High School's tennis and basketball courts. Anyone walking from either neighborhood took that short cut to get to the other side. Tywon was nearing his destination. He could see Money up the street running back and fourth to vehicles selling his Crack Cocaine. Money often encouraged Tywon to join him in the business, but every time, he declined. While sometimes considering the offer, Uncle Ed's words would replay in his mind.

'Cocaine is gon'na make the streets worse. Sell some weed, selling a little weed ain't never killed nobody.' In Tywon's mind, it was a sermon. Ed was right; cocaine was making the streets worse, especially in the rock form.

Tywon clearly seen the profit it generated, but he also could see the destruction it caused: Burnt out houses, childhood friends fighting over territory and even the parents of some of his friends were hooked. Money didn't give a fuck, he sold to them all saying, *'If I don't sell it to them, they'll just go somewhere else and get it.'* Tywon would have no part of it.

Tywon approached the block. "What's up Money?" giving him a five. "Damn, you got this corner banging with clientele. You're doing alright I see."

"And don't you doubt it," cockily replied Money. "I got the best shit on the east side. I'm a chef when it comes to cooking up dope."

He then pulled out a wad of cash. "I been told you what's up, but you bullshittin' Ty. Selling them nickel and dime bags of weed ain't go'on get you rich. You need to be re-thinking my offer of coming to work for me. What's up?" he again asked.

Tywon again declined. "Money, you're my man, but at the same time, I'm my own man. I look at it like this, as long as you've got bread, then I've got it too, right?"

Money's lips curled up like, *Shiiid...whatever. Yo' ass bet'ta grab a sack.* Tywon picked up on the gesture.

Right then, a car horn blew. "Bump! Bump!"

A white man pulled up in a Station Wagon. "Hold on Ty, let me serve this fool" said Money making his way over to the vehicle. Tywon stood waiting for Money's return. Then suddenly, he looked up. Money was pulling his customer out the car, kicking his ass. The customer screamed for help but then tried to fight back. That was a mistake. Money pulled out his pistol and bashed the man across his mouth. He fell to the ground. Blood began to spill as he spit a few teeth. Money angry was about to give him more, until Tywon called his name.

"Money! Money! Cut that shit out man, be cool."

The man saw that Money was distracted. He then got up and ran like hell, leaving his car behind. Money returned to the corner breathing hard with his gun in hand.

Puzzled "Man, what the hell was that about?" asked Tywon.

"Fuck that fiend!" replied Money. "That Bitch tried to accuse me of selling him soap."

"Soap? Well, what did you sell him?"

Money paused smiling, "Soap."

Tywon shook his head knowing Money wasn't right. This was another reason why he dared not to involve himself and Money in business affairs. Money was the definition of why it's said: Drugs and violence are joined at the hip.

He was slick, cunning and always trying to out hustle the next man. When doing business, he searched for the vulnerability in people. If he detected any weaknesses, he'd mentally strong arm the person. If that didn't work, he'd resort to physical force. Most times, he under paid his workers and then threatened them if they complained. Plain and simple, Money was a menace.

Tywon was tempted to tell Money about himself, but instead he threw his hand figuring, *'Why bother?'* He continued watching Money rave over the incident wildly waiving his gun. He figured it was now time to make his exit.

"Well, that was enough excitement for me in one day" said Tywon. "I'm about to go check on this ounce of weed, but first, I gos'ta go and see my lady," proudly.

"Your lady, who? I hope you ain't talkin' 'bout that stank ass bitch O'Sha. Ty man, you're wasting your time with that girl. I've been try'n to hit that ass, she ain't giving up no skins. You might as well forget it, you'd be better off trying to fuck her older sister Octavia, now she's a freak," boldly stated Money.

Tywon didn't appreciate the disrespectful comment about his girlfriend. Even though he knew Money didn't know any better, he went for a low blow himself.

"Money, you couldn't fuck my girl or her sister if you paid them to. Your rap and your game are both the same, weak. I'ma give it up to you though, when it comes to slangin' them rocks, you're number 1. But when it comes to romancing the females, you finish last."

Tywon laughed. "Money, a word of advice, don't you ever confuse yourself with me."

Money was burning with anger on the inside. He knew Tywon was right. He couldn't fuck either sister if he had paid them to, he'd tried that already. They both turned him down. Money didn't understand it. *Why does O'Sha like Tywon so much? That's my boy, but he ain't nothing but a nickel and dime ass weed pusher. Shit, I've got more Money than him. He can't do for her what I can. That's alright though, O'Sha better quit acting like she's too good from me. Because I'm gon'na get a shot of that pussy, even if I have to take that ass.*

Money then smiled at Tywon as if he never had any ill thoughts.

"Damn Ty baby, don't be so serious. I'm only bullshittin' with you," playfully grabbing Tywon around his back.

Now looking sincere, "But really, I know you care about that girl. I just called myself looking out for your feelings. Ty, you my man, you're like my brother and I don't wan'na see you get hurt, because, well you know what they say?"

Tywon stood touched but now confused.

"What who say?" he asked.

"You know, they, as in old sayings; 'Birds of a feather flock together.' In other words, if Octavia's a freak, what makes you think her younger sister O'Sha ain't one? That's who most young bitches learn that type of shit from, their older sisters."

Tywon threw his hand like Money was talking ridiculous but some of his negativity was seeping in.

Money went on. "Well, you ain't got'ta' listen to me. Just watch for the signs, you'll see them. All bitches start to act funny after a while, especially when they find a new dude. And their big sister ain't never too far behind it. Don't be nobody's fool."

Jealously and rage was blemished on Tywon's brain. Pain was imbedded into his soul. He never knew such feelings existed within himself. He was ready to explode.

Money nearly busted out laughing. He read the irritation across Tywon's face. He struggled to hide the malicious pleasure he was receiving. Manipulation was another weapon of choice Money often used to steer situations to his advantage.

Just then, Money's cousin named Big Daddy; also his worker came walking up the block. Money rolled his eyes as if the sight of his cousin disgusted him.

Big Daddy was a 19 year-old kid, 5 feet 10 inches, and 310 pounds. When he walked, you could feel the vibration from his steps. When he breathed, it sounded like he was on a respirator. And when it was time to eat, he feasted on meals like there were to be his last. But behind the beast, there was a gentle giant.

Big Daddy was smooth, clean and laid back with a charming smile. A lot of females found him attractive despite of his large size. He was a hustler when it came to making a dollar and honest with his business transactions, but Money being the person that he was kept a foot on his cousin's neck.

Smacking his lips, "Tywon, look at this fat muthafucka' coming up the street," said Money checking his watch. "His big ass late and he's eating again. I bet'cha if shit sandwiches were being passed out, his fat ass would be first in line to get one." Tywon stated no comment. He and Big Daddy were cool and had much respect for one another.

Big Daddy approached licking an ice cream cone. "What's up Ty man..? I ain't seen you in a while," he said ignoring Money's presence.

"I just left the mall from buying an outfit for the party tonight. I already know you're gon'na step in there fresh," lapping the cone.

Tywon paused. "Party, what par…?" Money cut him short.

Pointing to Big Daddy, "First of all, you speak to me when you step into my place of business. Second, this ain't no fuckin' porno flick, we sell crack on this block. You suckin' on that ice cream cone better than some bitches suck dick!" said Money slapping the cone from his hand. "Here," now handing him a sack. "Now get your ass on that corner and get that money, you're already late."

Big Daddy peered at his melting ice cream lying on the ground, then back to Money. If looks could kill, he'd be burning in hell. Big Daddy pictured himself effortlessly snapping Money's neck, but violence wasn't a factor included on his daily roster. He was a hustler and about his money. He simply waived to Tywon saying, "See you tonight." At that point, he stepped to the corner to serve approaching customers.

Money turned to Tywon smiling. "That's what I call cracking the whip, situation control, you know, being a boss," he said turning up his lips.

Naw, that's what you call being a dumb-ass. It's only a matter of time before your people leave or they turn against you. You need to have more respect for your workers, especially for Big Daddy. He's a money make'n muthafucka.' Personally, I think he could run this whole operation better than you can, thought Tywon. He wanted to voice his opinions, but he knew Money would only miss the point and view Big Daddy as a threat. He left it alone.

Still curious, "So Money, what party was Big Daddy talking about?" asked Tywon.

Money smirked. "Now why is the man always the last to know? If my so-called woman, my girl or my lady as you called her was throwing a party, she'd definitely tell me about it. Now how come you don't know?" he countered.

Tywon was dumbfounded. In a soft tone, "O'Sha's have'n a party tonight?"

Money mimicked Tywon laughing. "Yeah man, O'Sha's having a party and she must be inviting the new dude over tonight. That's why she didn't mention anything to you about it," he said convincingly. "Bitches can get real slick at times. They'll even go so far as to introduce you to the other cat they're fuckin'. It's like you gos'ta keep a third eye out on them hoes, but don't worry, don't even trip, I'ma tell you how to play it."

Money ran down a list of do's and dont's for Tywon to follow at tonight's party. He told him to be inattentive towards O'Sha. Act like he doesn't even notice her, and constantly laugh when conversing with other females. Money said bitches always get mad when you show other broads attention, especially when it looks like you're having a good time. He stated that would send O'Sha running to the new dude for comfort, exposing him. Then at that time, Tywon could confront the guy.

Money could see Tywon's brain was putty in this hand. It fascinated him how a person's mind could be easily controlled when vulnerable and emotional.

Money then sent Tywon on his way, but not before strongly advising him to avoid O'Sha, until tonight's party. The broken hearted protégé agreed saying, "That's not be a problem" and then headed off continuing his day.

Money was finally at ease; Tywon was gone. He didn't know how much longer he could hold out. He thought the constant sniffing and the brushing of his nose would give him away. But Tywon was too love-sick to notice a thing.

Money pulled out his silver compact with the large E engraved on top. He opened up the case. China was bent over, face down, ass up, making pleasure sounds. She was rubbing her white vaginal lips of ecstasy. She taunted Money stroking herself in circles, encouraging him to stick his face in for a dip.

Money's nostril hairs grew erect. He was 5 years familiar with this loving. He knew how good it was and how it made him feel. He first looked around to see if anyone was watching. He then dived in head first taking two nose full of China's scent, sliding the excess residue onto his tongue. China was the baddest bitch Money ever known, and he wasn't ready or about to give her up. He then closed his eyes letting the high rush him. Money wasn't even a minute into his high before interruptions came.

"Yo' Money! Money!" called Big Daddy.

Irritated, "Man what! What the fuck is it?" he answered looking up.

Big Daddy was pointing to a customer he'd refuse to serve anytime she came.

"Damn Big Daddy! Sell her whatever she wants. She's a V.I.P. customer." Big Daddy threw his hand gesturing; he wasn't selling her a thing. He sent the customer over to Money. She quickly approached.

"Hey Money, Hh…how you doin? Ugh…I know you told me not to bring my stankin' ass back around here beggin' for hand outs, but I've got money now" said Faye, Tywon's mother. "Here, look."

She brandished a fresh $50 bill. Money figured the crisp bill came from Tywon's stash but he accepted it anyway.

"Nonsense Faye, I didn't say that. Did I say that?"

She nodded, *'Yes.'*

"Well, you're welcome to cop from me anytime. I'm here to serve the public. Tell all your friends about me," he said handing her a few rock packets.

Money then grabbed her by the arm, whispering in her ear. "Hey, don't let Tywon find out you've been buying this shit from me. Otherwise, we go'on have problems. You understand me?"

Faye again nodded understanding him well. Money's pressure grip assisted her with the answer. He then flung her like a scolded child. Faye caught her footing and went on her way.

Big Daddy act like he wasn't watching the incident go down, but he seen it all. He didn't understand how Money could sell Crack Cocaine to the mother of his best friend: A woman who clothed and fed him when his own mother turned her back. It was totally disrespectful. Big Daddy knew the limits and he knew they'd been crossed. He also knew it was only a matter of time before Money got his.

The day fell into the night. Money closed up shop, not really wanting to. He tried to convince Big Daddy to keep working the block, but he refused. He explained to Money he had to get dapper for tonight's party. He voiced the ladies loved him and he had to be fresh to impress. Money laughed with disbelief. He told Big Daddy those broads were only using him for his money and the only woman that would ever love him is his fat ass momma. Big Daddy laughed at the joke, shaking his head like, *'Good one.'* He could stand the heat, he'd been taking it all his life. He then re-countered by saying at least he had a mother who cared for him and showed him affection. Money's momma was nothing more than a useless vacuum cleaner with a pussy hole. She was good for nothing but sucking up his cash and all the food around the house.

Money got mad feeling disrespected. He started talking like he wanted to fight. The hostile attitude made Big Daddy turn defensive. He quickly jumped into Money's face asking him, "What you wan'na do?"

Money never before seen this side of Big Daddy, he was slightly intimidated by his cousin's large size. Reaching for his pistol was out the question; Big Daddy was ready for that. Money then down played the situation by laughing.

"Damn Big Daddy, back off me. Give me three feet. You can't even take a joke anymore. Here, there's your pay for the night."

Money handed Big Daddy all his cash with no shorts. Big Daddy counted the money. He then gave Money a fierce glare before disappearing into the night.

Money gathered his composure. *Ol' punk muthafucka.' Big Daddy better watch his mouth. He's the lieutenant but his ass stills works for me.* Money then walked across the street and hopped into the white man's Station Wagon from earlier. He took off up the street like the car was his own.

****

Tywon had just jumped out the shower and dried off. He rubbed on his lotion, sprinkled on some baby powder and sprayed himself with cologne. He then took off his durag to check the waves in his hair. He rubbed in a little wave grease and brushed it down to make it tighter.

Damn, I look good, checking himself out in the mirror. Afterwards, Tywon slid on his black and white polyester Adidas Tracksuit, with the matching shell toe sneakers. He then placed his Gucci-link gold chain around his neck, along with his four-finger ring. Last, he put on his Cazel facial shades. He was ready.

Tywon was sure not to forget the 40-dime packets of weed he'd bagged up earlier. He was confident he would sell out as well as build some clientele at tonight's party. He then headed downstairs feeling good looking like cash money. De'Anne and De'Andre were smiling as if their hero just stepped in the room.

"Wow Ty, you're fresh!" complimented 10 year-old De'Andre. "I wan'na dress just like you when I grow up."

Enthused, "Thanks lil' bro, I appreciate that."

"Yeah Tywon, that outfit looks sweet on you. If you wasn't my big brother, I'd be all over you," seductively said De'Anne. Tywon didn't like that statement seeing it was from his 14 year-old sister, who was hot in the ass. But, since it was attached with a complement, he let it ride.

"Thanks y'all. Hey listen, we need to talk serious. Now, y'all know ever since Ronnie left momma, she's been all messed up and on them drugs. And we've done tried over and over and over again to help her with no success. I don't know, maybe she doesn't want any help. But I do know, calling momma a crack head all day ain't helping, De'Anne," he addressed. De'Anne turned her head.

"And Dre, you telling her she's no longer your mother ain't working either." De'Andre folded his arms, poking out his lips. "So when momma comes in tonight, try not to be too hard on her. Show her a little respect, she still has feelings. And yeah, momma's on drugs and it's an embarrassing situation. But the bottom line is, she's still our mother, and we all love her very much, right?

In unison, "Right...," the two struggled to say.

"Ok, good" said Tywon headed for the door. "Oh, I forgot to mention. Aunt Gladys is coming over tonight."

"Aunt Gladys! Awe naw, not the Reverend Alice Sharpton," pouted De'Anne. "All she talks about is how we're sinners and how the Lord is gon'na strike us down." Tywon laughed walking out the door.

****

The 10 o'clock hour fell. O'Sha's party got on its way and it was rocking. Trucks and cars of all types were pulling onto the block: Samauri Suzuki's, Wrangler Jeeps, Merkur XR4TI's, Sterlings and other types of flashy vehicles. Everybody from the neighborhood who was anybody was there, even a few unknown outsiders. Money did a couple of drive-by's to check the scene. It was more than he expected. He had no idea O'Sha and Octavia knew so many stylish people. He parked around the corner, not wanting to be seen in the Station Wagon.

O'Sha and Octavia were standing outside. The two were directing guests from their cars and off the neighbors grass and into their basement. When Money hit the corner walking, O'Sha's ass and hips in action created an erection in his jeans. From 20 yards away, his eyes were feasting on her breast. He nearly drew blood from biting on his bottom lip. He yearned for the day when he would spread open her flower and fertilize it.

Money approached, "What's up O'Sha. Damn, the party is off the hook. Where do you know all these people from?" he asked hoping the night camouflaged the bulge in his pants.

O'Sha turned, not seeing Money's approach. "Oh, hey Money. Those are all Octavia's friends. She's real popular down at the bar where she works." Money missed O'Sha's answer still focused on her breast. She then politely covered herself changing the subject.

"Money, I've been paging my baby Tywon all day, but he ain't returned none of my calls. You did tell him about the party, right?"

"Of course I did" he answered rolling his eyes. "But I didn't mention this being a celebration for both of you. I figured we should keep it a big surprise, plus he already thinks it's something else. But trust me, Tywon will definitely be here," smiling.

O'Sha also smiled, "Perfect, because I went though a lot of changes trying to put this thing together." She then went back to directing the guest.

Money walked away backwards lusting after her body. While doing so, he mistakenly bumped into someone standing behind him. He turned around and then smiled. "Oops my fault sweetie pie, I didn't see you behind me." he said.

"I just bet you didn't. You're to busy staring at my little sister's ass" said Octavia. "Your boy Tywon wouldn't like that, you checking out his girl and all." Money's lips tightened. He wanted to say, *'Fuck Tywon! O'Sha's my girl,'* but he kept that card hid.

Octavia picked up on his facial expressions. She knew game. She'd dealt with many types of men in her line of work to know when a guy's feelings were involved.

Money then redirected the conversation. "Octavia baby, I'm interested in experienced women only, like your-self. O'Sha's a mere child in my eyes. Now, a woman of your maturity, I can deal with. You're fine, sexy and beautiful with a pretty smile." Octavia blushed.

"But Octavia, it's just one thing about you I've gos'ta know."

"And what is that Money?"

"Is it slippery when wet? Because if it is, I got'ta hundred on it right now" he said laughing pulling out his cash.

Octavia didn't find a damn thing funny. "Money, if you had a little character to go with all that bread you've got, you probably could find out how wet it can get. But since you don't, just keep thinking about it," walking away. Money stood puzzled, trying to comprehend Octavia's statement. He then threw his hand thinking, *'Fuck her'* and headed into the basement.

Soon after, Tywon and Big Daddy simultaneously reached the block of the party. As the two strolled up the street, they also couldn't believe O'Sha's and Octavia's turn out.

"Damn Ty" said Big Daddy. "These girls really know how to throw a party. Shit, it's some fine ass females out here too. And look at the cars, damn!" Tywon agreed, thinking of the day he would drop a new ride.

Right then, a white dude came up street banging his music uncontrollably loud. "Damn..." everyone chimed as he crept through doing 2 M.P.H.

The 88' convertible Ford Mustang was impressive. It was custom burgundy with the beige leather seats, trimmed in gold detailing and accessorized with 15 inch, chrome and gold hammer rims. The burgundy fluorescent under carriage lights glowing on the ground set it off. The white dude stole the show and he knew it. All eyes were on him, until he reached the end of the block, making a left-hand turn at the corner.

Tywon and Big Daddy looked at one another shaking their heads. The ladies were impressed. They all conversed about how they'd like a taste of that cream in their coffee. The guys standing outside didn't want to hear it.

Soon as the two approached the party, Big Daddy spotted O'Sha. He nudged Tywon informing him of her presence. When Tywon laid eyes on her, his heart skipped a beat. It was like seeing her again for the first time. He wondered if what he felt was love. Right then, he decided to make an approach. Suddenly, some dude ran up to O'Sha giver her a tight hug and kiss on the cheek. She did the same in return. Tywon's mouth hung wide open, he was crushed.

"That must be the dude Money was talking about," he mumbled. He decided there was no reason for him to attend the party, until reaching into his pocket pulling out the bags of marijuana. At that point, he decided to stay. He figured since he was loosing his woman, he'd might as well stick around and make a buck. It would at least help ease the pain. The pair then headed into the basement.

In the basement, the party was filling in. The blue lighting set the tone and the D.J. was turning it out. Rob Base's, *'It takes two,'* was pumping hard. The D.J. then mixed in Run D.M.C.'s *'Peter Piper.'* The party people screamed, "Hhoooooo!" throwing their hands in the air.

Tywon and Big Daddy were posted against the wall bobbing their heads to the beat. Just then, Money came from out of nowhere.

"What's up boy?" giving Tywon a five. "I see yo' ass finally made it, huh?" Afterwards, Money looked to Big Daddy. No words were exchanged, but they both nonchalantly nodded to one-another.

Tywon looked towards the floor, then back to Money.

"Yeah man, I'm here but I was fin'na leave. You were right. O'Sha does have a new dude and he's here, I seen him outside," he said disappointedly.

Money's feelings were now also hurt. His earlier story of O'Sha having a new man was a hoax to make Tywon jealous. But it was now Money who was jealous from the tale being told to him.

Now bitter "You bullshittin' Ty? How's that bitch O'Sha go'on play you? C'mon, where's this dude at?" asked Money ready to confront the guy himself. Tywon grabbed him by the arms.

"Hold on Money, damn! You act like O'Sha's your girl or something. Chill out, let me handle this. Anyway, I've got business to handle." Big Daddy didn't say a word. He just shook his head thinking his cousin was sticking his nose where it didn't belong. Money got upset.

"Well fuck it then! You're just gon'na let this cat take your girl. I'm offering my help and you spit in my face!"

"Spit in your face? What are you talking about Money? Are you crazy? Man...you..."

Money walked away while Tywon was still talking.

Puzzled, "Wh...What's the matter with your cousin?" Tywon asked Big Daddy.

Big Daddy watched as Money rudely pushed though the crowd.

He then stated Money was just a hot head who needed cooling off. Just then, O'Sha and Octavia made their way into the basement. The alleged boyfriend closely followed behind them. The 3 formed into small group. They started talking and laughing amongst each other as if no one else was in the room.

Tywon snarled at the sight of Octavia. He figured she was behind this whole mess. It was killing him to see O'Sha giggling in some dude's face. Soon after, he reminded himself of why he was there. He then went off to push his weed. Big Daddy started talking to a trio of ladies.

Money was on the other side of the basement. He was drinking beer after beer after beer with no signs of stopping. Afterwards, out in the open he carelessly pulled out his compact and snorted a few lines. He staggered backwards as the high rushed him. *Whoo... shit!* he thought, *That was good.* Money downed his final beer and then continued watching O'Sha from across the room.

Tywon was already close to selling out. He wanted to run home to get more weed but O'Sha was too heavy on his mind. He felt the need to confide in someone about the situation. He spotted Big Daddy on the dance floor appearing to be having a good time. Tywon politely pulled him over near the wall and explained the matter. Big Daddy told Tywon any relationship ending needed closure. But he said, if this alleged information came from Money, 9 times out of 10, the information may have gotten twisted. He encouraged Tywon to approach O'Sha himself and receive closure if that's what it was he really needed. That's all Tywon wanted to hear.

As this was going on, Octavia made her way over to the D.J.'s booth. She announced she was gon'na perform a solo act for all the gentlemen in the house. On the low, it was to make some quick cash. Everyone kindly cleared the floor.

The D.J. put on Apologia's 'Nasty Girl,' Octavia's theme song. She then went to work. She grabbed the support beam, arched her back, dropped down low and shook her ass. The fellows in the house went crazy as she performed her act. Dudes were stacked on each other's backs throwing 5 and 10-dollar bills. But Money, he had to out do them all. He pulled out a thick rubber band stack of 20's and 50's and started peeling them off. Octavia started shaking harder like she was possessed. Money was loving it feeling like he was in control.

While everyone was focused on the show, Tywon took the opportunity to approach O'Sha, even though the guy was still standing next to her.

When Tywon approached, O'Sha didn't give him a chance to say a word. She surprisingly wrapped her lips around his.

Kissing him, "Ooh baby, I've been waiting all night for you to get here," she said. Tywon was moved, as well as shocked. She then introduced him to her cousin from Highland Park, *Terrell*. She said she hadn't seen him in over 4 years. Tywon was over-joyed to know his girl didn't have a new man. He shook Terrell's hand smiling like he'd known him for years.

Money now drunk just happened to look over in the trio's direction. He grew furious when he seen Tywon shaking Terrell's hand.

"What the fuck!" he slurred to himself. "Why is Tywon dumb-ass shakin' the hand of the man who's fuckin' his woman. If that's the case, I need to be fuckin' her myself."

O'Sha had just told Tywon she was afraid he wasn't gon'na make it to their surprise party. "Our surprise party?" he said unknowingly. "For us?"

Caressing his face, "Yeah baby, this is for you and I. Were celebrating six months together," she smiled. "Money knew all about it, I explained it to him last week: The plan, the lay out, everything. Money said he told you about the party, but he had you thinking it was something else. He insisted we keep this thing as a surprise from you. So, are you surprised?"

Tywon didn't know what he felt, but he was too heated to say anything. He then excused himself from O'Sha and Terrell to find Money.

Money watched as Tywon worked himself through the crowd on the right side of the room, appearing to looking for someone. He then took it upon himself to confront the situation circling from the left.

Money approached O'Sha. "Bitch! How you go'on invite another man to this party," he raved. "I told Tywon. I told him. Ain't none of you bitches shit. You, your sister, none of you Hho..."

"Wham!" Money was cut short from a punch to the mouth. Terrell floored him.

"Back your punk ass up off my cousin, who is this shit talkin' muthafucka!" he asked, standing over Money. O'Sha was confused. She couldn't understand what brought this hostility out of Money.

"Terrell, Terrell, calm down! This ain't necessary," she said pushing him backwards. Money staggered back to his feet. It was evident to the pair he was drunk. Octavia was just ending her show as Tywon was making his way back around. He looked past the partying people heads at Money's face, which again had that vicious look like earlier. He then peered at O'Sha who was holding Terrell back.

"Awe shit!" said Tywon knowing things were about to take a turn for the worse. He started pushing through the crowd, to get to Money. Big Daddy saw Tywon in action and started behind him. Some party attendees took notice of the developing drama and stepped out of the way. Then suddenly, Money pulled out his 9-millimeter pistol.

With no hesitation, "Bbooommm!" he shot. The music screeched to a halt. Terrell dropped to the floor. A horde of people started to scream and scatter.

Money was still aiming about to let loose another round, until Tywon and Big Daddy tackled him, knocking the gun from his hand. When the weapon struck the ground, this time it went off by itself.

"Bbooommm!" The bullet struck the gas pilot on the hot water tank. Suddenly, a loud hissing sound was heard, a half a second later, "Wwhhooommm!"

The blast blew out all the lights, which intensified the panic. People were stampeding over one another with no concern for anyone else but themselves, trying to get up the stairs.

When the traffic did clear, many laid hurt. The D.J. pulled out his flashlight to check the injured. Most injuries came from those who were trampled, a few from the explosion.

Terrell was back on his feet after the bullet grazed the side of his face. Octavia suffered the worse injury case. Her ear was severed from her face, cut by the flying metal debris from the hot water tank. Her ear was hanging on by only by an inch of flesh.

"Help me, help me please," she moaned laying in agony. O'Sha couldn't hold herself together. She was weeping uncontrollably. She blamed Money as well as Tywon for what happened. Octavia was then rushed out the house to Receiving Hospital. Terrell also took the ride to receive medical attention, but swore revenge against Money one day. In the mix of the black out and confusion, Big Daddy had long ago rushed Money out the house. Even though Big Daddy hated Money guts, he was still family.

O'Sha screwed in some white bulbs so everyone could see. She then looked around the basement for Money, not knowing he was already gone. She jumped in Tywon's face.

"Where's your boy at!" she asked grimly. "I don't know how his ass snuck out of here, but he's going down for what he done to my sister. Now when the Police get here, I want you to tell them where Money lives, so they can pick him up."

"The Police! Hold on," said Tywon. "I ain't no snitch. First, I got'ta hear Money's side of what happened. I can't just rat him out like that." O'Sha was now questioning Tywon's loyalty to her.

"You ain't rattin' nobody out, it's called doing the right thing. Money tried to kill my cousin and from the result of that, my sister's ear is off her face," she whimpered. "So, are you gon'na tell the Police or what?"

Tywon was in a tight spot. It was now a choice between his woman and his best friend. He then told O'Sha he was neutral in this matter. This was a situation between Money, Terrell and Octavia. He had nothing to do with it.

O'Sha grew very upset. Pointing, "You know what Tywon, fuck you! I need your help and you're siding with that nasty ass perverted friend of yours. You need to quit hanging around him, he's gon'na get you killed or either locked up one-day. But it doesn't mater, Money's ass go'on get his. He'll be back out on that corner like ain't shit happened. But you Tywon, you can get the hell out my house." she said pointing towards the upstairs. "It's over, leave!"

Tywon stood in the middle of the basement trying to plead his case to O'Sha. Right then, the Police arrived. They started asking questions of those who remained behind. Tywon started limping like he was one of the injured. He hobbled up the stairs and out the door. He didn't need O'Sha implicating that he was the best friend of the shooter, plus he still had weed in his pocket.

Lady Rock

The next morning, Money awoke. He opened one eye and then the other. He arose from the bed and sat on the edge, discovering he was still fully clothed. A throbbing hang-over suddenly hit him. "Damn," he grumbled holding his head not remembering the night before. It also didn't help that his mother was going through her regular bitching routine about her finances. Her screeching voice was increasing the pain in his head. Money opened his bedroom door and went into the kitchen. His mother was sitting at the table.

Clearing his throat, "Uh um... Good morning Ma'," he said in a groggy tone.

She snarled. "What's so fuckin' good about it? My bills are overdue, ain't no food in the house, and I ain't got no damn money. "What, you go'on gim'me some or somthin'?" she nastily asked.

Damn, is that the best way this bitch can ask me for some money? he thought rambling through his pocket. Money pulled out his cash and went into a panic.

"What the hell happened to my money?" he whispered to himself. He counted up only $300 of the $1500 he had yesterday. He then desperately started checking all his pockets. His mother was still standing in front of him with her hand out.

"Oh, now that I need some money, you suddenly ain't got none, huh?"

Money grew irritated. He threw his last $300 at her like it was nothing. She stuck the money in her bra and headed for the front door. Once she opened the door, she started yelling. "Somebody done lost their got-damn mind! Who the hell car is this up on my grass? Money do you know anything 'bout this?"

Before Money could answer his mother said she was calling the Police. Money hurried to the door and looked out. "Oh shit," clenching his teeth. The Station Wagon now wrecked was parked in the front yard. He rushed over to the phone and pushed down on the receiver.

His mother looked at him like he was crazy. "What is your damn problem? I was talking to the Policeman."

Money smiled innocently. "Ugh, I think I might know how that car got their Ma.' But don't worry, I'll take care of it" he said.

His mother slammed the phone down. She then looked him up and down calling him a, "Hopeless fool."

She then headed out the door, slamming it shut.

Money squint his eye shaking his head. "Her fat ass always trying to put me down, but she steadily stay begging."

At that point, he started replaying the last night's events in his mind, which could answer why the car was in the yard.

"Money! C'mon, c'mon man...Bring your dumb ass on. You done did it now. You really fucked up this time," said Big Daddy running Money from the scene. "Man damn, I think you killed that dude. What the fuck were you thinking about? Why would you shoot that man in front of all them people? That was just plain stupid. I suggest you lay low for a while, because if you don't, them go'on peoples lock you up."

Money suddenly stopped. "Lock me up! Ain't no jailhouse around these parts that can hold me. I'm muthafuckin' Money Bunny, you ain't heard?" he slurred, flicking vomit from his hand.

Big Daddy watched in disgust. Money continued. "You know Big Daddy, I think you wan'na see me locked up. Yeah...that's it. I can see it in your eyes. The way you be watching me. The way you be starring. You want it all, don't you? My money, the block and my style. Yeah... it's evident. You wan'na be me," he raved in Big Daddy's face.

Big Daddy pushed him. "Man, fuck you! One day Money, your mouth is gon'na land your ass into some shit that you can't get yourself out of. You done burnt the bridge with me for the last time. I'm washing my hands clean of you." At that time Big Daddy pulled out the gun that Money dropped on the basement floor. He disarmed the weapon and handed it to him saying, "Good luck cousin. Your gon'na need it." He then went on his way.

Money staggered. "Don't walk away from me muthafucka! I own you bitch! You work for me. Get your ass back here. Big Daddy! Big Daddy!" he called. "I'm only bullshitin.' Big Daddy!"

Big Daddy kept on walking. "Well fuck yo' fat ass then!" he yelled up the street. "I don't need you. I don't need nobody. I'm muthafuckin' Money Bunny, bitch!" laughing. "You'll be back. The weak always do."

From then on, Big Daddy promised himself to never deal with Money again. After 10 minutes of stumbling and falling to the ground, Money found his way to the Station Wagon parked around the corner. He repeatedly fumbled the keys trying to get into the car. Before exiting the parking space, he rammed both cars in front and in back of him. Afterwards, he side-swiped 10-parked cars up the street. But some how, he amazingly still made it home without a single bruise or scratch, parking the car in the yard.

Money came out of thought laughing, now remembering back to the lap dances he received by Octavia. "Damn, she was rolling that ass so...good last night. That's a bad bitch. She needs to let me hit that pussy. I'll tear it up," he expressed physically pumping the air. Money then snapped his fingers. "That's where my $2200 went to. That dirty ass broad hustled me. Fuck it though; it was worth the bread to see Octavia down on her knees, crawling like a dog for me." Money began to tingle on the inside, imagining she was still pulling on his pants zipper with her teeth. He couldn't wait to see her again. *But damn, I'm broke,* he thought. "Can't get no coochie without the loochie."

Right then, Money reached inside the kitchen cabinet to his stash spot. He pulled out an 8th of cocaine in a plastic bag. He sat it on the counter while he collected his other essentials. A pyrex dish, a box of baking soda, 1 fork and a mixer. He set the dope inside the cooking dish along with some baking soda. He added a little water and placed it on the stove to boil. Money kept a close watch making sure not to let it burn. Within minutes, the cocaine started to bubble into a gel like substance. He poured the excess water out the pot, then took the fork and added a little more baking soda. He inhaled the sweet aroma boasting to himself, "Yeah baby, can't nobody cook this shit up better than me," whipping the dope with the mixer. Minutes later, *"Walla!"* It was done. What appeared in the pot to be a hard round cookie was now, *'Crack Cocaine.'* Money let it cool, satisfied with the results. Afterwards, he weighed it. The Crack measured in at nearly 8 ounces. He smiled, rubbing his hands together yelling out, "Get money muthafucka's!" He then called his workers to let them know what time to meet him on the block. At that time, he would then issue out their packages. He explained Big Daddy was no longer a part of the team and everyone was to be there prompt and ready to hustle hard. Afterwards, Money sat the Crack on a plate, thinking of his soon to be $8500 pay day. He was excited, just as much as he was curious for a try. But for quite sometime, he'd been fighting the temptation of Rock Cocaine's said to be ultimate high. He was afraid of its demand and control over the body; its consumption over the soul, and its ability to over power the rational thinking of one's mind.

True Money was a user of powdered cocaine. But this drug cooked up in its altered form of crack, amplified the high 10 times more when used, he again shook of the temptation.

Money cut up the crack into small $10 rocks and packaged them up for sales. He then cleaned himself up for the day, ready to hit the streets. But first, he needed a little nose appetizer. He sat down at the kitchen table and snorted a few lines. The coke was good, but not as explosive to him like when he first tried it. Money needed something more potent. Something with a stronger hit. "Something like me," he heard a voice say.

Money looked around the room thinking his mind was playing tricks on him. The voice came again. "You heard right, over here."

Money jumped from the chair, startled. "What the hell! Who are you, and how did you get in here?" he asked the woman sitting at the table.

"Calm yo'self and sit the fuck down!" she said in the ruthless tone. Allow me to introduce myself.

DEX

"I'm the muthafucka' you'll desire in the morning before you eat
The muthafucka' that'll make you sell the shoes off your feet
Who am I? That's yet to be told
But if you fuck with me, be prepared to sell your soul
China White ain't the baddest bitch, that title belongs to me
Just gim'me five more minutes of talkin' and you'll see
I want you to get to know me, I'm that stronger hit
Pull my panties down, tickle me, play with my clit
I'm all pleasure; don't be scared, I'm not a disease
I'm here to serve you, make you feel good, I only want to please
Me, I'ma old hoe, I'm nothing new
I got a large following, bigger than congregations of churches do
Now c'mon Money, put the torch to me, light me up
Then wrap your lips around the glass dick and take a puff"
"Hold on bitch! Watch your mouth, I don't suck no dick"
"Well muthafucka I apologize, it wasn't meant the way it sounded
Now inhale, breathe, yeah... that's right
Let go all that pain, concentrate on that pipe
Slow it down, you chockin', you breakin' into a sweat
Blow that smoke, now you feel me, I'm better than sex
You and I are now one, by a kiss from your lips
Like husband and wife, joined at the hip
No need for hygiene, no need for a bath
Together we'll walk down a gutters path
Your respect is lost; your life is a waste
You're a crack-head now, your desire is to free-base
You'll deceive anyone; give up everything you're worth
Just to get a taste of this loving, you won't care who you hurt
You're a slave now, a victim of the trade
You've just been served, caught up in your own game
When your lips turn white and you scratch and you itch
People are gon'na wonder, Is Money on that shit?

It happens all the time, people sell me, then they use
You've become what you'd feared, you knew the rules
You ain't shit nah, yo ass belongs to me
I'ma play you like a trick, to get down requires a $10 fee
But keep up the good work, push and serve me on the block
That old hoe, the baddest bitch, you'll always want me, Lady Rock"

Money threw the pipe down. "What the fuck did I just do?" he asked himself. "Man, what's the matter with me. Why do I feel so weird?" At that point, the paranoia effect from the rock began to kick in.

Money started to feel anxious and jittery. He couldn't seem to sit still. He then began to swat at his shoulders like something was there. His eyes bucked and uncontrollably shifted back and fourth. Suddenly, jumping form his chair "Who that! Who that!" he screamed, looking from left to right. His high was now at its maximum point.

Money began hallucinateing images and hear voices. China White was at the table calling him a "Two timer." Lady Rock was in his face laughing. Other hard drugs such as heroin and various narcotic pills were pulling at his shirt. "Stop it! Stop it!" cried Money. "Get the fuck away from me!"

Without warning, Money snatched off his shirt and grabbed a knife from the utensil drawer. He then backed himself into the corner chanting, "They comin' to get me. They comin' to get me," sliding down the wall.

After 10 minutes or so, the high wore off. Money found himself on the floor, foolishly holding the knife in an upright position. He started laughing. "Damn! This some out cold shit, this the bomb. Now I see why them crack heads be on my line so tough," dismissing himself as one. "But never again will I mess around like that. That rock shit is just too damn good to be true." But that sermon was only a contradiction of what he was really feeling. He then smoked up 3 more rocks, finding himself 2 hours late for the meeting on the block. He there-after straightened himself out the best he could and headed out the door.

Money drove onto his block of business. Surprisingly, his workers were not out there. *Damn, where they at?* looking around figuring his 2 hour tardiness was to blame. "Shit! If you want somethin' done, you got'ta do it your damn self."

He aggressively whipped the battered Station Wagon around into the alley. He then got out the car and posted on the corner for business. It was the 15th day of the month. Besides the 1st this was the day most fiends cashed their government assistant checks.

Money just knew a slew of crack addicts were gon'na be lining up for his dope. But weirdly, a half hour had passed and not one fiend had approached.

"Man...I got all this shit in my pockets and I ain't served nobody yet. And where the hell are my workers?" *Something ain't right,* he thought to himself. The Police crossed his mind, but he figured if anything was wrong, he would've heard about it by now. Money was wishing he and Big Daddy had never fell out. He knew his cousin would've distributed all the packages to the workers by now and the block would be pumping. A reconciliation with Big Daddy crossed his mind, but then Money thought, *Fuck Big Daddy! This my show. He needs me. Anyway, it's best that he's gone. He was gaining too much respect amongst the workers. Their loyalty to him was beginning to bother me. Besides, Big Daddy is washed up without me.*

Afterwards, Money questioned that statement within himself. While waiting on a customer to show, he shorted his workers 4 rocks each out of their packages. He figured on blaming them of trying to cheat him after the nightly count. Soon after, he stepped in between the shadows of two houses. The lighter flicked and Lady Rock did most of the talking, 15 minutes later, he stepped out glassy eyed and fidgety. At that time, a familiar face was now approaching. Money instantaneously put on his game face to cover up his high.

"What's up Faye? What do you need?" he asked struggling to keep his composure.

Faye displayed a disturbing look. "Money, I've got somethin' to tell you," she whispered looking around. Money didn't catch onto her facial expressions. He figured she was trying to game him.

"Faye, I don't wan'na hear shit you got'ta say. All I wan'na see is that cash rolling out your pocket and into mine."

"But Money, listen."

"Naw bitch, you listen. I already told your crack-head ass, ain't no handouts around this muthafucka.' Now go'on, bring me back some money. Go and hit Tywon's stash spot like you always do. I'll be right here, I ain't going no-where," he said pushing her in the back.

Faye turned and gave Money a resentful glance.

Mumbling, "Yeah...that's what you think," walking away. Money grimed her until she bent around the next corner.

That fiend out bitch always begging, damn!

Just then, a scraggly looking white man approaching from the opposite direction caught his eye. *Who is this cat?* thought Money. *I ain't never seen him before.* The man walked up.

"Let me get $50 worth," he said.

"$50 worth of what!" defensively replied Money.

"$50 in rocks," he countered.

"Rocks, I don't know what you talking about. Ain't no rocks being sold around here."

The man pulled out a dingy $50 bill. "Awe, c'mon man. It's all over the 'burbs how you got the best shit in the city. My buddy John is always screaming your name. 'Money's got the best shit. Money's got the best shit.' That's all he talks about. So, if it is the best like John says it is, then you're gon'na be a rich man. Because I'm gon'na tell all my smoking buddies about you. So come on Money, let me experience the legacy of that rocket fuel," he voiced in an ego-stroking manner.

Money smiled with glorification. It made him proud to hear his dope was gaining popularity out in the suburbs. He always charged them double on the price. He was tempted to serve the man but was leery, not knowing if this guy was a cop. He decided to test the fellow.

"All that rich shit sounds good partner, but I ain't got no rocks around here. Check back in an hour or two. Somebody should be here by then to help you out."

Money figured by that time his workers would be on the block. They could then sale to him. If this man was the Police, Money himself couldn't be implicated for the sales.

"Fine," disappointingly replied the man. "I'll just take by business to the big fellow around the corner."

"Around the corner?" stated Money puzzled.

"Ain't nobody else serving around here. This my hood, I got this locked down!"

"Well, apparently you don't. Because it's about 5 other fellows on the next block selling to anyone approaching," he said pointing in the direction Faye went.

"From the looks of it, my buddy John was wrong about you. I need to be around the corner buying my dope."

It was now evident to Money why his 4 workers didn't show up. And he could only figure one big guy that was familiar and brave enough to sell in the hood, let alone on the next block. "Big Daddy!"

Damn, that must'a been what Faye was trying to tell me a minute ago. I should've listened to her.

Money was steaming mad. He whipped out his pistol, ready for war. *Family or not big boy gon'na feel this heat.* The scraggly man was caught off guard. His feet were planted with fear. He could only stare as Money stepped to him with the gun.

"A partner, I can't think of who your friend John is right now, but I do appreciate the dime you dropped. Here," he said serving the man the $50 in rocks. He then gave him an extra 2, as a reward for the information. The man sighed with relief saying, "No problem."

Money then took off running towards the alley for the Station Wagon. Retaliation against Big Daddy and his workers was on his mind.

At the same time, the scraggly man was screaming into his wiretap, "Move in! Move in! It's a go. Approach with extreme caution, suspect is armed and dangerous! I repeat, suspect is armed and dangerous!"

Money had no idea this was taking place. He reached the car, hopped inside and started it up.

Suddenly, "Scuuurredd!!" screeched the tires of the Police car now blocking the alley's exit.

Money was scared to death. He didn't know if what he felt between his ass was a wet fart or shit, but he was for sure that Police car was there for him. He slapped the wagon in reverse and stabbed the gas. Heavy white smoke burned from the tires.

"He's running! He's running! Suspect is running!" reported the Police car now taking pursuit. "He's in a brown and tan Station Wagon traveling north bound up the alley."

Multiple marked and unmarked Police cars sped up the street parallel to the alley. Sirens chimed the neighborhood. Sweat began to pour from Money's face. He was nervous but his hand was steady. He was relentless in his pursuit of escape, mowing down anything in his path. The howling 350 engine was pushing 45 M.P.H. in reverse. Money briefly turned around to look in front of him. Through the dirt and dust, he saw the red and blue disco lights of the Police car racing towards him fast. He then turned back around starring out the large rear window of the wagon.

"Awe shit!" he hollered.

Two other Police vehicles created a blockade out the alley's entryway. Uniformed and undercover cops were standing in front of the cars with their weapons drawn. But none of that mattered to Money; he had no intentions on stopping. He gave the old dinosaur model vehicle everything it had. Officers began firing their weapons as the car neared, now jumping out the way. The wagon burst out the alley plowing into the Police cars. The force spent the lightweight vehicles almost 3 times each. A fleeing Officer was struck by one of the cars, pinning him underneath.

"Officer down, call the medic!" was repeatedly being yelled over the C.B. Police frequency.

The wagon finally came to rest, smashing into a garage in the next alley. Surprisingly, the car was still running.

"Get that fucker!" Officers ranted. Police rushed in, approaching with caution. They were anxious to apprehend their suspect, furiously clearing the caved in debris. Money was briefly knocked out, now coming to. He looked around unsure of where he was, until hearing voices closing in.

Awe, hell naw. I ain't goin' out like this. Money pulled the sack of dope from his pocket and tossed it out the window. He then searched the dark car for his pistol but was unable to find it. *Where's it at?* "Fuck!" he voiced silently, feeling trapped.

On the outside, news of the high-speed chase had spread fast. The whole neighborhood appeared to be watching. Police created barriers to keep the residents back. People were discussing how they knew this day was coming. One woman even said she hoped the Police would kill his ass. Other rebellious gatherers were screaming, "Fuck the Police!" disapproving of their presence. A couple of thrown bottles emerged from the crowd. Officers quickly intervened, suppressing the mob.

Finally, the largest piece of garage wreckage was being lifted off the Station Wagon. The law stood armed and ready to kill just in case of any surprises. Money on the inside was ready. He sat in the driver's seat tightly gripping the steering wheel; incarceration wasn't in his future plans. From the voices and loud noise, he knew it was only a matter of seconds before the opportunity of escape presented itself, and then it came. A shine of light beamed through the busted windshield. Money again mashed the gas. Police began firing their weapons as the car bolted free of the rubble. A hail of bullets riddled the already beat up wagon. The neighborhood crowd began dispersing with screams getting out of the way. In fear of being shot, Money laid across the vinyl bench seat. Now unable to see ahead, he slammed into the Police cruiser he hit earlier. He forced the car into reverse, then back into drive, cock the wheel and sped off. Bullets were cutting and ripping through the seemingly unstoppable wagon. Police shot out all four tires. At all cost, they were determined to stop this mad man behind the wheel.

Money now, a half block from the scene was feeling a victory of escape, when suddenly, "Wwhhaaammm!" A crash bar equipped Police cruiser broadsided the wagon. The force hit sent Money crashing head-on into a telephone pole, ejecting him through the windshield landing him on the hood. Blood spilled from a wide gash on his head. He laid broke up and in pain. It appeared he wasn't gon'na make it. The neighborhood crowd once again gathered. Those who knew Money personally ran up to the wreckage.

"Damn! Money fucked up," said one of his workers. "He ain't go'on make it y'all."

"I'm hip, look at all that blood."

"I think he's dying," spoke another.

"I tried to warn Money. I tried to tell him the Police was watching him, but he wouldn't listen to me," said Faye shaking her head.

Big Daddy also stood shaking his head looking at Money, then over to the rookie cop who rammed him.

"Don't just stand there man, call a damn paramedic. That's my cousin laying on this hood!" he said loosing his cool.

The Officer gave no indication, but he felt intimidated by Big Daddy. At that moment, back up began to arrive. The rookie then turned brave.

Pointing, "You, you and you too! Get back, back up behind the line," he said in an authoritative tone. Faye and the others did as they were told. But, Big Daddy was rebellious. "Man...I ain't movin' no-where until you get my cousin some help. Look at him; he's bleeding the fuck to death, he's dying. He needs medical attention."

"Sir, calm down, we're gon'na call an ambulance. But at this time, this is a Police matter, so could you please step behind that line," he pointed. Big Daddy shook his head. "I told you already, I ain't going no-where. You step your ass behind that line. I'm standing right here, til' y'all do your damn job," looking the Officers in their eyes. "Sir, I'm warning..." Big Daddy aggressively cut him off.

"Move me yourself, if you bad enough!"

The rookie, along with 3 other Officers broke into a scuffle with Big Daddy. It was a struggle for the four, until two more Policemen joined in and wrestled him to the ground. He was then double-cuffed and placed in the backseat of a squad car. Money saw and heard it all, but he could only lay feeling lifeless.

At that moment, a familiar life saving tune danced in the air. Everyone turned to look as the sound neared. It was the ambulance. The music was joy to Money's ears. He felt new life creeping through his bones. Neighborhood gatherers were screaming and pointing "Right here!" The Paramedics came to a rolling stop, in which the driver peered at Money. His face showed concern, but the Police were steadily waiving him off. They directed Paramedics to the next block to the

Policeman who was ran over earlier. Big Daddy started raving and kicking the car door. Officers then hogged tied him with restraints. Adding insult to injury, Money still on hood was hand cuffed and searched.

"That ain't right!" the crowd stated over in anger. "He's hurt, he ain't going no-where!" The Police paid them no mind. The rookie Officer discovered incriminating evidence on Money, as well as inside the Station Wagon. He read off the items found, placing them on the hood.

"Here, we have the marked $50 bill used in the sting operation and we have what appears to be 11, 12, 13 loose Crack Cocaine Rocks, found in possession of the perpetrator's front pocket, also a 9 millimeter hand gun found underneath the passenger seat. In his back pocket, I came upon a silver compact with the engraved initials E.D. on top, 'What ever that means,' containing what I think is powdered cocaine, and last, a pipe used for smoking crack."

Proudly, "This guy is going away for a long time." Disrupting the moment, the undercover cop who purchased the crack from Money approached the rookie. He slyly handed the young Officer a small package and whispered a few words. The rookie immediately declined his colleagues request handing, him back the package. He stated there was no need for planting shady evidence. Their case was strong enough against the suspect. The undercover cop and senior Officers began questioning the rookie's integrity to D.P.D. with his job and reputation now on the line; the rookie did what he was asked. He re-entered the Station Wagon, acting as if he was conducting a second routine search. Big Daddy watched it all from the back seat. He knew the outcome from the second search wasn't going to be good. Then suddenly, the rookie emerged with a sack of crack. The same sack of crack Money tossed out earlier in the garage. The neighborhood gatherers were puzzled by what was found.

"Is that a bag of drugs the Policeman sat on the car?" asked Faye's friend. "Yeah, girl, they settin' Money up. You can't trust the Police nowadays," she replied.

The senior Officers on the scene knew the dope found in the garage wreckage belonged to Money. They also knew proving it in court was another thing. A good lawyer could easily have the charge dismissed, since the narcotics were not found in his possession. The Officers didn't want any mishaps or technicalities interfering with this case. They knew the planted dope would insure a conviction for Money.

There-after, a second ambulance truck arrived. Money was placed on a stretcher in-which he was handcuffed to. The medical technician then administered an I.V. into his arm. Money's head wound was severe and his vital signs were low. The paramedic could tell from the dried up blood, he'd been lying on that hood for quite some time.

The technician requested a Police escort to the hospital. At first, Officers refused but agreed after the paramedic explained the possibility of a negligent medical lawsuit. Money was then loaded into the ambulance truck and rushed off to Receiving Hospital. The Police escort led the way.

Soon-after questioning Big Daddy, along with the neighborhood folks, Police still didn't have a positive I.D. on their suspect, they only knew of his alias name, *'Money.'*

Just then, a teenaged girl emerged past the crowd approaching Officers. She told them Money's real name was Maurice Bonner, and besides his crimes committed today, he was also wanted in connection with a shooting at her party last night, as she then began explaining the details. The Police were thrilled about the new information.

"And what is your name young lady?" asked the Officer scribbling on his writing pad.

"My name is O'Sha, O'Sha Hood, and I'll testify to everything I told you."

Right then, Tywon inched on the scene. He'd just received the story on Money. He stood behind the crowd watching.

Now what is that bitch telling the Police about my boy this time? he thought to himself. The Officer then asked O'Sha if she knew Big Daddy. She glanced at him for a second but gave no acknowledgement of knowing him, not wanting to get him caught up in Money's mess. She then stepped back into the crowd, when Tywon grabbed her arm.

"What did the Police ask you? What did you tell them!"

"Get off me dammit!" she said snatching away from him. "Ooohhh…!" went the instigating crowd.

"I don't have to answer to you. I ain't your woman no more, besides, you wasn't concerned about what the Police asked me or what I told them last night. You were too busy sneaking your coward ass out the door." O'Sha's eyes began to water. "I suppose to have been your woman Tywon. You suppose to have had my back, been down for me. My sister and my cousin got hurt because of that maniac, menace, so called friend of yours. And it pisses me off thinking how you just stood there protecting him. Money ain't shit! He don't give a fuck about you. Why don't you see that? You act like you're his bitch or something. Hell, I wouldn't be surprised if you be wiping his ass too."

The neighborhood crowd broke into laughter.

Tywon was humiliated. The thought of himself being associated with a homosexual joke was degrading. O'Sha was about to continue, until Tywon suddenly lashed out at her.

"Don't you ever disrespect me like that again, I'aint nobody's bitch! You a bitch!" he said, as a couple of guys from the crowd held him back.

The reporting Officer noticed the disturbance and approached. "Is there a problem here?" he asked.

Upset, "I don't know." responded O'Sha. "Is there a problem here Tywon?"

Tywon smacked his lips. *I can't believe this broad said my name in front of the Police.* He then shook his head *'No'* insisting there wasn't a problem. Afterwards, the Officer stepped away.

O'Sha looked at Tywon with an evil glare.

"I'm just glad I found out who and what is really important to you in your life, because obviously, it wasn't me. It doesn't matter, it wouldn't have worked no-way. From what I see, you have family issues to deal with," she said now looking at Faye. O'Sha then walked off.

Faye looked around puzzled. "Who she talkin' 'bout? I know that heifer ain't talkin' 'bout' me," she repeated with her fists bald.

The neighborhood folks snickered as they began to disperse. Just then, the Police escort who lead the ambulance truck, radioed back to the scene. It was reported, a minute after their arrival to the hospital, their suspect in custody, *'Money'* had suddenly died. The paramedic stated Money's death was due to a possible brain hemorrhage suffered in the accident and doctors were presently trying to revive him, but his chances of survival were slim to none.

The listening Officer shook his head thinking of the young life just lost. He discussed the news with his colleagues who were not at all distraught about the death, then afterwards with Big Daddy who'd already heard the broadcast over the radio from the back-seat of the squad car. Slow tears streamed down his face as he wept silently.

Tywon standing amongst the last few gatherers caught the gossip rumor of Money's passing. At that moment, a shock ran through his body. "Money's dead?" he questioned in-disbelief. *'I must have heard wrong.'* "What did you say?" he asked the guy who first spilled the news. "Money's dead man, he's dead. I over heard it on the Police radio," he replied.

It was like an outer body experience as Tywon lost his legs. The confirmation of the story was too much for him to handle. He found himself sitting on the ground thinking of he and Money's childhood friendship; the good times and even the bad. But that didn't matter, in his heart, Money would truly be missed. Faye then pulled Tywon up by the hands and led him from the scene.

Soon after, Officers offered Big Daddy back his freedom with no charges, if he left the investigation sight peacefully, he agreed and was cut loose.

The only happy camper from this dilemma was the under cover cop. He felt justified from Money's death. He headed back to his squad car smiling. He jumped in his vehicle, looking to the passenger seat.

"Well John, he's dead. That black fucker is gone. Ah...the world is better off without him anyway," he said throwing his hand. "Just one less crack dealing son-of-a-bitch we won't have to worry about." John listening gave a slight grin. The under cover cop then became upset.

DEX

"Hell John, I don't know why you're so got-damn happy. Look at, your Station Wagon over there wrecked. Your fuckin' teeth are missing, and you look like shit. Jesús, and to think, all this ruckus over some kid selling you soap. Man...John, you need help," shaking his head. "Some days, I can't believe you're my little brother. If mom were alive today, what would she think of you?" John held his head in shame. Afterwards, the two men drove away from the scene.

Old School Rules

It had been 5 years since Black-Knight snatched away the life of Uncle Ed. A day later, he fled to Long Beach, California to lay low; to get away from the life, so he'd told himself. He knew it was really to escape the clutches of Sergeant Conrad Bantz. With 1 million plus dollars, he and his best friend K.G., who was also his hit man, were living the life of super-stars. From renting Ferrari's and Limo's, to eating the best steak, shrimp, and lobster in the most exquisite restaurants, to sexing the finest women, along with leasing a beachfront home with a pacific view, the two were down to their last 5 grand.

For the first time in a long time, Black-Knight was nervous about his financial situation. Periodically, he'd phoned old affiliates back home in Detroit to borrow cash, but bad seemed to always come instead. Many of his Old-School partners were dead, in jail or either indicted by the Feds. Others were broke, or on drugs, or just working jobs. Black-Knight always said, *'Fuck a job! A job ain't nothing but a ball and chain short of slavery.'*

Members from Black-Knights hit team were also doing bad or deceased. After running through a few hundred grand they each had stacked, the five-man crew took on the trade of robbing known local drug dealers. Word quickly got out who the men were. One of the robbers' girl-friend had discussed with them about how an old sugar daddy of hers had big money, and how much he still loved her and wanted her back. She told the crew she could get them access inside the home, but her sugar daddy had to be killed for her protection. The men agreed smiling and rubbing their hands together, eager to do the job. Two days later, the lick was set up and the men entered the back door of the home, but to their surprise when the lights turned on, the hit men found themselves facing a 30-man firing squad. Their lives were cut down and bodies dumped in a field. Rowe, a member of Black-Knight's hit squad amazingly survived his 13 burning bullets of death. Unfortunately, his injuries confined him to a wheel chair. He also lost a lung which sometimes required him to use an oxygen tank to breath. Rowe stays in touch with Black-Knight filling him in on the latest street news.

Black-Knight was on the patio laying in his robe. He was looking at the bright sky line beginning to set, then to ocean's waves coming ashore, finally, down at the beautiful palm trees surrounded by the thick grains of sand, which were starting to lose their shadows. He'd seen this sight many times and never wanted them to end, but the $2000 a month rent, now 3 months behind, attached with an eviction notice said different.

Black-Knight walked back into his plush decorated living room. He looked to K.G. who appeared not to have a care in the world. He was on the couch sliding his middle finger in and out the vaginal lips of his lady friend.

"What the hell, K.G.!" Black-Knight yelled loudly.

K.G. jumped up started. "W-What's up man? What's the matter?" he asked with attentiveness.

"Why are you playin' with her pussy on my $2500 couch? As a matter of fact, get that freak bitch out my house, we gos'ta talk," walking back to the patio.

K.G. gave a slight pause. He didn't appreciate the tone of voice Black-Knight had taken with him. He felt disrespected. "I'm tired of this shit," he mumbled under his breath.

"Well if you so tired, why don't you do something about." vindictively voiced the woman on the couch.

K.G. looked with anger. "Bitch, shut up! I've told you about your mouth before. You talk too damn much. Anyway, you heard my man. Let's go, get out!" K.G. snatched the woman by the arm.

"But, K.G.! K.G.!" she pleaded. K.G. didn't even give the girl a chance to put her panties on before he pushed her out the door. He then headed to the patio to accompany Black-Knight.

"So what's up man? What do you wan'na talk about?"

"For one, that broad you got hanging around the house. I don't like her. She talks too much and she be eating up every damn thing around here, plus she's always crying broke. She ain't never got no money!"

"Cheryl is a Hollywood makeup artist. She's going to be a big star one-day. She's just in between jobs right now," K.G. defended.

Black-Knight rolled his eyes and turned his head like, *'Whatever,'* looking out over the water. K.G. also looked over the water curious to what his partner was looking at, as Black-Knight then spoke.

"You see that K.G.? It's beautiful, don't you agree?"

K.G. agreed, not knowing what he was agreeing to.

"It's gorgeous. The sun-set, the air, this is the life; Best of the best food, driving fresh ass cars and the baddest bitches at our disposal."

K.G. smiled, thinking "Yeah..."

"But it's over, it's over now, we're broke.

K.G. frowned. "Broke! But how, what happened?"

"What do you mean how? I just told you how," thinking, *'Damn, were you listening?'* "Its crunch time again man. We gos'ta get on the hustle, get back onto our feet. I'm 36 years-old now and you're 37, we ain't gettin' no younger. Now, the plan is, we're gon'na sell all the furniture in this house. I figure we can get at least 10 grand for it easy. Along with the five grand I got, that should put us at about the $15,000 mark easy. From there, we'll get us a hotel room and then find us a connect on some dope or something. Shit K.G., I had hoped that street life was behind us but fuck it; we got'ta do what we got'ta do. What you think?"

Having no other plan or solutions, "Hell yeah! Sounds good to me," replied K.G., smirking. The two men then stood and shook hands, already knowing what the battlefield held for them.

Three weeks later, everything Black-Knight planned went accordingly. He sold all the furniture in the beachfront home, which brought in a little over 10 grand, on top of the $5,000 he already had. Also, he and K.G. settled into an inexpensive Long Beach motel in the heart of the ghetto. It was three steps down from what Black-Knight was accustomed to, but he knew it took sacrificing and patience to come back up.

Black-Knight was sitting on the old dingy motel room bed in a hot sweat. He was positioned in front of the air conditioner, which seemed to be blowing more hot air than cold, talking on the phone.

"So like I told you Rowe, don't let that wheel chair shit get you down. Me and K.G. 'bout to hit the streets of Detroit with a hard snow storm," said Black-Knight. "You're still part of the crew. You still down with me, and you gone eat again baby, don't worry. Just keep me posted on who's hot and who's not in the town. The last thing I need is to sell a kilo to an indicted muthafucka' and have the Feds on my ass. You feel me?" wiping sweat from his baldhead.

Taking a breath from his oxygen mask, "Yeah, I understand Knight," replied Rowe. "But aren't you afraid to set up shop here? I mean, back in the day that young white boy cop Conrad Bantz wanted you bad. Those killings down at Ed's bar sparked the investigation that led to the dissemblance of his task force, and that got his ass fired. And even though he didn't have a badge no-more, he still was kicking down doors of all your known drug houses looking for you, but nobody could tell him where you were, because no one knew."

"And that's the way I'm gon'na keep it," interrupted Black-Knight. "I'll never again sell bricks in the same city where I live. For what, so a muthafucka' can know my every move and try to kill me, or finger me for the man? Naw, I don't think so, I'm smarter than that. The way I look at it, Detroit's good for one thing, and that's gettin' money. When I step into town, it's gone be for one, maybe two days tops to handle my business. Far as hanging out with the fella's or kickin' it with the bitches, I'm not on that. But to answer your question Rowe, naw, I'aint scared to set up shop there. Detroit's my hometown. Fuck Conrad Bantz, I'll have K.G. put one in his dome."

Rowe laughed, loving to hear Black-Knight talk that raw shit, and he knew how his brother got down.

"Ok Rowe, get on your job up there and I'ma do mine down here."

Devotedly, "Ok Knight, I got you man," said Rowe, feeling he was back in the game. Black-Knight finished with a few last words.

"And just to be on the safe side Rowe, ask around and find out what came about Conrad. You know, if he's been promoted, demoted, or hell, even he's been deported," he laughed. "But seriously, I need to know if he's still working the streets. No need for me stepping back into a trap, you got me?"

"Ok, will do and tell my brother I said what's up. Until then, I'll talk to you later, peace." "Click!"

Black-Knight hung the phone up feeling disturbed. "Conrad Bantz, damn. I ain't heard that name in a while. Really, I was trying to forget about it."

He then laid across the bed remembering back to 1980, when he and Conrad Bantz first encountered. A then 28 year-old Black-Knight had just entered one of his three heroin houses. He seated himself on the orange couch in the front room and began counting his money. Then oddly, out the corner of his eye, he spotted an addict who was thought to be getting high, eyeing his cash. At first, Black-Knight thought nothing of it, but the addicts cold blue eyes kept replaying in his mind. He then whispered to K.G. who was seated next to him.

"A, who is that white dude sitting over there?" he asked pointing. "The one sitting on the dining room floor in the corner?"

K.G. looked in the next room. "Oh, I know him. I don't know his name, but he comes through about three or four times out the week. He spends good money."

"Good money, huh? Well, I don't like the way he looks. A matter of fact, he looks too damn clean to be a dope fiend to me."

"I'm hip," acknowledged K.G., as he further inspected the man. "He is kind'a clean."

Black-Knight didn't like the stabbing feeling in his gut. Whenever his stomach turned like that, he knew something was wrong. He then hit K.G. with multiple questions about the Caucasian man.

"Did he come alone? Did he ever receive credit? Does he associate with the other addicts?" anything for a quick investigation lead.

K.G. shrugged his shoulders to all the questions asked, gesturing, *'I don't know.'*

Black-Knight grew angry. "Damn K.G.! You supposed to be on top of shit like that," he snapped. "It's your job to know these things. Have you at least watched this dude shoot up before? For all we know, this cat could be the Man, sitting right up under our noses."

K.G. knowing he'd slipped up said nothing. Black-Knight shook his head. "C'mon, lets go check this fool out.

As the two neared, the Caucasian man calmly stood to his feet. K.G. was the first to approach with his fists bald. "What's up white boy? Something about you don't smell right," he said, sniffing around the man's neck attempting to intimidate him.

In fear, the other junkies detecting trouble, started clearing the room. The white man frowned. "What's the problem here? I always pay you guys for my dope."

Black-Knight folded his arms. "Would you believe that's one of the problems? Search him!" he ordered.

As K.G. reached for his pockets, the dope fiend slapped his hands. "Don't touch me man. Don't touch me!

K.G. felt disrespected. He furiously started taking off his jacket like, *'I'm about to fuck this white boy up.'* Black-Knight waived K.G. off, knowing it was more here than meets the eye.

"Who are you, and what the hell you doing in my house? You ain't no user." The man clinched his teeth, pulling a Police badge from around his neck. "You know what this is. Now, get your asses again the wall and spread your fuckin' feet.

Surprisingly, two more undercover cops in the house thought to be dope fiends pulled out their badges along with their guns. K.G. began talking shit about what he wasn't going to do, but the pistol strike across his head said different.

Black-Knight remained calm, hoping this was a simple robbery. The blue eyed Officer then stuck a gun to his back and steered him towards the cold dark basement stairs; the same dreadful dark basement where many had met their life's end. Black-Knight was nervous as hell. He just knew at anytime a bullet was going to rip into his back. As they approached the bottom of the stairs, he figured out of all the brutal crimes he'd committed in his time, his number was now up.

Fuck this, if I'm go'on die, I wan'na see it comin.' Then quickly, he snatched away from the undercover and turned around.

"Fuck you cop! You might as well kill me know. If you think I'm 'bout ta' plead for my life like a bitch, then you got me wrong."

"Kill you?" the under-cover laughed, raising his gun to Black-Knight's face. "If I wanted you dead, trust me, that's what you would be. Making a piss-ant low-life drug dealer like your-self disappear is nothing. I don't give shit about your life. Your demise is only a hair pull away of this trigger. I'm here on business. Now move you black motherfucker!

Reaching the middle of the basement, the cop screwed in a light bulb. Black-Knight stood silent with his lips trembling with anger. The cop smirked then went on to explain his name was Conrad Bantz, the youngest ever in charge of D.P.D Narcotics Division. He then added his father was the late Lucas Bantz, Commander of D.P.D., downtown precinct. "The most honored and respected Policeman who ever wore a badge." *'Yeah, and who probably wore pink panties and a bra to match,'* Black-knight wanted to say.

Conrad continued, "This heroin garbage you're selling is over. It's fuckin' up our families, our children, along with the community. It's too addictive, too hard to shake and it ends right here," he preached. The heat is on you man. You're going away for a long time for this poison you're pushing. Now, you can go get your fancy lawyers and try to tap dance your way out of this mess, but far as I can see, you're fucked. From our surveillance, we know who your supplier is, we know who does your cash pick-ups, everything. We even know about the two murders of the heroin dealers in this basement."

"Murders!" *But, hh-how...?* thought Black-Knight feeling the cop was fishing for a confession, but that wasn't going to happen. Still Conrad smirked, knowing he'd struck a nerve. He decided to lay it on thick. "Yeah, we know about all that shit. From the looks of it, it's over for you. You're looking at minimum of 50 to 60 years in Jackson State Penitentiary. You now have a promising future on being somebody's girl-friend." Conrad then stood back and let the terrifying thought of life in prison wreck Black-Knight's mind, not yet revealing his true intensions.

Black-Knight felt the wind leave his body. *50 to 60 years! Who is this white, pretty, blue eyed muthafucka'? He cain't be no older than me, tryin' to pull rank on somebody, that's bullshit. But if this white boy knows half of what he's done spoke on, my ass is hit,* he gasped, dizzy with fear. Conrad was loving it, seeing Black-Knight sweat. He figured the time was now.

"Or, or instead of jail," Conrad stated as a stipulation with his finger up. "We can work together."

Not seeing any other way to avoid prison, Black-Knight agreed to the unsaid offer. Conrad then put away his pistol and began explaining the new merger business plan. He told Black-Knight his heroin operations would be converting over to a drug not so detrimental hitting the streets called, "Cocaine."

"But I don't know nothing about no Cocaine," said Black-Knight. "I push boy."

"Well boy, I suggest you learn about it. That is, if you wan'na stay out of prison. Conrad then said, a man by the name of Uncle Ed from the east side of town, would soon be contacting him soon for the details. After further pep-talk, Conrad then reached up to the hot light bulb.

"Remember, you deal with Uncle Ed only. This will be the first and last time you and I meet. If we're ever to meet again, you and I must have a problem," unscrewing the bulb. The light went out. Conrad then proceeded back up the stairs leaving Black-Knight standing alone in the cold dark basement.

Suddenly, "Bblaamm!" The motel door was kicked open.

Black-Knight was startled as he came out of thought. "What the fuck!" K.G. came dashing in the room with buckets of sweat pouring down his face. A swollen eye and busted lip told of his scuffle. Black-Knight rushed behind him into the bathroom.

"Awe shit man! Are you alright? They robbed you, didn't they? I knew I should've went with you," repeatedly raved Black-Knight.

K.G. began washing the blood from his face. The white porcelain sink began to paint red. When he finished, he looked in the mirror. His heart sank. His head and face was disfigured with golf ball sized lumps. His jaw was enlarged, appearing to be broken and his left hand index finger nail was completely ripped off.

Black-Knight insisted K.G. receive medical attention, but he refused. Although he was in excruciating pain, he simply requested some aspirin, a washcloth and some ice. He then laid back on the bed. Black-Knight was pained about what happened to his best friend. He felt responsible, he nearly shed a tear. He never cared about any man like he did for K.G..

"K.G., I'm sorry man, I thought Les was solid when it came to business, but I just don't understand. We ain't never had no problems with him before."

K.G. simply waived his hand as to say, *'Don't worry about it, it's cool.'* But it wasn't cool by Black-Knight, he was infuriated. Still, he continued comforting his partner the best he could, at the same time, cussing himself.

Damn, my dumbass. Why did I let K.G. do this deal alone? I know the rules to this game: Trust no-one, nobody. Ignoring that, my boy is all fucked up now, and 80 g's of my money is gone. I should'da knew that muthafucka' Les was a snake in the grass when I first met him. Any many who's always bragging about what he has, or how much money he's got, or how many bitches he's fuckin', ain't really living that life. But still, his glitz and glamour conversations tricked me up. Well that's alright.

Black-Knight reached down inside a suitcase pulling out an A.K. 47 assault riffle, inserting the long 50 round banana clip. K.G. opened his eyes to the clacking sound of the weapon being loaded.

Mumbling through his swollen lips, "Knight, what you doin' man?" he asked struggling to lift from the bed. "Give me a few days to rest and heal up. We'll then get Les together. We know all his hanging spots. Don't be so quick to move, just chill out."

"Chill out! Chill out! Fuck a chill!" said Black-Knight with anger.

"That bitch rob us, and beat the shit out of you. Plus, we only got three funky ass thousand dollars left. You think I'm fin'na let this shit go down like that? You think I'm about to let that ponytail wearin' bitch play us? We from Detroit City, Motown, East side, we don't play! It's an old saying K.G. 'What goes around, comes around.' And what Les failed to realize is, I'm the type of muthafucka' to make it come around."

Black-Knight began tying an elastic cord around the wooden butt of the gun. He then slid it around his shoulder covering up with a black leather trench coat. Although K.G. was deeply in pain, he was resurrected by Black-Knight's inspiring words. He reached under the bed and armed himself with a rigid edge knife and his 45 automatic.

Black-Knight smirked feeling proud. Despite K.G.'s condition, he was ready for the fight. Regardless of his brave heart, physically, he was in no shape for a gun battle. Black-Knight encouraged K.G. to get some rest and assured him the situation with Les was going to be handled. K.G. briefly argued, but soon agreed and laid back in the bed. Black-Knight then took to the streets in search of Les for retaliation.

The Friday night air was muggy and stiff. The downtown Long Beach avenues were very much alive. Fancy cars of all types were streaming back and fourth, as the bar and club hoppers flooded the streets. Drunken men and women were off their guards, while the muggers and thieves patiently waited in the shadows. Two hours had passed since Black-Knight left the motel. He checked the inside of several nightclubs where Les was known to hang out. With no luck, he then asked the watching streets for Les's whereabouts. Unsurprisingly, no one was willing to talk. They all knew Les reputation and wasn't about to get themselves involved. Clueless and frustrated, Black-Knight was left to continue to comb the streets.

Soon after, he pulled to a stoplight in his mustard colored, 79' Chevy Monte Carlo. He gasped as he came to the stop. The one-mile per hour bumper-to-bumper traffic was increasing the rage in his gut. The hot 90-degree weather wasn't helping either, but Black-Knight knew it was imperative he calmed himself. He knew impatience and irrational thinking in a bad situation could get him killed. He then closed his eyes, breathed deeply in and out and counted to 10. When he reopened his eyes, a bum from out of nowhere was cleaning his windshield.

Black-Knight began waiving the man off, as to say, *No, I don't want my windshield cleaned,* but the bum ignored him. By this time, the light was now green. Aggravated, Black-Knight stuck his head out of the driver's window. "Yo! Yo' muthafucka, move! My windows are already clean. Get the fuck out the way." The man continued his job acting as if he didn't hear Black-Knight yelling. Cars in back were now blowing their horns, followed with obscene words. Black-Knight could no longer just sit there. He flung open his car door and ran over to the passenger side front. He grabbed the bum by the back of his head and smashed his face onto the windshield.

"Didn't I tell you I don't need my fuckin' windows cleaned? Huh, huh? Didn't I tell you?" angrily he raved, stroking the man's face up and down the windshield. Although glass cleaner was burning the bum's eyes, he caught a glimpse of the A.K. laying on the passenger seat partially covered by the leather coat.

Just then, "Woop! Woop!" sounded the black and white squad car pulling on the scene, blocking traffic. "Woop!"

Awe shit! thought Black-Knight releasing the man's head.

The two Officers exited their vehicle, sliding their Billy-clubs onto their belts. They approached from the front.

"What seems to be the problem here?" one of the Officers asked.

Black-Knight was at a loss for words as he looked up at one of the Officers who stood 6 foot 8. *Damn, he's a big muthafucka!* It was what most said when Big-6 stepped from the squad car. His large 300-pound frame was solid and intimidating. His monstrous biceps filled his short-sleeved shirt. His hands were over sized, along with his size 17 shoe.

Black-Knight didn't know what to say. He wanted to take off running knowing his assault riffle was in the car, but he knew Long Beach Police warning shots were often fatal. Lucky for Black-Knight his thoughts of running were dismissed. Big-6 was an elite handgun specialist who could hit the smallest target from 100 yards out. It also didn't help any that Big-6 was already giving Black-Knight that guilty look. Black-Knight then looked to the bum who'd just finished wiping his face. His nappy hair and scraggly beard also had the Officers passing judgment about him. He squint his eye at Black-Knight with a hateful glare. He then started yelling and pointing to the passenger seat.

"Yyoouu! Yyoouu! Yyoouu, Yyoouu! Yyoouu..!" he explained dramatically. The gibberish talk had the Officer's both confused. They didn't understood a word he spoke. The man was a death mute. Lucky for Black-Knight, he couldn't hear nor speak. The Officers found the bums display comical. But to Black-Knight, it wasn't funny at all. He knew exactly what the bum was trying to tell the pair. Black-Knight quickly started talking over the man, explaining the situation steering the Officers onto this side. The bum soon became hostile, as Big-6 tried to send him on his way. After a few more refusals to leave the scene, Big-6 manhandled the dirty fellow to the ground with one arm. He was then arrested and thrown in the back of the Police car. Black-Knight too was ordered to leave the scene with a verbal warning. He sighed with relief knowing he just escaped a weapons charge. He promptly put his anger in check and took off in his car. He made it half way up block, only to find himself again in bumper-to-bumper traffic.

The midnight hour was nearing. After practically searching in every downtown nightclub for Les, Black-Knight found himself at the city limits. He was ready to call it quits for the night, besides K.G.'s physical condition was heavy on his mind. He decided to head back to the motel room. Black-Knight quickly made a u-turn in the middle of the street, then a right hand turn at the next corner to by-pass the traffic. He was cruising up a downtown back street as the landmarks started to become familiar to him. *Damn, I ain't been down this way in a while,* looking at the many topless bars that sat across the street from one another. He then peered further up the road at the Grey Hound Bus Station. Suddenly, Black-Knight mashed the brakes looking to his left. The car came to a screeching halt, almost causing him to be rear-ended.

"The Perfect Beat Bar and Grill" he read to himself on the awning. It was the bar where he and K.G. had first met Les. Black-Knight second guessed himself, but then whipped up in the alley, parking just in front of the bar's back door. He placed the assault riffle on the back floor covered by his trench coat. Afterwards, he walked back up the long dark alley around to the front of the brightly lit bar. Black-Knight patiently waited in the line behind the 15 people in front of him. On any other occasion, he would have paid the V.I.P. cost to enter the premises, but with this situation of seek and prey, staying low key was a must.

The line to enter the bar was moving quickly, but the three obnoxious, loud talking ladies standing behind Black-Knight made it seem like an eternity. *Damn, I wish these bitches would shut up.*

The three women were conversing about how the owner of the bar loved to spend his money like there was no tomorrow. They also spoke of how fine he was and how he didn't mind licking a woman below her waistline. Black-Knight's eyebrows rose up. Just then, a longhaired, light skinned, dapper dressed gentleman exited the bar about to make his way across the street.

"Look girl, there he go right there," pointed one of the women.

"That's him? Mmph, he is fine as hell."

"Oh yeah, he can get all up in this," stated another.

Black-Knight looked away. He wasn't the one to be checking out another dude, until the ladies called out his name.

"Hey Les baby..." they chimed in unison.

Hey Les baby! Black-Knight slowly looked up, laying eyes on the man he'd been hunting for most of the night.

Sylvester Long, a.k.a Lavish Les, as he liked to be called, for years rumored himself to be a well connected South American Drug smuggler. To authenticate his character, he claimed to be part owner of one of the West Pacific Coast Import/Export docks which transported in his goods. Les lived accordingly to his nickname, lavishly. He wore expensive tailored suits, drove top of the line sports cars and spent generously in the local nightclubs, in-which he claimed to own. But, for those who knew Les well, knew he was nothing more than a street pirate with a damn good front. The high-end cars he drove were the car-jacked vehicles of out of town drug dealers, who came to cop dope. His expensive tailored suits were cheap imitations re-altered to fit and accessorized with flashy buttons and brand name tags. Les glitter and gold life style was only a mere trap to lower unsuspecting flies into web of deceit.

Les accompanied by his two-man entourage, turned around to see whom the ladies that were calling his name. Black-Knight himself turned away, shielding his face with his hand, not wanting to be seen. Les started in the ladies direction until they all got out of the line and ran over to him. Being the ladies man that he is, he directed the doorman to let the women inside the bar, V.I.P. Les then proceeded over to a 300 Mercedes Benz parked on the other side of the street. When he approached, the tinted driver's window rolled down. Black-Knight with an eagle eye saw the driver to be a woman now handing Les a tight wrapped package. He placed the package in his inner jacket pocket and kissed the woman on her lips. Black-Knight continued watching as the doorman opened the door and Les walked back inside the bar. The two men closely followed. *I'ma kill that pretty muthafucka,'* thought Black-Knight.

Black-Knight then refocused his attention on the woman in the car pulling from the curb. He took a non-blinking hard stare at her face, simultaneously, as the woman appeared to be looking at him just as the tinted window rolled up. Black-Knight's face got stiff. His bottom lip hung with confusion. He couldn't believe who he'd just seen. *What is Cheryl doing meeting Les? And how does she even know Les? And whose Benz is she driving?* Black-Knight punched his palm with his fists. Awe...hell naw. It's some shit in the game. *I just know that bitch had something to do with K.G. getting robbed,* he thought sure of himself. Black-Knight stood halfway out of line, watching until the Mercedes taillights faded up the street.

Just then, "Excuse me, the line is moving. Could you step up please?" Black-Knight turned around to the annoying voice. He gave the skinny long neck man a look that could kill. The man felt the eyes of his cold stare and got quiet. Suddenly, Black-Knights rational thinking kicked in.

Now smiling, "I apologize, it was rude of me to hold the line up like that," he said stepping forward.

Black-Knight and the skinny man began a friendly conversation. Soon-after, Black-Knight offered the guy $100 if he would open the bar's back door. The skinny man agreed, jumping straight at the financial opportunity.

Black-Knight headed back to his car. There he slid the rope attached to the A.K. 47 around his shoulder. He then put on his black leather coat, leather gloves and anxiously waited for the back door to be opened. While standing there, he listened as the music from the bar vibrated the door. Finally, after the seemingly forever 10 minute wait, the back door creaked open. The skinny man stepped into the alley, the loud music rushed out behind him.

Talking loud, "Sorry it took so long, I had to play it safe and make sure no one was watching me," he said as if opening the back door was a mission impossible. Black-Knight didn't say a word, as he handed the guy the $100 bill. He then closed the bar's door behind himself leaving the gullible man standing in the alley. "Sucka!"

Black-Knight had just closed the door when, "Hey!" called the security guard. "Did you just come in through that back door?" he asked suspiciously looking at the long leather jacket. Black-Knight was caught off guard. He gripped the butt of the A.K., ready to turn and cut loose, but suddenly released it. He then faced the guard with a fake laugh.

"Oh damn, I thought this was the bathroom door. My silly ass, it's on the other side of the room. Thanks for pointing that out to me" he said petting the guards shoulder, walking away. The security guard stood puzzled stroking the hairs of his goatee.

Black-Knight looked back to see if the guard was following, there was no sign of him. *Cool, that was easy.* Still making his way through the thick crowd, he spotted Les standing across the room at the bar. He was laughing and passing drinks to the trio of ladies that were standing outside. A group of other women were campaigning for Les's attention to also receive drinks, but they were being ignored. Black-Knight stood griming Les in disbelief.

This Ron O'Neil pimp wan'na be muthafucka' just robbed me out of 80 grand. How can he just be so calm, laughing, and laid back, like he ain't did shit? Black-Knight couldn't figure it. *Now where are those other two clowns that be with him*, he thought, further scanning the room. Finally, he spotted Les's two-man entourage, so-called bodyguards standing with the doorman. Surprisingly, they appeared to be pointing in his direction at him. Black-Knight squint his eyes.

"Awe...Shit! He again looked in Les's direction, locking eyes on his target. In the middle of the dance floor, he flapped open the right side of his trench coat, knowing it was now or never.

Black-Knight didn't want to ask any questions. He didn't want any explanations and didn't want his money back. The only thing he wanted was Les's ass. None of the bar guest seemed to notice the unfolding drama over the loud music. Then slowing, he began to raise the A.K. when suddenly; he felt a large hand from behind tightly grip his shoulder.

"Hey asshole, you've got a choice, you can walk out of this bar on your own two feet, or I can throw you out on top of your head," now clutching his shoulder harder, failing to see the weapon covered by the trench coat. "So, what's it gon'na be?" he finished.

Still facing forward, Black-Knight observed the doorman and Les's men now rushing his way. "Fuck!" he whispered in a cool panic.

Then hostilely, he snatched away from the guard and turned with the A.K. aimed at his stomach. "Back the fuck up off me before I open yo' big ass up, back up, now!"

The guard quickly raised his hands to his chest in shock, laying his eyes on the breathing holes on the assault riffle. His eyebrows turned down and his lips began to quiver. It was a silent plea for his life. Black-Knight could see the coward in his eyes. The guard slowly began to back away.

Just then, a second security guard snuck up behind Black-Knight and bear hugged his body, lifting him off the ground. His arms were immobilized. "I got yo' ass!"

The A.K. fell from Black-Knight's hands but the strap around his shoulder caught it.

"Get him man! Help me, get him," the second guard encouraged to the first, as Black-Knight wildly struggled to free himself.

The first guard continued to back away, his mind in a traumatized state. By this time, the bar guest began to take notice of the loud commotion. Even Les caught sight of the drama. He began moving in for a closer look.

"Let me go man! Get the fuck off me!" demanded Black-Knight, trying to reach his finger around the trigger.

The security guard refused. "Take it easy man. You're makin' it hard on yourself. Calm down," he said in Black-Knights ear.

"Fuck you, I'm go'on kill yo' ass."

The doorman and Les's bodyguards were now less than 10 feet away with their pistols out.

Suddenly, Black-Knight's finger grasped hold of the trigger. "Wwhockk! Wwhockk! Wwhockk!" he fired at the ground, blasting the security guards foot off his ankle. They both fell to the floor. The guard screamed in agony. People in the bar began running and screaming in a panic in every direction trying to take cover.

"He's got a gun! He's got a gun!" was echoing throughout the room. Just then, the doorman and Les's men approached firing their guns towards the floor at Black-Knight. They hit everything and everyone passing in front of them except for their intended target.

Black-Knight immediately sprung to his feet, thinking if or not there was a rabbit's foot in his pocket. He knew it could have only been luck that kept his ass from being shot. Thereafter, he ran towards some tables and chairs. The long length leather flared out behind him like a dark hero as he dived for cover. Women were crying and screaming. Victims laid shot and bleeding. Everyone was in a panic trying to get out of the front door at one time.

Les nervously approached his men pulling out his gun.

"Who is the muthafucka' shootin' up the place?" he asked.

"Les we don't know who this cat is. We haven't seen his face," they answered, looking down at the mangled remains of the security guards foot, who was in a cold sweat going in and out of consciousness. The doorman was applying pressure to the wound with his jacket when suddenly, the guard died.

Black-Knight was laying low, thinking how fucked up his simple plan had just went, and how the hell he was going to get out of this mess. True, he had an A.K. assault riffle, but he figured he was out gunned by 4 to 1 odds. Les and his men were ready with their guns aimed, periodically firing 4 to 5 shots just to keep him pinned down. Right then, Black-Knight over heard, "The Police have been called, they're on their way."

"The Police?" *Awe shit Knight, time to make a move baby,* he told himself.

Black-Knight untied the rope from around his shoulder. He then checked his ammunition clip. It appeared to be full minus the three earlier shots. *I'm good.* He then grabbed a chair and flung it against the wall in the far corner. Everyone shot their guns in that direction except for the doorman. He wasn't so easily fooled.

"I'll get his ass." Suddenly, he heroically ran in Black-Knight's direction firing his weapon. "Bboomm! Bboomm! Bboomm Bboomm!" sang the 38. caliber handgun. The bullets were ripping through the flipped over wooden table.

Oh shit! Oh shit! This fool is gon'na kill me, thought Black-Knight ducking down on the floor. The closer the doorman got, the closer his bullets came to being fatal shots. Wood splinters were shredding from the table onto his face. Black-Knight had enough.

"Fuck this!" He took three quick breaths, then emerged running and firing the A.K. "Wwhockk! Wwhockk! Wwhockk! Wwhockk!"

The 10-inch flame exploding from the barrel of the A.K. 47 made Les and his men hit the floor, but for the doorman, it was too late. Two of the high-powered riffle shots struck him in his stomach, completely blowing is entire mid-section out.

After witnessing the destructive damage the A.K. had caused, Les looked at his men with the, *'I want to live look.'* They both gave the same look in return. They all then took off running towards the front door, at the same time firing their pistols behind themselves.

Black-Knight could see that they were trying to work their way out the front door. He kept on firing giving them everything the A.K. had. Both of Les's bodyguards took fatal shots to their backs, but Les managed to make it out the front door. "Dammit!"

Black-Knight then rushed towards the door. He was ready to take this fight to the streets even though he could hear Police sirens nearing the scene. As he neared the front door, K.G. surprisingly rushed inside the bar in a panic.

"Knight! Knight! C'mon man, lets get out'ta here. We got'ta go! This Police are coming! Where's the back door?" he urgently asked, pulling Black-Knight by the arm.

Black-Knight was dumbfounded, confused and a little suspicious.

"K.G., what are you doing here man? I thought you were..." K.G. cut him off.

"Knight, I'll explain everything to you later, but right now, we got'ta get out'ta' here. C'mon, lets hit the back door," he urged with persistence. Black-Knight's mind was already made up.

"Fuck that K.G.!" snatching away. Pointing, "You see all these dead muthafucka's in here?"

K.G. looked around the bar. "Damn."

"Yeah, that's right, damn. And ain't nam one of them Les. I want his head. Now I know you saw him run out of here, you had to. Which way did he go?"

"Damn, that was Les who ran out of here. Yeah, I saw him. He went that way," pointed K.G. to his left. Black-Knight was about to go after Les. Just then, 3 black and white squad cars quietly pulled up.

"Shit, lets go!"

Black-Knight and K.G. hauled ass through the bar, busting out of the back door. In the alley, Black-Knight handed K.G. the assault riffle, as he fumbled the car keys. He was opening the car door when he heard, "Clack! Clack!," hoping it wasn't what he thought it was.

Black-Knight slowly turned around only to see the barrel of the A.K. pointing 2 inches from his face. K.G. was biting on his bottom lip and shaking his head.

"What? Don't tell me you didn't see this day comin'. Looking all surprised and shit," snatching the car keys. Black-Knight held out his hands.

"K.G., whatever problem you have with me, we can discuss it later. But right now ain't the ti..." K.G. shoved the assault riffle up to his cheekbone.

"Shut up! Shut the fuck up right now. You see, that's the problem with you Knight. You're always trying to control the situation or tell somebody what they is or what they ain't go'on do. I'm sick of your shit, every since we were kids. It was your way or no way. Everyone thought you were always the man with the plan, but when it came to us hittin' licks back in the day, it was me putting in all the work, not you. When you wanted a muthafucka's ass whooped or killed; who did you call? Me. You didn't even sell your own dope, my brother Rowe handled all your business and he always brought you back your money faithfully. He made you rich, not yourself. And what did he get from all that work? Nothin', that's what; nothing but a steel framed chair to roll around in all day. That shit is your fault," he said wiping the sweat from his eyes.

My fault? I set Rowe up with a few hundred grand before we left. It's his own damn fault, he ran through his own money. I didn't tell that idiot to start robbing his old customers. That was his own doing, stupid muthafucka! Black-Knight wanted to say, but the A.K. 47 still pressed to his face kept those words silent.

K.G. continued, "At times Knight, I resent yo' ass. I hate that I let your wants, needs, and dreams stand in front of my own. I hate that I allowed myself for so many years to walk in back of you in your shadows. Not once have you ever given me the opportunity to stand or to shine alone. It was always about you. Well, it's my time now, it's all about me." Black-Knight barked back.

"Is that what all this bullshit is about, shining?"

"Mmm…basically. And the fact that you used me, my brother and everyone else around you to get what you wanted. I peeped that about you a long time ago. You ain't shit, but a selfish arrogant muthafucka.' You think I don't know how much money you were running through a day? Shiiid…I knew, but who was I to question the great Black-Knight? I wasn't nothing to you but a flunky, your gofer, a do-boy."

"It wasn't like that K.G."

"Yeah, that's exactly how it was. So this time, the user got used. Do you remember Cheryl? My so-called 'freak bitch' you kicked out the house, the make-up artist? You know, the girl you saw in the Benz tonight? K.G. paused, expecting Black-Knight to look surprised but he gave no reaction.

"Well anyway, that's Les's sister and my supplier. She's the one who came up this whole plan to act like I got robbed for the money. She even put this movie make up art on me so everything would look real, and your dumb-ass fell for it," peeling the make up art off his face. "I've been coping dope from her and sending it back home, I'm doing damn good. Who's Benz you think that is she's driving?"

Damn, thought Black-Knight, *I didn't see that coming.*

"Shit, with a $12,000 per kilo price tag here in Cali,' and a sales price of a $24 g's back in Detroit, me and Rowe is getting' paid. And you think I'm fin'na let you fuck that up 'cause you wan'na get back on? Nah, you're just in the way. But really Knight, I didn't expect for you to find Les, not tonight anyway. 'Ol Les," he laughed. "He's probably somewhere scared to death trying to figure out who's tyrin' to kill him."

"Well K.G., it looks like you got it all planned out. You get the girl and the money too, huh?"

"That's right, it's my time to shine."

"So let me ask you this; where is the money, my 80 grand?"

"You mean my 80 grand? It's in a safe place, not that it concerns you anymore."

"K.G. listen man, Cheryl is playing you. I saw her hand Les the money earlier tonight. Yo' girl is double crossing you, I'm telling you."

K.G.'s eyes rapidly began to blink. He got a little nervous.

"Naw, naw, you lying Knight. Cheryl is loyal to me, she wouldn't do that to me. You just stalling for time."

Black-Knight could see his persuasion tactic was working. He then poured it on.

"This is no bullshit K.G., I'm serious as hell. Cheryl is screwing you over."

Just then, a light colored Benz pulled into the opposite end of the dark alley. K.G. smiled, showing all of his teeth.

"See Knight, you were wrong. There's my ride now. See you in the next life, muthafucka!" K.G. slid his finger around the trigger and then took one step back positioning himself.

Black-Knight took a hard swallow but stood militant. He couldn't believe he was about to die like this. He always thought it would be in a gun battle like earlier in the bar, or in a drug deal gone bad, never by his childhood best friend. *Fuck it,* thought Black-Knight. *I'm ready to die.* Now at peace with himself, he closed his eyes.

Two seconds later, "Bbooomm!" Blood spattered across Black-Knight's face. He fell against the car, then to the ground. Oddly, he felt no pain and for some reason he could still hear. He figured his death was just moving in slowly. Suddenly, the Mercedes Benz tires screeched and sped away.

Just then in a distance, "You got 'em 6! You hit 'em! Got-damn you're a hella'va shot!" heard Black-Knight which forced him to open his eyes. Checking himself over, *I'm alive?* Afterwards, he looked to K.G. who was laying next to him bleeding out of a large hole in his head. His eyes and mouth were wide open, as if he couldn't believe he was dead. The A.K. 47 was lying underneath his body. Afterwards, he peered up the alley. Multiple flashlights were heading his way.

Black-Knight jumped to his feet. Suddenly, another shot was heard. The Monte Carlo's driver window shattered behind him. It was a warning shot. "Down, stay on the ground! You're under arrest!" yelled Big-6, the sharp shooter Officer whom Black-Knight had an encounter with earlier. *Under arrest?* That was enough to get Black-Knight's feet moving. He'd rather be killed than to do life in prison.

In a zig-zag motion, Black-Knight ran hard and fast down the dark alley, slinging the heavy leather jacket off his back onto the ground. The Officers were in hot pursuit firing their guns along with Big-6 leading the pack. His sprints were long and wide. For every one stride Black-Knight took, it equaled two for the 6 foot 8 Officer.

Finally, Black-Knight bent the corner onto the sidewalk. Already his wind was getting short, but the adrenaline of fear kept his speed steady. Half way up the block he looked back. Big-6 was now charging up the sidewalk coming on fast.

Breathing hard, "Man…this big muthafucka' still chasing me?" and wasn't showing any signs of giving up.

Black-Knight was yelling to the late night pedestrians to move out of his way. He then took to the street running against on-coming traffic. Cars passing by were blowing their horns. He nearly got hit twice. It didn't matter to Black-Knight. He knew if he got caught, it meant a life sentence. Big-6 less than 20 yards away, was already picturing him-self beating the shit out of Black-Knight after he caught him. Even though heavy sweat was pouring from his face and his chest was getting tight, only his heart bursting could stop his determination. But Black-Knight had determination too, and that was to get away.

Right then, he ran back onto the sidewalk, then back into the street, again onto the sidewalk. Nothing he did could shake Big-6. He was so winded and so tired, he wanted to just sprawl across the sidewalk and give up, but Black-Knight wasn't a quitter. The distance gap between the two was now only by inches. Police sirens chimed the crowded downtown streets. Pursuing Officers radioed Big-6 for the perpetrator's location, but he wasn't answering back. He wanted to bag this suspect on his own. "Your ass is mine! Your ass is mine!" 6 repeated to him-self reaching out his hand. Suddenly, Big-6 felt a nagging pain at the back of his thigh. His sprints quickly turned to gallops. His gallops turned to hops. He then grabbed the back of his leg and stopped.

Gritting his teeth, "Shit! Dammit!" he raved, upset with him-self.

Black-Knight couldn't believe it. He felt new life. He felt like a free slave. *Big ass horse finally broke down,* he smirked looking behind himself. Big-6 was bent over looking at the ground. He was disgusted. This had never happened to him before. This was the first time a murder suspect ever evaded his capture. *Damn, how am I going to explain this?* he thought radioing in the suspects description and location. He then took a last look as Black-Knight faded away into the dark streets of Long Beach.

Tell it All

Inside the Federal Building, "You think you're smart? You think you're so damn smart, hhmmm Maurice? You think you're really above the law," stated the female federal agent with a vindictive grin. "Okay, Mr. Smarty Pants, you've had your last chance to accept this 60 month plea deal. It's out of my hands now, but there's another agent very interested in talking to you. He'll be in momentarily."

"Whatever! Let him bring his ass in here. I still ain't taking no 5 year plea," said Maurice.

"Oh, you're right about that. That deal is out the door. You should've accepted my offer," she said shutting the door.

"Damn, I don't like the way she said that."

Maurice looked around the interrogation room. It was nothing there but four walls, a table, one chair and a long mirror built into the wall. He got up from the chair, walked around the table and up to the mirror. Then suddenly, he started ranting.

"Y'all can kiss my ass!" he said pointing to the mirror. "5 years, for what? That dope sack wasn't mine; that belonged to the Police, they put that shit on me. I'll do 2 years for the gun, but that dope charge, I can't see it."

The agents in the next room looked at one another. "Well, at least this young asshole is smart enough to know it's a double sided mirror he's looking into, but it's too bad he doesn't realize he's now in the hands of the Federal Government." The agent picked up an evidence envelope from the table. "Let me go over here and burst this kid's bubble."

The Federal agent entered the room. "Sit down!" he ordered Maurice pointing to the chair. Maurice was breathing hard.

"Naw man, I don't wann..."

"I said sit down..!" he hollered as if he was talking to a dog. Maurice hesitated but then took a seat. *I don't know who he thinks he's talking to.*

The agent loosened up the tie around his neck. He then walked around the table several times looking at the scar that ran across Maurice's head from front to back.

"How did you get that ugly scar?" he asked.

"I fell, why?" Maurice answered with attitude.

"I'm just asking, just asking."

The agent suddenly stopped, threw the envelope on the table and folded his arms. "Well, if there's one thing that I know about you now, I know that you're a big liar. You didn't get that scar by simply falling."

"I didn't? Well, tell me Mr. Federal Agent man, how did it happen?"

"It happened 3 months ago in a high-speed chase with the Detroit Police. A young rookie rammed the car-jacked Station Wagon you were driving with a Police cruiser. You hit head on with a light pole and was ejected through the windshield. Is that how it happened? Do you remember that day Maurice? Maurice Bonner, or shall I call you, Money Bunny!"

Money looked into the agent's cold blue eyes. *How does he know my nickname?* he thought with a quiver.

The agent smirked. "Whoa kid, that didn't strike a nerve did it? You look like you've just seen a ghost. Relax, I'm your friend. The only friend you've got now." The agent then leaned across the table extending his hand. "I'm Federal Agent Conrad Bantz."

Money jerked his head. "Oh, so within 5 minutes of conversation and calling me a liar, you're suddenly my friend now, right? Get the fuck out'ta here with that!" he said refusing the handshake.

"Eeewww!" chimed the other agents watching behind the mirror.

Conrad felt insulted. He lightly stroked the stubble hair on his face. Then out of nowhere, he reached across the table, grabbed Money by his shirt collar and pulled him up from the chair.

"Listen here, you got damn black ass, porch monkey, baby killer, crack rock selling son-of-a-bitch! I could give a fuck less about how much of that poison you sell to your own kind, or even how many pistols you carry around to shoot up one another. But for me, this case is personal. I'm not going to let it get cold like it did 5 years ago. Now, if you don't know, you flat lined in that hospital three times on that operating table, something kept you alive so that this case could come across my desk. I guarantee that you're going to tell me everything I want to know before I leave this room."

Afterwards, Agent Bantz reached inside the envelope pulling out an silver compact with the large initial's E.D. engraved on top, placing it in front of Money. A frightening shock bolted through Money's body. His eyes got big and his posture became limp.

Awe...shit Awe...shit, he thought, putting his face in his hand wondering what other surprises were to come. The agents behind the mirror could see Money's distraught appearance.

"He's a user," they openly agreed with one another.

Conrad stood stern feeling his blood rush from Money's grief when he spoke. "Money, you don't look so tough now. What happened with that lingo shit talk? Don't catch feelings on me now. Let me ask you, do you know anything about this compact here, opening it up. It was found in your possession. When the compact opened, China waved.

"Hey Money baby, it's been quite some time. I missed you. When we hookin' back up?" she asked rolling her tongue.

Money was ready now. He slyly stroked his nose desperate for a hit. So desperate, he unknowingly was ignoring Conrad's question. Suddenly, Conrad pounded his fists onto the table. "Do you hear me talking to you? I asked did you know Uncle Ed?"

In cases like this, Money usually would have lied, but the distraction of China White somehow made his head shake, *'Yes.'*

"Okay good. Now, how did you know Uncle Ed, and what was your relationship with him?"

Just then, Money frowned. "What the hell me knowing Ed got to do with the 5 years y'all trying to give me?"

"5 years? Oh no, you've got it all twisted son. Like the other agent told you, that plea for 60 months went out the door when she did. You should've taken that deal. You're now looking at a 240 months, which is about 20 years."

"20 years!" Money stood up and hollered.

"That's right. I'm giving 5 years for the gun, 10 years for the Crack Cocaine and the other five is up in the air, depending on what valuable information you can provide me with." said agent Bantz taking a seat on the edge of the table. He now had Money's total undivided attention.

"Do you think I'm playing Money? This is not a game. The rest of your life is in the air. Now, you can refuse anymore of my question if you like, you can stick with your plea of innocence and take this case to a jury trial. But, I'ma warn you," said Conrad with an eye-to-eye stare.

"The Federal Government has a 90 percent conviction rate against drug cases. That means if you lose, the federal government will seek to give you the maximum penalty time of 30 years in a U.S.P. (United States Maximum Security Prison). Maybe even a life term depending on the judge in this case, either way, it makes me no difference. Like I said before Money, I'm the only friend you've got."

Conrad then stood from the table and placed the compact back in the evidence envelope. Afterwards, he exited the interrogation room giving Money a chance to think. Money's brain was twisting in knots. He could barely sit straight in the chair. His mouth turned white and his throat became dry. He could hardly swallow. After watching Money's world spin out of control in the next room behind the mirror, Conrad returned back in the room. He'd seen this white ghost, pale face look that Money displayed many times. Thereafter, Agent Bantz went through his regular routine of offering water, comfort and advising one to make it easy on them-self by cooperating. He then stood patiently waiting for Money to sing like the stool pigeon he knew he was. Finally, Money halfway regained his composure. He felt as if his back was against the wall. There was no way in world he was about to do 30 years for withholding information about a dead man, or for that matter, nor for any man that was alive.

Money began to tell of everything he knew. He explained of Uncle Ed's murder in full detail by Black-Knight. He told of the names of

Black-Knight's associated accomplices, but he failed to explain the where-abouts of Black-Knight because he didn't know. He then mentioned the role he played with the 44. Magnum handgun and how the silver compact came to be his. Money began to volunteer extra information that wasn't even asked of him. He spoke of Tywon's marijuana dealings and Big Daddy's crack selling on the block. Money told it all in hopes to get back down to the 5 year plea. Overnight, he reduced from a pistol toting, crack selling, gangster, hustler, down to a common jail-house snitch.

It was no surprise to Conrad Bantz, he seen it all time and time again. When it was said and done, Money still received 144 months, which equaled to 12 years. After awaiting 4 months for inmate placement, Money was shipped off to Milan Federal Correctional Institution, Medium-Low Prison in Milan, Michigan to serve his time.

LIFE GOES ON

Early Sunday morning, a knock came at the front door. De'Andre answered, "Who is it?"

"Big Daddy" the voice replied. "Is Tywon in?"

De'Andre opened the door smiling.

"What's up Fat Daddy" he overly emphasized.

Big Daddy walked in, playfully on the defensive. "I know you ain't talking Dre. Look at that lil' gut you got" he smiled poking De'Andre's stomach.

De'Anne laying on the couch inhaled the scent of Big Daddy's cologne. *Mmmph,* she thought walking over to give him a brotherly like hug, or so he thought.

"Dang Big Daddy, if you wasn't Tywon's friend, I would be all over...," suddenly cutting herself short, letting out a deep sigh. She then laid back on the couch giving Big Daddy the, *'I'm all woman,'* look.

Big Daddy knew it was little De'Anne he was looking at, but his mind was caught up in the moment. Her high-cut shorts revealed her toned and firmed shaped legs. Her spaghetti strap top displayed her petite shoulders along with her perky nipples that bulged through her shirt. Big Daddy tried to hold it back, but felt a slight erection. He was now wondering if the rumors he heard were true. De'Anne herself was getting off on the adult attention she was receiving. Just then, Faye walked in the room.

"Hey Big Daddy, what you working with?" Before she could even get out another word, he quickly looked to De'Andre cutting off any feed back.

"Where's your brother?" he asked.

De'Andre pointed towards the basement. Big Daddy rushed down the stairs. *Damn, why Faye wan'na front me off like that?*

In the basement, the mildew aroma slapped him in the face. *Wheph!* turning up his nose and lips. The basement air damp and stale. Big Daddy looked around the room. *Damn, how is they livin' like this?* he thought, referring to the clothes that were laying everywhere. Clothes were stacked on the floor, the chairs, and on an old pool table. Dirty clothes, wet clothes, it was endless. Big Daddy decided not to take another step.

"Ty, it's Big Daddy, you down here?"

Tywon hollered across the basement. "What's up Big? Yeah, I'm over here."

Big Daddy pushed passed more clothes on hangers to where Tywon was sitting.

"What's up man?" they greeted giving one-another fives.

"Shit man, I ain't doin' nothing, just bagging up this weed. Getting it ready for my house later," said Tywon.

"Yeah, I see," replied Big Daddy looking at over 100 small baggies stuffed with marijuana. "But anyway, you heard how much time Money got, right?"

Tywon looked up curious as to why he asked. "5 years, right?"

Big Daddy sadly shook his head. "Naw...man, 12."

Tywon choked, "12 what! 12 years?"

"Yup, they hit his ass in the head. I don't know what Money said or what he did, but they gave that boy 12 years."

Tywon exhaled as if he was facing the time himself.

"Man...12 years... So, what is his momma go'on do?"

"Shit!" said Big Daddy. "Unfortunately she's coming to live with me and my moms. There's no way she can make it on her own. She's too big to work, and she done spent up all of Money's emergency cash on bills."

"Damn, well tell her to let me know if she needs anything, I got her," said Tywon feeling like Money's mother was now his responsibility.

"Are you sure?" said Big Daddy knowing his aunt was a money hungry pest. "I'm sure, just let her know."

"Ok."

Tywon then continued to bag his weed. He suddenly took notice of how observant Big Daddy appeared to be. "Big Daddy, you starring at this weed pretty hard. Are you alright?"

"How much is that?" he asked. "I mean not to be in your business or anything, just curious."

"It's cool, I understand. Thinking about a career change, huh?"

Big Daddy smiled thinking, *'Possibly'.*

"Well, right here," Tywon pointed. "This is over $500 worth of weed. These are my $5 baggies, those go fast. I will sell out of those in about an hour and a half in my spot. Down here," pulling out a shoe box full of larger baggies. "These are my 10's. These bags are for those who don't wan'na keep running back and forth buying nickel sacks." Big Daddy picked up one of the marijuana baggies. "Damn, this a fat-ass bag of weed. You get all this for $10?" Tywon shook his head. "Yeah, that's what keeps my customers coming back to me. My plays are big. I give good deals. Plus, I got quality shit. Let me show you."

Tywon pulled out two different types of marijuana in one pound plastic bags. He gave Big Daddy a quick education on the quality of weed, how much weed was to be sold in grams, per ounce and by the pound. Big Daddy calculated the numbers in his head. In disbelief,

"Damn Ty, you make 4g's a pound."

"Well, yeah and no. I pay $2200 per pound, so my profit be about 2g's minus the $300 or $400 I pay my workers. Sometimes I sit in the weed house and sell my own shit."

"Shiidd...man, if you sell two or three pounds a day, that's hel'la bread," excitedly said Big Daddy. "I need to get on your team. Sounds like this weed game is better than that crack bullshit I be selling. Dude, ever since Money was arrested, the neighborhood is hot. The Police are everywhere. First, they ran us off the corners, so I got a crack-spot. Since then, they've raided the crack-spot four times within the last three months, two of my workers got arrested, luckily they only received probation. Before that, the streets said the Police was asking, *"Who's Big Daddy?"*

"I heard that myself," butted in Tywon.

"Yeah, and somehow they must'a found out who I was. I've been stopped and searched five times in the last two months. Thank God, I ain't have nothing on me. Tywon, you know me man, I plays it low-key out here, but this whole situation is foul. I ain't sure, but I think Money probably said something."

Tywon quickly defended Money. "Naw, naw man. Don't think like that. That's yo' own cousin. Money may have been wild, but he was a stand-up kind of guy. I really don't think he would put you out there like that. *Tywon, if you only knew.*

Big Daddy continued, "And the fiends Ty, ssshhhh...! They're so terrible." Them fiends be stankin' and beggin' and don't be feedin' they kids and shit. They be giving me their food stamps, their jewelry, their cars. They even be trying to give me pussy," he frowned. "Ty man, it's depressing. I'm tired of this shit."

I know what you mean, thought Tywon, looking around the basement.

"Check it, I even had this one fiend give me a Police badge for a dime rock."

"You lying?" replied Tywon.

"I ain't bullshittin.' Look," throwing the badge on the bed. Tywon picked up the badge and looked it over.

"It's real alright."

"You can have that if you want it," said Big Daddy. "I ain't got no use for it." Tywon threw the badge back on the bed figuring he had no use for it either.

Just then, "Tywon!" called Faye from the top of the stairs. "Tywon!"

Tywon got quiet. He put his finger up to his lips. "Ssshhh," he told Big Daddy fiercely waiving his hands to hide. Big Daddy was in a frenzy confused on where to hide. He then ducked behind an old refrigerator. Tywon hid on the side of his bed.

After not receiving an answer, *They must be gone,* figured Faye. She slowly crept in the basement. Her steps were so quiet that Tywon or Big Daddy wasn't sure if or not she was down there. Finally, Tywon peeked over the edge of his bed. He saw his mother rambling through his personal belongings. Big Daddy could see this as well, shaking his head. *I knew sooner or later I was go'on catch her ass, and she always swearing she ain't took nothing. That's why I moved here in the basement,* thought Tywon. Suddenly, he bolted from his hiding spot. "What the hell you doin' Ma! Why you in my shit!"

Surprised with shock, Faye fell backwards onto the bed, landing on top of the Police badge. She had that wide eyed zombie look on her face.

"Why are you hollering?" she gasped holding her chest. "You scared me half to death."

"Scared my ass Ma! What you down here lookin' for?"

In a feisty tone, "I ain't looking for nothing, why you think I'm always looking for somethin? Shit, this my damn house. I can come down here if I want to. I was just seeing if you had some dirty clothes over here you wanted me to wash for you," she spoke as if that was the God honest truth. Tywon looked to Big Daddy in-disbelief as to say, *'Do you here this shit?'* Big daddy fought back his laughter knowing the situation was serious.

"Bullshit Ma! This whole basement is filled with dirty clothes, you ain't trying to wash no damn clothes. You need help, that's what you need. You need to let me, Aunt Gladys and Francine take you back to the Harbor Light Treatment Center downtown. Those people can help you get off that shit."

Faye snarled, *Harbor Light Treatment Center? We tried that drug program shit already, it doesn't work.* Faye knew she'd been busted, but the treatment center lecture was the last thing she was trying to hear. She hated that place and never wanted to go back. Besides, Faye liked getting high. She then conjured up some tears to avoid any further treatment center talk.

Emotionally, "I don't have a drug problem Tywon. I'm a recreational user. I can stop at anytime I'm ready. Just say you don't want me around the house. De'Anne and De'Andre disrespectful asses say it all the time," she said standing up from the bed.

"I can deal with the finger pointing and the name calling, but the language you used with me today young man, was un-called for," walking away.

Tywon threw his hand knowing Faye was playing him. But, he couldn't help but to feel bad, this was his mother.

"Come here Ma,' I'm sorry. Let me talk to you real fast," he said, but Faye continued up the stairs. Big Daddy looked to Tywon.

"Damn man, she's crying. I think you hurt her feelings."

"Man, don't let my momma fool you. She's always on some slick shit."

At the same time, Faye was entering her bedroom. She quietly closed the door behind herself. She then opened her hand, laying eyes on the Police badge she palmed on Tywon's bed. *It appears there's a new sheriff in town,* smiling, holding the badge up in the mirror.

Back in the basement, it bothered Big Daddy that Tywon was so naive to Money's vicious ways. He threw that conversation of Money possibly being a snitch to see how Tywon would respond to it. The response wasn't what he hoped for. If it had been different, he would've exposed Money for the dirty dog he really was. Big Daddy would've told Tywon of how Money 5 years ago claimed to have killed his Uncle in a bar. He would've spoke about how Money disrespectfully sold Crack Cocaine to his mother. Finally, he would've delivered the crushing blow of how Money claimed to have had relations with his younger sister, De'Anne. Big Daddy knew hearing all of these vile acts would've hurt Tywon, possibly even make him break down and cry. He just couldn't continue to sit back and watch him play Money's fool. Regardless of his feelings, Big Daddy decided to let Tywon know about the transpired incidents.

"Hey Ty, can we talk, man to man?" he asked with a look of urgency. Tywon halted any further bagging of his marijuana. From the wrinkles on Big Daddy's forehead, he figured whatever was about to be said, had to be serious.

"Yeah Big, what's on your mind?" he responded in a soft tone voice.

"Ty, me and you are cool right?"

Yeah, Tywon nodded.

"Okay. I know you and I basically associated through Money, but I have always liked you as a person myself. You're a cool guy. You don't be involving yourself in a bunch of unnecessary drama. You stay focused when it comes to your business affairs. I like how you ain't let no-one pressure you into selling that crack shit. You stuck to your weed game and it's working out for you, and I got'ta lot of respect for you because of that."

Proudly, "Thanks Big Daddy."

"Oh yeah, but that's what it's all about Ty, respect. When someone loses that for you, then what's left? There's no value there, you understand? That person will do or say anything to play on you. They will mess you over and fuck you over, they don't care."

Tywon knew how deep Big Daddy could be. The rounded conversation was appreciated. Tywon understood him well.

Big Daddy laid his opener conversation on thick, but he figured it was now time to drop the bomb, until Tywon interrupted.

"I feel that respect convo' Big. That's all me and your cousin had for one another is respect. I'ma miss ol' Money. You got the address of where he's at Big Daddy? I got'ta write my boy this week coming up."

Big Daddy's over-sized jaws dropped. *What the Ff..? I just...*

Big Daddy felt as if he could just slap the shit out of Tywon. He figured to even continue this conversation was pointless.

Just then, De'Andre came downstairs throwing the cordless phone on the bed. Afterwards, he began taunting Big Daddy. Suddenly, the two began slap boxing one another. Tywon, sitting on the bed watching the non-violent slapping contest, kept hearing a faint voice. He started looking around, until he peered down at the phone. He picked it up.

"Hello?"

"Hello! Hello!" The voice rudely responded back. "Tywon! This Aunt Gladys. Why De'Andre leave me on hold so long? I'ma spank his tail. I done told y'all momma to send him to church with me. That lil' boy soul needs to be cleansed of the devil. I'll tell ya..."

Tywon sighed rolling his eyes. He removed the phone away from his ear, wishing he'd left his aunt on hold as well. De'Andre pointed at Tywon laughing knowing Aunt Gladys was chewing him out.

Playfully looking at his brother, "I'm go'on beat yo' lil ass," he said placing the phone back up to his ear.

"You go'on what, Tywon!" responded his aunt.

"Oh, oh, I'm sorry auntie, not you, De'Andre..."

De'Andre and Big Daddy were cracking up. After hearing that profane statement, Aunt Gladys really started preaching. Suddenly, Tywon clicked the button on the receiver, turning off the phone.

"I ain't got time for that shit," throwing the phone back onto the bed. He then pointed. "Dre, grabbed these two shoe boxes. It's time to go."

De'Andre picked up the boxes opening them up. "Ssmmm, aahhh..." he expressed after taking two deep whiffs of the marijuana baggies, loving the smell. Tywon slapped him in the back of the head.

"I said pick em' up, not open em' up, now c'mon here before your young ass catch a contact." Just as the trio were heading up the basement stairs, the phone laying on the bed began to ring. Tywon ignored the phone smirking, thinking, *The Reverend Alice Sharpton.*

At this time, Faye was just leaving her bedroom from getting herself together. She had on her favorite red dress, her high heel shoes, make-up and her best wig. Before hand she'd went into De'Andre's room and got an old 'Walkie Talkie' radio, sticking it into her purse. She was now creeping from the upstairs down to the living room. Simultaneously, Tywon, De'Andre and Big Daddy were exiting the kitchen walking into the living room as well. Faye at the bottom of the stairs again jumped at the site of the trio. She just knew Tywon was about to say something about the Police badge missing from his bed, but his mother was the last thing on his mind. Tywon was taking notice at how De'Anne was still carelessly sprawled out on the couch half-naked. He immediately walked over to his sister and quietly checked her. He told her, *'In the presence of any man, regardless if there family or not, always conduct yourself as a lady.'* De'Anne got up from the couch and walked away with an attitude. Tywon then turned to Big Daddy.

"Damn, do I have to be the big brother and play the daddy around here too?" Big Daddy had on his signature quiet look, as if he hadn't noticed a thing. Afterwards, Tywon looked to his mother.

Pointing, "That's your fault Ma. You've supposed to have taught her better." Faye threw her hand dismissing any responsibility.

"De'Anne knows better. Anyway, where y'all going? Drop me off," she said.

It didn't surprise Tywon that his mother had a careless attitude about the situation. Nowadays she seemed not to care about nothing, but getting high. Ever since her husband, Ronnie (De'Andre's father) had left 5 years ago, drugs had become her sole outlet for coping with life. "Boy...I can't stand her ass sometimes," Tywon mumbled underneath his breath.

Everyone then began making there way outside. Tywon opened the trunk of his car, while Big Daddy and De'Andre hopped inside.

"Ma, I ain't got time to drop you off nowhere. I got business to handle," he said securing the two shoe boxes underneath the spare tire. *Man that weed strong. I hope we don't get pulled over.* Tywon closed the trunk, expecting some argumentative comments from his mother, but when he looked up, she was nowhere in sight. *Cool,* he thought. He then jumped into the driver's seat ready to start the car. But something kept telling him to look into the rearview mirror. His eyes shifted upward. The bouffant hair-style wig in the rearview mirror explained Faye's sudden disappearance. She was in the backseat seated behind Tywon. Tywon's head dropped, letting out a deep sigh. His first thought was to put his mother out of the car, but he changed his mind knowing if Faye remained at home without his presence, she would again go rambling through his personal belongings. The last thing he wanted was for his mother to find the new hiding where he kept his money.

"Where you want me to drop you off at Ma?" he asked in an aggressive tone. Faye pointed as if that showed the way. "Take me off Woodward Avenue down to Harbor Light. I need to speak with a counselor." Tywon turned around in the driver's seat ecstatic.

"For real Ma'? You fin'na get some help? That's what I'm talking about," cranking up the car.

Big Daddy, still trying to get comfortable in the passenger seat was smiling, happy for Faye. De'Andre posted in the backseat next to his mother also smiled. He grabbed and held her hand for the first time in a long time to show his support. Faye herself gave a slight grin, appreciative of the support. But, her true intentions set a dark cloud over her head.

Tywon was slowly driving up the street nearing the alley's entryway when he stopped and pointed.

"That's the place right there I was telling you about Big: Ed's Night Lounge. Damn, I hate that it's burnt down now. I use'ta be gettin' paid in that joint. Money did too," he exaggerated. "And Uncle Ed, that was my man. He use'ta let me do whatever I wanted to do in there. He was like a daddy to me. Remember Uncle Ed Ma?" he asked looking into the rearview mirror. Faye shifted her eyes away not saying a word. She remembered Uncle Ed, she remembered Uncle Ed very well. Better than Tywon knew.

Now looking up the alley-way, Faye pictured herself 18-years ago stepping into Ed's Night Lounge for the first time.

"Hi," said a much younger Faye approaching the bar. "Are you guys hiring for any positions?" she asked the bartender.

The bartender was standing face forward towards the mirror wiping out glasses when he heard the soft voice. He looked in the mirror, smiled and then turned around. The bartender with his large afro and butter-fly collar shirt sucking on a tooth-pick, walked from around the bar and slowly looked Faye up and down.

"Mmmph, Mmmph, Mmmph. Now, what position do you want to be put in, I mean work in baby?" he chuckled removing the toothpick. Faye quickly caught on to the freakish comment.

"Is the owner here?" she asked having no time for games.

"I am the owner, but at this time..."

Ed, sitting over in the booth just finishing a narcotics pill deal, overheard the bartender, 'Day-Break' claiming to be the owner.

"Day-Break!" Ed yelled. "What yo' jive turkey ass over there lyin' 'bout nah'? You don't own nothing but them raggedy stretch pants on yo' ass. I done told you about harassing the customers. Leave that young girl alone. Come here baby," Ed called to Faye waving his hand. "This my place, what you need?"

Faye walked over to Ed's table and sat down.

Day-Break was pissed, he felt a little envious. He couldn't believe how Ed pulled rank and fronted him off like that. "I saw her first," he mumbled walking back behind the bar.

Faye started off by introducing herself to Ed with a hand shake. She then desperately began explaining how bad she needed a job. Ed asked Faye what were her qualifications and where did she work last. She explained that she never before worked, but she said she could scrub floors, wash dishes, cook, clean and take out the trash. Most of Faye's qualifications sounded like household chores to Ed, but from her ambition and determination to work, he continued to listen.

After 20 minutes or so of conversation, Faye became personal with Ed. She spoke of her mother's illness 6 months ago following her death. She said she really had never known her father and she was now being raised by her two older sisters: Gladys and Francine. Faye told Ed, Gladys was a self proclaimed preacher. She'd argue down any minister in the middle of his sermon if she didn't agree with his spoken word. It was no surprise when almost every church on the east side of town disband her membership.

Faye stated she and her other sister Francine were a little more closer, ever though Francine was a complex person. She was something in between a battered Vietnam Veteran, a border line gangster, and a compassionate lover. Ed was confused.

"What do you mean?" he asked.

"Well, one minute Francine would be cooking for her man, massaging him, making wedding plans and telling him how much she loves him. And the next, she would pull out her pistol, whip him with it, tie him up, and then ask him his name, rank and serial number."

"Are you serious?" Ed laughed.

Faye was dead serious. She further explained that Francine was recently diagnosed with a mental illness called, 'Schizophrenia' and was now on medication. *Schizophrenia?* thought Ed. *That bitch must'a got hold of some bad dope.*

Day-Break, still feeling humiliated was behind the bar drinking up a storm. He watched in a jealous rage as Faye and Ed giggled away. He hated biting his tongue when Ed talked shit to him. It seemed to Day-Break that Ed always pulled this stunt when it came to a female.

"So what if this is his damn bar. He thinks he has to have every woman coming through that door." Day-Break couldn't hold it back any longer. He slammed down his glass and stepped to the middle of the floor. "Fuck you Ed!" he fiercely pointed.

Ed stood up pushing the table away unknowingly pinning Faye in the booth. "Naw Day-Break, fuck with me!" he responded exposing the pistol on his waistline.

Faye, unable to breath was scared to death. *Oh my God, what have I gotten myself into?* she thought bracing herself.

Day-Break peered at the curved handle of the revolver, then into Ed's yellow coated eyes. He could see the seriousness on Ed's face. Day-Break knew the outcome of this situation for him wasn't going to be good. "Oh, so it's like that now Ed?"

"It's like that muthafucka! Get'ta steppin'!" he said petting his pistol. Day-Break slowly started walking backwards toward the door. He was afraid of being shot in the back. As he approached the exit, he gave Ed a sailor's salute and then went on his way.

Ol' simple son-of-a-bitch. Jealous over a broad. Ed then looked to Faye. "Oh damn baby, I'm sorry," pulling the table from Faye's chest.

Scared, "Thank you," she said standing from the booth, taking a breath. "I think I should be going now."

"Why? I thought you was lookin' for work."

"I am, but not for a job that endangers my life."

"So being my bartender is go'on endanger your life?"

Faye smiled. "Your bartender? You're hiring me?"

Ed nodded. Faye was so happy. It was her first job. It was her chance to prove that she could make it on her own. Suddenly it dawned on her. "But Ed, I don't know anything about makin' drinks, nothing."

"Calm down sweetie pie, I'ma show you. A matter fact," he paused looking at time on his watch. "Right now is perfect. My 12 o'clock afternoon drinkers should be here any minute."

Within 4 weeks time, Faye was mixing and serving drinks like she'd been doing it all her life. She was making mega tips on top of the

$100 a week Ed was paying her. Faye liked working at the bar and she really liked Ed. He was like a confidant, a protector and a father figure all in one. Ed just seemed to understand her so well. Faye slowly felt herself falling in love with him. Then, one late night after the bar closed.

"Ed, how do you think I look?" casually asked Faye wiping down the bar. Ed was doing his nightly count ignoring the question.

"Ed!" she again called.

"Whud...What is it?"

"How do I look daddy?" now perking her breast.

Ed folded his arms and took notice. "Good Faye. You look good. I'm sure one-day you'll make some man very happy," he answered, again starting to count his money.

Faye put her hands on her hips. She took Ed's comment as a insult. *Some man, huh?* She suddenly became aggressive. She poured two drinks, walked over to Ed's table and sat down. She then reached inside of his upper pocket, pulling out two narcotic pills. She placed one under his tongue and one under her own. "Let's see how I look to you after you swallow this."

Faye took a few sips of her drink as Ed downed his. Afterwards, he shook his head. "Damn Faye, you just fucked up. You just crossed over. Your rollercoaster ride has just begun."

Faye smiled, happy to have Ed's attention. "Let me worry about that," she said springing onto Ed's lap. The last thing Faye remembered was passionately tongue kissing Ed.

It was now the morning. Faye awoke to find herself in a strange bed ass naked. *Where am I? What is this place, and where are my clothes?* she thought, looking around the room. It was the apartment, which sat over the bar. Faye suddenly heard laughter nearing the bedroom. Ed himself walked in naked talking on the large base phone. He didn't say good morning, hi, hello, not a word. He simply tossed her a wet rag, pointed to her clothes and then to the door. He afterwards proceeded back to the room he'd just left.

Faye's feelings were a little hurt. She was hoping for a morning kiss or maybe even a hug. "Ed's just busy," excusing him to make herself feel better. She then wiped herself clean of the sticky, crusty, glaze that lay against her thighs. "Uuugghhh...," she snarled throwing the rag in the corner.

The next night, Ed and Faye repeated their encounter. The same drink, same narcotic pill, and the same morning outcome. But this time, Ed could see how deep Faye's feelings were into him. Soon-after, Ed told Faye he wanted to keep it strictly business between them. Faye of course didn't want it this way, but just to be in Ed's presence was enough satisfaction for her. Then, a couple of months later one day before work, "Ed, we need to talk," said Faye.

Ed sighed already knowing what it was about. "Faye baby listen, like I told you before, I don't need no woman, I don't want no woman, I ain't go no time for a woman. I can cook, clean, wash and do all that other shit myself. And besides, it ain't safe for no woman to be around me. Because I'm..."

"Still in the streets," Faye harmonized along with Ed. "Ed, I understand that already sugar. You've made that perfectly clear to me. But, that ain't it," she spoke excitedly.

"That ain't it? Well, what the hell is it then? C'mon with the c'mon Faye, I ain't got all day."

"Ok, ok. I think I'm pregnant. Ed, I'm going to have your baby," she said placing her hands over her mouth, hoping Ed was excited as she was.

"Pregnant!" Ed walked over to Faye snatching her by the shoulders. "What the fuck you mean pregnant bitch! Tell me you lyin'! Tell me you lyin'!" shaking her. Faye was shocked.

"Ed! Why are you treating me this way? I thought you would be happy about this."

"Happy! How do I suppose to be happy bitch! You come from two pennies. Now you thank cause you pregnant, you bout'ta rub together a dime and a nickel. I already know how the shit supposed to play out. You think I'm fin'na take care of yo' ass, some got damn baby and them circus clown sistas' of yours? Shiiid...uh uh bitch! You got me fucked up!"

Faye was hyperventilating. She then calmed herself down.

"Now Ed, I know you don't mean those things, you're just upset. I don't want your money, or anything from you. I only want you to accept this child. Ed, this baby can be the better part of you."

"Faye, the better part of me and that baby ran down your leg."

Ed then peeled off $150 from his stack and crammed it into Faye's hand. "Get rid of it, and get yourself some help. The last thing a kid needs is a pill poppin', junkie momma," waiving her off towards the door. Faye cried, pleaded and begged for Ed to accept their child. She claimed she would discontinue her pill usage if he just gave it some thought, but Ed's mind was made. After a hard backhand slap to her face, Faye respected Ed's decision and went on her way.

Tywon was still watching in the rearview mirror, as a single tear rolled down his mother's cheek.

"Awe...Ma, don't cry. You go'on be alright. I'll hold down the household while you're away in rehab. Don't you worry about a thing."

"Huh? Hhmm? Oh," said Faye coming out of thought, wiping away her tears. "I ain't worried about it. I know you'll keep it under control."

The one thing Faye was worried about was how to tell Tywon after all these years that Ed was really his father. She didn't know where to start or where to begin. *Do I tell my son his daddy denied him even before he was born? That he didn't want anything to do with him? And were my reasons of not telling Tywon Ed was his father just as selfish of me because I grew up without my daddy? Or, was it shame for myself because I was too high off pills to even remember the night he was conceived?*

About the time Faye's thoughts and emotions finished scrambling, she found herself pulling in front of the Harbor Light Rehab Clinic. She stepped out the car giving both Tywon and De'Andre hugs and kisses and waived goodbye to Big Daddy.

"I'm proud of you Ma," said Tywon laying $20 eating money on her, as she walked in the clinic. Afterwards, Tywon pulled off. Within one and a half minutes time, Faye walked back out of the rehab clinic throwing the visitor's tag on the ground.

"That shit ain't for me," she mumbled looking around for any signs of Tywon's car. Soon-after bending a couple of corners, Faye ended up at her intended location: The Cass Corridor, A four to five block stretch of streets where you could find every kind of drug, prostitute or trick ready to satisfy your desired needs; The revolving door as the staff of Harbor Light entitled it, from it's unfortunate location of only one block from the rehab clinic. Forty percent of those patients in Harbor Lights drug treatment program often flirted with the Cass Corridor. These flirtatious actions most of the time resulted in the relapse of a patient upon his or her completion of the drug program.

Faye approached one of the dealers in the corridor. She bought two dime rocks with the twenty Tywon had given to her. She wasn't worried about being broke, she knew tonight's hustle would make up for the expense. She then asked the dealer where could she smoke her dope? She explained she was leery about doing out it in the open. The dealer pointed to an abandoned apartment building up the street. He told her that's where most of his customers got high. Faye then strolled up the street and entered the building.

On the inside, the old apartment building was dusty and dim. Every crack-head and prostitute in the city of Detroit seemed to be roaming around that building. *Damn!* thought Faye felling a little uncomfortable. "This place is running itself." Still, she managed to find her an empty room. Faye pulled out her glass pipe, slid the rock inside, put the pipe to her mouth, flicked the lighter and began to smoke. For her, it was relaxation in its ultimate form. Unfortunately, the high was short lived. She then pulled out the other baggy, badly wanting to smoke. After a hard stare with the baggy, she shook her head. *Naw, naw Faye, don't do it, it ain't for you,* she shook her head, returning the crack baggy back to her pocket. It was still early but Faye figured it was now time to put her plan into effect. She began to stroll around the abandoned building looking in and out of different apartments, until she finally found what it was she was looking for.

"Eewww...aahhh..." pleasurably released the trick into the prostitute's mouth. She quickly spit.

"Nasty muthafucka! That's go'on cost you extra." The trick was smiling as he zipped up his pants. He then paid the whore her regular fee. She counted the money.

"Where's my extras!" aggressively she asked.

"Hold your breath until I come back with it," he laughed walking pass Faye out of the apartment. The prostitute ran out into the hallway behind the trick ranting and raving about her money, which did her no good. She then returned back to the apartment when she suddenly noticed Faye.

"Whoa! Whoa! Honey, I'm a girl who gets down and dirty for her money, but I don't do bitches," thinking Faye was a homosexual trick.

Faye smirked. "Well that's good to know, because I don't do bitches either. But anyway, that was disrespectful of your trick. He could've at least warned you by tapping the back of your head or something, ol' dirty bastard. If that was me, I would've bit his dick off," she said with a bold faced expression. Suddenly, the two women began to laugh.

Soon-after, Faye and the prostitute, *Wanda* became better acquainted. The pair discussed their marriages, separations, their kids, problems, how they came to be, and the two even swapped their worst tricking stories. There were a lot of hardship similarities between the pair. Faye wasn't looking for it, but she found a friend in Wanda. It now made her feel awkward about even running down her hustle plan to Wanda. She would hate to put a friend in jeopardy over trying to make a dollar, but *hell* thought Faye. *I'm bout' that money.*

Faye then told Wanda of her plot. Wanda at first was hesitant, knowing Faye's plan was risky. She knew a scheme like this could take a wrong turn at anytime, or even become deadly. But Wanda too was about that money. She then agreed to the plan, telling Faye, "My safety is in your hands. Don't fuck me over." Confident without a second thought, Faye told Wanda not to worry. She assured by the end of the night, they both would have fat pockets.

"Good," said Wanda. "I'm ready to blow this hell hole anyway." As a gift incentive Faye pulled out her last crack baggy. She displayed it to Wanda as if asking, *'You wan'na smoke?'* *'Hell yeah!'* excitedly Wanda shook her head. She wasn't about to pass up a free high.

At this time, Tywon was also feeling high. High off the heavy traffic that was flooding his weed spot. He, De'Andre and Big Daddy were sitting in the car three doors down observing the spot.

"Ty man, I ain't even go'on lie," said Big Daddy. "Your spot is bumpin' like a rock house. You're definitely onto somethin' big."

"Yeah...," simply responded not wanting to seem like he had the *'Big Head.'*

Just then, the trio heard the echoing sound of bass. They all turned around in their seats and looked out the back window not seeing a thing.

"Dang! Where is it coming from?" said De'Andre.

The louder the bass became, the more Tywon's car vibrated. Not two seconds later, the burgundy Mustang now with its camel colored, convertible top up, bent the corner.

"Eeewww...that's fresh!" exclaimed De'Andre.

They couldn't hear the words to the music, but the hard hitting recognizable baseline of Eric B and Rakim's, *'Paid in Full'* was enough. Tywon filled in the rest. "To now test to see if I got pull, hit the studio, 'cause I'm paid in full!"

Just as he finished, the Mustang was passing. Tywon, De'Andre, and Big Daddy focused their undivided attention onto the driver. After the car passed, Tywon snapped his fingers.

"That's dude! That's the white-boy, from uumm...uumm..."

"From O'Sha's block party" dryly finished Big Daddy not wanting to appear like a groupie. Tywon heard Big Daddy's confirmed answer, but his mind was on the female passenger he caught a glimpse of, in the Mustang.

The convertible stopped in front of the weed spot. The white dude exited his car with the music still on full blast. He then ran up on the porch of the marijuana house skipping two steps at a time, holding his gold chain. As he approached the armor-guarded front door, he was let inside the house. De'Andre grabbed both the driver and passenger seat, pulling himself forward.

"Tywon, do you know him?" curiously he asked hoping he did, so he could possibly get the chance to sit in the Mustang.

Hell naw! I don't know his ass. And I don't care what he's drivin.' Tone-Tone, '*Tywon's worker*' knows not to let no customers in my spot. Stay here De'Andre, c'mon Big Daddy, it's bout'ta be some shit," stepping out the car.

De'Andre sat disappointed, wanting to be a part of the action.

Tywon hurried across the grass onto the sidewalk with Big Daddy just behind. In a flash, he was at the porch ready to walk up the stairs, when suddenly, he remembered the girl in the car. He turned around and looked to the passenger side window. Tywon's heart froze. His legs became like butter. A dizzy feeling of excitement came over him. All of his anger seemed to be washed away after seeing that familiar face. Big Daddy also recognized the sensuous face. He nudged Tywon.

"That's your girl O'Sha, ain't it?"

Love struck, Tywon couldn't find the words. Just then, O'Sha looked up to see the pair. She excitedly began to waive. Tywon suddenly came alive. Ecstatically, he waived back. O'Sha then turned down the music and began exiting the car.

Awe...man, thought Tywon with a love jones. *She must have forgiven me,* approaching for a hug. But before Tywon knew it, O'Sha was in the arms of Big Daddy, telling him how much she missed him, rubbing his large stomach.

Envious, "What about me? Where's my hug?" he asked, with his arms to the side. O'Sha snarled. "Hey Ty," acknowledging his presence.

At that moment, the white guy came walking out the house with Tone-Tone following. "Oh shit!" said Tone-Tone under his breath, not expecting to see Tywon.

Tywon looked up to the porch with an evil eye stare. Tone-Tone quickly got to explaining. "Ty, this White Boy-J, J, that's Ty. This is the dude I was telling you about with the bad ass Mustang who be coping the weed."

Tywon and J shook hands, but Tywon was thinking to himself. *Tone-Tone ain't never said nothing bout no White Boy with a*

Mustang who be buying weed. He's on some slick shit, and I'ma find out what it is.

Tywon looked to the shoe box in J's hand. "It looks like you done bought me out. You like that weed, huh?"

"Man, yo' weed is the bomb," emphasized J. "You don't serve nothin' no-less than quality. No sticks, no seeds, no stems, the weed be all green. That's how I like it. I buy up at least 50 bags a week for me and my people. At $10 a piece for these fat ass bags, you can't beat that."

"$10 huh?" replied Tywon, now looking to Tone-Tone who just crept back in the house.

White Boy-J finished. "I need more weed if you got it."

"Oh yeah?" Tywon directed J over to his trunk. He sold J the entire $5 baggy shoe box for $7 per bag, and the $10 baggy box for 12 bucks a piece. Tywon folded the stack and put into in this pocket. Afterwards, the two stood talking for another hour. Big Daddy was still in conversation with O'Sha. De'Andre got his wish of sitting in the Mustang, and Tone-Tone had the hectic job of telling pissed off weed customers they were all sold out.

Thereafter, the conversation ended. Tywon and White Boy-J exchanged pager numbers. Tywon told J to call him for his weed only. There was no further need for him to come to the weed house. J agreed, as he and O'Sha then took off. Big Daddy approached Tywon smirking.

"I see this weed game is a dirty game too. Your boy Tone-Tone was hittin' the white boy for an extra $5 a bag. It's the game. How can you knock that?"

"I can't knock it, but when I don't get my cut out the deal and it's my shit, then we got a problem. I'll take care of Tone-Tone's ass in a minute. But what's up with O'Sha. Did she say anything about hollering back at me?"

"Naw, nothing like that, she's still mad at you. She feels that you chose Money over her that night. I tried to smooth it out but you know how women are. They run deep off their emotions. Just give her a little more time."

Tywon set his thoughts for another question, but Big Daddy beat him to it. "And no, the white boy ain't her man. He's kickin' it around with Octavia's promiscuous ass. You know she'll take em' purple, black and green as long as they got that bread."

Tywon laughed. "Yeah, Octavia is a hustler. How's her ear healing up?"

"O'Sha says it's healing good. Octavia's just waiting for the hair to grow back to cover her surgery scar."

"That's cool. What about their cousin Terrell, the one Money tried to shoot?"

"You mean the one Money dumb-ass did shoot. O'Sha didn't get too much off into that; Terrell is her cousin. But, I think that boy was go'on try to kill Money. Luckily Money's locked up, them Highland Park boys is wild. Them cats be killin' up each other."

Tywon shook his head again in defense for Money. "Naw, it would'na went down like that. We all just would'a been some shootin' muthafuckas!"

Big Daddy quickly switched the subject. "Yeah, well, it's getting dark, I'm tired and I'm 'bout to sit in the car," he said standing up from the hood, tired of the heroic Money tales.

Tywon gave Big Daddy a puzzling glance, but dismissed it, thinking it was nothing. He then headed off into the weed house. He wanted to check-out on Tone-Tone about why the $5 over charge against White Boy-J was never mentioned to him. De'Andre followed.

After the brief scolding, Tywon and De'Andre exited the house, hopping into the car. Tywon displayed $300 of the $500 he had taken from Tone-Tone. "Pay me, don't delay me," he stated, snapping off the bills. Big Daddy smiled. "That's right dog, get that money!"

De'Andre in the back-seat whom witnessed the scolding, admired his older brother's hustle skills. "Roof! Roof!" he barked as a sign of victory. Afterwards the three headed back to Tywon's house.

****

Faye's hustle skills were also taking place. Between she and Wanda, they both had already accumulated almost $2000 a piece. Wanda insisted on stopping while the getting was good, but Faye was persistent for one more lick.

"C'mon Wanda girl, just one more time," pleaded Faye, felling an addiction for the easy money. She hadn't seen this type of cash since she started using.

"I don't know," Wanda shook her head. "One of those guys was my best trick and plus, my damn jaws hurt."

"Well quit trying to suck everybody's dick. Get on your back for a change. C'mon girl, let's get this money."

"Alright," agreed Wanda lighting a candle for light. "Get into position."

Faye silently hid in the dark apartment bathroom. Periodically, she peeked out the bathroom door only to see Wanda still patiently waiting in the flickering shadows of the candles.

Impatiently, "Is anyone out there yet?" she ask already knowing the answer. Wanda threw her hand as to say, *'No, now get back in the bathroom.'*

After another 30 minutes of waiting, Faye finally heard, "Hey Baby, how you doing?" It was a trick entering the apartment. Faye cracked the bathroom door for a better look. Wanda rolled her eyes.

"Awe...man, not you again. Didn't I tell your clown ass not to come back around here? I didn't like the performance you put on the last time I saw you and plus, you still owe me money. It's plenty of action around here," she pointed. "Go some place else."

"Awe... baby, don't be like that. I apologize for how I acted the last time I was here. I was upset at my wife and I made the mistake of taking it out on you. I didn't mean to hit you, I'm sorry."

The trick could see Wanda wasn't convinced. "Look, look. I got money," he stated taking a different approach. "This is $1500. I'll give you $300 of it, if you just suck me good like you do."

$1500? thought Faye. *Shiiid, Wanda bet'ta get down on her knees and start sucking before I do.*

Wanda acted as if she had to think about it. "Make it $400, and if you cum in my mouth, that'll be an extra hundred. Pay me now," she demanded.

Faye witnessed the exchange of money. Soon-after, Wanda got into position. The trick then pulled himself out as she took him in. Faye could only think of the $1100 the trick had left in his pockets. She then reached inside of her purse pulling out De'Andre's Walkie-Talkie toy radio along with the Police badge. She sat her purse behind the toilet and turned the radio on. *It's show time,* now busting out of the bathroom door.

"Freeze! Don't move! Don't move! Detroit Police Prostitution Task Force!" Faye yelled. "Get against the wall!"

The trick appeared to be in total shock. He quickly pulled up his pants and began whimpering. "I got a wife and two kids. I can't do no jail time." Wanda also claimed detriment, saying this third offense would violate her probation.

Faye heard none of it, as she spoke into the C.B. radio. "This is task force Officer 2-3-4-5-6 requesting backup."

2-3-4-5-6? Wanda gave Faye a look as if to ask, *Are you serious?* Faye hunched her shoulders like, *What?*

She continued, "I have in custody a male and female suspect I caught engaging in oral sex. My location is the abandoned apartment complex on Cass Street in apartment 3-D. Send backup immediately."

Faye then released the receiver as if she was waiting on confirmation feed-back. Only a static frequency was heard but Faye played it like help was on the way. "They'll be here any minute." She then pressed her hand in the middle of the tricks back, applying pressure.

"You just stand right there Mr., and don't you move." She began petting him down. "Wife and kids, huh? Your nasty ass ain't fit for a wife and kids. Why are you running with filth like that?" Faye pointed to Wanda.

Wanda squint her eye. "*Ok bitch! Act like you see me standing here.*"

The trick began to stutter when Faye hollered, "Silence! I don't wan'na hear that shit! Now, I'ma be nice tonight. I'ma cut you a break seeing that you have a family and all, but the whore, she's going to jail. And of course freedom ain't free you know, so my question to you is; how much money do you got?"

Suddenly, the trick strong armed his way around towards Faye. "Naw bitch! The question is how much money you got!"

"Find her purse, the money's in her purse!" yelled Wanda, grabbing at Faye's legs. Faye jumped backwards, breaking the heel off her shoe, which caused her to fall to the floor. The badge and Walkie Talkie radio fell from her hands. Wanda and the trick started punching and kicking Faye in the face. "Where's the money at?" "Where's your purse bitch!" the two repeated.

Faye was in such disbelief to what was going on, she couldn't even scream. She could only think of how that fast, her life was in jeopardy.

In a panic, laying on her back in the fetal position, Faye jabbed both her feet upward into the trick's neck. The sharp end of the high heeled shoe broke the skin nearly crushing his windpipe. He fell to the floor kicking, gasping for air, and screaming the little he could. Wanda looked to her man who appeared to be dying.

"Charles! Charles!" she called, but he was unable to answer back. She then peered at Faye. "Awe...Bitch! I gos'ta kill you nah, you done hurt my man."

Catching her breath, "Fuck you and yo' raggedy ass man! Y'all set me up." Just then, Wanda pulled out a large pair of toe-nail clippers.

Still breathing hard, Faye joked. "What you go'on do with those bitch! Give me a pedicure?"

Wanda then suddenly flicked out a large knife from inside. "Naw, just a little trim up," swinging the knife. Faye jumped back dodging any contact.

"Why yo' ass running? You scared or something? Stand still so I can stick yo' ass," again jabbing the knife. Faye didn't understand.

"Why are you doing this to me Wanda? I thought you and me were friends?"

"Friends? Bitch, I don't know you. Just because we shared a couple of laughs and smoked a rock together don't mean were friends. You a snake ass bitch, plain and simple. You wan'na hit licks on my tricks, so now I'ma hit a lick on you. You better recognize the game you playing hoe! And this the last time I'm go'on ask you, where's the money?" now backing Faye into a corner.

Faye knew Wanda was right. You don't make friends with nobody in one day. This whole situation was a game, and the set up was just part of it. Faye figured if she was to survive the game, this game had to be finished. Right then, Faye began fighting her way out of the corner. In the act, she received cuts and slashes to her hands and arms. Her wounds were badly burning. She could feel the blood dripping from her hands onto the floor. *This bitch Wanda is trying to kill me.* Faye just wanted to get the hell out of that apartment, but not without her earnings.

"Ok! Ok! You wan'na fight dirty? Ok then!"

Faye darted over to the candle and snatched off her wig. She lit it on fire and threw it at Wanda. Wanda ducked from the burning wig which landed on the dirty mattress setting it a blaze. From the fire, the two could now clearly see one another.

Wanda looked around the room for the purse, now making her way towards the bathroom. Faye scanned the floor for any type of weapon when suddenly, she spotted one. As she jumped into motion to retrieve the weapon, her ankle was grabbed. She again crashed to the floor. Wanda turned and took notice. She could see Faye on the floor kicking Charles in the face. The fire was now making its way up the walls. Wanda charged Faye screaming, "Stop kicking him!" Faye desperately reached for the weapon, but Charles still had a hold of her foot. With one last kick to the head, Charles was knocked out cold. Faye, crawling on her stomach finally palmed the weapon, when Wanda approached. Wanda knelt down on her knees over Faye's back.

"Turn over bitch! I want you to see me cut your throat."

Faye slowly turned over onto her back, only to feel the knife pressed against her neck. She then looked up. Debris from the fire was falling from the ceiling. Faye was feeling for the sharp edge of her weapon, at the same time logically pleading.

Coughing, "Wanda this is crazy. Can't you see this room is on fire, we all go'on die in here."

With her left hand, Wanda gripped underneath Faye's jaw. With her right, she pressed the knife harder to Faye's throat drawing blood.

"The only thing in this room dying tonight is you. You dead bitch!"

Faye heard every deadly threatening word Wanda was saying, but for a second her mind zoned out. *Is this it? It's over? Is this how I'm gon'na die? In a burning abandoned apartment building with my throat slashed open? And who's go'on look after my kids, my precious babies? They need me in their lives. No!* thought Faye. *No! No! No! This is not how I want the final chapter in my life to end.*

Suddenly, screaming erupted. "Uugahh...!Uugahh...!" Charles awoke in a ball of flames. From his unconsciousness, he didn't realize his clothes had caught fire. Wanda looked to his direction.

"Oh my God, Charles!" she screamed ready to run to his aid. But then, Wanda dropped her weapon and felt her neck. Weirdly, both of her hands were filled with blood. She drastically started making gagging sounds, gasping for air. She then fell onto the floor kicking and rolling around like a fish out of water. Her throat was slashed wide open. Faye stood up letting the bloody jagged edge Police badge fall to the floor. It was the only thing that saved her life. Wanda kicked a few more times and gurgled her final breath. Faye never before killed anyone, but she felt no remorse for Wanda. *It was either me or her,* she thought.

A faint sound of fire trucks nearing the scene could be heard. Just then, Charles engulfed in flames ran towards Faye screaming, "Help me! Help me please! I'm burning?"

Faye wasn't interested in helping anyone but herself. She took off running out of the burning apartment into the fiery hallway. The loud crackling sounds of the fire swallowed Charles high pitched screams. After running down three flights of stairs, Faye finally made her way outside in front of the apartment building.

"Are you alright? Are you ok? Is there anyone else in there you know of?" asked the firemen running the water-hose into the burning building. "No," Faye shook her head to the last question.

After receiving medical attention at the scene, Faye disappeared through the crowd. She thought deep about Wanda's and Charle's death, she even thought about the money she left in the purse behind the toilet. She cried about it all, still in disbelief to what had happened. No less than five minutes later, Faye walked around the corner and admitted herself into the Harbor Light Treatment Center.

1996

THE WRONG GUY

"Man! I'm tired of this shit! 23 hour lock down, can't use the phone, can't see shit in here. I only get out once a day like I'ma damn dog, and ain't nobody in here to talk to. I'm tired of living like this."

Just then, the clattering sound of keys could be heard chiming the prison hallway. All inmates in the *'Hole'* were pleading their case for freedom. The correctional Officer ignored them all. He unlocked and opened cell door 23-B. The hallway lights shined inside the dark room like heavens gates had just been opened.

"Gather your belongings, you're going back into population," said the Correctional Officer. He didn't have to say it twice. Money hopped straight to it, happy to be getting out of the hole.

"Bout damn time, I thought y'all forgot about me and threw away the key," nonchalantly exiting the dark room. The C.O. looked to Money in-disbelief.

"Forgot about you! Money, you're one unbelievable character, do you know that? You're lucky not to be on your way to a U.S.P. for an additional 30 years right now. We can't prove it, but we know it was you who stabbed that guy up in the shower."

Money laughed. "Why y'all suspecting me? This is jail, shit go on in here everyday. Besides, my two witnesses swore in the investigation that I was working out with them on the weight pile."

"Yeah, you somehow got them two clowns wrapped around your finger. Sean and Tootsie are two hopeless souls in the world, especially if they're being led by you." The C.O. then looked upward. "It's the blind leading the blind," he harmonized in a folk tale. With that said, Money kept silent the rest of the way back into population.

Eight years had now passed since Money was incarcerated. In that time frame, he fell into the house rules of the prison system, or what another inmate would consider it to be, institutionalized.

Everyday Money's bed was made no later than 6:15a.m. His prison issued uniform was crisp, his black boots were flawlessly polished. Perfect was an understatement for his underwear arrangement in his dresser drawer. And, all the labels on his necessities had to be face forward. He would even buff and wax the floor twice daily, so any inmate who entered his cell had to remove their shoes. He was very meticulous. At the same time, Money was still Money, nothing about him had changed. He often found himself in the middle of meaningless drama, petty beefs, and prison house gossip. Since his 8 year incarceration, he's fought over a dozen times about the television, slapped inmates over the microwave, and did his first stabbing 6 months ago over a gambling debt owed to him. Regardless of prison, in plain term, Money was still a menace.

The C.O. led Money to the Officers station. There, he received his property and was awaiting to be assigned to a new cell. The C.O. behind the glass smirked glancing over the inmate roster. *Billy Paige.*

He then looked to Money. "You're assigned to Unit 2, 1st floor, Cell 32, top bunk."

"Top bunk! I don't do top bunks!" protested Money.

The Officer's word was final. He turned his back with nothing more to say. Money grabbed his property bag and went on his way. When he arrived to his assigned cell, he threw the sheets and pillow from the bottom bunk onto the top.

"I'm taking the bottom bunk! You got'ta problem with that!" he asked feeling tough, but there was no one in the cell to respond back. "I thought not!" he stated now making up his bed.

Word had quickly spread around the prison that Money was back in population. Inmates were strolling back and forth pass his new cell just to see. Money was catching them out the corner of his eye.

"Ol, nosey ass bastards."

After making the bed, Money inspected the cell for cleanliness. The room checked out A-1 if he'd one it himself. He was impressed now wondering who his new cellmate was.

"Billy Paige?" He read on a bookmark now scanning over the book titles. "Oppression of the Black Man. Power to the People. The

Day Whity Falls, and several others. "This cat must be into all the black movement bullshit," carelessly flopping the books down.

Right then, "What's up dog! Whut up killer!" greeted Sean and Tootsie, Money's prison buddies who were standing at the cell's entrance, like dogs happy to see their master. As if the two were trained, they began taking off their boots to enter the cell. Happy to see the pair, Money smiled.

"What it be like ba-by... The mic controller is back...," displaying his hand in a D.J.'s scratching movement. They all gave one another 5's and shoulder greetings. Soon after, the three began a whispering conversation about the stabbing. Doing so, they didn't notice Billy Paige standing at the cell's entrance observing them.

Bill Paige was one of the south side Chicago's biggest drug dealers in the late 1970's. He profited over 5 million dollars in cash and assets in his time. The Federal Government built a weak drug case against Billy with no chance of conviction, until his own jealous brother whom turned informant, assisted the government with strong incriminating evidence to prosecute him. Billy was crushed after the forfeitures and seizures of all his homes, rental properties, and hard currency. Billy was left with no choice, but to except a plea of 360 months or take an option sentence of life in prison. Since his 18-year incarceration, Billy has read many books on the hardships of black men beginning with Africa. He has also studied and observed how a form of apartheid is being practiced amongst African Americans in the prison system. He speaks about how the U.S. government continuously finds ways to turn the black man against himself. Under his wing, Billy teaches one to close their eyes to the false illusion of America, and open them up to the evils of the real world.

Billy casually walked in the cell. "Which one of you is Maurice Bonner?" he asked looking the three men in their faces. Money defensively stood from the bed.

"Who the fuck wants to know?"

"No need for hostility my brother. I'm Billy Paige, your new cellmate. It's nice to meet your acquaintance," extending his hand.

"Your brother!"

Money disrespectfully looked past Billy's hand to his African Kofia styled hat.

"What's that different colored pork-chop looking thang on your hat man?" Sean and Tootsie broke into laughter. Money smiled. Billy took off his hat and pointed.

"This is Africa. This is the motherland from where our descendants were born, a place where our people once stood strong as Kings and Queens. The red, the black, and the green colors you see, represents the nation's flag. The red is for the blood, the blood that has been shed; the black is for the people, the people that stand strong and proud; and the green, the green is for the fertility of the land. Here," he pointed on the hat to where Ethiopia would be. "There are millions of our people dying everyday of starvation. Africa's government deprives our people of clean drinking water, the aid of medical supplies, housing, vaccines, the simple necessities of life, it's despicable. You name it, Whity won't provide it. There are other nations here as well; Zambia, Somalia, Zimbabwe, Angola, Kenya..."

Damn, thought Money standing with his arms folded. *This is the reason why I dropped out'ta high school. This shit is boring.*

At the same time, Money noticed Sean and Tootsie inching their way out of the cell. They too were not interested in history class today.

"Hh...hold on Martin Luther King!" said Money with his hand up. "Me and my boys was kickin' it, and you done ran them off with that Kunta Kente' shit you talking." Billy quickly struck back.

"Your boys ran themselves off, not I. They're just afraid."

"Afraid! My people ain't scared of shit! We down."

Billy shook his head. "No, not afraid of anyone, but afraid of the truth," picking up a book. "Do you know why you are here Maurice? Here, locked up in prison?" Money took a seat onto the bed. He then looked up to Billy. "Yeah, I know why I'm here."

"Ok, Tell me. Why are you here?"

"I fucked up, caught a gun and a dope case."

"No, wrong, and incorrect. It may seem unreal to you, but the reason you're here Maurice is because you're black."

"Because I'm black? Man...what is you talkin' 'bout?" asked Money becoming interested.

"It's true, you were born into slavery and don't even know it. You were locked up even before you came here. Let me explain. Your social security number and your zip code both are numbers that able the government to know how and where to find you. Most of the blacks in America live in urban areas of the city. Whity knows in these urban areas, young blacks distribute the drugs that they fly in across the water. These drugs create profits. Most times, the profits generated by these drugs are by black men who protect their profits most times through violence. The violence leads to murder; the murder leads to investigations, the investigations leads to imprisonment time for over 35 percent of the blacks in these urban areas, but not before Whity strips them of the profits generated by the drugs. Now this is the killer part, after you're incarcerated, you are now a ward of the state. There-fore, your inmate number used to identify you is now recognized as your social security number and politicians can use your head for their State Census Count, which brings them lots of money. It's nothing more than modern day slavery, and it's a repeat cycle for us blacks."

Money took a hard swallow. His undivided attention was focused on every word coming past Billy's perfect white teeth. Billy could see this as well. He decided to test his newfound protégé.

"So Maurice, let me ask you. Why are you here?"

"Because I'm black."

"Who flew the drugs in?"

"Whity!"

"Who put the drugs in the neighborhoods?"

"Whity!"

"And now who's paying the price?"

"Me!"

"That's right my brother, it's real. You just have to open your eyes to see it. Allow me to assist you in your journey to find out more about the truth."

Money was hesitant. He was a little afraid. "What is the truth?" he repeatedly asked himself. "Can I handle it? Will it change my life?" He was destined to know.

An hour later, Money consulted with Sean and Tootsie. He spoke about Africa, apartheid and the truth. Close-minded, they both laughed at him. Sean said the truth was no more than a lie. He also told Money to be careful of Billy, before he knows it his name would be turning into, "Moony of Africa." Tootsie began laughing. The joke upset Money.

"Fuck you Sean!"

He then looked to Tootsie who was still laughing with tears running down his face. He angrily pointed at Tootsie but said nothing. Afterwards, he walked away annoyed by the hard laughter.

Money ended up back at his cell. It took him sometime to calm down. After some thought within himself, he gave in to the idea of allowing Billy to show him the, *'Truth inside the real world.'*

Money smiled thinking of the respect he had for Billy. He never heard a black man speak so profound and intelligent, and never saw anyone with such dedication to anything but selling drugs. Billy never swore, he never got upset and he never complained. He just spoke knowledge to make one think. Money wanted to do the same. After many months and many late nights reading and studying black literature under Billy's guidance, Money felt he was ready to spread the truth himself.

One day after the inmate roll call, Money proudly stepped into the Mess Hall. His black movement handbook was tightly tucked in his right hand. His black Kofia styled hat symbolized with Africa's continent was snug on his head. He scanned the lunchroom searching for any face that may want to hear what he had to say. He first approached a set of inmates who claimed to love Africa but wasn't interested in hearing the truth. "No problem my brother, stay black, stay strong and proud," throwing up his right fists.

Afterwards, Money stepped to another group of men not knowing they were the friends of the man he stabbed. Still, his knowledgeable words seemingly grasp their attention. Money then asked each of the inmates the question of why they thought they were in prison, when he was interrupted from his name continuously being called. He turned around. Sean and Tootsie were waving their hands as to say, *'Come here.'*

Money politely excused himself from the inmates unknowing if he stood there any longer he was about to be stabbed himself. He then made his way over to Sean and Tootsie's table and took a seat.

"Now what do I owe my brothers for allowing me the pleasure of joining them for a meal? Seeing that they haven't consulted with their brother in over four months time," asked Money with his chest out.

Sean looked at Tootsie. "See, that's the shit I was talkin' 'bout Toot. The voice, the attitude, you ain't the same man," he said now looking Money's way. "Billy said this, Billy said that. It's Billy, Billy, Billy, that's all you talk about. I mean, the brother is deep and all but damn. And where did this Billy muthafucka' come from anyway? Until you came out the hole, I ain't never seen him before. What about you Toot? You ever seen this Billy cat?"

Tootsie shook his head, *'No.'*

"But since his ass came into the picture Money, you don't talk about no bitches no-mo', making no money, coming up, none of that shit. You ain't even mentioned shit else about the lick we suppose hit on that Big Daddy cat who suppose to have three or four hundred thousand dollars stashed. Shiiid...,we gos'ta get that. I got 19 months left; you got 14, and Toot fin'na bounce in 3. You need to be letting us know something!"

Money just sat listening, letting Sean blow off his steam. Tootsie as usual was bias about the situation. He was with whatever decision that was made by Sean.

Sean continued, "Like I said Money, your man speaks knowledge, but you talk about him so much, if I didn't know his name was Billy, I would think it was Belle," biting into his sandwich.

Money couldn't swallow the milk he was drinking fast enough, he almost choked. "So what are you saying Sean? That I'm Billy's cheerleader or something? That I'm his broad!"

Sean then gave Money a hard stare. "I don't know, you tell me. You and Billy do sleep in the same cell at night, and he did let you have the bottom bunk. Maybe 'Ol Belle likes to be on top," snickering.

Tootsie's black gums and horse like teeth showed, but not one peep of laughter came out of his mouth. He could see the raging bull in Money's eyes.

This man just disrespected me. I should bust his head open, thought Money. He then closed his eyes. *What would Billy do?* Suddenly, as quick as it came, it went. A settled look appeared over Money's face.

"Look brother Sean," he said standing from the table. "That life style of robbing, stealing, using and selling dope and shoot 'em up bang-bang is over for me, I don't even want to indulge in conversation about it. I'm reformed now. This is a new me, a better me. I'm happy now. I'm into opening up my brothers eyes to let them know that there is a better life awaiting for them after prison, a better life if they choose. Can't you see? I want our people to understand that we as black folks, we can provide ourselves with meaningful work, an equitable distribution of resources, and a healthy environment for us to live and understand one another. But right now, we're suffering. There's injustice, inequality, racial hate, oppressive relationships, and this is just amongst our-selves. Until we recognize the truth and understand us as a people, we'll never live vibrant pluralist lives." Money again threw up his fists. "Power to the people," and walked away.

Tootsie looked to Sean. "What did he just say?"

"He just said he ain't down wit' the program nomo', but I know one thang. Money go'on either fall back in line or fall by the way-side," brandishing the sharp end of his shank.

Billy was back in the cell rambling through Money's dresser drawer. Doing so, he came across Money's '*P.S.I. Pre-Sentence Investigation Report.*' Billy read everything about Money's case. The dope, the plea, the names, the snitching, he read it all. This reminded Billy of his own brother who'd told on him years earlier.

'*Ol snitchin' muthafucka,*' he frowned. The papers were suddenly snatched from Billy's hand.

"I am what I am, so now what?" asked Money eye to eye with Billy. Billy took a deep breath and stepped back to recapture his composure.

"Br...Brother Maurice. I didn't expect you back from lunch so soon," trying to place his hand on Money's shoulder.

"Don't touch me," slapping Billy's hand. "A snitch muthafucka, huh? But you're the same one who said, "Judge my brother not by his condemned past, but by the stature of his character in present day."

Billy chuckled. "I did say that, didn't I? But did you really believe that my brother, honestly," in a preachers tone. "What you do in the past is always go'on play into your future. Life is like a credit report; your past history means everything."

Money wasn't hearing that slick talk today. He snatched off his Kofia hat, throwing it on the floor.

"Shut your fake ass up Billy! I can't believe I fell for all that righteous brother, see the truth bullshit you ran down on me. The Apartheid speeches, stories of starvation, and that love thou brother crap. Damn man...This was the only thing in my life I ever felt apart of. It was real to me and it was all a lie," he said almost coming to tears. "Shit, I even lost my boys Sean and Toot behind this shit."

Without warning, Money backhanded Billy across the mouth losing respect for him. Billy did an over dramatic fall to the floor. A couple of inmates walking past the cell took notice of the unfolding drama, but kept on moving minding their own business. Money then stood over Billy, bent down and poked his finger in his chest.

"You made me look like a real fool, a real idiot. It's cool though, I needed this wake up call. But, if you speak one word about that P.S.I. outside this cell, I'll cut your throat wide open in yo' sleep, do you understand me?" Money's lips were trembling tight exposing the hair under his lip.

The two were so close; Billy could feel the heat from Money's breath on his face. Billy afraid, told Money not to worry, not a word of the P.S.I. would leave his lips. He then stood up and ran out the cell.

Afterwards, Money stripped the bottom bunk of his sheets. He moved up to his assigned top bunk giving Billy back the bottom. He then laid back on the bed in disappointment thinking how this whole thing was just some game.

SLIPPIN'

I don't believe this shit, I let this cat sell me a dream
He lowered me to talkin' 'bout Apartheid, starvation, and Africa's Kings and Queens
Rappin' to me about the white man, the truth, social numbers, and zip codes
Had me off my square, like a puppet, following his roll
But damn, I got'ta admit, the struggle he'd preached seemed so real
Nothin' ever touched me like that, I loved how it made me feel
Like I was apart of something, something where I couldn've made a difference
But wouldn't it turn out, all the preachin' was just a bunch of bullshit
Even had my silly ass out there talking about the so-called truth
Brothers doing double takes asking, "Money is that you?"
"Correction, it is Brother Maurice," I would respond in my righteous voice
Them cats turned their backs on me, they didn't wan'na hear that noise
"Get the fuck out my face!" I heard it so many times
Knowing any other time, that knife ah'be in they spine
Just because I've seen a lil' light, these boys think I done turned friendly
All I can say is they better recognize, I still keep that tool handy
But I can't believe Sean raised up on me, I don't know why he's frontin'
Throwing that gay shit out there like that, that boy got it comin'
And that fake ass Billy, yup, that's his new name
He knows sneaking and reading someone's P.S.I. can be a dangerous thang
My safety here in prison now lies on his lips
So that means partner gos'ta go, I got'ta sink his ship

I'd rather be a snitch muthafucka', than a dead muthafucka' any day
Because I ain't ne'va met a dead muthafucka' that had anything to
say
And Sean was right, Billy is suspect, he just popped up out'ta thin air
If he's workin' for them peoples, his ass is out, his life won't be spared
But fuck 'em all, Billy, Sean, the inmates, I ain't trippin'
I'm just go'on lay low, stay out the way, play it cool, and try not to be
slippin...

"Money, yo' Money!" called Tootsie shaking his foot. "Money!" Money came out of thought looking down at the foot of his bunk.

"Toot? What's up man?" lifting from the bed.

"You man, are you alright? Your eyes were wide open, but you weren't there."

"I'm straight, just got a lot of things on my mind. But what are you doin' here?" suspiciously. "And where's your punk-ass boy Sean at?"

"C'mon Money, y'all still boys too. It ain't like that."

"Yeah it is, anytime a cat accuses you of some homo shit it jail, it's like that. Sean disrespected me."

"You're right," agreed Tootsie. "But Sean said he was just teasing you. He was just tryin' to get you to see Billy for the fake he is."

Too late, thought Money. *I already know.*

Tootsie continued, "Sean wants to talk to you tomorrow, clear up the air between you two."

"Why didn't he come himself to talk then?" Tootsie paused as if he had to think of a reason.

"Sean has a new cleaning job over at the control tower. One of the C.O.'s hooked him up. He's over there now."

Money wasn't totally convinced. *Tootsie holding something back. I bet'cha Sean sent his ass here to see what my thoughts are about him, to see if or not I plan on stickin' his ass with that blade. That means he's planning somethin' against me, so I better watch my own ass. I got'ta keep Sean and Tootsie closer to me, especially Toot. If I tell him the sky is red enough times, he'll believe it.* Money smiled within himself. *See, that's what keeps me one up on these two clowns, I know how they think.*

Money smiled as if he had no questionable thoughts.

"Ok Toot, Tell Sean to meet me on the yard tomorrow after the 4 o'clock count."

"Cool," returned Tootsie with a smile. "I'll let Sean know," exiting the cell. Just then, Tootsie peeked back inside the cell. *I thought Money slept on the bottom bunk. He mus'ta switched beds.*

At that very moment, Sean was just walking into the control room. The C.O., his new boss, greeted him at the door. He explained in detail to Sean of what was to be cleaned, and the do's and dont's of the job. Last, he told Sean to never touch the telephone switchboard. All inmate calls were to be screened by federal employers only.

Sean explained that he was a trust worthy and model inmate who would never violate the Federal Bureau of Prisons Policy. The C.O. had his doubts about that. After 15 minutes into the cleaning job, the C.O. grabbed a magazine and told Sean to keep on working while he took an emergency lavatory break.

"No prob boss, I'll hold down the fort while you're gone," he said. As soon as the C.O. left the room, Sean locked the door behind him. He quickly placed the over-sized headphones on his head and began listening on the inmates phone calls. Sean was in tears of laughter from some of the conversations he was hearing. He heard inmates begging, crying, and pleading for their women to stay with them through their prison bit. He even heard a woman over the line telling an inmate she was leaving him for his best friend.

"Awe...that bitch cold blooded!" Sean voiced to himself.

After a few minutes, he took off the headphones, ran to the door, unlocked it, and looked out. The C.O. was nowhere in sight.

Looks like I got time for one more call, he thought, running back to the switchboard. It was only one phone in usage, Sean switched on the line to listen.

"But Mr. Bantz, my cover is blown, you got'ta get me transferred out'ta here! Money's go'on kill me!" exclaimed Billy. "He jut put a knife to my throat," he lied.

"Well, he should've cut your ass!" countered Conrad. "I didn't tell your stupid ass to go and read his P.S.I., Money's P.S.I. is useless to me. I already know he's a snitch."

A snitch? Who Money? thought Sean listening closer.

"Billy, your job is easy, simply gather information about the connections Money's making while in that prison. What's so fucking hard about that? All you have to do is watch him and report to me every 30 days, that's it. You need to quit all that fight the power, righteous black man bullshit you do, its' just confusing things. I can't get your jail time cut if you can't deliver. You do still want your time cut, right?"

"Yeah!" eagerly responded Billy.

"Like I told you, Money's bite ain't as big as his bark. He plays tough, but he's soft as doctor's cotton. One thing about him though, he's sly as a fox. Most times, Money can convince people to do his dirty work for him. Why do you think he's out of the hole and didn't get more time for that stabbing?"

Billy sat holding the phone clueless. Sean sat hoping the answer wasn't what he thought, but after hearing his name being implicated with the stabbing, he was on fire like the devil was on his back. *That rat bastard is a snitch.* Sean's lips along with his right eye twitched with anger.

Suddenly, "Bam! Bam! Bam! Bam!"

"Who locked this fucking door!" hollered the C.O. pulling out his keys. He quickly entered the room, looking around. Sean was mopping the floor in a hot sweat like he wasn't guilty of a thing.

Innocently, "Sorry boss, I must'a brushed up against the door while mopping," he said wiping sweat from his forehead.

The C.O. had no argument. The switchboard was free of calls and nothing appeared to be out of place, plus Sean was hard at work. Soon after, Sean was dismissed for the day.

Later that night, Sean explained to Tootsie what Conrad told to Billy. Tootsie couldn't believe it. "Damn man, Billy is an informant?" he asked.

Sean looked at him cockeyed. "Man, were you listening? Fuck Billy, I'm talkin' 'bout Money's ass. He implicated us in that stabbing.

Them peoples know we did it." *We?* thought Tootsie. *You mean you. I had nothin' to do with that stabbing,* he wanted to say, but he played along.

He just sat with his mouth hung, nervously rubbing his head.

In disbelief, "Are you sure Sean? It got'ta be some type of explanation for this. I'm fin'na ask Money," he said about to stand from the bed.

Sean pressed his hand down on his shoulder. "Naw, don't ask him nothing.' It's been too much talking done already. This go'on stop right here," pulling out a homemade shank.

Tootsie protested any violence, he liked Money. He didn't want to see him get hurt. Sean didn't like what he was hearing. He then turned the knife on Tootsie as if he was the snitch.

"Are you protecting him or somethin'! Are you two muthafucka's in ka-hoots against me, huh!"

Both of Tootsie's hands were to his chest.

"C'mon Sean, you already know."

"Naw, I don't know shit! I do know Money set us up for a fall and you acting like you don't wan'na do shit about it! You two muthafuckas' ain't boyfriend and girlfriend are you?"

Tootsie smacked his lips. Sean then backed off.

"Listen Toot, you're either down wit' me or you're against me. Ain't no in betweens," stated Sean.

Tootsie was in a difficult position, but he knew Sean meant business. He could only think back to the day when Sean stabbed up the guy in the shower, in-which Money was accused of doing. Just the thought of it made his skin crawl. Sean was still awaiting an answer.

"You in or you out?" he again asked with the knife in an upright position. Feeling his life was now threatened Tootsie replied, "I'm in man, I'm in." Soon after, Sean began explaining of how Money's murder was going to take place tonight.

Money was laying in the bed tired of listening to Billy's repeat apologies. It seemed the more he ignored the apologies, the harder Billy tried to apologize. He offered everything from food, to cigarettes, to magazines, to books of mailing stamps. He even offered back the bottom bunk, but nothing was working. Billy was desperate, more or less thinking of his freedom. He knew some how he had to get back in good with Money. He figured the only way now was the truth. He stood from bed, looking to the top bunk.

"Ok Money, I'ma keep it straight-forward with you. You and I aren't bunking by chance. I was put here to watch you; to record your moves."

Money lifted from his bunk. "What! Record my moves," his voice silently cracked.

"Yeah man, to see who you're associating with. It's this Fed. This guy has a hard on for you. He wants you bad, he wants to give you life. I don't know the details, but it's about something that goes way back to 1983. Do you know anything about that?"

Money's twisted face gave the answer. Just the thought of Conrad Bantz had Money wanting to shit on himself.

Like any other time when the pressure was on, Money started babbling. After 15 minutes of listening, Billy knew just about everything Conrad did. The whole time while Money was talking, Billy was in thought. *This can't be the dude who slapped me and threatened my life. Mr Bantz was right, this guy is a pussy.*

Billy then suggested to Money that they should work together. He told Money to find some new associates around the prison. Some people who had a history of dealing with drugs. He said this would benefit them both. Conrad would still get his monthly report, Billy's time would still be cut and Conrad would totally be thrown off Money's trail. With no other ideas in mind, Money agreed. He then checked the time.

9:46 p.m., I got 14 minutes before the 10 o'clock inmate count. Money hopped off the bed and headed for Sean and Tootsie's cell. He knew their meeting was set for 4 o'clock tomorrow, but this news about Billy couldn't wait. Besides, Money felt he needed all the friends he could get now knowing Conrad was on his back.

Walking up the hallway, Money saw the same group of guys he'd spoken with earlier in the mess hall. The friends of the man Sean had stabbed. As Money neared, one of the men pointed in his direction. Suddenly, three more men poured out of their cells.

Awe...shit, thought Money becoming a little nervous. *Why all these muthafucka's coming out of they cell?* He wanted to turn back around, but didn't want to seem like a punk. As Money approached, he spoke. "W-sup, W-sup," head nodding. None of the men spoke back. Only their mean mugging, hatred facial expressions spoke their greetings. Unfortunately, the narrow hallway offered Money no room to walk around the group. As he turned himself sideways to pass, one of the men grabbed him forcing him into a cell. The others watched as the two broke into a scuffle. Money fought the best he could. Unlucky for him, he was up against an ex-pro street fighter. After three quick combination hits to both sides of his face, Money was dazed. One final hit to the sternum floored him. He dropped to the floor holding his stomach gasping to breathe.

"Damn Lil' Moe!" the group cheered. Just then, another man pulled out what looked like an oversized screwdriver. He put his left hand on top of Money's head. The other held the large weapon to his throat. "Ssshhh!" silently expressed the man's lips seeing Money was about to scream.

"Do you know me?" he asked looking Money in the eyes. Money on his back looking up fearfully nodded, *'No.'*

"I didn't think so." He then pulled up his shirt revealing the multiple stab wounds around his stomach. He looked back to Money.

"Do you think you know me now?" Money was afraid to answer, unsure as to if his neck would result in the same way, but he slowly shook his head, *'Yes.'* It was the man Sean had stabbed.

Just then, the 10 o'clock count time bell sounded. Money was quickly lifted to his feet and rushed out of the cell. The man pointed the duck-tape wrapped screwdriver at Money's eye.

"Tell that bitch Sean not to sleep too hard at night because one of these days, he just might not wake up."

Then, as quick as the men appeared, they all scattered back into their cells. Money sighed with relief, running back to his cell. That was the closest he'd been to death since being in prison.

After the inmate count, Money just laid in bed. His knife was tucked tight in his right hand. His eyes were wide open on the alert.

Nothing or no-one was getting close to him, no-one except for Billy who wouldn't shut the fuck up. He was going on and on about how they were going to play Conrad Bantz for a fool. Oddly, Money didn't mind. He was worn out from his 10-second brawl, and Billy's gibberish talk was keeping him awake. But, after continuously nodding in and out for three hours, Money fell asleep.

Suddenly, he awoke to a loud muffled out cry from underneath him. He could hear heavy breathing, along with something being punctured.

In a loud whisper, "Hold him Toot! Hold him!"

Money's eyes widened. He was paralyzed with fear. *Toot?* he thought. *This hit was meant for me?*

Just then, Money looked up only to see the two familiar silhouette figures running out of his cell. He slowly but quietly eased from his top bunk to the floor. He looked at the double wrapped white towel covering Billy's face, then down at his chest which was drenched in blood. He figured there was no sense in looking at Billy's face, he knew the end result. Right then, it hit Money.

Tootsie saved my life. He saw me on this top bunk earlier. He could've easily told Sean, but I guess decided not to, damn... with a frightening twitch.

The drama was becoming way too real for Money. He quickly disposed of his knife and any other contraband he had. He knew this investigation over Billy's death was going to be big. Big enough to where Conrad Bantz just might show his face.

Money already decided he was not going to say a word.

"I ain't seen shit, I ain't heard shit, and I don't know shit. As far as Sean dirty ass goes, he's go'on get his at a later date. I'm just glad he got the wrong guy."

PABLO

Life for Black-Knight took a 360-degree turn. By a foot, he evaded capture from Big-6 and half of Long Beach California Police Department. After maneuvering his way past numerous Police blockades, he snuck on a Grey Hound Bus carrier bound for Tucson, Arizona. During his late night ride, uncertainty and disbelief ran deep in Black-Knight's thoughts. He just couldn't understand why his best friend K.G. turned on him. *We were on our way back up. It just don't make no got-damn sense,* he thought punching the seat.

After a few hours into the bus ride, the morning sun began to rise. Black-Knight was in a comatose like sleep. Several passengers were annoyed by his grumbling snore.

Soon-after, the bus reached its destination at the Grey Hound bus station in Tucson. Everyone began exiting the bus. The driver himself was about to exit, until looking in the far back. He could see someone slumped over, appearing to be dead, but the grizzly bear like snore said different.

The bus driver approached Black-Knight, immediately taking notice of the blood spatter across his clothes and face. The driver then took a step back, worried whether or not Black-Knight was some type of slasher. *I don't recall this guy boarding the bus*, ready to call the Police.

The driver not wanting to involve himself, headed back towards the front of the bus when he suddenly stopped and yelled out.

"Hey young man, the ride is over! We're here at the station," continuing towards the front.

Black-Knight unsure of where he was frantically awoke wiping the drool from his mouth. He then looked out the window to see the driver and passengers had already exited the bus, now entering the bus-station. He then himself hurried to exit the bus when he took notice of his face in the passenger's side mirror.

"Awe…shit!" now looking at his clothes. "I got'ta get cleaned up, and fast."

Afterwards, he peered towards the bus station wondering if anyone had noticed the blood on him and were they calling the Police? He quickly fled away from the bus station.

After making himself scarce, Black-Knight found himself hungry, hot and broke, with nowhere to go. He did manage to steal himself a t-shirt from a street vendor entitled: *'I Love Mexico'* which was almost too small of a fit.

Half the day had passed. The Arizona heat was doing a number on Black-Knight. He was dehydrated and feeling a bit sluggish. Every diner and restaurant with air-conditioning threw him out because he couldn't purchase a meal. Rambling through his pockets, *Damn, I ain't even got a quarter,* pissed that his last $3000 was left back in his Long Beach Motel room. With no hygienic tools or financial resources, Black-Knight badly wanted to call home to Detroit for some financial aid, but he was too afraid. He wasn't sure if Long Beach Police had yet identified K.G.'s body. If they had, he knew an investigation would lead them straight back to Detroit. He quickly scratched that idea. He figured there wasn't any sense in risking a chance of getting caught up over a simple phone call. *I ain't that damn dumb,* he thought staying cautious.

After another hour had passed, Black-Knight couldn't take it anymore. He felt like he was on the brink of starvation. Cups of water from the local restaurants wasn't cutting it anymore, he needed food. He decided to try his luck at one last diner. There, he offered to wash the dishes, mop and take out the trash for a meal, but the restaurant owner turned him down. He claimed his full staff of employees was capable of those jobs.

Black-Knight looked over his shoulder to the back of the diner. *Full staff of employees?* He saw no one but an old fat Mexican woman working the grill along with the dishes that were piled a mile high. And the floors had more grease on them than the fryers. Black-Knight was about to plead his case, but threw his hand like, *Fuck it!* and walked out. He soon-after found himself standing at the restaurant's garbage can when he did the unthinkable. He reached inside the trash and pulled out several paper bags with left over food in them. He immediately tore away the bit off parts. After a hard stare with the sandwiches, he began to eat. The first initial bite disgusted him, he couldn't believe life had dealt him these cards, but the last thing he was going to do was feel sorry for himself. He knew in life only the strong prevailed. One thing though, Black-Knight swore to God if he got back onto his feet, he'd never turn his back on another person in need again.

After his salvaged meal, Black-Knight went on his way to nowhere. He combed the neighborhood streets of Tucson which seemingly had nothing to offer. He soon found himself sitting under a tree waiting for the sweltering sun to go down.

"Weph! The devil must be workin' overtime," he said wiping his chest of the pouring sweat.

Black-Knight sitting under a tree observed his surroundings. He didn't see anything but dirt, palm trees, mountains and a lot of Mexicans. From further observation, he noticed something else.

"I've only seen a handful of black folks since I've been here," rubbing his head. "I better not make too much noise in this town. Don't need the local cops on my ass."

Black-Knight figured he might as well make the best of Tucson since California was out of the question and Detroit was off limits.

The sun soon fell and the moon arose. The desert like heat still remained though the sun had gone. Regardless, Black-Knight was back on the move. His mission now was to find somewhere to sleep for the night. If worse came to worse, in which it was, he would sleep outside. Yet, he kept telling himself he wasn't homeless. The thought of it was degrading to his character. Just then, he came upon the homeless shelter. As quick as he stepped in, he stepped out fanning his nose. The blasting aroma of under-arm funk along with the echoing sound of crying babies was too much to bare.

Smirking, "Man, even the women smell like they've been workin' hard," walking away.

Black-Knight decided to take refuge in a field on some tall, soft grass. As he lay and became more comfortable, he laughed thinking of how he once was a millionaire.

Yawning, *Damn, I took everything in my life for granted. I never thought I would be homele...* Before his thought was finished he was asleep.

As Black-Knight slept, he began to replay the shoot out back in the bar in his dreams. Then about how K.G. was laying on the ground with his face half blown off. The sounds of the bullets replaying in his mind were so loud and clear, he felt as if he again was right there. "Bbooomm! Bbooomm! Pow!" crackeled the guns. His head jerked from every sound he heard, suddenly, "Boof!"

Black-Knight awoke opening his eyes. A body lay dead next to him. Right then, he realized the gunshots he was hearing were real. He laid stiff and motionless listening to gibberish Mexican talk float back and forth. After a few more cracks of the guns were heard, it was over.

Black-Knight peered through the tall grass. He saw four men running away with two and three large duffle bags a piece across their backs. He then looked back to the young boy who lay dead. It was clear he was of Mexican descent. The only thing now on Black-Knight's mind was to get the hell out of there. Two nights in a row of killing was more than enough for him. As he began to walk away, he tripped over another body lying in the grass.

"What the...?" he began counting.

To his surprise, six more people lay dead, or so he thought when he heard a moan. "Mmm...mmm..." lightly. It was another kid.

Black-Knight's first instinct was to make like a ghost, but his second thought was, *'This is someone in need,'* remembering back to his earlier statement. He then looked to the sky.

"Lord, I said when I got back onto my feet I would help!" The moan came again. Black-Knight shook his head. "That must be the sign," rushing to his side.

The boy was shot in his shoulder. The injury wasn't bad as it looked, but it hurt like hell. Black-Knight turned him onto his back.

"Who-are-you? Where-are-you-from?" he asked breaking it down into syllables.

Whispering, "My brother, where's my brother?" he responded speaking perfect English. Black-Knight knelt down giving it to him straight up.

"Your brother's dead. Now lets get you out'ta here. Which way you live?" waiting for directions.

From the disturbing news of his brother's death, the boy laid motionless ignoring the question.

Growing impatient, "Hey got dammit, I'll leave yo' ass here. I don't know you from a hole in the wall. I owe the Lord a favor, not you. Now tell me the way or I'm gone."

The boy still said nothing; only his tears wept his response.

"Ok, fine then bleed to death," he said standing up looking across the grass. He could see the trampled path from where the Mexicans had come from. Just then, sirens could be heard from a far. Suddenly, the boy resurrected.

"That way my friend, my house that way," he pointed thinking the fire truck sirens he heard was the Police.

Black-Knight bent down. "I thought so," picking up the 140 pound, 5 foot 4 youngster throwing him over his shoulder. The two took off towards the Mexican border.

After four hours into the journey, Black-Knight was cussing himself. He again dropped the boy 'Elmundo' on the ground for the 20th time.

Tired, "A man, I didn't sign up for this shit. I thought you lived maybe three or four blocks from where I found yo' ass. Now, you tellin' me you live a day journey through the desert. Man...we go'on die out here. We ain't got shit! No water, no pop, juice, kool-aid, nothing! I just signed my own death warrant."

He then looked to the sky. "Lord, you done set me up."

Elmundo could only mumble. "It'll be worth it my friend."

"Yeah, whatever."

On top of the night heat, the sun was now rising. Black-Knight and Elmundo had serious doubts about themselves surviving this journey. Things looked very grim with no shade or water supply, plus Elmundo was slipping in and out of consciousness. The front and the back of his shirt was covered with dark dry blood. Time for him was running out. 19 year-old Elmundo had made this trip though the desert many times. He knew this desert like the back of his hand. He'd been running marijuana across these parts for years. He knew where and when to stop and rest. Of course he was always prepared with food and water. This time for the first time, he'd brought his 15 year-old brother *'Jesús'* along to teach him the family trade. Unfortunately, Jesús first time was his last time and their thousand pound marijuana shipment was hijacked before it could reach the Tucson safe house.

Now six hours inside the desert, Black-Knight's knees started to buckle. His back and feet were numb. His dark skin began turning a pale white. Right then, he again lost grasp of Elmundo who hit the ground like a brick. Then Black-Knight himself tipped over. He laid on his side dazed and delusional. His lips were chapped with sunburn. His arms and legs just locked up, they wouldn't move. He knew then, he and Elmundo's fate was sealed.

At that moment, Black-Knight heard the faint sound of a roaring engine. He dismissed it figuring the heat exhaustion was playing tricks on his mind. He suddenly heard it again, staggering to his feet looking upward. Something was coming off the mountain fast. Only the dust cloud trailing it could be seen. Now on leveled ground, the vehicle started heading in their direction. Black-Knight still bent over like a broken tree twig, mustard up some energy to waive his arms. Suddenly, he shielded his eyes from something shining bright. It was the sun reflecting off the chrome mirrors' on the Border Patrol's Bronco. Still watching the truck approach, Black-Knight didn't see a break in its speed, now jumping out of its way as it skidded sideways to a halt. Simultaneously, a shotgun riffle peeked from out the passenger window.

"On the ground! On the ground!" repeatedly yelled the two Mexican Border Patrol Officers' in Spanish exiting the truck. Black-Knight didn't understand a word of their language, but he did understand the shotgun pointed in his direction. With no hesitation, he placed his hands behind his head and got down on the ground.

The two Officers were in a frenzy. They seemingly already knew who Elmundo was. Elmundo being shot intensified their anger towards Black-Knight.

Over and over the Officers slapped him asking, "Who shot the boy? Who shot the boy?"

Weakened by the hot sun and the repeated abuse, Black-Knight passed out. When Black-Knight awoke, he thought he was dead. The only thing he could see was white. He then brought his eyes into focus. Weirdly, he found himself clean, clothed and laying in a comfortable bed with soft white sheets. In fact, the entire windowless room was in white, down to the linen outfit he was sporting.

"Ok, part 2 to this fairy-tale," he voiced getting out of bed.

Black-Knight headed towards the door rubbing his sore face. He also kept stroking his nose smelling a hint of shit.

Opening the door, "Somethin' stank bad," stepping into a long hallway. The doors were endless up the foyer. He noticed he was in some kind of mansion. *But who's mansion and where?*

Black-Knight remembered Elmundo and the Border Patrol Officers, so he knew he was still in Mexico. He just needed a physical person to talk to. He began checking all the rooms yelling, "Hello…!"

Strangely, every room was unoccupied. He did notice that he was on some type of farm. The sounds of chickens and the smell of manure made it evident.

After checking 12 to 13 rooms, Black-Knight opened a door to where he saw over 25 people of Mexican descent, including the two Border Patrol Officers. They all were standing around what appeared to be an operating table. Right then, a man broke down into tears as the doctors pulled the sheet over Elmundo's face. The doctors said his blood lose was just too great. The man who everyone kept calling *'Pablo'* was in rage. The lost of his two young sons was unbearable. He kept pounding himself in the chest screaming, "Why!" on his knees praying to the Lord. Everybody in the room knew to give Pablo his space. No one wanted to piss him off no more than he already was and end up on the meat hook in the barn.

Black-Knight quietly crept out the room just as he crept in. Grieving for Elmundo, *Damn, the young fellow didn't make it,* slowly walking back up the long foyer.

Not long after, Black-Knight found his way out in front of the Villa. The scenery was beautiful, green grass, exotic trees, cattle, horses, chickens, goats and snow covered mountains in the far distance. Black-Knight smiled turning in circles with his arms out.

"Now this is what the fuck I'm talkin' 'bout! Living large!" looking out over the acres of land.

He decided to take a walk and further inspect the scene. He roamed the acreage land for over an hour coming across endless fields of marijuana.

"Oh…so the farm is a front, and the shit smell is to cover up the scent of the weed," feeling as if he'd uncovered something.

When he returned back to the farmhouse, it was no surprise that Pablo and his men were waiting for him. *All shit,* thought Black-Knight. *Let me get my story straight,* thinking.

When he approached, a much shorter Pablo stepped to him looking upward. "Did you see anything interesting out there my friend?" he asked without a blink of his eye.

Without hesitation, "Yeah…I saw the weed plants," he replied knowing a lie would insult the man. Just then, seven of Pablo's men surrounded Black-Knight.

"Follow me," he stated leading the way.

"Follow who! Shiiid…y'all ain't fin'na kill me!" Black-Knight took off running towards the weed fields when one of Pablo's men, "Bbooomm! Bbooomm!" shot him in the back. Unable to picture himself dead with large holes in his back, Black-Knight shook off that idea. He instead followed behind Pablo as instructed even though the worst happening to him plagued his mind. *Lord, don't let me die in Mexico,* he prayed.

Soon, they all approached the barn. Black-Knight was spooked. Behind the clucking chickens, he could hear the faint sounds of clacking chains and distressed moaning coming from the inside. Pablo with his grieving blood shot red eyes approached one of his men. He whispered something in his ear. The man went on ahead in the barn. Afterwards, Pablo approached Black-Knight.

"The Border Patrol Officers who brought you and Elmundo to me," kissing his hand along with a crucifix across his chest, "Says you claim to see the guys who shot and robbed Elmundo and Jesús last night. It this not true?" he asked, feeling Black-Knight could give him the much needed closure.

Black-Knight was about to explain that he didn't exactly see the faces of his sons' killers when Pablo's man came trotting out of the barn. In each of one of his hands, he had a large ridged edge machete' and a brown rubber apron used for cutting cattle meat. As Pablo began putting on the apron, Black-Knight re-thought his statement of what he was about to say.

Now fitted with the apron and machete' in hand, Pablo rephrased his question. "Would you be able to point out these men if you saw them again?"

"Oh definitely, without a doubt," answered Black-Knight. "No doubt what-so-ever, I'll point 'em straight out."

Pablo squint his eye with a hard stare shaking his head. "Ok then, come with me," walking inside the barn.

Inside the barn, Black-Knight laid eyes on four naked men suspended in the air by chains hooked through their hands. Screams and moans uttered through the tape across their mouths. Blood from their hands traveled the length of their bodies dripping into the fire below their feet.

Black-Knight sighed knowing he'd just stepped into hell. He was ready to say whatever it took to ensure he didn't end up hanging by those chains.

Pablo then waived Black-Knight closer to him. With his Spanish accent, "A, you see these mutherfuckers? They kill my two boys then try to sell my product to my American connection. They say 'No, not your product. We buy from someone else.' I say who? They say different names." Pablo hunched his shoulders like, *What do you think?* Black-Knight hunched his shoulders in return as to say, *I don't know.*

"They lie!" yelled Pablo swinging the machete' gashing open the thigh of one of the men hanging. The man let out a foreign out-cry. Blood oozed from his would like thick gravy. The chains started shaking as he went into shock. Pablo stood gritting his teeth in anger. Black-Knight displayed no emotions. And Pablo's men were all laughing at the sound the bleeding man had made, it was nothing to them, they were use to these type or torture killings. Then, without warning, Pablo swung the machete' at the heads of his men as they all ducked missing them by inches.

"You think this funny! You think this funny! This no funny! Elmundo and Jesús are dead. Have you forgotten about Enrique, Emilio, Felix, Ramiro, and Lino? They dead too..." he explained calling the names of his deceased marijuana mules. "It's my fault, I'm to blame for this tragedy. I sent them to their deaths." Silence filled the barn besides the chickens and the grunts of agony.

Just then, "Sss...Santos," faintly whispered one of the men hanging. Sweat and saliva freed his mouth of the tape. "Santos, you promised." Pablo's eyes widened, looking to Santos, the man who he had fetch the apron and machete'.

"Santos! How do you know this man?" fiercely asked Pablo. Santos began stumbling backwards shaking his head.

"Pablo, believe me. He's lying, I not know him. I...I..." Santos took off running for his life.

It wasn't long before he was caught and dragged back inside the barn. After being beaten near death, Santos told almost everything. Anything Santos didn't say, his cousin, the man hanging who called his name told the rest. He explained that for quite some time, Santos wanted to come to power over the marijuana farm. He said the only way to do it was to first kill Elmundo and Jesús, who were to take over the trade in years to come. Afterwards, the plan was to kill Pablo making his death also look like the work of robbers. Santos's cousin then began to plead.

"Please, forgive me Pablo, a 1000 apologies for my sins against you and your sons'. I never..."

Pablo put up his hand as to say, *Speak no more, I've heard enough.* He then took a seat to think. He couldn't believe Santos, his partner for the last 15 years plotted to kill he and his family. It was all unbelievable.

Black-Knight stood aside, relieved the situation played itself out. He didn't have to implicate no-one in nothing. Pablo's men continued to abuse Santos. They were always jealous of him because of his close relationship with Pablo.

Soon-after, Pablo signaled his men to bring Santos over to him. He looked him the eyes.

"Santos I loved you like a brother. I trusted you. How could you betray me like this?" rubbing his face. He then stood. "Now, how do you wish to die?"

With puppy dog eyes, "Hang me Pablo! Hang me!"

Pablo then pulled out his pistol. "Bbooomm! Boommm!" shooting Santos in the head. "Hanging you would take too long."

His ass deserved that, thought Black-Knight.

Afterwards, Pablo put out the fires below the hanging men feet. Charred and blistered, their feet looked as if they had been cooked. He then cranked the chains lowering their knees to his head length.

Pablo ordered Black-Knight and his men to line up. He paced back and fourth for a minute and then introduced himself.

"Ello, I am Pablo Fernando Jose' Warez, the 1st," he added. "I am standing here now to let you know: Don't fuck-with-me. Now, as you know, these men are guilty, guilty for the deaths of my two sons'; Elmundo and Jesús, and why? Because of one mans greed, so now, he dead, his cousin and he friends, they soon be dead too. They take my marijuana and boom, boom, boom, kill my boys. They no real men like me. They pirates, they thieves, they murderers. And what do we do with thieves and murderers?" he asked looking to Black-Knight in a deranged manner. Black-Knight was caught off guard. He answered in question.

"We kill 'em?"

"That's right!" agreed Pablo. "We cut their fucking hands and feet off and then we kill 'em."

Suddenly, with several hacks of the sharp edged blade, Pablo severed the hands and feet of each man from their bodies. Only the hoofs of their wrists and ankles remained. Each man screamed for mercy. Pablo ate off their pain to feed his grief.

Still alive, but unable to crawl or walk, Pablo ordered his men, along with Black-Knight to throw each of the bodies along with the hands and feet into the hogs pen. The hogs wasted no time feeding on the men. Their screams and cries soon went silent. Afterwards, Santos was stripped naked and also thrown in the pen. The hogs welcomed him as well. Even though his sons' murders' were brought to justice, Pablo was still saddened. He dropped the bloody machete' and the apron and returned inside his home. His men then gathered amongst each other to discuss what happened. Black-Knight walked off towards the back of the barn unbuckling his pants as if he had to urinate. When he reached the back of the barn, he threw up. The blood and guts scene inside the hog's pen was horrifying. He'd killed many men in his time but nothing to where body parts were being tossed around. He then smiled as the vomit dribbled from his lips. *I think Pablo and I are gon'na get along just fine.*

Several months had passed and not one word of what happened in the barn was spoken, at least not from Black-Knight's lips. Before time, he had no plans or anything financially solid, so he made due of himself around the farm. Not long after, he was invited by Pablo to work the weed fields. Black-Knight was sure not to get too friendly too fast. The last thing he wanted was for Pablo to think he was trying to get close to him to harm him. Black-Knight didn't want to wake up one day to find himself dead like Santos.

One day during lunch, "B.K.!" called Pablo walking out the front door of the mansion. "I want to talk to you!" Black-Knight detected urgency in Pablo's voice. He stood up from the table.

"What's up Pablo? Is everything ok?" walking over to him.

"Yes and no my friend, business is slow and I have much product. You say you from Detroit town?"

"That's right, Motor City baby."

"They smoke the marijuana there in Motor City?"

"Awe...hell yeah," replied Black-Knight with a frowned face. "A lot of cats I know smoke this shit."

"Ok good," smiled Pablo. "How much can you sell?"

"Mmm...I can sell 'bout four or five."

Pablo eyes lit up. "Four or Five hundred pounds? That's good, good my friend. You be my new American connection. I set everything up," running back up to the house.

Black-Knight stood in confusion. "Four or five hundred pounds? I meant four our five ounces. If I'm gon'na sell four or five anything, it's go'on be some keys of cocaine. I ain't got no market for all that weed. I wouldn't even know where to start. Shit, I better let Pablo know," walking up to the house. He then stopped. "Naw, naw, I can't do that. Pablo go'on think I'm here just free loading, he go'on think I'ma fraud. C'mon Black-Knight, you're still a hustler. Think baby, think."

Black-Knight stood staring past the green pasture up to the snowy mountain caps. Suddenly, an idea hit him. He second guessed himself but it was the only thing he could think of. Black-Knight decided to call back home to Detroit to speak with Rowe, K.G.'s brother. He convincingly told himself the phone call was to find out how K.G.'s funeral turned out, but deep inside he knew the truth.

But when Black-Knight talked to Rowe about the funeral, he wept saying he knew nothing of K.G.'s death. It was a shock. Rowe said he noticed he hadn't heard from the pair in a while, but he assumed they were handling business as usual. Black-Knight asked Rowe if anyone from Long Beach Homicide Department contacted him or any members of his family.

"Hell, fuck naw!" answered Rowe. "But I'm fin'na call down to California and find out why."

Black-Knight strongly suggested to Rowe not to do that. He figured if the Police weren't looking, it made no sense to make them start asking. So, with no choice, he explained to Rowe the chain of events that led to K.G.'s death. Rowe first denied what he was hearing, but after thinking back on some of he and his brother's conversations, and the business transactions, he knew Black-Knight wasn't lying. Still, he didn't acknowledge the story to be true. After a brief silence on the phone, Black-Knight went on to tell Rowe he still was working on a big plan, which could financially set he and his family for life. Even though bitter about his brother's death, Rowe knew money talked and the rest walked; he was all ears.

Black-Knight told Rowe enough just to wet his beak. Black-Knight said he would contact him in another day or two to fill him in on the details, afterwards he pushed down the receiver.

"Rowe knows more than he's letting on, I just know it," now hanging up the phone.

Black-Knight didn't trust Rowe, especially from what K.G. had told him. But he really didn't have any other sources in Detroit he felt he could trust. He had to take the chance with Rowe.

Just then, Pablo came walking up. "Ay...B.K. ...," he expressed with excitement. "Everything set up for you my friend. My people in Arizona have 500 pounds and transportation waiting for you. You leave in two days. You sell marijuana for whatever you want. You bring me $150 a pound, ok? Good deal? You like?"

Black-Knight smiled shaking his head in agreement. He didn't exactly know what marijuana sold for in Detroit, but he knew damn well it was for more than $150 per pound. He felt the excitement of again about to come up. He was also glad to be directly connected. He then took a deep breath. "It's on again," feeling new life.

Hello and Good-bye

The year was now 1998 in Detroit, Michigan. Besides the auto industry, marijuana was playing a big role in Detroit's flowing economy. Hustlers were now pushing this product in large volumes. Money was being made and money was exchanging hands. Because of its risk factor and the time it carried, cocaine slowly began to take a back seat to marijuana. Marijuana was proving itself to be safer and more profitable than cocaine, if sold in quantity. Even though large and bulky when distributed, with the right connection, marijuana could turn a person into a millionaire with-in a six month period. This persuaded many cocaine pushers to convert over to selling weed.

Riding down I-75, "You know that weed my man showed us in Memphis was some bullshit, right?" repeated Tywon to White Boy-J for the 30th time.

J exhaled, "Damn Ty, I know man. I'm sorry, I mean, what do you want me to do? It was a bad run."

"I'm just saying, I'm sick of this shit; riding all over the damn country looking for weed. Like I said before, we need a plug out west, some place like California or Arizona."

"I'm hip," agreed J as he and Tywon both noticed the Michigan State Trooper posted at the Michigan/Ohio border.

Tywon and White Boy-J had taken a one-day trip to Tennessee. Their mission was to purchase 100 pounds of marijuana through a connection of J's. Like the last two times, the trip was a disappointment. The weed was greenish black, flat, and compressed, not at all up to their quality standards. The $800 per pound price tag was right, but they had to pass. So, they again found themselves heading back to Detroit empty handed.

In fear of the State Trooper, "Is he coming?" asked Tywon afraid to look in his rearview mirror.

Fully turned around, looking out the back window, "Nah, he still sittin' there," replied J.

"Damn J! If he was coming, you already got us looking guilty. All turned around and shit. Sit yo' ass down."

J laughed, "Calm your paranoid ass down Ty. Man... you trippin'. I see what O'Sha be talking about now. You worry too much."

"O'Sha ain't got nothin' to do with this," Tywon pointed back and fourth between himself and J. "Her ass already got one foot out the door. And hell yeah I'm worried. We got $105,000 in the trunk to lose. That's our come up money. We can't afford to take no loses."

J had no argument for that. He knew Tywon was right. A financial loss like that was not included in their program.

During the past 10 years, Tywon and White Boy-J became close friends. Their friendship developed as J dated Octavia, O'Sha's older sister. J was in love with Octavia. He romantically showered her with cards, flowers, hand written poems, clothing, jewelry, and cars, financially breaking himself. He even went against his own mother who didn't like Octavia after she stated, *'That black bitch ain't no good for you. She doesn't love you. She's just after your money!'* J wouldn't hear of it. Soon after, their seven-year relationship slowly ended after Octavia was drawn back into the street life of strip club dancing and periodic tricking. White Boy-J was crushed.

Also at this time, Tywon and O'Sha again began dating on and off after he pleaded for her forgiveness. But during their on time, Tywon was learning a scorned woman was anything but forgiving.

Just then, "All Shit J!" mumbled Tywon in a panic making sure his seat belt was fastened.

"Whud...Whud..." responded a puzzled J again ready to turn around. Tywon pinned him to the seat with his hand. "Don't move, don't turn around, don't do shit. Troopers!" Tywon eyed his driver's mirror. He could see the State Troopers coming on fast. He started perspiring. J shook his head knowing this wasn't good. The so feared royal blue enforcement vehicle with its red rotating flash bulb on top was now in direct line with Tywon and J.

Stuttering, "Ugh... Ugh...Ok J. Ok man, be cool. Let me do the talking. I got this," said Tywon signaling to pull off on the high-way shoulder. As he began pulling to the side, the State Trooper flew past them as if they were standing still.

Tywon and J looked at one another with a sign of relief. They both then bust out laughing. Pointing, "Yo' ass was scared," giggled Tywon.

"Naw... yo' ass was scared," returned J.

Tywon took a deep breath agreeing. "Yeah, you right. I was scared." Afterwards, the two continued on.

****

"Ok, sign here for your $121.95 cash refund remaining from your commissary account." The paper was signed. "Alrighty then, that's it," said the C.O. "You're here by a free man now. But, if the devil permits, I'm quite sure we'll be seeing you again."

Money gave a grim stare. "Shiiid, whatever, I'm out this bitch! You won't be seeing me back up in this joint again," cockily walking away.

Just outside the barbed-wire fence, Money spotted a white Cadillac Escalade truck sitting out front in the parking lot. From the large figure sitting in the driver's seat, he could tell it was Big Daddy.

Money threw up both his hands as to say, *'What up?'*

Big Daddy honked his horn indicating it was him. Money smiled, now high-stepping towards the truck when suddenly, he heard, "Yeah motherfucker! You did your time, but this shit ain't over with!"

Money looked to his side unsure if or not that statement was directed at him. He almost passed out at the sight of the Caucasian man's familiar face just slightly aged.

Looking around, "Wh... Wh...What you want? I did my time already. Leave me alone," said Money picking up his pace.

Conrad Bantz trotted along side of him. "What! I know you don't think you're gon'na just waltz your black ass away from me after killing my informant?"

"Killed your informant! Who? I ain't killed nobody," hunched Money. "What are you talkin' 'bout?" Big Daddy sitting in his truck leaned forward taking notice of Conrad's ranting.

"What the Fff...," now exiting his vehicle.

Just then, Conrad slammed Money up against the wire-fence, then to the ground. "Don't you toy with me you son-of-a-bitch! We both know you had Billy set up to be killed."

Money's face was twisted. "Billy! I ain't have nuttin' ta' do with that killin' Sean and Too..."

"Sshh...sshh..., uh, uh Maurice," cutting him short.

"Billy was your cell-mate therefore I'm holding you responsible for his death. Do you remember me telling you that I was the only friend you had?" Money nodded. "Well Maurice, I don't feel you're being my friend right now, but we can still make good on all of this," sliding a business card into his shirt pocket. "All you have to do is give me Black-Knight. He's out there somewhere. The son-of-a-bitch just hasn't peeked his head high enough to where I can see it."

Big Daddy 100 pounds heavier than 10 years ago was slowly approaching.

Money was looking up from the ground. "Mr. Bantz, I don't know where Black-Knight is. I'm telling you the truth."

"I know you don't know, but I want you to find him for me. I want you to keep your ear low to the ground. I'm giving you a pass to hustle these streets. Go on out there and make your money. Sell all the dope you want, get yourself a fancy car, fuck every broad you can until your dick falls off, I don't care. But, you will deliver Black-Knight to me. Understood, fair enough?" negotiated Conrad extending his hand to officiate his offer.

Instantly, Money began to fantasize about himself driving in a Cadillac truck and receiving a blowjob at the same time. Without a second thought, he latched onto Conrad's hand accepting the offer as he was pulled up.

"Besides Money, what else is a low-life like yourself gon'na do out here," finished Conrad. Money's face stiffened up.

Right then, Big Daddy approached.

"Ahh...Well if it ain't Money's cousin, Vernon Tarpley, a.k.a., Big Daddy," jokingly said Conrad pointing to his chest. "I've heard lots about you. The indictment papers are in the mail. We'll be seeing you soon," walking away.

Big Daddy's eyes widen like golf balls. "Yo' Money, who the fuck is he! What he mean indictment papers! What you tell him 'bout me?" he asked ready to swing on Money.

Money threw his hand. "Cut it out man. Oh, what? You think I'm some type of snitch or something Big Daddy? You're my own blood, my first cousin. This me man, Money Bunny. Act like you know. Ol' boy is a C.O. inside the prison, he just messin' with you. He knows your name because you're down as an emergency contact for me," he lied. "Now c'mon, lets go. I done did ten of the damnest years of my life here. I've stayed long enough.

Big Daddy squint his right eye. "Yeah, ok Money! Let me find out! I'm telling you!"

"Find out what Big Daddy?"

"You know what! You just let me find out," ended Big Daddy walking back towards the truck. Money followed.

****

Tywon and White Boy-J pulled up to Tywon's mother's house. De'Andre now in his early twenties came bolting out the door.

"Weph! I'm glad y'all back," he said walking towards the back of the car. "We out dog, totally dry, ain't none of the weed houses got shit in them. I was just about to go holler at the cripple dude up there at the car wash. He got pounds for $1800, but since y'all back, for get 'em. Open up," knocking on the trunk.

"For what?" said Tywon exiting the car. "It was another dry run thanks to you know who." They both then looked to J as if he was to blame.

"Awe, y'all ain't go'on put that on me. At least I did try," he explained.

De'Andre disgusted, shook his head. "Damn J, I thought white people were connected in the world. You might as well be black like us, 'cause you don't know shit!" he smirked.

Tywon laughed.

Upset with the statement, J took a seat on the porch. *"Man, that De'Andre is always talking trash. I don't see him making any effort to do nothing but run his mouth."*

Just then, a loud bass sound was heard beating up the block.

"That must be Big Daddy's fat ass coming this way?" said De'Andre. Tywon confirmed it seeing the truck.

"Yup, that's him."

Before Big Daddy completed his turn into the driveway, Tywon was yelling. "I know that ain't who I think it is! I know that ain't my homeboy!" smiling.

Before the truck even came to rest, Money hopped out. "Whut up though baby! Yo' boy is back...," giving Tywon handshakes and hugs.

"Damn clown," uttered Big Daddy.

Money then pointed. "I just know that ain't little De'Andre. Damn boy...you done, you...he's a grown man now Ty," he stated looking De'Andre up and down.

De'Andre not really wanting to, tried to give Money a simple handshake, but Money grabbed him taking a hug.

Releasing him, "Boy! You're like my lil' brother that I ain't seen in a long time. Damn I missed y'all."

"Yeah, and you're like my stepbrother that I would never trust," thought De'Andre concealing his feelings. De'Andre desperately tried to hold his composure, but just seeing this scoundrel Money standing in front of him, shot his mind back into the past.

"C'mon De'Anne, just one lil' kiss on it and then I'll leave you alone," begged Money with his penis in his hand.

"No...Money, stop it. Put it up and quit grabbing my head," warned De'Anne. "I told you, De'Andre's right upstairs."

Money smacked his lips. "De'Andre ain't comin' down here. I just left him. He's all into that video game up there. So c'mon nah, just suck on it a little."

"Are you deaf Money? I said no, now go'on and get your dick out of my face, ugh."

Money was pissed. He then stood back with his dick still in his hand starring at De'Anne. "This young bitch must don't know I will take that ass. 'Ol hoe, actin' like she's sanctified. She's lucky Ty my boy, otherwise I'd rape her ass and dump her body."

Now desperate and sexually frustrated, Money pulled out a 50 dollar bill and brandished it towards De'Anne. The crisp 50 caught her attention, but she quickly negotiated another $25. Without hesitation, Money put the cash in her hand. De'Anne then scooted on to the edge of the couch and took him in.

The anticipation already had Money's toes curling. He held his ass cheeks tightly together and gritted his teeth trying to hold back the feeling. He just couldn't figure how this girl so young was so skillful in what she did. With no hands, De'Anne slowly twirled her head with all of him positioned into the right side of her jaw. The moisture and slow grind of her mouth now had Money's eyes blinking along with drool that was escaping his lips. Only one minute and a half into the session and numbness already was starting to set into Money.

No, no, oh please no, strongly he thought, holding himself back. Amazingly, it was working. Money then made the mistake of watching De'Anne's top lip slowly retract back and fourth off of him. The sight was so seductive holding back was no longer an option.

Just then, "Money! Hey Money!" called 10-year-old De'Andre. "Where are you?"

From hearing the startling sound of her younger brother's voice, De'Anne tried to pull of Money, but Money wouldn't have it. He strong-armed her head into place until every last drop of him was gone. De'Anne fell to the floor spitting and throwing up just as De'Andre arrived at the edge of the stairs.

Looking over the railing, "De'Anne! What's wrong? What's the matter?" he asked sprinting down the stairs.

Money was bent over De'Anne looking as if he was consoling her.

As De'Andre approached, he could see the $75 laying in the vomit along with a clear-white, snot looking substance.

Confused to it all, *Why is that money in her throw-up? And what's that weird looking white stuff?*" He then knelled down to his sister. "De'Anne?" questionably he called.

De'Anne said nothing. Afterwards, De'Andre looked to Money who mysteriously had a dried up glazed looking film across his hands. From further inspection, he noticed Money's pants to be unzipped with his pubic hairs slightly exposed. Suddenly, De'Anne bolted form the floor to the bathroom, crying. The last image of that dreadful incident De'Andre remembered was Money fixing his pants, walking out of the front door telling him to take care of his sister. De'Andre didn't understand what happened that day, but he did now as he stood feeling he could just whoop Money's ass.

Tywon directed Money's attention towards the porch. "Money, that's my partner J. The coolest white boy you'd ever meet."

White Boy-J threw up his hand. "What's up Money? Tywon told me all about you. You're a wild boy."

Money paused for a second, grimly looking White Boy-J up and down sizing him up. "*Ppsss... this white boy don't know me.*" He then nonchalantly nodded turning back to Tywon.

Well fuck you too, thought J grabbing his crotch.

"Yeah man, but it's good to be home, that's all I can say. A Ty, you still kickin' it with baby girl?" asked Money.

"Who, O'Sha? Yeah... naw... yeah... Shit, I don't know what it is. Right now, we're beefing."

"Oh," responded Money, feeling he now had a chance for O'Sha. He then snapped his fingers. Excitedly, "Awe... what about her sister, that fine ass bitch Octavia? That heifer was a freak. Man...I use ta'..."

As Money was into detail, White Boy-J stood. That was twice Money had already rubbed him the wrong way. Hearing enough, he retired inside the house. Tywon then nudged Money.

"Cool it man. Octavia was J's lady. I told you that in one of the letters I sent you."

"All man, bump that white boy. You said the key word 'Was his lady.' He knows what she was when he got with her. That's his dumb-ass fault. He needs to be on his own side of town anyway. Looking like an albino monkey in the ghetto," he laughed. "You feel me?"

Tywon didn't at all like Money's comment. He felt the statements were disrespectful.

Stepping closer, "Hold on Money, J is cool, you're the one who ain't been around in a while. I can see jail ain't changed you a bit. On the real, you need to check yourself. And you need to apologize to my man J."

"Apologize! To who, the white boy? Man, that white boy can kiss my ass. I ain't apologizing to him. And anyway, who is you Ty? His damn daddy or somethin?"

Tywon looked to Big Daddy who hadn't said a word since arriving. Big Daddy simply hunched his shoulders, shaking his head, as to say, *'Ain't no hope for him.'*

Money continued, "So now what? Y'all siding wit' the white boy over me now? I done lost my spot with y'all?" he stated eyeing everyone. "Money done did ten years in the joint, so he's threw, he's finished is what y'all thinking now, right? Ok, alright then, it's cool. I'ma show all of y'all," walking backwards towards the truck.

Tywon exhaled. "Money, you're trippin.' It ain't even..."

"Naw, naw Ty! You said it loud and clear my friend. I'm on my own now. Like I said before, it's cool, I understand. The white boy is the new Money in the crew now," hopping inside the truck. "C'mon Big Daddy, take me to see my momma before I go to the halfway house."

To hell with him then, thought Tywon reaching inside the trunk. Let Money's ass think what he wants to think."

De'Andre saw his brother grab a packet of cash. He immediately whispered to him. "Ty! I just know you ain't finna give this fool no money? After all that shit he just talked to us? Fuck him, leave his ass broke."

"Dre, Money just got out after doing ten years. He ain't got nothing. Regardless of what he said, he's still family," expressed Tywon.

"Mmph, family don't fuck around with other family members."

"Huh? What you say?"

"Nothing man, nothing."

Tywon walked over to the passenger side of the Escalade. "Money, you got the whole situation all wrong, but hey, it seems your mind is already made. Who am I to argue with that? So here bro," handing Money the packet containing $5000. "That's some start up cash to get you going since you fell like you're so alone."

Money was totally surprised. He didn't know what to say. He badly wanted to say, *'Thank you,'* but his dumb pride stood in the way.

"Ok Money, take care of yourself and be safe. Alright then Big Daddy, talk to you later," finished Tywon tapping the door, walking away.

Money had that, *'I just lost my best friend look on his face.'* He was now wishing he had a rewind button to reverse this whole day.

As Big Daddy was pulling out of the driveway, Money noticed De'Andre had his middle finger up towards him. Money did nothing to counter the action. He only stared at the cash Tywon put in his hand feeling as if he was just bought to go away.

Feeling his old friends put him down, Money looked up an old familiar lady friend of his own: China White. China bragged to Money about how over the last 10 years, she's traveled the world. She claimed to have mixed and mingled with men and women of different races, creeds and colors. Money seemed intrigued by China's adventurous stories as she licked him around his nose. Money there after enquired about Lady Rock, but China warned him about what happened the last time they met. Fearing Lady Rock's destructive effects, he dismissed the thought. Money however did invite another friend to listen to China's adventurous stories: Tootsie. Tootsie at first accused China of falsifying her ventures. He wasn't convinced about the things she said people do while in her presence. But after further conversation alone with China, Tootsie found himself in love. He claimed no other woman in the world touched his heart like she had. Soon, she became the number one priority in his life. Such a priority, at times, Money hates that he even introduced the two.

Money was standing on the porch of the blow house when he knocked on the door. The mail shoot on the security door popped open.

"What you need," the person on the other side asked.

"Gim'me a gram," replied Money.

"They're a $100."

"Damn, a $100!"

Down to his last $300, Money peeled off five 20's sticking it inside the mail shoot. When the shoot reopened, he received his package. He then hopped back into the passenger seat of the car Tootsie was driving.

"Did you get it?" asked Tootsie.

Money aggravated, "What you think, I was on the porch asking for a job? Yeah, I've got it."

"Chill man, I'm just asking," pulling from the curb.

Taking a deep breath, "Naw man, I'm just frustrated. My boys done cut me loose. My cousin won't fuck with me, he thinks I'm hot. I'm living in a halfway house, I'm broke again. And the worst thing is I'm about to be working at a car wash with yo' dumbass. Can things get worse for me?"

"Thanks but no thanks Money. You can ride the misery train alone," replied Tootsie. Disgusted by his life, Money sunk deeper into his seat.

It was only a total of three weeks since Tywon handed Money the $5000. After continuously getting high, partying, tricking, and just spending money like it grew on trees, Money found himself down to his last $200. Having nothing to show for his spent cash or a back up plan, Money decided to take on a job at a local car wash.

Pulling into the car wash, "We're right on time Ty. The car wash jumpin'," excitedly said Tootsie. "We can make some real good tips, c'mon man."

"For real!" acted Money as if he too was excited. "Well, what are we waiting on Tootsie? Lets go!"

Tootsie hurried from the car. He quickly grabbed a wash-mitt and went to work.

Fuck out'ta here, thought Money laying back in the passenger seat. *I ain't no damn slave, washing nobody's car.*

A half hour had passed, still lying back with his arm covering his eyes, Money heard someone approach the car. He assumed it was Tootsie. "Did you get rich yet?" he asked.

"I've been rich, but I doubt if you will be just sittin' around on your ass," cockily an unfamiliar voice responded.

Money lifted from the seat. He first laid eyes on the man's familiar face but couldn't quite place it. Then down to this paralyzed legs and at the wheelchair that supported him. The man's lip curled.

"Brother man, you're starring at me like you ain't never seen nobody in a wheelchair before."

"Oh, my fault," apologized Money exiting the car. "But I know you from somewhere."

"Yeah, you look familiar too, but check it, if you came to work for me, then that's what I need for you to do. I've got a lot of people lined up to get their cars washed. If you're down, then lets get on it. And then we can talk about where we know each other from later, cool?"

"Ok" agreed Money seeing the guy was straightforward.

Money picked up a wash-mitt and began his job. After cleaning a few cars, the job didn't seem so bad. And the tips were pretty good too. Money made $25 after washing only four cars. *This might work out."* Just then, "Bump! Bump! Bump! Bump! Bump! Boooomm...!" carried the extended bass line.

"Damn...!" simultaneously expressed everyone turning around. The white Escalade pulled into the car wash like it was a monster truck. It was Big Daddy accompanied by De'Andre who was bouncing to the music.

At the first sight of the two, Money ducked down and ran like shots were being fired. He couldn't allow himself to be seen, not like this, not working at a car wash. Especially not after Tywon just gave him $5000 to get back onto his feet. He'd rather die than to face up to the embarrassment.

Money quickly cut through the lounging area where customers were awaiting their cars and into the bathroom where he slammed and locked the door behind himself.

"Weph, he must got'ta go bad," said a lady. "He sure does," giggled another.

But that wasn't on Rowe's mind, the man who sat in the wheelchair. It was déjàvu for him when Money enclosed himself inside the bathroom, it reminded Rowe of where he knew him from.

"That's the kid who was in Ed's Night Lounge that night, in the storage room. Damn, after all these years. I gos'ta call Black-Knight about this."

Just as he picked up the phone, "What's up Rowe?" greeted both Big Daddy and De'Andre in unison.

Hanging up the phone pointing, "Hey fellas, meet me around the back."

In the back stashed away in his van, Rowe showed Big Daddy and De'Andre three large bundles of marijuana, equivalent to 100 pounds. The three wrapped packages all had numbers on them specifying their weight. Big Daddy whipped out his knife, cutting into one of the packages.

The marijuana he pulled out was light green, fluffy, and it smelled good. "Damn...Rowe. This shit like popcorn. This shit smell like it's straight off the farm. You must got'ta hella'va connect. You keep some good ass weed," admired Big Daddy.

Rowe shook his head, "Yeah..."

De'Andre agreed, but he was concerned with the price, hopping it was less than the usual $1800.

Rowe then quickly made up a fabricated story of what it took for this particular type of marijuana to end up in his hands. "He yelled out an inflated price of $2000. The two looked at Rowe like he was crazy.

"Damn Rowe, I see why everybody quit messin' with you. Your prices are ridiculous," said De'Andre.

Rowe countered the usual $1800. De'Andre pressed for $1700. Rowe wasn't budging. Big Daddy then stepped in. He agreed to Rowe's $1800 price tag if he would front another 50 pounds at the same price.

Rowe agreed to the deal not wanting to take the chance of the Police or robbers hitting his stash.

To keep the attention low, Rowe handed De'Andre the keys to his van. "Bring it back after y'all unload." De'Andre refused giving Rowe back his keys.

"I ain't driving that handicap van. That's like walking on another man crutches; It's bad luck. We got it Rowe."

Big Daddy pulled his truck up next to the van. De'Andre loaded the truck with the weed. Big Daddy counted out $90,000 to Rowe. The two then went on their way.

Ass-holes, thought Rowe watching the truck pull away. Rowe was wheeling himself back into the lounge, when he saw Money coming out of the bathroom, suspiciously looking around.

"A partner!" he called. Money was startled. "You've been in there all that time?"

"Uh...yeah" answered Money.

"Did you spray? Like I told all the other workers, from now on, if you got'ta shit. You go across the street to the McDonald's."

"Ok," said Money putting up his thumb. "Got you," walking away. Rowe then called Black-Knight to tell him about Money, but he didn't answer the phone.

Stepping outside, "Where you been?" asked Tootsie. "Man, you're missing all the action. I done made $30 in tips already."

Money wasn't concerned with no tips. He was making sure Big Daddy and De'Andre were long gone. He then went back to work periodically looking around.

After the car wash closed, Money and Tootsie counted up their earnings. They made a total of $180 between themselves. They had plans of grabbing a bite to eat, then afterwards going to the blow house. They both hopped in the car ready to pull off when Rowe called out.

"A! A man! I didn't catch your name," rolling up to the passenger's window.

"Money, my name is Money," replied Money.

That's right, Money Bunny, he thought to himself. "Ok Money, nice job today." *Besides that long ass bathroom break.* "Are you and Tootsie coming back tomorrow?"

Money looked to Tootsie. Tootsie shook his head.

"Yeah, we'll be here," finished Money. They then took off.

Cut Me In, Or Cut It Out

It was now six months since Money had been out of prison and working at the car wash. In this time, he made the position of manager. He ran the car wash like it was his own. He always made sure supplies were in full stock and the customers were happy. This new prioritized position made Tootsie a little envious of Money. He felt he should've had that position, especially since he was the one who turned Money on to the job.

It was also evident to Tootsie that Money and Rowe had become very close. Money was now his right hand man. Whatever Rowe needed done, Money handled it. Not long after, Rowe gave him the job of serving the customers who bought pounds of marijuana. This gave Money a chance to familiarize himself with the weed pushers. Within one month's time, Money counted a half of a million dollars that passed through his hands into Rowe's. Money knew it was money in the marijuana game but not like that.

Shit, I'm handling all this grip and ain't none of it's mine?

Right then, Money quit getting high and began strategizing a plan. He was ready to get paid, but he'd just been invited into the game. He didn't want to rock the boat by pushing Rowe's hand too fast. So, Money continued serving and closely observing and making crumbs.

Then one day, Big Daddy and De'Andre pulled into the car wash looking to cop a hundred pounds.

Stepping inside, "What's up Rowe?" spoke the pair.

"Alright now, what's going on fellas, y'all boys' alright? Where's my man Tywon?" asked Rowe.

"Ty good, we chilin'," simply returned Big Daddy.

A brief silence filled the room. Everyone stood looking at one another.

Playfully, "We're waiting Rowe, c'mon and roll your cripple ass out here and serve us before we rob yo' old ass, said De'Andre.

From out of nowhere, Rowe pulled out a 9 millimeter pistol and a 45 automatic. "Unless a muthafucka wanna be sittin' in one of the chairs or worse, he'll think twice about robbing me."

"Damn!" De'Andre bust out laughing. Big Daddy smirked at the playful scene but knew Rowe was somewhat serious.

"But hold on, my man Money gon'na hook y'all up," finished Rowe.

He then called Money's name. Big Daddy and De'Andre looked at each other. *Money? Naw, couldn't be*, they thought.

Money doing inventory check had no idea of Big Daddy's and De'Andre's presence. If he had, he would've directed Rowe to serve the two himself.

Money stepped out. "What you need Rowe? I was in back checkin' the..." his words died as he laid eyes on Big Daddy and De'Andre. The two did double takes making sure it was Money they were looking at.

Rowe eyed them all with questionable thoughts. "Do all y'all know each other or something?"

Big Daddy as usual said nothing. He couldn't bring himself to claim his own cousin. Though unable to prove it, his gut was still telling him Money was a snitch. De'Andre on the other hand couldn't hold it back. He smirked with a grunt. "Money? Yeah...we know 'Ol Money. We know Money real well." he emphasized. "He knows Tywon too."

All shit! thought Money. *This young punk finna fuck up all my plans.*

De'Andre continued, "Rowe, if it's one thing I can say about this guy right here. He's the best car wash manager you ever had. Money be having your people clean the shit out of some rims. You need to keep this cat on your team."

Rowe smiled happy to know his choice in manager was appreciated. Big Daddy stood looking out the window wondering how long would it be until the feds raided the car wash, and were his indictment papers really in the mail. De'Andre stood hoping his positive words about Money would help get the price reduced on the weed. And

Money, he was thinking how much of a threat Big Daddy and De'Andre were to his plans. He didn't need any of his past life surfacing around Rowe's ears.

"Money, take care of these guys for me, will you?" asked Rowe. "These are Tywon's boys, good customers. In fact, whatever they buy, you front them the same, they always pay."

De'Andre smiled. He now felt no need to hustle the price. Big Daddy was cool with the front as well, but he wasn't about to allow himself to be seen in no type of drug transaction with Money. Handing De'Andre the truck keys, he walked out front. Money let out a loud huff, really not wanting to do the deal.

"C'mon man." He and De'Andre then headed out the backdoor.

At the van, De'Andre couldn't stop smiling. Money looked.

"What are you grinning at?"

"You, I'm trying to figure out how you worked your slick ass here into this spot. This could be a gold mine for you if you work it right. Yeah...you in, but I can see you ain't all the way in."

Defensively, "What! What do your young ass know?"

"I know Rowe cripple ass ain't the man like everybody thinks he is. Shit, this B.K. weed. And I know you didn't want me or Big Daddy to know you're up here serving half the city."

"Hell naw I didn't, especially not you. The last time you saw me, your finger was up saying, 'Fuck you,'" imitated Money.

De'Andre huffed. "Damn right. That was for the shit you did to De'Anne years ago. Had my sister sucking on yo' grown ass dick and all. You knew she was under aged. She ain't worth a damn now," looking at the ground shaking his head.

Money said nothing, he just continued checking the weight and unloading the packages. De'Andre then dropped the bomb.

"You did the same shit to my momma too, only it was for a few rocks. That was fucked up Money. I was young, but I saw things." Suddenly, Money stopped. The blood rushed to his face. He felt as if he was about to pass out. He couldn't believe how bluntly De'Andre spoke about the incidents: Like it wasn't shit to him.

"Do you know how that feels as a kid Money? Kids teasing you and shit; 'Your momma's a crack head, your momma's a crack-head,' they would sing. 'No she ain't! Stop sayin' that,' I would yell back. But I knew it was true. Hey...fuck it though. If you didn't serve Faye, she just would've got it from somewhere else, right Money? It's just part of the game, you know?"

Money was fucked up. He turned to De'Andre not knowing what to say. De'Andre had delivered some head crushing blows from the past but he wasn't threw yet. Rowe looking out of the back window couldn't hear their conversation, but he knew it was more than just a car wash relationship they had. He then went to answer the ringing phone.

Money continued, "De'Andre man, I'm... I'm..."

"Uh, uh, Money, hold those thoughts," said De'Andre who was looking inside the van to the plentiful packages of marijuana. "In fact, no need for an apology, 'cause the way I'm hearing it, you got'ta bad case of diarrhea of the mouth. You got white folks in suits hanging 'round you. I'm not saying it's true, but if word like that gets to Rowe, then you might lose this here gold mine or worse. So, on top of the 200 pounds you got laying there, throw in an extra 20 pounds just between you and me."

I can't believe this punk is trying to shake me down. But Money knew he had no leverage for negotiations. He slyly looked up at the back window. There was no sign of Rowe. He then grabbed a 20-pound package of marijuana placing it on top with the other load.

Money pointed, "Alright you dirty mutha..."

"Money!" called Rowe interrupting him.

Shit! Busted.

"Telephone man, some dude about an apartment you trying to get?"

Relieved, "Oh, ok. I'll be right there."

Money turned back to De'Andre. "Stay here, I'll be right back." He then retired to the phone. Picking up the receiver, "Hello?"

"Long time no hear slick. Where you been? Did you find my guy yet?" asked the man on the line. Money cringed at the tone of the voice.

Frantically whispering, "How did you find...Where you...Why you calling me here?" he asked looking out the window.

"I'm checking on your progress," answered Conrad Bantz. "It's been six months, you know? What do you got for me?"

"Uh...nothing right now. Still asking around, plus I just got out the halfway house. I'm just working now."

"Yeah, I see. What are you guys selling in there? That place is busier than any other car wash I know."

"Nothing man, just some joints on the side. Everything is cool."

"Ok Money, you still have my card right?" Money called out the number. "That's correct."

Conrad then told Money he would be checking back soon. Money hung up the phone filled with anxiety. He took a few breaths to regain his composure. He suddenly, remembered, "Dre!"

He ran back outside only to see Rowe had already wrapped things up. Money was more worried than ever, hoping Rowe didn't add up the weight of the packages.

Holding the door open, "Everything cool Rowe?" asked Money.

"Fine," he replied, rolling himself back inside the lounge.

Money stayed outside. He pulled out a cigarette and lit it. He inhaled and exhaled the cigarette into extinction, thinking how messed up this day had been for him. He felt his come-up plans were in deep jeopardy, but the time was now to put it into effect.

Money approached Rowe telling him, he felt it was now time for him to be pulled in closer to the business, or even be made a partner. Rowe simply told Money he wasn't ready. Money insisted that he was. He voiced to Rowe, he had restructuring plans on how things should be ran around there, especially for their safety. He said serving customers out the van was all wrong. Any one with enough nerve and firepower could just demand the keys and the entire load would be lost. He then spoke of Rowe's high prices that were pushing customers away making them find new connections, some even taking their own trips to Arizona.

"I'm ready Rowe, pull me in. I know the in and the outs," Money ended, just knowing his speech was bond.

Rowe looked at Money, he knew he was right. He knew his product was wide open to thieves and his prices were high. He also knew folks were finding new connections and making their own trips. But Rowe was old-school, he didn't care as long as he got his slice of the pie. And he definitely didn't like anyone trying to tell him how to run his business.

"Money, you just ain't ready," again said Rowe.

Money was heartbroken. He didn't understand. "C'mon Rowe man, I've earned it."

"Money let me explain something to you. Anytime a customer has to tell me my server gave him more product than he paid for, then I have a problem with that server."

Nervously, "Hugh, what are you talking 'bout Rowe?"

I'm talking about Tywon's little brother, De'Andre. He added the weight of the weed as he loaded into the truck. He found that yo' ass gave him 20-pounds too much and gave it back to me. Shit, if that was me, my ass whud'da been gone with that extra 20. That would've been over $35,000 out my pocket!" angrily slapping his leg. "Now, I'm through with it Money! You ain't ready!"

Money stormed out of the back door, pissed off. Rapidly pacing back and fourth, *"Ow... I can't believe I fell for that shit! That young punk set me up. It's personal between me and De'Andre now. And this ol' cripple bastard Rowe talkin' 'bout I ain't ready yet. Bitch, I was born ready, he's the one who ain't ready. Thinkin' I don't know who his ass is. I knew who he was from the first day I saw him. I never forget a face. And it's too bad for Rowe he can't hold his liquor. I'm quite sure Black-Knight would like to hear who Rowe thinks is responsible for his brother, K.G.'s death."* Money snarled. *"Yeah... it's only a matter of time. I'ma take over all this shit."*

* *

"Please, give her a big round of applause. I like to welcome our guest speaker here today, Faye Nelson," ended the counselor.

Faye walked out on stage up to the podium. The crowd along with Tywon, De'Anne, Francine and Gladys, stationed in the front row, were already standing and clapping. Faye nodded to the members of N.A., *Narcotics Anonymous.*

"Thank you, thank you. But give yourselves a big round of applause as well for attending this meeting. It's a struggle itself just coming here, I know."

The members all clapped for themselves. Faye scanned over the 20 or more people sitting in the chairs.

"Alright, wow. It's bad to say, but I haven't seen some of these faces in so long, I thought they were dead," she laughed along with the crowd. "But seriously, hi! I'm Faye Nelson, an addict. Clean for 10 years, yet still an addict."

"Hi Faye...!" they all greeted together.

"I'm here on behalf of Harbor-Light Treatment Center, other addicts, and for the love of life to tell my story."

"Alright now!"

"Go'on 'head girl!"

"Well, my drug addiction started with pills. From that first pill I swallowed, I was told my roller coaster ride had just begun. Me, being young, fine, naive and thinkin' I knew it all, didn't take heed to the warning. From the pills, I graduated to cocaine. From the cocaine, I received my P.H.D. in smoking crack," Faye smiled. "Baby, when I put that pipe to my lips and that haze of blue smoke left my mouth, there was nothing you could tell me. I was the cracks hoe and that pipe was my pimp. What I'm saying is, I liked getting high. It made me feel perfect inside. It gave me fantasy away from the real world. Away from the problems and the bullshit, excuse me."

"Uh, uh, you alrite, tell it how it is!" she heard from the members.

"You know? And using drugs also done took me in some dark places. I done had my ass kicked up and down the street. Hit in the head with bottles, kicked, cut, stabbed twice, and my teeth cracked. But y'all would thank from hearin' all that I would be ready to quit, right?"

"Naw..."

" Nope..."

"Uh, uh, you wasn't ready."

"Y'all know it, y'all been there before, I wasn't," she agreed. "It wasn't until I saw the bottom start to fall out from under me that I was ready. But still, I continued to get high. I pawned the TV's, the stereo, my vacuum cleaner. Hell, I even tried to pawn my pots and pans."

Faye pointed. "I stole from my sisters, my kids, I tricked, licked, sucked, you name it, I did it for the high."

Embarrassed, Tywon put his head down in his lap. He felt his mother's last statement was too much information. De'Anne paid it no mind, she and the counselor were to busy winking at one another. And Francine and Gladys didn't care what their sister said, they both were just glad she was off drugs.

Faye continued, "But then one day, I escaped this huge apartment fire with minor scratches and bruises. Even though I survived the blaze, I couldn't help but to think of my get high money that burned with the apartment, *'Careful not to mention the whore Wanda, and her boyfriend Charles, who died in the fire.'* Right then, I knew it was time for some help. That near tragic incident made me realize I was in love with life, I wanted to live. I wanted to wake up in the morning, smell fresh air, and have breakfast with my children. I couldn't do that chasing that high all night."

"Mmm, mmph, sho caint!" chimed the audience.

"But y'all know what? It still ain't a day that goes by that I don't think about getting high. There's only one reason that I can think of why I should: Because I like it. But, I have a million and one other reasons just to say no. My disease is Crack-Cocaine. It still calls me. It still knocks, and it's still in them streets killing. I know some of y'all who have one or two days clean, or even a month are saying, wow! Ten years clean, she's strong. And the answer is no. I'm not strong, in fact, I'm just of flesh and blood like the rest of you. The only difference is, I'm in love with life, and you can be too. Now, I don't care who you are, what you done, or who you done it to. If you want help, I personally, along with the counselor here," she looked. "Will ride the road to recovery with you, one day at a time. But first, you have to accept God. You have to have a conscious contact with him, and again get to understand him. I did. I sought him through medication and prayer. It's time for your spiritual awakening people. Please, carry this message with you to other addicts and practice these principles in all of your affairs," putting up two fingers, "I'm Faye Nelson. Peace, God bless, and I love you all," she ended blowing a kiss to the crowd.

The N.A. members all stood giving Faye a standing ovation. Whistling could be heard throughout the room. Faye and the counselor hugged. As the two released, Francine and Gladys were already up on stage. They too wanted to congratulate their sister on her speech.

De'Anne sat in her chair focused on the counselor who just head-nodded her, directing her to meet him in the hallway. Tywon twisted his lips, picking up on the counselor's gesture.

De'Anne 'ol freak ass will talk to anybody she think has a dollar. She go'on learn the hard way. Simultaneously, Tywon's cell phone rang. He picked up walking out into the hallway himself.

"J! What's crackin' baby? Tell me somethin' good."

"Everythang is everythang Ty. We plugged. Five dollars a peezie," White Boy-J coded for $500 per pound.

Excited, "For real! Awe, hell yeah! It's on now! Ain't no turning back from here. We fin'na come up hard. Yeah boy! Yeah!" *Damn, Let me calm down,* seeing that he was getting loud. "So J, how did you find a connect out there in Arizona?"

As White Boy-J went into detail, Tywon was watching De'Anne across the hallway who was smiling all in the counselor's face. Suddenly, her smile took a stiff look as she laid eyes upon another man coming up the hallway. *What she starring at?*

Puzzled, Tywon focused on the gentleman himself. The man was clean and dapper and walked with a slight limp. Tywon was just about to dismiss him as one of De'Anne's infatuations until he took a closer look.

Surprised, *"That's..."*

DEX

"Hello Tywon, hey De'Anne," the man waived entering the N.A. meeting. Tywon hung up on J, forgetting he was on the phone. He and De'Anne then followed the man back into the meeting.

Faye was speaking to the N.A. members when she suddenly heard a commotion at the entrance. Francine and Gladys were telling the gentleman he wasn't welcome there. Faye immediately rushed over.

"Hey! Hey! Please, calm down," she said to her sisters. "I invited Ronnie here today to speak. He's a recovering addict too, you know? He has a right to be here. This is important to him."

"I don't care what's important to him. He's nothing but a servant of the devil," voiced Gladys tightly holding her bible. "Mmph Faye, I guess you done forgot about the past?"

Ronnie was about to defend himself when Francine blurted out. "I ain't forgot, and I still got one with Ronnie's name on it," inviting him to step outside.

A few N.A. members laughed.

Tywon snickered himself admiring his aunts' heart, but he knew this conflict needed refereeing. He first calmed his hostile aunts, then De'Anne who started barking on the ass end of the argument. He explained to the trio what happened in the house was 15 years ago. He said in that time span people sometimes change. Tywon gazed towards Ronnie. He quickly scanned over the burn scare on his face, left from the hot pot of water from years earlier. He then looked back to the upset ladies. He said sometimes when the fight is over, the scars still remain, and even though our minds will never forget, our hearts are willing to forgive. "I'm sure if y'all give Ronnie a second to repent, you'll see him in a different light. He's De'Andre's dad. Give him a chance?" asked Tywon.

De'Anne, Francine, nor Gladys rejected. Tywon then offered Ronnie the floor. As Ronnie poured his heart out to the angry trio, Tywon pulled Faye a side.

"Ma, I think it's cool that Ronnie's coming back around. I mean, for De'Andre's sake." Faye smiled. "I also think every son wants to know who his father is, no matter how old he gets. You understand me Ma?"

Uh, oh. Faye knew where this conversation was leading.

"We'll talk later Ty," she said attempting to walk away.

Tywon grabbed her arm. "No Ma, now. I've waited long enough."

Faye exhaled as she took a seat. She knew Tywon was right. He had waited long enough. Faye gently stroked his face. She then began a candy-coated version of she and Ed's relationship. She spoke highly of Ed. She only spoke of his positive side to deter any resentment Tywon may have felt from hearing the truth. She dared not to mention that Ed at first denied Tywon. She also failed to mention that in later years Ed wanted to claim him. Faye told Tywon she could see traits of his father in him: His dedication, his drive and his leadership skills. Tywon smiled. She also compared their doggish ways towards women, which she didn't like. Tywon simply hunched his shoulders saying, "It's in the blood." After speaking so highly of Ed, Faye told Tywon she banned their relationship because of Ed's lifestyle. The game he played was dangerous, at the same time influential. She didn't want him growing up being a part of that. Upset, Tywon argued her different. He voiced to his mother that she was wrong and selfish and should have allowed their relationship to be.

"Maybe," she somewhat agreed. "But who told you about selling marijuana Tywon? Who told you it was ok or safer than selling any other drug?"

'Who told you about using crack Ma?' he wanted to say.

Tywon didn't answer his mother's question, but Faye knew it was Ed.

She continued, "And now, whose younger brother is running around the city buying up hundreds of pounds of weed and managing four and five weed houses? Who is he doing for, and where did he learn it from?" asked Faye. Tywon still remained silent. "It's simple Tywon: Influence from your surroundings. It's a cycle, that's all I'm saying son. You're a grown man now, and this is the game you've chose to play. But ask your-self," with a frowned expression. "How long can I continue to play the game, before the game plays on me?"

Faye stood. She then headed back over to De'Anne, Francine, Gladys and Ronnie who all were releasing from a group hug.

DEX

Tywon sat confused. *How in the hell did we go from discussing who my daddy is, to De'Andre selling weed for me?* he thought missing Faye's point. He then called White Boy-J back.

"Yo!" answered J.

"J, how long before the shipment arrives?" asked Tywon.

"About a week, we're still getting the transportation together. I'm flying home in a few days to give you all the details."

"Alright. Me, De'Andre and Big Daddy will be waiting for you," hanging up the phone.

****

Money along with the help of Tootsie was putting his plan into effect. The two were out plotting robberies against Rowe's marijuana customers whom Money had served many times. The pair had circled a particular block five times, now coming to a stop. Money leaned onto the steering wheel. "Are you sure this is the house?" he asked looking up at the address.

"Yeah, I'm sure. I checked ol' boys registration when I was cleaning his car," replied Tootsie. "And, I went and got keys made from his key ring just like you told me to."

"Good, now we go'on do this fast and smooth, so nobody gets hurt. This cat bought 150 pounds from me four days ago, so I'm sure he's sold most of it by now. I over heard him telling Rowe that every night, he takes his baby son out for a 9:30p.m. car ride to make him sleep."

Tootsie laughed. "Lil' bastard won't shut up, huh?"

Money then checked the time. "9:30."

Like clockwork, the man and his child exited the house and rode off. Rubbing his hands together, "Alright Toot, lets g..."

Money slapped the cocaine capsule from Tootsie's hand. "What did I tell you 'bout that gettin' high shit! Are you trying to get me killed? You got'ta be focused man?"

Tootsie gave Money a look he never saw before. "Don't you ever do that again, and I do what I wan'na do. I'm grown. I like getting high. If you don't like it Money, then find someone else to help you do these robberies."

Money could see he was losing control of Tootsie. *That China White got 'em.* He knew part of it was also due to his position at the car wash that Tootsie felt he should've had. *This petty thinking muthafucka.'* Money still pushed his authority.

"You heard what I said Toot. Now let's go."

Parked three houses down, Money armed with a pistol and Tootsie with an assault riffle, crept along the grass and onto the porch.

Money whispered, "Where's the hand gun Toot? Why you got that big ass chopper?"

Tootsie smiled from behind his mask. "You never got too much fire power."

They began fumbling the keys trying to gain entry inside the home, when the wife, thinking it was her husband without checking, opened the door. Money and Tootsie busted in rushing her to the floor.

"Where's the money! Where it at bitch!" they ranted making her assume an, 'X' style position across the floor. She was so choked up she could barely speak. The large gun Tootsie held to her head was terrifying.

Money checked all the rooms, making sure no one else was in the house. *All clear.* He then rushed back to the front room.

"Listen baby, we just want the money. Give us what we want and we go'on." She pointed to the bedroom. There, Money flipped, tossed and tore up everything in the room coming up with only $8,000. He pocketed the money and went back into the front-room.

"I'aint find shit in that room! She thank we playin' man! Beat her ass!"

"No... please, no..." she cried.

Just as Tootsie began attacking the woman, "Bbooomm!" Money shot; missing the woman's three year-old daughter who startled him only by inches. "Where'd that baby come from!" said Money. "I didn't see her before."

The way the woman rushed over and held her child, touched Money. "Damn, this ain't for me. C'mon, lets get out of here."

Just as they were about to leave, the headlights of a vehicle pulling into the driveway shined through the front window.

"It's him," said Tootsie stepping back. He then pointed the chopper at the woman and her child, threatening to cut them both down if she screamed. Her tears stated her plea.

Money cracked open the front door, just as the wife did before. When the man entered his home, he received the shock of his life. He was nothing but cooperative. He told Money about the $8,000 in the bedroom which Money still denied finding, but it was enough to suspiciously raise Tootsie's eye browse.

"That's all I've got," the man insisted.

Money head nodded Tootsie, who began kicking and stomping the woman senseless. The children couldn't do anything but cry. After hearing five minutes of torment from his family, the man finally gave in. He directed the pair into the basement. There, he opened a large dummy space inside the furnace with over the $300,000 in it.

Jackpot! "Now see, wasn't that easy?" said Money.

Disgusted, the man rolled his eyes.

"No need for attitude partner, you've got 60 pounds of re-up weed right over there," he pointed

Still high, Tootsie tied the couple up with telephone cord. Money bagged up the cash, while the children were left to roam free.

The two then headed out the door. Overwhelmed by the biggest lick they'd ever hit, Money and Tootsie hauled ass to the car. Tootsie hopped in on the passenger side, as Money opened the back door, tossing the bag on the seat. He then opened the driver's door when suddenly, someone ran from behind the car putting the gun to the back of his head.

"Break bread muthafucka! Y'all boy's fin'na eat good. Cut me in or cut it out!"

"Huh?" softly spoke Money scared and confused.

"You heard me! I didn't stutter!"

Money was stalling just knowing at anytime, Tootsie was going to cut the perpetrator down.

Tootsie then leaned over the driver's seat with the chopper.

"Quit bullshittin' man. Do 'em and lets go," he said.

Awe man, it's a set up. Money closed his eyes and grit his teeth, waiting on the shot to end his life. Then weirdly, he heard laughter.

"Toot, look at your boy. All hunched over, shittin' his pants." Tootsie chuckled.

Somewhat relieved by the laughter, Money turned around and to his surprise, it was Sean from prison.

Just then, the man who was supposedly tied up in the basement ran onto his porch with an AK-47. "Wwhhockk! Wwhhockk! Wwhhockk! Wwhhockk! Wwhhockk! Wwhhockk! Wwhockk!" he shot.

"Ddoommm!!! Ting! Ting! Ting! Ping!" sounded the bullets ripping and cutting into the car.

Money and Sean dropped to the ground. Tootsie tucked himself under the dashboard. The bullets continued to fly. Suddenly, the firing stopped.

Crying, "No baby, please stop! Just let them go!" pleaded the man's wife trying to pull him from the porch. That's when Tootsie jumped out with chopper, squeezing the trigger.

"Ssscccrrr!! Ssscccrrr!!" squealed the rear wheels of the airplane awakening Money. *Damn, we here already?* he thought wiping the drool from his mouth.

"Enjoy your stay here in Arizona," said the flight stewardess as he exited the plane.

"Thanks." *Eeww..., she was fine.*

Money strolled through the airport with his overnight bag finding his way out front. There, he hopped in a cab.

Looking in his rearview mirror, "Where to buddy?" asked the cab driver.

"Ugh...take me to..." Money looked on a piece of paper with the directions. "To the Ameri-Suites Hotel off I-17 highway."

"You got it."

As the driver began pulling off, Money looked to another cab pulling up. *Is that White B...* A passing bus blocked any further view. He wasn't sure, but the person he saw looked to be White Boy-J. He dismissed it thinking, *Why would J be in Arizona?*

As they drove, Money took in the sights of the tall palm trees and the wide 6-lane highways. He also noticed most cars had tinted windows with carpet padding on the dashboard. Money laughed never seeing anything so ridiculous. The cab driver explained it was for protection against the scorching sun.

Soon, they arrived to the hotel. Money paid his tab with a tip. When he exited the cab into hot sun, he understood why people covered their dashboards. The weather was 101 degrees plus.

"Shit! It's hot," sprinting inside the hotel.

The lavish Ameri-Suites air-conditioned lobby cooled his body. Money stopped at the front desk. The hotel clerk seemingly already knew who he was.

"Maurice Bonner?" she questioned without checking his I.D.

"That's right, do you know me?" he asked giving the clerk a funny look.

She handed him a key-card. "You're all set."

Money was puzzled. "Do I owe you anything?"

"It's all taken care of. You're all set," she repeated smiling.

Ol' friendly ass bitch, he thought walking away.

Arriving to the room, he slid the key-card downward. The red light turned green. Entering the room, he again was slapped in the face by the cool air. He then stretched across the bed hollering, as if someone was killing him. "Whew! This bed comfortable. I could lay here all day."

Just then, Money heard a knock at the door. He opened the door to find a woman of Asian descent.

"Damn baby, me so horny," flirted Money. The petite built woman was not amused.

"Mr. Knight will see you now," she spoke.

197

"Oh, oh, you're with Black-Kni... my fault baby. I'm sorry," he apologized.

"Follow me please."

Money grabbed his over night bag and followed the woman down to the limo parked in front. After a short drive, she pulled over. She raised down the tinted glass divider handing Money a blindfold, instructing him to put it on. After a brief conflict over the blindfold, they continued on their way. Money of course inched the blindfold down catching a glimpse of a sign that read: Welcome to Scottsdale, Arizona. Not long after, they came to a stop. Money was told not to remove the garment from his eyes until he was inside the home.

When inside, the blindfold came off, Black-Knight stood with his had extended. "Money Bunny... it's been a long time. Two martinis," he told the Asian woman. Money shook Black-Knight's hand scanning him over, remembering him in his younger day.

Petting his hand, "Black-Knight, it's a pleasure," he said taking in the sights of his large beautiful home.

"Man, you got your 40 acres and a mule."

"No doubt, and I plan on keeping this mule, but the mess that I hear jumped off the other night with the husband and wife shot dead on their porch, jeopardizes my way of living. What kind of home-invaders take the money but not the weed?"

"Some stupid ones," co-signed Money.

"For real, that type of dumb shit brings heat on the weed game. Did you hear about that?" he asked.

Money shook his head out of pity. "Yeah... man, I heard about it. Dude was one of Rowe's customers. I use to serve him. He was cool," thinking Tootsie and his drug habit were way out of control.

Toot didn't have to kill that woman. He shot her after he shot ol' boy. My man was already laying dead in the bushes, and the nerve of him inviting that bitch Sean on the lick. I don't like him, and he doesn't like me. Shit, the way I remember it, that fool tried to kill me back in prison. Giving him 50 thousand dollars just because he was there at the robbery, shit, I didn't invite his ass. Tootsie's actin' like this his operation. Sean knows too much and Toot is out of control. They both gos'ta go.

The Asian woman returned with the drinks. Money took a sip. "But down to business Black-Knight. I'm not here to speak bad on Rowe, but I am here to let you know his operation isn't being ran right."

"Oh no? How so?"

Money began telling Black-Knight about the weaknesses and vulnerabilities of the weed operation. He talked about the expensive $1800 ticket price that Black-Knight thought Rowe was retailing for $1500. Money then contradicted himself, he went into detail about how Rowe gets drunk and claims Black-Knight killed his brother K.G. and one day swears for revenge. Black-Knight took it all in with no facial expressions. He knew what Money spoke was true; still it was nothing he felt threatened by. But, a change in the operations had to be put in place.

Money was in thought. *Damn, I can't read this cat. He ain't blinked, flinched or nothing. It's got'ta be something I can say to get a reaction."*

Money knew Black-Knight would eventually contact Rowe with these accusations. Money had to think fast. Something had to be said to ensure himself a position. Quickly, he concocted a story.

Rubbing his chin, "Black-Knight, do you know of a white dude named, uh... Comroy, Conray..." Black-Knight spit his drink across the table coughing, hoping he was hearing wrong.

"Conrad Bantz?" he corrected catching his breath.

"Yeah! That's him. He comes up to the car wash regularly," he lied. He and Rowe will go in the office and talk for hours. Rowe says he's an insurance agent, but dude looks more like a federal agent to me."

After those words, Black-Knight appeared to have gotten sick. He sat back in his chair. He then scooted back onto the edge. Afterwards, he got up with his drink, walked around, and then downed it. His mind was running in a million directions.

That got his ass, thought Money. *Now to reel him in slow.*

"Listen Black-Knight man, I think they're plotting something against you. I've heard your name mentioned too many times. Rowe is still upset over K.G.'s death, you know?"

Distraught, "Yeah, yeah," was Black-Knight's only response. "Excuse me for a second." He turned his back using his cell phone. When the answering line picked up, he told someone, "It's me man, I got a job for you to handle."

Over hearing the conversation, Money interrupted the phone call, explaining to Black-Knight he owed him for sparing his life years ago. He said if needed, Rowe's demise would be met, "Don't worry."

Afterwards, Money began to negotiate himself for the position of running the marijuana operation. Black-Knight briefly thought about it. He then told Money after Rowe's death, they would need at least six months to lay low. Money questioned the long six months, but agreed.

The next day, Money flew back into Detroit. He was inside the airports lavatory using the urinal, when Conrad Bantz walked up to the urinal beside him.

"So, who did you visit in Arizona?" he asked unbuckling his pants. Looking downward, shaking himself off, Money was startled by his presence.

"A Conrad man, you got'ta stop this poppin' up shit. A brother caint even shake his dick off without you being there."

"Hey, watch your mouth. Be nice. Now, I asked you a question."

Zipping his pants, "Who do you think man? I went to go see Black-Knight"

"Good work kid. So, ol' Black-Knight's residing in the desert lands of Arizona, huh? Ok, gim'me his location. I'll have some agents down that way to pick him up."

"Uh, uh, hold on Conrad, you're movin' too fast. You pick up Black-Knight now, and I'm a dead man," he said appearing to be worried.

Conrad was holding his head back making pleasure sounds, farting, as he relieved himself.

Money turned up his nose. "You nasty!"

"Whatever. Listen Money, after Black-Knight's in custody, you won't have to worry about him. Besides, the agency will protect you."

"The agency? Conrad, don't talk to me stupid. This some personal shit you got going with him. Now check it, let me work on Black-Knight for another six months, maybe even a year to get him comfortable. And I promise, when you take Black-Knight's ass down, you'll also collect an empire worth over 50 million dollars."

Astonished, "50 million dollars! What's he selling? Who's his supplier?"

Money laughed on the inside but stood firm. He could see the dollars signs in Conrad's eyes. *This white muthafucka ain't nothin' but a thief with the government backing him up.*

"On everything Conrad, if you want a slice of this pie, be cool and let me work my hand." Writing on a piece of paper, "Now, here's a number, so when you wan'na talk, you can just call. All that James Bond pop up shit you doin' is gon'na mess around and get me killed. Please, cut that out." Money picked up his overnight bag from the floor. "We good?" he asked.

Conrad didn't want to appear eager. He stood acting as if it was a hard thought. He then nodded, as to say, *'We're good.'*

In front of the airport, Money watched as Conrad Bantz took off in a Crown Victoria.

He then took a deep breath. "Shit, I'm telling so many damn lies, I'm just hoping I can keep em' all straight."

Who could it be?

Tywon pulled up to the house of his lady friend in his new Ford Expedition. He turned down his radio. She approached his driver's door.

"Hey sweetie, I missed you. Gim'me kiss," she said as they locked lips.

Releasing from the kiss, "Damn girl, you got that fire," he laughed. "Shit, got me wantin' to do something."

"Something like what?" she asked exposing the cleavage of her breasts.

Tywon immediately felt an erection. "Eeewww...baby damn. C'mon and get in. Let's grab a spot and do the nasty."

A look of disappointment came over her face.

"I can't sweetie, not today. I just came on."

Tywon didn't want to hear that shit. He quickly made up an excuse to leave.

Less than a minute later, he was on his way. Only a block away from the previous female, he spotted another woman walking up the street. Loving the way she walked, "Damn she got ass," pulling over to the curb. He leaned over, looking out the passenger window. "A, a baby! It's gettin' dark out here. You need a ride?"

She stopped and checked out the truck. "Naw, I'm alright. But you can give me your number."

After hollering out his cell phone number, Tywon turned towards the backseat, thinking he'd heard something. He saw nothing. Now putting the truck in drive, he suddenly heard.

"Ain't shit! Ne'va been shit! And ain't go'on be shit!" ranted O'Sha climbing from the trucks third row seat.

From the sound of the voice, Tywon turned white in the face. His bowels softened. It was as if a 1000-pound weight was hanging from his bottom lip. If he ever wanted to die, it was now.

Now sitting in the passenger seat, "You know what Tywon? Over the years I done heard so many stories about yo' nasty ass, but because I loved you, I refused to listen to the rumors. I guess I had to see and hear it for myself." In a rage, "I've stuck with you for the last 10 years! And this is all the respect you have for me? I can't believe this Tywon! You out here tryin' to pick up nothing ass neighborhood hoes, females on their cycles and only God knows who ever else. If that girl wasn't on her period, I know you would've fucked her."

Tywon remained silent as he drove. He was still in disbelief that O'Sha camped out in the back of his truck and heard all the things he said.

O'Sha continued, "No wonder you ain't trying to marry me. You're out here feedin', fuckin' and financing all these other females. Always talkin' 'bout, 'But baby, I'm out takin' care of business," she mimicked. "Whatever Ty, it's over. I'm sick and tired of being dogged out. You don't value me. My sister told me years ago. I should've left you alone like she did J. The both of y'all just some male whores."

Whores! Bitch! Yo' sister Octavia is the biggest whore walking the streets of Detroit. I can name 10 dudes before J that hit that ass. And she talkin' 'bout somebody should'a left somebody. A matter of fact, she's still out here playin' the game raw! That's the problem now, her blind ass leading your dumb ass. For some reason you think Octavia's shit is candy coated, but her shit stank just like everybody else's, Tywon wanted to say. Instead, he just remained silent as he pulled up to their house.

O'Sha stepped out the truck. "I won't be here when you get back Tywon, so please, don't call my cell phone. I won't be answering."

"Yeah, whatever," mumbled Tywon, tired of the bitching and whining.

Frowning, "Yeah, whatever? Is that all you have to say to me?"

Tywon then pulled off screeching his tires. O'Sha watched with scorned feelings as he bolted up the street.

Walking up to the house, "Alright Mr. Whatever, you go'on pay for this big hole in my heart," closing the door behind herself.

Twenty minutes later, Tywon received a phone call from De'Andre telling him the marijuana shipment had arrived.

"I'm on my way."

Within five minutes, he arrived to the stash house. De'Andre, Big Daddy and White Boy-J were in the living room separating the weed by weight.

With a serious look, "Man, I smelled this shit all the way from the street," said Tywon inhaling the scent. "We got'ta get some air conditioners in here to suppress the weed smell. It's strong."

"It is funky," agreed Big Daddy.

White Boy-J smiled, "This that chronic."

By this time, De'Andre had rolled a Philly blunt full of marijuana. It was to test the quality of the product, so he claimed. He lit it and took a few puffs. He made a few gagging sounds. "Oh yeah, oh yeah, this that deal," he claimed barely able to speak. He then passed it to Big Daddy, who turned it down. He said weed was a gateway drug to using cocaine. Everybody bust out laughing.

"Ok, Mr. former crack dealer."

"Gateway? Man...fuck that. Pass that blunt over her Dre," said Tywon. "I'm the one who needs to smoke. O'Sha caught me up again."

"Again?" smirked J.

"Again," with disappointment. Tywon then went into detail about what happened.

As the four continued to converse, the subject was changed. They began discussing the random robberies of marijuana dealers. They talked about the husband and wife robbery, murder. Another, where a dealers parents were held hostage until a $50,000 ransom was paid, and the most recent shocker, the death of Rowe.

"Man, he was a cool ass dude, but that shit was bound to happen," said De'Andre. "His weed stash was right there in the van. If you bought from Rowe, you knew that. That was an easy ass lick."

Big Daddy shook his head. "Yeah, Rowe did leave himself wide open."

"I heard they found him burned up strapped in his wheelchair?" unsure said J.

"I heard the same thing," added De'Andre. "They burnt up the van too. Police found it one block from the car wash," still thinking, *'Somebody hit a lick.'*

"It took some dirty muthafucka's to do that to a cripple man," voiced Tywon passing the blunt to J. "So where's Money? Any of y'all seen him? Big Daddy?"

"I ain't seen him, but my momma said he came by the house telling my auntie, if anything happened to him, he loves her. Now she done got my momma all worked up and scared."

Tywon displayed a look of concern. "Do you think the dudes who killed Rowe are after Money?

Big Daddy hunched his shoulders. "Ain't no telling," knowing Money was some how tied into this mess.

"You got a phone number on Money?"

"Naw, but I'ma hunt 'em down and see what's going on."

"Alright, let me know," ended Tywon.

Not long after, the four-man crew loaded each of their vehicles with enough marijuana to fill their customer orders.

****

Since Rowe's death, Money had received many phone calls in question to his murder. *'When and where did he last see Rowe? Did Rowe discuss any beefs he had? Who did he think killed Rowe?'* And the number one questioned most asked: *'Had he ever heard of a man named Black-Knight? And did he think Black-Knight was responsible for Rowe's death?'* Money had one or three words. "No," and "I don't know." He would then play fearful of his life and request for the calling line to pray for him.

Everything for Money was going according to plan, except for Sean and Tootsie. The two were out spending money like it grew on trees. From jewelry, to cars, from cocaine, to clothes, the pair was drawing unwanted attention. Money tried to talk to them but it was useless. The combined $175,000 between the two had them feeling financially invincible. Money of course knew better. He knew their heavy spending was going to leave them broke, and that's when his third eye in the back of his head would have to open up. He already suspected Sean and Tootsie of plotting against him. He knows when anytime two parties get quiet when you step into the room, you're the topic of their discussion. Money experienced it with them one too many times.

A week prior, Money also confronted Sean about trying to take him out back in prison. Sean defended himself saying he knew it was Billy who was on the bottom bunk the night he and Tootsie came into their cell. He claimed to have protected Money.

"Protected me?"

"Yeah, protected yo' ass. ol' boy Billy was an informant for this federal agent named Conrad Bantz, who claimed you told the C.O.'s in prison that it was really me and Toot who did that stabbing in the shower, that federal agent also said a few other things about you that I ain't go'on mention," grunted Sean with a look as to say, *Got yo' snitch ass.*

It was now Money who was in defense for himself claiming the accusations were false. Sean listened to Money babble, but he knew the real. He also knew Money was his meal ticket right now, but if or whenever that stopped, Money was going to have problems.

It had only been two weeks since Rowe's death and already, Money was tired of sitting in the house. Six months seemingly was taking forever to pass. Lying on the couch, he could hear Sean and Tootsie upstairs having a conversation. He couldn't quite make out what they were saying, but when he walked upstairs, the two became quiet.

Irked, "What's up, I'm bored," said Money concealing how he really felt. "Let's hit that titty bar Double 07 and check out some females."

"Double 07! Oh hell yeah, I'm wit that," responded Sean wiping cocaine residue from his nose.

Tootsie checked his money pulling out a $5,000 wad. "Yeah, this should be enough for the bitches."

Not long after, they all hopped in Sean and Tootsie's newly purchased Range Rover. Sean got into the driver's seat, Tootsie in the passenger, and Money as usual sat in the back. He never let his back face the two.

Soon after, the trio pulled into a gas station. Money was headed back from paying for the gas when Big Daddy riding by spotted him. He whipped into the gas station's lot slowly riding pass the Range Rover, making full eye contact with Sean and Tootsie.

"Fuck he looking at?" grimly said Sean starring back.

"That's Money's cousin, Big Daddy," answered Toot.

"Oh...but back in prison, Money was talkin' 'bout stickin' homeboy up, and that's his cousin? Money's scandalous."

"Yeah, but they're cool now."

"Well, not with me. And fat boy looks like cash money. That lick still might haf'ta go down," looking at Money getting into Big Daddy's truck through the passenger side mirror.

Money looked to Big Daddy rolling his eyes.

"What you want man?"

"Pppsss...! Trust me, your presence ain't no pleasure either, but what's the deal?" he asked.

"The deal, with what?"

"Cut the bullshit Money, this me. I'm talking about that bogus ass story you ran down at mom's crib. Why you wan'na trouble them with yo' street shit? Leave them out of it. Secondly, this Rowe business, it's fishy. That man toted two pistols. It had to be somebody close to him to disarm him," he said giving Money the eye. "But I admit Money, you're good. You playin' scared, you layin' low, ain't bought shit. You're playing a good game."

Money badly wanted to smile, loving the praise.

Big Daddy continued, "But, you know what's going to get you caught up?"

Money twisted his lips as to ask, *What?*

Big Daddy eyed the Range Rover. "I don't know that other cat in the truck, but your boy Too Too, or whatever his name is go'on be your down fall. He's a car wash clown, so how is it now that he's shining so hard? He's all geared up, jewelry blinging and he's riding shotgun in a Rover. All this possible after his boss gets killed, right? It don't look good Money," he said shaking his head.

Damn, I knew somebody was go'on peep these fools. I know the streets is watching. Flat-out, I'ma tell Sean and Tootsie it's over. I'ma...

Big Daddy interrupted Money's thoughts. "Somehow you mus'ta got in touch with the big man, Black-Knight. And me knowing you manipulated him into thinking Rowe was some type of threat to him, and you offered to off Rowe for the weed connect. Am I right so far?"

Money had the dumbest expression on his face ever. He felt as if he had just been put on trial. His eyes began to shift and his mouth tightened.

Defensively, "Why your fat-ass always thinking I'm involved when some shit happens, Big Daddy? I didn't kill Rowe. Every since we were kids, you've always thought the worst of me. You never said nothing, but I could tell by your eyes you were thinking it. Even my own momma," he said becoming emotional. "She blamed me for everything that went wrong; if her lottery numbers didn't fall, if her check didn't come in the mail, all kinds of dumb shit. She would cuss me out, slap me in front of my friends, talk about me real bad, you remember, you was there." Big Daddy agreed. "And the only time she asked about my day or how I was feeling was when she needed some money. That woman never gave a damn about me. I guess that's why there's so much hate in my heart."

Suddenly, Money bent forward into a ball. Big Daddy's lips and cheeks tightened. He remembered Money's traumatic childhood events. Those were sad times for him. Consoling him, Big Daddy petted his back.

Just then, Money sat back up laughing.

"See, yo' big soft ass fell for that sob story just like everybody else. My point being, fuck what people think about Toot, I don't care.

I'm representing me. I'm stickin' to my guns and playing my roll, and as long as I do that, I'm good. Don't look at me like that Big Daddy, you know what it is. I'm still Money Bunny, Maurice Bonner. Ten years in the joint up under my belt and nope, I ain't changed and ain't go'on ne'va change. I'm like this 'cause I wan'na be. It wasn't my childhood upbringing, it wasn't 'cause I grew up without my daddy or 'cause my momma treated me like shit. I'm like this because flat-out, I just don't give a fuck! All I want is the riches, the bitches, a fat ass ride and to get my dick sucked. I'll shoot 50 muthafucka's in the head to get there if I have to, including them two clowns up there in that truck. Father time, he can kiss my ass. Mother nature, she can suck my dick, and the reaper, I've offered him my soul many times but his punk ass just won't take me. There is no lesson to be learned Big Daddy. You've got life and you've got death," he explained with hand gestures. "Everything else in between is already written." With that said, Big Daddy was speechless. *This boy got serious issues.*

Right then, "Bump! Bump!" Sean blew the horn.

Opening the door, "I got'ta go," said Money.

"Alright then Money Bunny," he emphasized. "Oh yeah..." snapped Big Daddy as if he'd forgot, "Remember some years back you told me you shot up some old cat named Uncle Ed?"

With attitude, "Yeah, and what about it?"

"Well, it turns out that old cat was Tywon's father. He found out last week. I guess when some shit does happen Money, you are always some how involved."

Disgusted with himself, Money slammed Big Daddy's truck door. He then jumped into the Range Rover with Sean and Tootsie, where they pulled off.

Soon-after, the trio pulled into Double 07 topless bar where they valet parked. The pink colored neon lights made the bar appear high classed and extravagant.

Inside the bar, Sean and Tootsie with $600 in singles each, headed straight for the V.I.P. section to receive lap dances. Money by himself took a seat at the bar. He needed a stiff drink. The news of Uncle Ed being Tywon's father was a jaw-dropper. He couldn't help but to think how fucked up the situation was, how bad he'd done members of Tywon's family in the past, how he presently was planning revenge against De'Andre, and also, how he witnessed and somewhat participated in the death of his so called best friends father. It was all too much, but the betrayal wasn't about to end there. As Money downed his second shot of 1800, he spotted Octavia. She was fully clothed, but still hustling lap dances. *Now that's a good, good freak right there. I wonder what she'd charge for a shot of head.* Money wanted to make an approach, but this was the first time he's seen her since the shooting in her basement. He was thinking of a good apology line.

Just as he came up with the right words, a females voice chanted, "I heard they'd let the dog out the pound. And it looks like he's sniffing up a tree."

Money turned to his left. It was sight for sore eyes that put a smile upon his face. "O'Sha, hey...baby. How you doing?" he asked looking around for Tywon. "Where's my boy at?"

"Mmph!" she expressed turning her head up. Money picked up on the careless gesture. *Oh, yeah... I'ma play this just right.*

"What you drinking sweetie?"

"Gim'me a...double shot of Hennessey on the rocks."

Whoa!

Money ordered their drinks. After 45 minutes of O'Sha pouring out her heart about Tywon, and her third double shot, the conversation became personal.

Turning her glass, "So Money, where's your girlfriend?" she asked.

"Uh...you know me, a friend here a friend there, nothing steady."

"Yeah I know, just being a hoe, all y'all the same."

Money laughed. "Naw baby, it ain't like that. But can I tell you something O'Sha?"

"What you wan'na tell me Money?"

"That you have the most beautiful set of lips hiding those gorgeous white teeth. Smile for me baby," he said making her blush.

Hitting his shoulder, "Stop it Money, you're embarrassing me."

"For real O'Sha, you're a special girl."

"Naw, I don't know about all that."

"I just wish you could see yourself through my eyes," licking his lips. Suddenly, there was a deep stare between O'Sha and Money.

The time wasn't right, the place wasn't right and the person definitely was all wrong, but O'Sha was in a vulnerable state. She was hurt and needed the comfort of a man.

"Scoot closer," she told Money. "Just to let you know, don't think it's the liquor acting out, I know exactly what I'm doing." O'Sha then laid a kiss on Money so deep, he instantly became erect. The bulge through his jogging pants told the story. O'Sha had stroked him a few times to calm the matter, but that only intensified the situation.

Octavia, looking around the bar for O'Sha, caught the releasing of their kiss. "What the hell! No she didn't."

Already not liking Money for what happened ten years earlier, she walked over to the pair.

Slapping her hand, "Pay me! Pay me Money, or I'm tellin' Tywon. And what you thinking about O'Sha?" looking to her sister. "Them two is best friends."

O'Sha smacked her lips. "Octavia, do you really want me to tell you about yourself? I got this, finish doing your thang."

Money intervened. "Octavia, calm yourself down. Here," handing her $200. "O'Sha's a little emotional, that's all. We just kickin' it, there's no need to bother Tywon with this. Now, my fella's over there got a lil' somethin' waiting for you," he pointed to the V.I.P. section. They all looked. Sean was flipping off dollar bills to the music as if it was raining. Tootsie was lap dancing for a dancer he'd paid to lap dance for him.

Octavia laughed. "Damn, they live as hell!"

"That's right, go'on and get that bread girl," encouraged Money. He then signaled Sean and Tootsie to take care of Octavia. They both waived her over.

O'Sha smiled. "Money, you sho' know how to work your hand, don't you?"

"All the time," cockily he spoke, thinking, *This pussy's mine.*

O'Sha giggled, standing up from her chair. "I'ma go to the ladies room Money. Watch my drink for me?" laying a napkin over her glass.

"Then after that, you wan'na get out'ta here with me?" he asked.

"Mmm, not tonight Money, lets take it slow, we've got time."

Disappointed, "Alright," spoke Money watching her walk towards the restroom. Turning back toward the bar, *Damn, that girl got'ta ass on her, knowing she should let me hit that, talkin' 'bout not tonight. Well, why not bitch?* he thought frustrated. *We're already in the wrong. We might as well just fuck and get it over with. Shit, plus I got a $200 credit line with that ass.* Money then reached inside of his jacket pocket, pulling out an ecstasy pill. *I'ma guarantee myself that pussy tonight,* slipping the pill into her drink.

Just then, O'Sha returned. She thanked Money for his patience. She thanked him for his listening ear. Finally, she thanked him for just being a friend. She told Money, if they were ever to become involved, she wanted it to be right.

Whatever that means, thought Money. He then insisted they toast to their new friendship. As the two chimed glasses, O'Sha's drink dropped to the floor. She then took off running towards the V.I.P. where Octavia was into a fight. Money watched in disappointment as the glass rolled across the carpet. *Damn!*

Suddenly, security took notice of the brawl and the music was shut off. Two minutes later, "The bar is now closed! Dancers, report to the dressing rooms! Everybody else, lets go!" the staff announced over the loud speaker.

Outside, Money stood against the truck pissed. He could only think how close he came to having O'Sha.

Sean and Tootsie were laughing. They were still in excitement how Octavia whooped the other girls' ass.

"You should'a seen that shit Money!" said Tootsie.

As Tootsie explained the fight, the three were unaware three men in a green 4-door Malibu, parked across the street from Double 07 were observing them.

One of the men in the car pointed. "Ain't that ol' boy right there?" he asked.

"Yeah, that looks like him. She said his boy been bragging all night that they ridin' a Range Rover," spoke another. "And that's the only Rover I see."

"Alright, bet. Get those masks and gloves on. Hand me that tech-9, we go'on roll on they asses at the end of the driveway just as they're pulling out."

Still laughing, Sean and Tootsie climbed into the truck. Money sobbing was already in the back.

Starting up the truck, "Man! Quit whining over that bitch! You'll see her ass again," said Sean pulling out the driveway.

Suddenly, "Ssscccrrr...!" screeched the Malibu.

Sean mashed the brakes. "Who is these mutha..." before he could finish his sentence bullets riddled the windshield.

In fear, Money laid across the backseat. The three armed men weirdly noticed their bullets ricocheting off the truck but kept on firing. Double 07 patrons scattered, running back inside the bar as bullets flew in their direction. Just then, Sean forced the truck into reverse, smashing into a car behind him. Then, back into drive plowing the 4-door sedan out of its way.

Speeding away, "Yeah! Yeah muthafuckas, bulletproof windows! I'm built for war baby!" hyperly yelled Sean giving Tootsie a five. "Them boys wasn't ready! That ain't nev'a seen no shit like that Toot!" Tootsie laughed feeding off Sean's rush. He now had more respect for Sean than ever. Money was just lifting from the seat, pepping out the rear window. He could still hear the loud, thunderous sounds of the bullets striking the windows. He took a deep breath glad to be alive. He then frowned thinking of who wanted to kill any of them.

Was that hit meant for Sean? Naw, the only beef he had was in prison. Couldn't be Toot, any beef he had died on the porch that night. The only person left is me, but who...?" Suddenly, Money lost his breath, *Black-Knight*!

Money began thinking of any possible way he was a threat to Black-Knight. He knew he was the only thing linking Black-Knight to Rowe's murder and the only thing linking Conrad Bantz to Black-Knight as well. He then thought, S*hit, and if anything ever jumped off to* *wheres I would have to testify against Black-Knight about that murder, best'a believe, I'ma tell it. Wheph! That would be a life sentence for him. It's bad to say, but if I was him, I'd be trying to kill me too.*

Right then, Sean turned towards the backseat. He saw the distraught appearance on Money's face.

"A Toot, look at this cat back here. He's scared as hell. He got pussy written all over his face, but I know one thang, he bet'ta straighten it up before it gets fucked."

Tootsie began laughing harder, Sean right along with him. Money didn't at all like what he heard. He was about to voice his thoughts when Sean again mashed the brakes in the middle of the street, coming to a halt.

Turning on the interior lights, "What Money! You don't like what I just said? Breathing all hard out your nose and shit, I hear you back there. I just said saved your got damn life. Far as I see it, you owe me. Them shooters back there didn't come for Toot, and damn sho' not for me. I wonder who that leaves Money. You know that hit back at the bar was meant for yo' ass. Your past is chasing you dog; whole new ball game now. The hunter is now the hunted. But hey, this is the life you chose, right?" he pointed. "So all that sensitive, gettin' wet in the face, actin' pussy type shit go'on stop. You're a gangsta' son, ah killa' man, you got murders up under your belt, ain't no turning back now and ain't no bitches rolling on my team."

Your team? thought Money.

"Only hard dick hittin' pistol packers, and if you ain't one of them Money, then you can get the fuck on out this truck. Step yo' game up or step the fuck off."

Tootsie came around to the truck's backdoor and opened it up. Right then, Money knew it was him alone against the world. It didn't take to long for him to figure out what he wanted. He pulled the truck door close. Sean snarled his top lip.

"Thought so! And Money, I don't know what this Conrad dude looks like, but if I see any white boy with a suit or sunglasses on hanging around you, ball game over." He then turned back forward, cut the interior light off, put the truck in drive and sped away.

The Wolf

The relationship between Tywon and O'Sha wasn't getting any better. The more apologetic and caring he became of her feelings, the more she seemed to pull away. Often when he advanced towards her for sexual relations or even a kiss, he'd be rejected. Feeling he'd lost her, Tywon many times asked O'Sha if there was another love interest in her life. Without hesitation, she would defend her respect for him by saying, *No*, but her actions spoke differently. Because of their familiarity with one another and their time together, the two still remained to live under one roof.

Seated at the table counting, "Ok, I've got 398, 99, $400,000 here. What's your count Ty?" asked Big Daddy tying rubber bands around the bills.

"Uh... uh... about $350,000?" he guessed.

Big Daddy sighed. "C'mon Ty man, you're off by at least $50,000. We got'ta re-up this month. Where's your mind at?"

Stressed, Tywon began hitting his head with his palms. "Uuuhhh...! man, O'Sha!" he exhaled. "She's got me dog. I love that girl, can't think straight. Check this out, I done bought her ass a new car, clothes, a diamond watch, sent her and her sister on trips and cruises and still, ain't none of the shit workin.' I done nearly spent up a $100,000 trying to make her happy. Dude, she's only giving me the pussy once a month."

"Oowwee...! That's bad," commented Big Daddy. "You've got problems."

"What should I do?" desperately asked Tywon.

Big Daddy sat back in the chair, laying his hand across his large stomach. He then went into counsel mode.

****

In Arizona, Black-Knight placed a call to Pablo in Mexico. He asked if Pablo had any other marijuana dealers in Arizona who sold to other marijuana dealers from Michigan. Pablo said he had three in Tucson and two in Phoenix. Black-Knight then requested a big favor. He asked Pablo to cut off their marijuana supply for a three-month period. He explained that he'd put together a team of weed-pushers to corner Michigan's marijuana market. He told Pablo his new team would sell five tons of marijuana per month if not more. Those numbers to Pablo sounded astronomical but very profitable. He agreed willing to take the chance. All Black had to do now was figure out how to get in touch with Money. Eight months had passed by and Black-Knight hadn't heard from him. He repeatedly called the cell phone number he had for Money but the line went unanswered. If Black-Knight had to, he'd make the trip to Detroit to find him.

****

"And remember Ty, just give O'Sha a little room to breathe. The less you chase, the more they wan'na be caught."

Closing the door behind him, "Alright Big Daddy, thanks man. See you in the morning," waived Tywon.

"See Toot, here comes big boy right now on schedule," said Sean keeping a close surveillance. The two watched as the Cadillac truck leaned to the side as Big Daddy climbed in. He then pulled off.

"What you waiting for Sean? Follow him, he's leaving," pointed Tootsie.

"Chill Toot, I've been watchin' these boys' moves and layouts for the last three months. I got their schedules down packed."

Using his fingers, "From Tywon, to Dre, that white boy and big boy, I know the times and when and where they go'on be. Watch this."

Sean went in the opposite direction of Big Daddy, cutting down onto 94 free-way. Within a 8-minute period, he was pulling into a 31 Flavors Ice Cream Parlor parking lot.

Tootsie was puzzled. "What are we here for?"

Aggravated, "Just watch!" said Sean.

Just as he predicted, the white Escalade pulled into the parking lot.

Amazed, Tootsie smiled. "Man Sean, you're like some kind of detective."

"Naw baby boy, this wolf just ready to eat."

After ordering his triple chocolate ice cream sundae, Big Daddy went on his way. Already knowing his next move, Sean and Tootsie went their own way, planning for the home invasion on Big Daddy within the next few nights.

* *

"Baby, we having a real good time here in Vegas, but I'll be home tomorrow. Oh, Octavia? She's in the bathroom throwing up again, she's still sick. She says thank you for the trip though. Ok, I will. Love you too Tywon, bye," said O'Sha hanging up the phone.

"Mmmph mmph mmph, you's just a good girl gone bad," smirked Money laying across the hotel bed ass naked. "Got that man sniffin' yo' panties over from 2500 miles away, damn...shame."

"Shut up Money," laying underneath his armpit. "Don't start. You've been sniffing for some years too."

"Yeah, but now I'm fin'na drill that ass," rubbing her booty. Money then positioned O'Sha onto all fours, laying eyes on her perfectly arched back, her flawless skin, her wide spread hips, and dripping wet pussy that was just waiting for the stabbing. Simply from looking at her body, Money knew the loving was good with a condom on, but without it, he could only imagine. Over anxious and already hard, he was leaking.

"Are you just go'on stand there and look, or you go'on hit this good pussy?" said O'Sha, horny and growing impatient.

"What the...girl...I just...hold on," he said reaching for his condom. Money tore open the package with his teeth, pretending to put the rubber on. He then gripped O'Sha's curvy, more than a handful hips, sliding his naked penis into her warm body. O'Sha climaxed on contact, feeling his downward curve.

Passionately, "Eeewww...!" she moaned seductively looking back at Money. "It feels so hot, long and good baby. You got your condom on, right?"

Money sounding as if he was walking on a floor of hot rocks, lied, jittering his head, '*Yes.*' He then looked downward watching her body lotion lubricate his shaft. It was a scene he'd pictured doing for so long, and now, it was happening.

Just then, Money's back stiffened, his ass tightened, he began taking mini-strokes trying to fight the feeling. It did him no good. If O'Sha didn't know it was Money behind her, she would've swore it was a wolf from his loud out cry. After releasing inside of her, he fell onto her back.

"Mmm..., sounds like it was good to you baby," she spoke.

Arrogantly, "It was alright."

O'Sha's eyes opened. "Alright? Get yo' ass off me!"

Money laughed, "Just bullshittin' girl. It was the bomb, now lay down."

"Naw, uh, uh, and where's your rubber at," seeing the flaky glaze on his penis.

"Huh? Over there, I threw it."

"Over there where?" continuing to look. O'Sha didn't see a thing. She then smacked his leg. "Money, I just know you didn't cum in me! I just know your nasty ass didn't cum in me!"

Money again had the dumbest look ever on his face. "What you trippin' for O'Sha? You on the pill, right?"

"Pill! You asked me that before Money and I told you no. Oh my God, I don't believe you. This trip is over!"

"*Over? Ok then,*" thought Money, hunching his shoulders. *I got what I wanted and your man paid for it, stupid bitch!*

Upset, O'Sha called the airline to switch their flight dates. Within three hours time, they departed Las Vegas headed back to Detroit.

The next day, Tywon awoke to his ringing phone. The caller I.D. revealed it to be White Boy-J. He answered the line immediately starting to talk. "J, everything is ready? Me and Big Daddy counted the ends twice. The trucks are on standby. We've just been waiting on you to give the word."

Disappointed, "Well, it still go'on be a wait," responded White Boy-J.

"Huh, what you mean?" asked Tywon worried.

"I just talked to my chili pepper (Mexican) here in the Z-town, (Arizona). He said it's gon'na be at least three months before it's back on."

"Damn, three months? Why?"

"He didn't say. That might'a been a warning. He might be hot, you know?"

"I'm hip," agreed Tywon. "That is possible. It's a good thang he put you up on it, 'cause a milly (Million) was ridin' on it this time."

"I know, and a loss like that would cripple us."

Tywon again agreed. He then told White Boy-J to stick around Arizona for a few more days to see if he could find a new connection. J said he was already on it, now hanging up the phone. Tywon figured this small break might be exactly what he needed. It would give him some time to spend with O'Sha, who'd just left going to the doctor saying something on the trip must have made her sick.

* *

Money also just received a phone call from a blocked number. Out of curiosity, he answered the line but held the phone.

"Hello, Money? Is that you baby?" whispered a sexy voiced woman.

Amused, *Baby*? "Yeah this me, who this?"

"It's Black-Knight!" the voice changed. "Why are you avoiding my phone calls man! What's the problem?"

Cowardly, Money again held the phone silent, not knowing what to say.

Black-Knight continued, "Everything is in place man. I got the state of Michigan locked down. You wan'na get this bread or what?"

Puzzled, "So, you and me don't have a problem with one another?" asked Money.

"A problem? Hell naw, but we will if you ain't got the semi-trucks and the crew you told me you had. Do we have a problem?"

"No, there's no problem at all. We're good," answered Money not so quick to wash away his dreams.

Black-Knight then told Money he had 3,000 pounds of marijuana waiting on stand by just for him. He explained that he needed Money and the tractor-trailers to be in Arizona one week from today. Money countered saying that he didn't have the funds to cover such a large load.

"Not to worry," re-countered Black-Knight. "The 3000 pounds will be fronted do you, I just need you to get it there."

Outdone by the proposal, Money told Black-Knight he and the semi-trucks would be there by next week.

Sitting on the couch, Money was trying to figure out how he was going to pull this off. *The only person I know with some trucks is Tywon, but between Big Daddy and De'Andre, they're gon'na down play this shit. The white boy, I ain't sweatin' him. But it got'ta be a way I can convince Tywon to fuck wit' me on this trip.*

Just then, the phone again rang displaying a blocked number. Thinking it was Black-Knight, Money answered. "Yo..."

"Yo! Your god-damn self!" hollered Conrad Bantz. "You're just gon'na stick your thumb up my ass, right?"

"What!"

"You're fucking me over Money! It's been over 6-months. You haven't called. You haven't answered your phone. You haven't produced me Black-Knight. You haven't done a god-damn thing you said you would. I guess that's 'cause you're too busy goofing off in Las Vegas."

Damn, thought Money, *this man tracking my every move. I need a fake I.D. or something.*

"Where's our boy Black-Knight, and where's the 50 million you promised me? If you're shittin' me, then you're shittin' the government, which can result into some serious charges for yourself."

Money knew Conrad's threats were bullshit itself. Still, he began providing information to back him off. He told Conrad about he and Black-Knight's earlier conversation. He spoke about the semi-trucks and how much marijuana was going to be on them. He was careful not say whose trucks would be transporting the weed, or when and where this large transaction was supposed to take place. He did tell Conrad he heard through a confidential informant, that Sean and Tootsie were the perpetrators who murdered the husband and wife on their front porch 8-months ago, and the two were also responsible for the death of his boss at the car wash, Rowe.

"Did you have any involvement in Rowe's death?" asked Conrad.

Offended, "No!" replied Money. *I can't believe he asked me that shit!*

Conrad had his doubts about that. "Is that all you have for me today Money?"

"That's all," he ended.

"Ok, keep in touch." Conrad cleared the line. Money then turned off his recorder.

"Yeah white boy, we'll see who walks away when all this is over."

****

A couple of nights later, Sean and Tootsie were staking out Big Daddy's house.

"Damn Toot, somethin' ain't right," said Sean trying to figure out the situation. "Instead of shootin' moves, Tywon's been taking that tramp lady of his to every expensive restaurant in town. The white boy, he ain't no-where to be found. And instead of doing his usual drop offs and pick-ups, De'Andre's been hangin' 'round all the neighborhood peons. And big boy in there," he looked to the house. "He ain't made not one move either, what you thank Toot?"

Tootsie heard not one word Sean spoke. He was to busy with his face down on the cocaine tray.

Upset, "Gim'me that shit!" snatching the tray. "That's why we're damn near broke now, you and that cocaine habit." Sean then snorted the rest. "Now c'mon, the big bad wolves got a pig to catch."

Sean opened his trunk. He grabbed a roll of duck tape, a hammer and some rope. He and Tootsie then crept along side of Big Daddy's house into the back-yard. There, they both peeked inside of a bedroom which allowed them to see straight into the front-room. Big Daddy was laid back in his recliner watching television. Sean ordered Tootsie to stand watch as he began placing the tape strips across the bedroom window. After he was done, he tapped the window lightly with the hammer, shattering the glass onto the tape. He then peeled the tape back along with the broken glass attached to it, now having an entry inside the home. Sean hand signaled Tootsie telling him, *'I'm going in.'* Tootsie nodded keeping watch. Big Daddy not hearing a thing was still posted in the recliner. Now inside, Sean again signaled Tootsie. *'C'mon.'*

As Sean pulled him up through the window, Tootsie's pistol fell from his waistline onto the floor. A loud thump was the result of it.

"Maybe he didn't hear it," whispered Tootsie.

Just then, the T.V. and lights were turned off. *Awe shit.*

Sean grabbed Tootsie's gun as well as his own, laying quiet on the side of the dresser. Tootsie sweating bullets, hid inside the closet. From the total darkness, along with his cocaine high kicking in, he was becoming more frantic by the minute. The heavy breathing and the ponderous footsteps nearing the bedroom didn't help either.

I'ma give it to his ass soon as he steps through that door, thought Sean.

Suddenly, "Bbbbbbbbbb...Bbooommm!!" shot Big Daddy with the semi-automatic, ripping the bedroom door to shreds. The fire coming from the barrel of the weapon lit up the room. As Big Daddy kicked open what was left of the door, Tootsie in a panic sounding like a whining puppy dog jumped out the bedroom window. Startled, Big Daddy jumped backwards again firing away. He destroyed the entire window frame and some brick structure. Sean was still holding his breath beside the dresser. Even though he had two guns in his hands, he knew they were not match to whatever weapon Big Daddy was firing off.

Big Daddy looked out of the window. "Missed his ass! I'll get 'em though!"

Haven't seen Sean, he rushed back towards the front of the house in hopes to catch Tootsie running up the street. Sean took a deep breath, ready to jump out the window when he heard a loud crash.

"What was that!" He waited a minute before investigating the noise. Through the darkness, he could see a silhouette figure of someone lying on floor. Turning on the light, he saw it to be Big Daddy foaming at his mouth. His eyes were bucked and his head was twitching. Sean could see he was having a seizure. He knew it was only a matter of time before Big Daddy swallowed his own tongue. He could easily prevent this fate, instead he knelt down whispering, "Oink, Oink fat muthafucka. Yo' house is blown down," throwing a sofa cushion over Big Daddy's face.

Then quickly, Sean ransacked the house finding only $14,000.

"Shit, this is only his ice cream money, I know it's more here somewhere." But there was no time to look. The neighbors were starting to come out of their homes. Along with the $14,000, Sean took the semi-automatic weapon from Big Daddy's hands who now laid dead. He then jumped out of the rear bedroom window. Tootsie picked him up on the next block.

The Plan

The news of Big Daddy's death hit hard. No one could believe it. The gentle giant as everyone called him was gone. The community was shocked and they wanted answers. Neighbors reported seeing two men flee from the scene, but the Police investigation found no evidence of any finger print traces. Therefore, they had no leads.

Outside of the funeral home, the long rear door of the Hearse was just closing. Honorary Pallbearers Tywon, Money, De'Andre and White Boy-J standing amongst one another were distraught.

Grieving, "I just talked to him," said Tywon wiping his eyes. "This city is just full of haters."

"That shit ain't ridin' like that! Somebody knows something," angrily spoke De'Andre.

Money and White Boy-J shook their heads in agreement. But in Money's mind, Big Daddy was gone. He was hurt by his cousins' death, but his thoughts were focused on getting those semi-trucks down in Arizona, also getting Tywon aside to discuss his plans.

Just as he was working up the nerve to pull Tywon away, O'Sha and Octavia approached expressing their condolences.

Kissing Tywon's tear dried eyes, "Are you ok baby?" asked O'Sha giving him a warm hug.

"I will be soon. Thanks baby," returning a kiss onto her cheek. Octavia did the same for J. Money was heated by O'Sha's affection for Tywon.

What about me? I'm the cousin! he thought in a jealous rage.

Curiously, "So Octavia, I hear you were sick on the last trip? Are you okay now?" asked Tywon. Octavia gave him a look as to say, *'What are you talking about?'* Money quickly cut in.

"Hey Ty, let me holla' at you for a minute," he said pointing towards the corner.

Weph! O'Sha was relieved as quickly as she'd felt faint.

As the two walked towards the corner, Money ran down his plan with urgency. Tywon said the plan sounded good but the time wasn't right. This was Big Daddy's final hour, and any further business affairs would have to be discussed another day.

Money frowned, "Another day! Fuck that, I need to know right now!" Fed up, Tywon tried to walk away, Money grabbed his arm.

De'Andre, White Boy-J, O'Sha, and Octavia looked to the corner from the loud disruptive conversation. Suddenly, they all saw Tywon hit Money across the mouth. He fell to the ground. Tywon then began stomping Money as if he didn't know him. O'Sha held her hands up to her mouth, hoping the brawl wasn't over her.

Octavia looked to her sister. "Girl, you done got some shit started. I told you fucking best friends wasn't right. I did it before."

The reason for the fight wasn't even confirmed, but O'Sha was feeling like a whore.

It was as if this was the opportunity De'Andre had been waiting on. He ran to the corner joining in with Tywon on the stomp fest. It took White Boy-J along with help of some funeral attendees to pull the two off of Money.

Big Daddy's mother along with Money's mother riding past in the funeral limo cried from seeing the fight. Faye, De'Anne and Ronnie also invaded the circle to calm Tywon and De'Andre down.

"What is the matter with you?" asked Faye slapping both their faces. "You're disrespecting Big Daddy's family."

Just then, "Money emerged up to his feet staggering. "Fuck all y'all!" he ranted sounding like he was drunk.

"Fuck who, me?" Tywon pointed to himself.

"Especially you, bitch!"

After that insulting comment, Tywon broke loose from White Boy-J's grip. Money then took off running up the street fearing another beating.

Octavia laughed, "And that's your piece on the side, right?"
O'Sha smacked her lips feeling her world was collapsing.

On the next block, the Range Rover pulled up to Money who'd ran out of breath.

Sean rolled down the window puffing on a blunt blowing out the smoke. "Hey, hey playboy, looks like you lost your voters support back there."

Money breathing hard and sweating approached the truck. "What y'all doing around here?" he asked haven't seen Sean or Tootsie for months.

"Oh...nothing," casually spoke Sean. "Me and Toot was just checking out the bitches at your cousin's funeral. That boy knew some women. But then we noticed you and your boy fightin,' or should I say him and his brother kickin' yo' ass. So after you ran off, we thought you might'a needed a ride."

Just then, screeching tires were heard coming around the corner.

"You thought right," said Money climbing into the back seat.

"Where to?"

"It don't matter, just drive."

As they drove away, Money began telling Sean and Tootsie he and Tywon's fight was over O'Sha. He said she confessed her love for him to Tywon.

Confused, "Hold up, I just saw the bitch hugging my man," said Sean. Money thought fast.

"Yeah, they just were saying their goodbyes to one-another. Anyway, that's my bitch now! That girl is down for me, and she's been telling me where Tywon stashes his bread. That boy got 3 million put up."

In unison, "3 million!"

"Yup, and I know exactly where it is."

Sean was in thought. *Damn, 3 million dollars! I should to put a bullet in these two fools and kidnap O'Sha myself.* Smiling, *then fuck her brains out and make her tell me where the money is.*

Tootsie was in thought as well. *Lord, please don't let Money ask me do I know anything about Big Daddy's death. Between using this cocaine and my guilty conscious, I might not hold up.*

Money's mind was racing as well. Suspiciously, *Checkin' out some bitches, whatever. I can't prove it, but I know these two had something to do with Big Daddy dying. Still, I need them for this one last lick.*

After his thoughts, Money told of his plan to obtain the 3 million dollars. Sean and Tootsie had no objections, but they did have plans of their own.

They pulled back up to Money's car. The funeral home was deserted.

Exiting the truck, "Tonight, it's on," said Money. "Be ready. Oh, and one last thing. Have either of you heard any word on the street about who did this to Big Daddy?"

"Naw, but we go'on find out," confidently spoke Sean.

"Toot?"

Tootsie sat silent looking out the window. Money then closed the door. "That was enough said without Tootsie saying a thing."

As Money drove away, the same three men from Double 07 were observing him.

The day moved on. Tywon went home avoiding Big Daddy's family gathering. He felt he and De'Andre's earlier actions were unexplainable. Right then, a knock came at the front door.

Opening the door, "Ma, what are you doing out this way?" curiously asked Tywon.

"What, I'm not welcomed at your house?"

"Of-course, I'm just...what's up Ma?" knowing it was purpose for her visit.

"Well Tywon, you and De'Andre were wrong for what you'd done to Money today, and in front of his people?" feeling ashamed. "That incident could've turned into something real nasty."

"Yeah Ma, but let me expl..."

"No Tywon let me finish. And shamefully, I think I now what this is all about."

"You do?" Thinking, *How?*

Faye held her face. "I should've told you years ago myself. I knew this was a long time coming. De'Andre finally let it go, huh?"

Tywon had no idea of what his mother was talking about, but he was now curious.

Playing along, "Come on Ma, you know De'Andre, once he gets pissed off, he tells it all.

Regretfully, "Yeah, I know. I was wrong for taking him with me when I use to cop from Money."

Tywon stood infuriated. "When you what from Money!"

Faye was startled. "Why are you screaming? Isn't that what you and De'Andre beat the crap out'ta Money for?"

"Naw...Ma!" Why haven't you been told me about this? All damn, I don't believe this. I'ma kill Money!" wildly ranted Tywon pacing back and forth.

After Tywon calmed down, Faye went into detail about how she many times purchased crack-cocaine from Money. She repeatedly apologized to her son. Tywon didn't get a chance to express what he thought or how he felt. O'Sha accompanied by Octavia were just walking through the door. Tywon whispered to his mother.

"This is family business only." Faye understood.

As Faye greeted the pair coming through the door, Tywon was in thought. *That dirty son of a bitch Money done went too far. He sold dope to my momma? What kind of shit is that? That supposed to have been my boy. I've always known he wasn't shit, but I didn't think he'd do nothing like this to me. Since we were kids, everybody around us use'ta talk bad about Money, but me like a fool always defended him. Even De'Andre and De'Anne never like his ass and she likes all men. I now understand why Big Daddy never dealt with him. He knew his cousin was low-down and now that I think about it, he indirectly tried to warn me. Damn, how could I have not seen this? I can only imagine what other dark secrets there may be about Money. Shit, I'm afraid to go digging, might find out somethin' that'll make me wan'na kill his ass.*

Suddenly, a frown came over Tywon's face as he looked to O'Sha. *Money talked about Octavia but he's always had a wondering eye for O'Sha.* He then dismissed it. *Naw, O'Sha would never mess around that close. Anyway, I'ma roll with Money's plan. We definitely can put my trucks on the road, but after I meet his connect, I'm go'on make it mine.*

Finally for Money, the awaited day came and went. He, Tywon, De'Andre and White Boy-J were 24 hours into their road trip to Arizona. They started in Detroit down I-75 highway into Ohio. Afterwards, onto I-71 through Kentucky, catching the 40 in Tennessee, a small part of Arkansas and were now traveling through Oklahoma.

Frustrated, "Shit!" exclaimed Money. "I ain't use ta' all this drivin.' How much longer we gos'ta go before we reach Arizona? I ain't brushed my teeth, I'm hungry as hell and my ass is stickin' together."

"Damn Money, T.M.I." spoke De'Andre.

"T.M.I.? What's that?"

"Too much information!"

White Boy-J smirked. "Yeah Money, this is roughing it to the road to riches. Hygiene takes a back seat."

"Yeah, well if I don't tend to this hygiene, y'all go'on be throwing this back seat out onto the road."

They all laughed, except for Tywon who was driving the van. His thoughts were on the drama which occurred three days ago.

"And y'all make sure y'all kill Tywon's ass dead. Because if he gets wind of me being involved with this robbery, I'ma dead woman," said O'Sha.

"Don't worry baby, he won't" assured Money taking the set of keys from her hand.

"Ok, drop me off here," she pointed to an upcoming restaurant. Money pulled over. Before O'Sha exited the vehicle, she laid a deep, hard French kiss on Money, so hard and deep, Sean and Tootsie in the back seat felt it.

"Damn baby, can I get one of those?" asked Sean gripping his crotch.

O'Sha winked her eye. "We'll see after I get my share of the money, good luck," closing the door. Sean getting into the front seat watched O'Sha's ass as she walked away.

He then looked to Money smiling. "Looks like yo' bitch is choosing. I'm fin'na be swimming in that ass."

Money twisted his lips. "Whatever, anyway y'all heard what O'Sha said. We got'ta knock Tywon's ass off. Ain't no games to be played here. I'm trying to get paid."

"Yeah, yeah, we know the drill. We ain't new to this shit!" interrupted Sean. "Just get us to the house."

Tootsie chuckled. Money feeling humiliated, want to slap the shit out of Sean, but that wouldn't happened without consequence. He recognized the M-16 military style assault riffle in Sean's hands that once belonged to Big Daddy. *I knew it.*

As Money was driving up the street, Tywon was leaving the house.

"Damn!" pounded Sean on the dashboard. "He's leaving. Roll up on his ass, I'ma snatch him back into the house."

Just then, Money parked. Sean felt as if he'd been defied.

Angrily pointing the gun, "Didn't you hear what I just said!" slapping Money. "Boy! If you fucked up my chances of gettin' that 3 million, I'm tellin' you..."

Tootsie could see Sean had lost all respect for Money.

Defensively with his hands up, "Hold up Sean, think about it. What sense would it make for you to pull a gun on him now, when I got the keys to the house and the safe? Besides, Tywon stays strapped. It would just be a shoot out between you two and won't nobody get nothing."

Sean thought about it. *This punk-muthafucka is right. A gun battle would bring the heat. I guess Tywon gets a pass this time. But this boy Money, this is his last day on earth.*

Sean then openly agreed. "You're right Money, and I'm sorry for hittin' you. It's the money, make'n my nerves bad, you know?"

Money accepted the apology knowing it wasn't genuine. Tywon then drove off.

"Alright, lets go, and bring the duffle bag."

The three exited the vehicle into the dark night, appearing as if they were about to engage in a war. Sean handling the M-16, Tootsie equipped with the AK-47 and Money with two 9mm pistols in each of his hands, walked mean and hard up the middle of the street.

Just then, the trio found themselves on opposite sides of the street. Sean pointed in a shouting whisper. "This is Tywon's house here!"

Money argued. "Yeah, but this is his safe house over here. He ain't go'on have his money where he lay his head, you know that."

"He's right," co-signed Tootsie.

"Shut up!" Sean snarled. They both followed.

Money was the first upon the porch. He pulled out the keys, opening the door. The three stepped into the fully furnished house.

"Where's the safe at?" asked Sean cutting on the lights. Paranoid, Money turned the lights off.

Avoiding the question, "If Tywon pulls back up and sees these lights on, he's going to know we're in here. Then, he'll be waiting outside for us." It made sense, but already Sean was tried of Money's logic.

"Fuck this, where'd O'Sha tell you the safe was?"

"In the basement."

"Ok, gim'me the keys," he demanded. Money handed over the keys. The trio then cautiously headed down into the basement. Neither of them could see a damn thing, the windows were covered. Tootsie repeatedly pulled the light switches, but there were no bulbs in the sockets. He then pulled out a lighter, flicking it.

"Good thinking Toot," said Sean. "Over here" he pointed spotting the safe. He took the key from his palm kissing it, hoping this was the lick to put him over the top. He then laid down the M-16. Tootsie did the same, holding the lighter up to the keyhole. He inserted the key, turned it, opening the safe. Sean and Tootsie couldn't believe their eyes. There were thick rubber band mountains of cash stacked on top of thick rubber band mountains of cash.

Excitedly, "Hello! Gotdamn! Jack-pot baby!"

The two began filling the duffle bag with the money. Already the pair were discussing their plans for new cars, clothes and islands they were going to visit, excluding Money who they had forgotten about.

Right then, a bright light came on. Sean quickly reached for the M-16 which surprisingly was gone. He then nervously turned his head looking out the corner of his eye. He could see Tootsie with his mouth hung open standing in shock. At that very moment, Sean knew the ball game was over. He exhaled standing to his feet. He saw Tywon, Money, De'Andre and White Boy-J all pointing weapons in his direction. Right then he knew it all was a set up; from the fight at the Funeral home, down to O'Sha playing her part. He then watched as Tywon held a cell phone to his ear.

"Ah, yes, I'd like to report hearing gun shots across the street from my home."

"Awe...please...wait a min..." The last thing Sean and Tootsie saw was the 20-inch flame coming from the M-16.

Suddenly, "Tywon! Tywon!" called De'Andre.

"Huh, what?" coming out of thought.

"Don't you see the squad car behind us?"

Tywon peered in his driver's mirror. The red, blue and yellow lights on the Oklahoma State Trooper car were wildly flashing. Tywon pulled over to the side of the road followed by the trooper. The four began making up a story as to say where they were going. They all quickly agreed on Texas seeing it was the next state over. The trooper stepped from his vehicle dressed in all green with a ranger styled hat, tall black boots, and dark round sunglasses.

He approached.

Tywon smiled. "Hello Officer, what seems to be the problem?"

With a southern slave master appearance, he just stared. He then stood on the rocker panel of the van looking inside to where Money, De'Andre and White Boy-J sat.

Suspicious, *Three Monkays and uh pecka'wood? I wond'a...*

In a southern accent, "Where ya' boys headed ta'?" he asked.

"Texas..." they sang.

"Texas, whut part?"

Suddenly, there was jibberish talk.

"Sounds like you boys don't know where ya' headed."

"Yeah we do, El Paso, Texas," blurted Money unable to thing of any other Texas City names.

"El Paso? Is that where you boys goin' ta?" the trooper asked the others. It sounded good, so everyone nodded in agreement. "Yeah..."

"Mmm...well ta' my knowledge, the only thing in El Paso is a bunch of Mexicans and a lot of cocaine comin' out'ta Mexico. None of ya' look Mexican, so ya' must be plannin' on pickin' up some of that cocaine and travel it back up north."

"No sir, not at all sir, uh uh," they spoke.

"Naw, let me see some I.D."

The trooper looked their identification over.

Taking off his glasses, "Michigan? But y'awl license plate back there says Tennessee. Ohh..., this story just keeps gettin' bet'ta."

The trooper pulled Tywon from the van for questioning, then Money who yelled, 'El Paso,' afterwards, De'Andre and White Boy-J, separating them all. The trooper received four different answers from four different people until Tywon admitted their destination was Phoenix, Arizona. He was questioned if or not they were picking up weed. Tywon of course answered no. Their names were then ran through the system for any outstanding warrants. Money was sweating bullets hoping nothing federal showed up. After running their names, the trooper returned back to the four sitting on the grass with his hand on his pistol.

"Damn, we goin' to jail," mumbled De'Andre.

"Ok, I'ma let cha' all go this time. But, don't think ya' got'ta away with nothin.' Yer see fellas, I do this everyday. This here in Oklahoma is my road. Money goes this'a way, and the drugs go back that'a way," he pointed. "Now ya' boys wouldn't happen ta' have a ton of money hidden in that van would ya?"

"No," simply answered Tywon.

"Ya' wouldn't mind if I checked would ya?"

"Awe...man! We've been out here for 2 hours already," blurted Money.

"It's eitha' me, or I can call in the dogs."

Tywon threw his hand. "Go'on head man," tired.

After another hour of the trooper checking the spare tire, the T.V., the captain chairs, and disassembling the custom wood trimming finding no money, the group were finally on their way.

Riding up the road, "Man, that was some bullshit. That's why I'd rather fly," complained Money.

"Yeah Money, but next time we get pulled over, just don't say shit," said Tywon. Rolling his eyes, '*El Paso, Texas.*'

12-hours later, the group came out of the Arizona Mountains traveling down I-17 into Phoenix. Money just caught a signal on his cell phone. He called Black-Knight telling him, he, the semi-trucks and his crew were now in Phoenix.

"Bout time," voiced Black-Knight. "Didn't think you were going to show."

Money explained the delay came due to his cousin's death. Personally, Black-Knight didn't care, he was just ready to meet and make the deal. "How long would you need to put your people into place?" Money placed Black-Knight on hold as he consulted with Tywon.

"Give us two hours," he said coming back on the line. "We got'ta meet with the truck driver's, then freshen up at the motel."

Black-Knight agreed. But Money wanted to stop at the motel first. The 40-hours of funk was making him feel nauseated. Tywon then instructed White Boy-J who was driving to drop Money off at the, "Where?"

"The AmeriSuites Hotel, in fact, there it is right there," he pointed. J pulled up, Money stepped out. Tywon handed him his bag.

"We'll be back to pick you up after we meet with the truck drivers."

"Ok," said Money walking away in a hurry. Soap and water was his only concern. They then pulled off.

De'Andre watched Money from the rear window of the van as he entered the hotel. Shaking his head, "I can't stand that muthafucka," he whispered to himself.

While soaking in the bathtub, Money called O'Sha telling her play-by-play of what happened on the road. Just then, she placed Money on hold. After a minute, she came back on the line, "This is Tywon, I'll call you right back."

Frustrated, Money threw the phone. "Bitch!"

On the other line, O'Sha began telling Tywon the Police investigation stated Sean and Tootsie's deaths were the results of a robbery gone bad. She said they were suspected to be in connection with over 12 other robberies and murders around the city.

"Yeah, but you see that shit stopped right here!" cockily said Tywon. *But damn, not before they got to Big Daddy*, he squint his eyes in pity. "Alright O'Sha, let me handle my business. I'll call you later," hanging up the phone.

O'Sha then called Money back as he was getting out of the tub, but he ignored her call. He was jealous that he came second to Tywon. Behind her call, Money's phone rung again but this time with a blocked number, his gut was telling him it was Conrad Bantz. Money wasn't in the mood for his shit talk today. It then dawned on him.

"If I fly the plane back to Detroit, I just know Conrad is gon'na be at the airport waitin' on me. And that's the last thing I need for Tywon or De'Andre to see. Shiiid, I guess I'll be driving the van back home with the white boy." Money just let the phone ring.

At the truck stop, Tywon and White Boy-J briefed the truck drivers on their loads. The pair explained to the drivers they would be carrying 1000 pounds of marijuana each. Their pay would be $100 off of each pound they transported which equaled $100,000. Tywon then added he would give them an extra $10,000 each simply for their loyalty to the cause. It was really to create some eagerness amongst the drivers. Their last few runs to Arizona for Tywon were dry runs. After the meeting, the three headed over to White Boy-J's condo to clean themselves up. Tywon then called Money who'd been ready for over an hour.

"Where y'all at?" he asked worried.

"We're on our way," responded Tywon. "Did you talk back to Black-Knight yet?"

"Yeah, he gave me the location of the loading dock."

Tywon then tested Money. "Where's it at?"

Money became silent. *Tywon trying to play me for my connect?* Suspiciously, "Just come pick me up. We'll all ride over there together."

"Alright, we'll be there in a minute."

Tywon hung up the phone laughing. "Money might be a fool, but he ain't a damn fool."

After picking up Money, they all headed to meet Black-Knight.

During the ride, Money observed how fresh and clean the trio were. He kept asking them what hotel they cleaned up at. The three just laughed. They would never tell Money of White Boy-J's condo.

Finally, they arrived to the loading docks. Tywon and J's semi-trucks were pulling up simultaneously. The dock was long with 30 truck ports, surrounded by nothing but desert land: The perfect cover.

"Damn, if somebody wanted to kill you out here, they'd definitely get away with it," spoke De'Andre looking around.

Right then, Money spotted someone on the far end of the dock waiving their arms. "That's him, over there," he pointed.

They drove over. Everyone exited the van.

"Hey...Money, glad you fellas could make it," said Black-Knight shaking Money's hand.

"I told you I would be here," as if he had no doubt. "This is my crew," introducing them. "This my boy Tywon, that's De'Andre, and the white dude, we picked him up on the highway."

Black-Knight was confused, "Huh?"

Money laughed. "I'm just bullshitin', that's White Boy-J."

Tywon couldn't believe it. *It's millions of dollars at stake here and Money's ass is crackin' jokes.* Tywon then took over.

"Excuse me, Black-Knight? Which of these loading stations would you like for my drivers to pull into?"

"Uh... stations, 28, 29, and 30," he directed.

Tywon whistled to the drivers, pointing to each station. The drivers backed in up to the ports. "Ok, now lets check out the product."

Hhmmm, authority. Black-Knight gladly led the way.

As they all walked through the building, Money couldn't stop starring at Tywon. *Tywon foul for that shit he just pulled. He's trying to take my connect.*

De'Andre fought to hold back his smiles. *Ol' Sucka muthafucka!*

White Boy-J was eyeing Money. *This bum called me straggler.*

Tywon checked his phone. *What O'Sha want now?*

And Black-Knight glanced behind himself at Tywon. *Damn, that young boy reminds me of Uncle Ed.*

After a two minute stroll, they reached a large door. Black-Knight slid the door open to the right. The air-conditioned warehouse like room held over 12,000 pounds of marijuana, neatly wrapped, numbered and sitting on wooden pallets. The cool temperature room kept the weed scent faint.

Shiiid, I would've killed Rowe my damn self for a connect like this, thought De'Andre looking with amazement.

Black-Knight took his pocketknife cutting open one of the bundles. He then pulled out a handful of weed. It was light green, fluffy and seedless with a strong odor. He held it up to their noses.

"Weph!" White Boy-J frowned. "That's some fire ass weed."

Tywon agreed. "It's tight, that's go'on sell fast."

"And it's a drought back home," finished De'Andre.

Black-Knight then directed their attention through-out the room.

"Most of the weed you see in here is already sold. I got some Georgia boys coming through here to grab 1000 pounds, some Tennessee cats coming to get 2000, another 1000 by St. Louis. I cut them Ohio muthafuckas off, they still owe me money. D.C., New York and Michigan, which is y'all."

"D.C. and New York?"

"Hell yeah, them east coast cats travel for this Mexican weed. That Jamaican weed down the way ain't of the same quality," schooling them. Money then tried to recapitalize on the situation.

"So, what's the price on 3000 pounds?" he asked Black-Knight.

"For y'all..." looking upward, thinking. "$800 on the front."

"That's cool," responded Money.

"Hold up! $800?" said Tywon shaking his head. "That's too much." Money again felt his toes were being stepped on.

"What you mean Ty? He's throwing the weed to us."

"Chill Money, I got this," doing the math in his head.

Tywon took Black-Knight's $800 price subtracting it by his wholesale price of $1200. That left $400 minus the $100 per pound the drivers were to be paid cutting the margin to $300, in which he then multiplied that times the 3000 pounds giving him a projected profit of $900,000. It was a good lick off a front, but it wasn't good enough.

Tywon held up his finger to Black-Knight as to say, *Give me a minute*. He then stepped to De'Andre and White Boy-J, whispering. Afterwards, the pair went back to the van. When the two returned, they dropped 3 gym bags in front of Black-Knight. Tywon then reached inside of his pocket pulling out a 100-dollar bill handing it to Black-Knight.

"What's this for?" he asked.

"Well, in each of those three gym bas is $330,000. The 100 bucks is to make it an even million I'm paying you. I want the whole 3000-pound load for $400 per pound."

"$400! C'mon now young blood, you're tryin' to stick me up without a gun."

Young blood? thought Tywon. *Uncle Ed, I mean my daddy use to say that.* He shook it off. "But wait a minute Black-Knight, let me finish. If you give me the load at $400 per pound, that'll be 1.2 million. I'm paying you a million up front, which'll leave me owing you a balance of $200,000. Then, front me another 3000 pounds at $700 a piece. And I promise you, in a months time, I'll bring you the 2.3 million I owe you, and plus another million-five to recop.

Black-Knight impressed, gazed at Tywon, afterwards down to the million dollars at his feet, then to Money who looked like the bottom had just fell out from underneath him. It was no doubt, Tywon had strong-armed him for his connect. But after hearing all the comas and point millions Tywon was throwing around, he couldn't do anything but respect it.

"You've got a deal," smiled Black-Knight.

Everyone cheered as if they'd hit the lottery. They all knew this was the beginning of something big. Black-Knight then shook Tywon's hand.

"You're a real business man."

"I know, it's in the blood," Tywon laughed.

After another hour, the semi-trucks were loaded. Each truck received 2000 pounds of marijuana. Then another 500 pounds of boxed onions were loaded. It was to cover the marijuana scent and camouflage the load if the driver was ever stopped. Tywon then handed the drivers their Manifest (Cargo) sheets, telling them he would meet them back in Detroit. Soon after, the drivers took off.

"Alright then Black-Knight, it was good meeting you," waived De'Andre and White Boy-J hopping into the van.

Tywon got into the driver's seat. "I'll see you in 30 days," he spoke with confidence.

"Ok, sounds good."

Money feeling salty threw up the peace sign about to hop in the van when Black-Knight stopped him. "What's up Money, we cool?"

In a dry tone, "Yeah, we straight."

"Good, I threw you in an extra 200 pounds for putting this deal together."

Money brightened up. "Thanks Black-Knight."

"No problem, but let me ask you. Have you heard anything else about that federal agent, Conrad Bantz?"

"Nope, not a thing," he answered with a straight face.

"Rowe?"

"Nobody talks about a dead man."

"Last thing, what's up with Tywon?"

Puzzled, "What about him?" asked Money?"

"How long have you known him?"

"Since we were kids, why, you don't trust him or something?"

"That ain't it. Ah...don't worry about it. I'll see you guys next month."

"Alright Black-Knight, next month then, peace," hopping into the van.

As they drove away, Money felt awkward. On top of selling Tywon's mother crack, molesting his sister and fucking his woman, he'd just knowingly introduced him to the man who'd killed his father, simply for financial gain. *Damn, and I suppose to be his best friend.* When they reached the airport, Tywon and De'Andre exited the van. Money was just mentioning he was going to ride back to Detroit with White Boy-J.

"For what reason when you can just hop on the plane with us?" asked Tywon.

"No reason, I just want to see the sights."

"See the sights!"

That excuse sounded suspicious. It didn't lay right with Tywon, De'Andre or White Boy-J. And too much cash was involved to take any risks with Money.

Tywon waived his hand. "C'mon J, get out the van. Take the plane home with De'Andre. I'll drive back to Detroit with Mr. see the sights here."

White Boy-J got out the van, Tywon got in.

"We should arrive the same time the weed does, see y'all in two days," driving off.

On the road, Tywon dared not to take the same route back home. After traveling through the state of Arizona, he cut upward in New Mexico, making his way through Colorado. At that point, Money took over the wheel riding through Nebraska and was just now entering Iowa when suddenly, he began to cry.

Tywon asleep awoke to the whimpering. "Man...what the hell is wrong wit' you!" witnessing the large tears.

Crackling voice, "Nothing man."

"C'mon now Money, what's up?"

"I'm just saying Ty. Y'all done black balled me out the crew."

"Black balled you, how?"

"Like when I asked you where did y'all change clothes at, y'all laughed at me, then the million dollars, how come I'm the only one who didn't know about the money?"

"Dude! You crying over that shit! I don't believe this. If you must know, the million dollars was sent in the semi-trucks and we changed clothes at J's house. You don't like him and he doesn't like you, so why would he invite you over to his place. It's your bad attitude and fucked up ways that keeps you in the dark."

Money didn't want to hear all that; it was the hard truth. But hearing of where the million dollars came from satisfied his curiosity. Still acting, he conjured up more tears.

"You're right Tywon man. I do have some doggish ways. But since we've been apart, I mean not kicking it like we use to, I've been lost. Then on top of Big Daddy dying and shit, it made me realize... I miss you dog. I want us to be back tight, like we use to be. But first, before you say anything, I got something I wan'na confess to you."

"Confess to me? What?"

Money began telling Tywon about the times he sold his mother Crack Cocaine. Money only confessed because O'Sha scolded him for the act after Faye told it to her, the night she mentioned it to Tywon, who told his mother, *'This is family business only,'* but girl talk always spills the beans.

Angered, Tywon hit Money with an unexpected blow to his jaw. The van swerved wildly off the road, cutting off cars on the side and in the back of them. The offended cars blew their horns and flashed their high beams at the out of control van. Now on the grass, Money cut back onto the highway kicking up dirt and rocks.

After regaining his composure and control of the van, Money wanted to hop off that steering wheel and kick Tywon's ass, but Tywon was starring back at Money as to say, *Try it!*

Money then smiled, shaking his head. He knew he deserved the hit, probably more. Even though Tywon already knew about the incident, hearing if from Money's mouth only pissed him off more.

He then pointed, "Money, I loved you like you were my brother. There was no limit to what I would've done for you, but now, you're just like shit on the bottom of my shoe; disgusting and something I can do without. So as of now, we're threw. The only thing keeping us associated is that weed. And after that's gone, you're gone."

Tywon then retired to the back to lay down.

Oh! So after we sell this load, you think you're gon'na deal with Black-Knight direct without me? Bitch you crazy! Money wanted to say. Instead he apologized to Tywon, as he continued driving up the road.

Myrtle Beach

Ballin' out control was the definition of the life-style Tywon, De'Andre and White Boy-J were leading. Their spending went beyond simple cars and jewelry. They were buying million dollar estates. Tywon settled on a 1.2 million home off the water in the suburbs of Michigan. Money fixed his eyes on a $500,000 home in the 'burbs as well, but instead, remained in the hood. De'Andre spent $350,000, while White Boy-J trailed Tywon with a 1.1 million dollars spent on his home. There wasn't any frontin', and no games were being played. This crew was making celebrity dollars.

Pointing downward, "That's tight as hell J," emphasized Tywon, checking out the diamond bezelled Rolex watch.

The jeweler pulled it from the display case. "Here, try it on."

When White Boy-J put the watch on, his wrist lit up like a disco ball. The watch complimented the large diamond ring he was wearing.

"Damn J, you the flyest white boy I know."

"I hear that all the time," he smiled.

"How much?" he asked the jeweler.

"$50,000"

White Boy-J didn't complain or try to hustle the price. He pulled out five, $10,000 stacks placing them on the counter. The price didn't bother him at all. He and Tywon just received a weed shipment that would make them 4 million dollars each. Within minutes, the jeweler handed J his receipt. He and Tywon afterwards went on their way.

At the old stash spot, Money was just confronting De'Andre about the theft of his marijuana clientele.

"A De'Andre man....I done told you about selling weed to my customers. Now that's 400 pounds I'm stuck with. You go'on quit fuckin' with my bread!" he hostilely said.

De'Andre jumped up. "Whatever dog! Your peoples called me to serve them. Besides, they don't wan'na fuck with you no more anyway. Word is gettin' around the streets you was a stick up kid with yo' boys Sean and Toot, so don't blame me, you've fucked yourself."

Money didn't have any argument behind that. It also didn't surprise him. He'd heard the same rumor in the street himself, but he was hoping it would fade away. He then pointed, "You heard what I said Dre, don't toy with me," walking out the door.

On the porch, Money had a fit with himself.

"Fffuuuucckkk...! Shit is goin' from bad to worse. I told them two dead ass clowns to quit braggin' about them robberies, now my name hot all over again. But that De'Andre, fuck him, he's gon'na get his. In fact, fuck Tywon and that white boy too. Fuck the whole squad, it's on! Using me for my connect."

Angered, Money flipped out his cell phone, calling Black-Knight. When Black-Knight who was in Detroit picked up on the line, Money began telling him an ear full of lies that would forever change all their lives. But before acting on the life threatening accusations, Black-Knight questioned it.

"I just don't understand Money. Tywon and I make a lot of paper together. Are you sure he has people out here that wan'na kill me?"

"Black-Knight, this ain't about the money. This is about revenge. It's about you killing his daddy years ago. If someone you knows killed your father, would you let that shit ride? Would it matter to you how much money y'all made together?" Black-Knight remained silent. "I didn't think so, and that's the same way Tywon feels." Money then poured it on. "And I just found out, the last time Tywon, his brother and the white boy were there coping, they were talking about busting you out and taking all your weed. De'Andre was the one who was gon'na do it."

"Who, the young guy?"

"Shiiid, don't slip on him. That young boy a cold killer, wake up Black-Knight man, you done got too comfortable. You go'on fuck around end up like Uncle Ed. Wasn't you the young cat years ago who got closer to the old cat and did him? Well time is repeating itself and this time, you're the old cat."

Suddenly, the image of Black-Knight standing over Uncle Ed with the shotgun replayed in his mind. Just then, it was as if lighting struck him and the images changed. Black-Knight now saw himself lying on the floor with De'Andre pointing a shotgun at him.

"Bbbooommm!" he jumped, picturing the gun blast blowing his face off. It all made sense. The dots were connecting. Black-Knight didn't question it any further.

Money had laid it on thick. He couldn't see Black-Knight's face, but the breaks in his conversation and the prolonged silence let Money know his words had gotten through. He then advised Black-Knight on what should be done.

****

Two months prior, "Sssssshhhhhhh!" released the pressure from the air brakes on the 18-wheeler. Money hopped out from the passenger side, now walking along side of the tractor-trailer approaching Tywon, who was closing the door of a second truck, fanning his face from the Arizona heat.

Excitedly smiling, "Damn baby! This the biggest load ever. Ain't nobody in the 'D' pushing as much weed as we are. Not those west side boys, them Highland Park cats, none of 'em. We got the game on lock. They caint fuck with us!" boasted Money.

"What did I tell you? Didn't I tell you years ago weed was where the money was at?" stated Tywon, far exceeding his own expectations.

"It's 3000 pounds here in this trailer. 2500 in that one," he pointed to the truck Money just exited. "And another 1500 back there," looking to the air-conditioned rig, White Boy-J was seated in talking to the driver. "That's a total of 7,000 pounds. At the wholesale price of $1200 apiece, we're talkin' about a grossed amount over 8-million dollars. Now, can you touch that!"

Money grabbed the crotch of his pants. "Eeewww shit! We fin'na get paid, but hold up," he said with a disturbed look. "So, how much of that has to be paid to Black-Knight this time?"

"Shit, the usual. 2000 pounds of this weed is his, so at $700 a piece on the front, that equals 1.4 million he gets."

"1.4 million! For what! 'Cause he fronted some shit! Fuck that! These are your trucks Ty, don't be nobodies fool, we the ones doin' all the work, we the ones taking all the risk. Out of all the runs we done made, Black-Knight has made his money; at least 10 to 12 million. Talkin' 'bout he's retiring, he's gettin' out the game. Shit, I would be too, if I had some damn fools like us bringing me millions. Fuck Black-Knight! I wouldn't pay him shit. If he wan'na go to war about it, then lets take it to the streets!"

"Take it to the streets!" Tywon yelled in disbelief. "Man..., is you stupid! We make'n millions fuckin' wit' Black-Knight and you wan'na start war over a funky ass million dollars! You know Money, I should've cut you loose months ago like I said in the van. You ain't fin'na fuck this up with that dumb shit. This is your last time comin' down here to Arizona with me. You can send your money down here for how much ever weed you wan'na buy, but that's it. Damn idiot!" walking back towards the truck.

****

Returning from the jewelry store, Tywon and White Boy-J pulled up in a 500 Mercedes Benz. They observed Money on the porch appearing to be talking to himself.

"Looks like your boy is losing it," pointed White Boy-J.

"He might be, you know he hasn't sent any money on the last two trips to Arizona?"

"Yeah, but he's still spending money like he's making it. He even bought me a plane ticket for bike week in Myrtle Beach."

"Now that surprised me more than I think it did you J. But I'm looking forward to going to Myrtle Beach myself, seeing all those fine ass women in bikinis."

"I'm hip."

Spotting the Benz, Money walked up to the passenger side of the car. "Can I roll wit' the real play'as of Detroit?" he jokingly asked checking out White Boy-J's watch. "Damn J! You done upgraded to a Roly I see," feeling a bit envious.

"Just a lil' somethin' for the trip tomorrow, you know?" spoke J.

Money then directed his attention on Tywon. "Well everything is set. The bikes are on the way to Myrtle. All we got'ta do is fly in, meet with the trailer hauler, pick up the bikes and we're ridin.'"

"Cool," replied Tywon about to exit his car when some unfamiliar guys pulled up. They pulled so close, Tywon hurried to get back inside his car. With the window already down, he pointed his gun.

"What's up! You tryin' to hit me man!"

"No! No! I apologize," smirked the driver.

Oh, he finds this shit funny, thought Tywon.

"We're realtors," the man pointed to himself and the other three men in the car. "We're surfing this area for property and we heard this house is for sale. We would like to buy it. Can we see the inside?"

Tywon looked to White Boy-J with is pistol still drawn on the men. Mumbling, "Get ready man, these muthafuckas ain't no realtors." White Boy-J was already on it, along with Money who pistols were aimed. Even De'Andre was out the upstairs window with the shotgun.

"Naw man, this house ain't for sale. But we are passin' out these bullets, y'all buying?"

The man's face wrinkled up.

"Bust they asses Ty!" hollered Money.

"Oh...that's Tywon," the driver whispered quickly pulling off.

De'Andre yelled out, "What was that about?"

No one answered, too busy trying to figure it out themselves. Money was in thought. *Man, I just made the call 10-minutes ago.*

Black-Knight got killers on stand-by like that? Tywon my man, you bet'ta duck for cover.

The next day, "Please fellas ride sensibly and stop the wheelies," said the traffic cop. "Every year around this time we have at least 20 motorcycle related fatalities here in Myrtle Beach. So keep that in mind, ok Mr. Frank White? Here you go," handing Money back his license.

Frank White? Ain't that the king of New York? comically thought Tywon. The traffic cop then pulled away on his motorcycle.

Curious, "Money, let me see those license."

Tywon and White Boy-J scanned over the I.D.

"This looks real as hell," Tywon laughed. "And they let you on the airplane with this?"

Money nodded. "It is real. I ain't goin' through that shit no mo' like we did in Oklahoma. $500 get you a license, social security card and a birth certificate."

"For real? I need that plug," stated J hopping back onto his motorcycle.

Tywon then checked his cell phone down on his hip. He saw that he'd missed 10 phone calls from De'Anne.

Throwing his hand, *She don't want shit,* figuring his sister wanted nothing more than some money. He decided to return the call anyway. De'Anne answered the line ranting out of control. He couldn't understand one word she spoke. Her hysterical screaming blocked any comprehension. This nearly sent Tywon into a panic.

"Calm down De'Anne, take a deep breath! Now tell me, what's the problem?

As her words became clearer, he learned De'Andre had been shot. Money and White Boy-J stood from their bikes in shock.

"De'Andre! Shot!" looking at one another.

Tywon then went on trying to find out if or not De'Andre was dead. De'Anne repeatedly told him she didn't know.

In a reserved tone, "De'Anne, don't worry. I'll be there in 2 hours, you hear me? I'm on my way. But check around and find out what hospital De'Andre was taken to." He then warned his sister not to alarm their mother.

"Ok, but hurry Ty and be careful," hanging up the phone.

Tywon's world was spinning out of control. His knees felt like they were about to give away. He wanted to scream out, *'Lord have mercy!'* in his brothers name, but he couldn't. To break down and cry in front of those who were in his presence would only show his weakness.

Enraged, Tywon kicked over his motorcycle. "Damn man! Them muthafucka's done shot my brother!"

"Who shot him?" asked White Boy-J concerned.

"It had to be those dudes from yesterday who came by the house. I've repeatedly told De'Andre to stay out them streets. I just hope..." Tywon took a breath shaking his head. "I'm tellin' you, if Dre's dead, it's on. Muthafuckin' heads go'on roll behind this one! I'm taking whole families, no questions asked. It's go'on be a lot of head bussin' and wig splittin' goin' on."

Tywon then took a last look at the burnt orange colored sun as it began to set over the Atlantic Ocean.

At that point, "C'mon y'all, we got'ta get back to the D," he voiced with urgency to Money and White Boy-J.

On the airplane, "Just try to relax until we get home Ty. Trippin' will just make this flight seem forever. But trust me, my ear is low to the ground on this one. If them cats did do this to Dre, then they got it coming. Be cool though, I got your back. I love you man," assured Money reaching for a hug. Tywon needed those words of assurance as he stood up embracing Money.

Turning around, seated in the row up front, J shook his head in thought. *Look at this fake ass shit here. I love you man, I got your back,* he mimicked to himself. *Yeah right, this dude is a true actor. Money don't give a fuck about nothing or nobody, especially not Dre. From what I've seen and heard, those two don't even like each other. A matter of fact, now that I think about it, De'Andre's death would only benefit Money. He could then reclaim all the clientele Dre had took from him. But then again, don't too many of them dudes like dealing with Money. It don't seem right after a cat done spent $150 to $200,000 on a load of weed, and a hour later muthafucka's in your house with ski masks on robbing you and threatening to kidnap your kids. Bad word like that* *travels quick. And weirdly, Money always has this yellow eyed, glossy glare look about himself. I don't know what he's on, but he looks like he's tweaking off that shit. Personally, I don't like this muthatfucka, but Tywon's my boy and Money's his boy, so it is what it is, but Money better not try no shady shit with me, because white boys probably can't jump, but this white boy will smoke yo' ass,* lying back in his chair.

The flight stewardess had just walked down the isle instructing everyone to fasten their safety belts. The plane was now on the run way gathering speed to take flight, as their backs implanted into the seats. Soon after, the plane took to the air. After 10-minutes or so, "Bing!" came a sound followed by a red light.

"It is now safe to move about the cabin," informed the captain over the intercom.

Money remained in his chair praying for De'Andre's death, thinking of the half of a million dollars worth of marijuana customers he was about to regain. He also was in thought about which of them he could set up first, for a quick lick.

White Boy-J was thinking why a rich, street smart and intelligent guy like Tywon still associated himself with a shit for brains, back stabbing son of a bitch like Money? And why he kept him so close? J desperately wanted to ask, but he wasn't one who pried in the personal affairs of others.

Tywon also was in thought. *Please Lord, let De'Andre pull through this. My brother was only following my footsteps. Damn, I feel as if I sold him to the game, traded his life for riches. On everything, I'll trade all this material shit and the money for his life. Just let me talk to him again, see his eyes open, hear him laugh, hear him crack a joke. If either of us has to depart from this earth, please Lord, let it be me.*

All the praying in the world couldn't grant Tywon his wish. De'Andre Lamar Nelson was laid to rest June 2, 2002. He was survived by his mother; Faye Nelson, father; Ronnie Nelson, brother; Tywon Miller, sister; De'Anne Nelson, two aunts; Gladys and Francine Miller, and many other family and friends.

2003

My Daddy Told Me

The marijuana game was now what the cocaine game once was: Murderous. Detroit's city street's was a war zone. Almost everyday for the last 7-months after De'Andre's death, marijuana dealers were falling victims to the game. Black-Knight was sending murderous messages to anyone who associated or bought weed from Tywon. He even went so far as to put hits out on those who were pallbearers at De'Andre's funeral. Tywon of course didn't lie down on these deadly threats. A psychotic side of him seemed to erupt after his brother's passing. Being 25 million dollars strong, he formed his own assault team of killers, who'd tried numerous times to take Black-Knight out. Tywon most times went along for the ride himself. Their only problem, they couldn't kill a target they couldn't see. Black-Knight wasn't a resident of Detroit, but he was still putting down hits from out of state. The back and fourth retaliations kept Tywon fearful of his life and constantly on the run.

As the motel door began twisting, "Wake up Money, get off of me! Don't you hear the doorknob turning? It's him, Tywon! I told you not to tell that bitch O'Sha were you were!" ranted China White.

Money frantically awoke. He quickly but quietly armed himself with two 40-caliber pistols and ran to the door. He leaned against the door jam just as Tywon burst into the dark room aiming his pistol. Money behind him placed one of the guns to the back of Tywon's neck and the other up under between his ass and dick.

"Unless you want a sex change operation, you'll drop that gun."

Tywon's pistol hit the floor, his hands went midway into the air. Money slammed the door shut with his foot. He then walked Tywon over to the bed, guns still pressed to his body.

"Sit down!"

With his pistols still aimed, Money walked backwards towards the wall switching on the light. Tywon looked around the room in disgust.

Pizza boxes, beer bottles and condom packages were scattered throughout the room.

"Is this where you've been hiding out for the last 6-months?" Money shrugged. "Maybe."

"So what do you have to say for yourself," asked Tywon with a grim look.

Money smiled taking a seat sitting one of his pistols on the table. He kept a close watch on Tywon as he sniffed a nose full of the white ecstasy. He then brushed his nostrils free of the powdery residue.

"Fuck it!"

"Fuck what?" asked Tywon.

"You asked me what do I have to say for myself and I'm telling you fuck it, shit happens."

"You got my brother killed behind some bullshit lies, and all you can say is fuck it! Mutha...," jumping from his chair.

Money again aimed both pistols. "Sit yo' ass down Ty! Don't be a tough guy. Act like you see these two guns in my hand."

Enraged and breathing hard, Tywon took a seat. "You got me moving my family all over this got damn city! That muthafucka Black-Knight is trying to kill me! And all you can do is sit there and sniff that shit!"

Money then held his hands to the side displaying himself like a crucifix. "China is the only one who understands Ty. She loves me. She loves all. C'mon and join us. Be one, be free, like me."

"Mmph, sounds like that same shit you told O'Sha."

Money came back to his senses. "What did O'Sha tell you?"

"Everything you dirty bastard! How do you think I found you?"

Tywon smirked in disbelief. "My main man fuckin' my woman. Weph, that's a hard bullet to swallow. I expected some shit like this from you Money, but not from O'Sha. Out of all the men she could've messed around with, she did it with you."

"I told you years ago the bitch wasn't shit," Money justified.

Tywon put up his hand, shaking his head as to say, *Please, say no more.*

"But let me ask you Money, why did I have to find out from O'Sha who killed my father? You were there. You witnessed his death. Why wouldn't you tell me? You've known this for almost 20 years, and you tell a woman over me! Are you that weak to the flesh? That weak to where as you'd discuss my personal life with a woman just to get a piece of ass? Dre was right, you are a sucker."

Money's face tightened. He felt insulted, but continued to listen.

"Oh yeah, and De'Anne told me how you did her back in the day. That's so fucked up Money. You a straight predator, a sicko! You done fucked over everything I love. It's like you hated me or something, like I was your enemy. I guess I was the big joke in your life, huh?"

Money jumped from his chair slapping the tray of cocaine off the table. "Fuck you Ty, bitch! You think you know me! You don't know how I feel. The joke is me walking behind you. The joke is everybody recognizing your accomplishments over mine. Around you, I always came second. I always had to try harder, be something that I wasn't, but over time, I accepted that. But when I got home, your albino wan'na be black, white friend replaced me. I felt like I had been pushed out the picture. So yeah, you can say I hated you. Even my own fat ass cousin respected you more than he did me. You got the looks Ty, the girl and the money. And yeah, me and O'Sha fucked around, but that bitch still didn't look at me the way she did you. Her heart was always with you. She even called out your name sometimes when we fucked. That girl made me hate her." Tywon didn't know if that statement should've made him feel good or bad.

Money continued, "And Black-Knight, fuck that black, bald headed eagle looking muthafucka too! That was my hookup! My connect! I finally had did right putting something big together and you stole it!" he pointed with the gun.

Tywon put up his hands covering himself.

"As soon as Black-Knight saw that million dollars, I knew then again you were pushing me aside. Nothing I've done in my lifetime can compare to you Ty. And on the real, I'm tired of trying."

Money then aimed both pistols at Tywon. "That's why you gos'ta go!"

Shielding himself, "Hold on Money! C'mon now, we still boys!" pleaded Tywon. "You go'on take both of my momma's sons from her?"

"Yo' momma!"

"Bboooff!" The motel door unexpectedly was kicked open.

Money ducked as White Boy-J shot at him, missing.

Money returned fired out the door, letting the two 40-calibers rip. During the exchange of fire, Tywon made eyes with his gun that was still laying on the floor. Without a second thought, he sprinted towards the weapon. As he did so, Money turned around spotting him. Tywon now had no choice but to rush Money. As he neared him, Money aimed his pistol, but Tywon was too close up on him, disabling the gun from his left hand. But unfortunately, that wasn't enough.

"Bbooomm! Bbooomm! Bbooomm!" three times to the chest with the pistol from the right.

Tywon's mouth hung wide open. The pressure felt as if a horse had just kicked him in the chest. All the strength in his body seemed to give away. Suddenly, he fell to his knees, then looked up at Money. Tywon saw the same deranged appearance on his face as before in O'Sha's basement. Right then, the same gun he'd been shot with was now in his face. He was starring eye to eye with the barrel of the gun. Weirdly, he couldn't find the strength to move out of its path. He then heard, "Die bitch!"

"Click! Click! Click!" The gun was empty.

Afterwards, Tywon fell to the floor. He gasped for air continuing to hear the shoot out between Money and White Boy-J. Finally, Money shot his way out of the motel room with Tywon's gun. Thereafter, White Boy-J rushed into the room.

Looking to the floor, "Awe shit Ty! Hold on man, stay calm," rushing to his side. "Everything go'on be..." Tywon began to fade away.

"Damn, so your boy Money tried to ice yo' ass, huh?"

"He sho' did," answered Tywon looking out through the barbwire fence of the Federal Prison. "If I didn't have that bullet proof vest on, my ass would'a been out'ta here. Like cube said, I rather be judged by 12 than carried by 6."

"True that," stated Merv, the inmate Tywon was telling the story to. "So what happened with ol' boy you went to war with, Black-Knight?"

Tywon gave a malicious grin. "That bitch got life in the Feds. They hit him with the Rico Law. He's in U.S.P., never to see the streets again. Feds charged him with all those bodies, and running an international drug smuggling operation from Mexico into the United States. I heard the Mexican government in co-operation with the United States government took his mans Pablo down too. It's said they confiscated all his shit and then executed him in front of a firing squad."

"Awe... now that's fucked up."

"Naw, that's the Mexican way," they both laughed.

"What happened with your girl O'Sha?"

"Shit, she was like any other bitch when the Feds came asking questions. She told them everything and testified to it to save her own ass. My daddy told me the woman you share your bed with can sometimes be your worst enemy."

"Damn, but what about your boy, the white boy?"

"Who J?" Tywon smiled. "That was my dog, my man. Last I heard J accepted a plea for 10 years. Shit, the lawyer damn near broke him gettin' him down to that."

"Oh, so the white boy didn't snitch you out?"

"He got 10, I'm doing 20. What do you think?"

"Yeah, muthafuckas talk that tough shit, but once them peoples come throwin' them football numbers out there, you gone say something."

"Fuck it, I ain't mad. I got a out date from this joint."

"That's for real," stood Merv fixing his nuts. "A lot of these guys are go'on die in here. But that's out cold how you said your moms still ain't talkin' to you."

Tywon threw a rock over the fence. "Like she said, I got her baby killed. My sister says my mom's is holding up well though. She's about to remarry my stepfather and they're going to start their own drug rehab clinic. I think they're going to be happy together this time."

"That's cool man, but now you know what my next question is right?"

Tywon snarled, "Money?"

Merv nodded, *Yeah...!*

"Well... last I heard about Money..."

Speeding down I-94, "It's just me against the world baby," Money mimicked along with the song. As he bobbed his head to the beat, he looked over to Octavia seated next to him in the convertible Corvette, with her hair blowing in the wind. He then turned down the radio yelling.

"Now this is ballin'! This is livin' girl! We ridin' in a drop-top, we're dressed fly as hell, and I got a pocket full of money!" pulling out a wad thinking, *Yeah...! I'm finally the man.*

Octavia gave a prissy like smile as if she was impressed. *Ugh, I can't believe I'm fuckin' with this clown, especially after how he dogged my sister out. But he's cashing me out, so I can't complain.*

Suddenly, red and blue lights danced from the grill of a Crown Victoria. Octavia turned around. "See there Money, I told you to slow down.

"Don't trip, I got this," he said pulling onto the shoulder.

Conrad Bantz walked up, leaning onto the door.

"Money Bunny, Maurice Bonner. You think you're a pretty smart guy, huh? You think you're a slick cat? Somehow you managed to come out clean and free, while all your buddies drowned in that river of shit you created. How did you pull that off?"

Money laughed with glorification. "Conrad, I'm gon'na be real with you. You and I are alike in many ways. You're a liar, you sneaky, you conniving and you're manipulative just like me. You'll make a bunch of promises that you don't even plan on keeping. And you'll tell a muthafucka' anything they wan'na hear to get what you want."

Conrad smirked knowing it was true.

Money continued, "But I was already one up on you. That's why I recorded damn near every phone conversation we had. Fucked you up when I gave you them copies of you conspiring to take that money from

Black-Knight. I figure that's why I'm still out here, 'cause if I was goin' down, yo' white ass was comin' wit' me. But look on the bright side Conrad, you received high appraise for taking down one of Detroit's biggest marijuana rings in history, thanks to me. And if it'll make you feel any better, just look at me as the one who got away."

Conrad sucked his teeth, "The one who got away, huh? Nah... Money, I got a feeling you'll be biting the bullet real soon."

Grabbing Octavia's thigh, "Conrad, the only thing I'ma be bittin' into real soon is this fine piece of ass. Now, are you threw? Can I go? Me and baby girl here go'on be late for dinner."

Without another word spoken, Conrad stood aside. Money pulled up waiting for traffic to clear.

He then looked back yelling. "A Conrad, I thought you and I were supposed to be friends. Conrad put both his hands to his mouth like a funnel yelling. "No! With a friend like you Money, who needs enemies?"

Money laughed, recklessly pulling away onto the freeway.

After dinner at the restaurant, Money fell ill. It seemed every five minutes, he was throwing up or either shitting. A couple of times it was a combination of both. He figured his sickness was due to the cocaine usage and the heavy drinking he'd been doing all day; not at all suspecting Octavia who despised and hated him. Her long time plan for revenge against Money kicked into affect, after the explosion in her basement with the hot water tank. She knew the opportunity for revenge one day would present itself as if just had, sprinkling rat poison over his food while he went to the bathroom. Money was so busy plotting against everyone else, he had no idea someone was plotting against him.

Helping him into the passenger seat, "Don't worry baby, let me get you home. I'll take care of you," claimed Octavia now getting into the driver's seat.

"Uuuugghh..." was Money's miserable response.

Octavia drove for about a mile when she pulled to a red light. No cars were on either side of her, when suddenly, a green 4-door Malibu pulled up next to them, the same green 4-door Malibu from Double 07.

The driver looked over to Octavia. "Hey sweetie, how you doin'?"

"I'm fine," she replied.

What the fuck! Hey sweetie? thought Money ready to check the dude, but first, he had to throw up. He opened the passenger door again letting his dinner go. "Uuuuggghhhh...shit," wiping his mouth.

With his eyes bloodshot red from vomiting, he looked up only to see a handgun pointed in his face.

"Hey Money, remember me?"

"Bbbooommm!"

Octavia rushed from the Corvette hopping into the Malibu. She and the perpetrator then took off, leaving Money hanging out the car door.

I Forgot to Tell

I don't believe this shit, this fool done shot me in the head
Now here comes the puddle of blood, starting to paint the street red
I screamin' for help, but my lips are tight, closed and stiff
I'm going into shock, my body startin' to twitch
My eyes are closed, but I'm aware of what's going on
Some cat walked up yelling, "That boy all fucked up, trust me, he's gone
Black on black crime, don't make sense, that shit needs to stop!"
Please sir, call for some help, my body temperature startin' to drop
My life is leaking, spilling fast into the streets
My name is Money Bunny, local celebrity, you've probably heard of me?
I'm known for high-speed chases, slangin' them rocks and them pounds of weed
I use'ta ride that road for 2 days on a mission to cop them greens
We brought it back, bust it down and bagged it up
Astronomical paper was coming in, had me trippin,' like what the fuck?
But after a while, that bullshit Ty, Dre and the white boy pulled got old